The Best American
SCIENCE FICTION
and FANTASY
2017

The Best American
SCIENCE FICTION
and FANTASY™
2017

Edited and with an Introduction
by **Charles Yu**

John Joseph Adams, *Series Editor*

A Mariner Original
HOUGHTON MIFFLIN HARCOURT
BOSTON • NEW YORK   2017

hmhco.com

ISSN 2573-0797 (print)   ISSN 2573-0800 (ebook)
ISBN 978-0-544-97398-5 (print)   ISBN 978-0-544-98067-9 (ebook)

Printed in the United States of America
DOC 10 9 8 7 6 5 4 3 2 1

Contents

Foreword

WELCOME TO YEAR three of *The Best American Science Fiction and Fantasy*! This volume presents the best science fiction and fantasy (SF/F) short stories published during the 2016 calendar year as selected by myself and guest editor Charles Yu.

After more than fifteen years working in the SF/F field, I found 2016 to be an entirely new challenge, as I threw myself into the world of novel-editing, launching my own imprint—John Joseph Adams Books—with the publisher of this fine anthology, Houghton Mifflin Harcourt. I'm very proud to have published novels by Hugh Howey, Carrie Vaughn, and Peter Cawdron thus far, and look forward to the publication of Molly Tanzer's JJA Books debut in November. Those will be followed in 2018 by the release of books by Bryan Camp, Ashok K. Banker, and Todd McAulty, along with second books by Molly and Carrie.

So while for much of 2016 I've been immersed in the long form, it's always a pleasure to return to my first love: short fiction.

Our guest editor this year, Charles Yu, is a writer I've been interested in for many years, ever since I first heard about his amazing novel *How to Live Safely in a Science Fictional Universe,* which came out in 2010 to major acclaim. It was published the same year I launched my magazine, *Lightspeed*—and much to my delight, when I reached out to him about writing a story for my fledgling magazine, he agreed, and sold me the superb tale "Standard Loneliness Package" (which you can read online at lightspeedmagazine.com); thus our collaborative relationship was born. His short fiction has also appeared in *Playboy, Esquire.com, Wired Magazine* and *Wired.com, The Oxford American,* and *Vice.com,* among other anthologies and magazines, as well as in two collections: *Third Class Superhero* and *Sorry Please Thank You.*

I've also published his work in a number of my own anthologies, including *Robot Uprisings, Dead Man's Hand,* and *Press Start to Play.* Fun fact: if you mashed up his stories in the latter two volumes, you'd basically get HBO's hit TV show *Westworld,* for which Charlie worked as a scriptwriter and the story editor on season one.

I feel like I would be remiss if I didn't point out that Charlie had a fantastic story in *The New Yorker* this year called "Fable," which surely would have been on the best-of-the-year list I passed along to the guest editor if it weren't written by that guest editor. If you like genre short fiction—and I know you do, since you're reading not only this book but this foreword—then do yourself a favor and definitely check it out. (And lucky you, it's available online on *The New Yorker*'s website for free.)

Science fiction and fantasy, though they seem to be about the future or fictional worlds, are always at their core really about the problems and issues of today. Even in the best of times, genre writers find inspiration in injustice, or in the flaws found in an otherwise well-functioning system. In the worst of times . . . well, the one silver lining of living through the dystopian hellscape of contemporary American politics is that such strife tends to generate great art—and no one embraces the ability of literature to critique and debate our daily truths by considering it through a different lens more than writers of science fiction and fantasy.

If there's one story in this book that I fully expected to resonate strongly with our guest editor—speaking of writers finding inspiration in injustice—it's "The Venus Effect," by Joseph Allen Hill. Like *How to Live Safely in a Science Fictional Universe* (and, erm, Charlie's introduction to this anthology), "The Venus Effect" breaks the fourth wall and has the author intruding on his own story, to similarly great effect. Though it also should be completely unsurprising that Charlie loved this story because of the audacious brilliance of it and the way it tackles an extremely thorny issue—police brutality—with such aplomb while staying within the framework of a fun adventure story that is somehow both excessively clever and enormously poignant.

Charlie often employs other meta techniques in his stories as well, so it was an equally safe bet that he would also love the Nebula Award finalist "Welcome to the Medical Clinic at the Interplanetary Relay Station | Hours Since the Last Patient Death: 0," by Caroline M. Yoachim, which uses the structure of a choose-your-own-adventure-type narrative to critique and have some fun with the completely unfun health-care system.

"This Is Not a Wardrobe Door," by A. Merc Rustad (also a Nebula Award finalist), and "Not by Wardrobe, Tornado, or Looking Glass," by Jeremiah Tolbert, in addition to both having *wardrobe* in the title, are, unsurprisingly, both portal fantasies. Portal fantasy is a subgenre that is more or less illustrated by Jeremiah's title, which references the Chronicles of Narnia (wardrobe), *The Wonderful Wizard of Oz* (tornado), and *Alice's Adventures in Wonderland* (looking glass)—all three everyday things serving as portals to a magical otherworld. I've observed an uptick in portal fantasy recently—there are some great portal fantasies on the Notable Stories list—and I can't help but wonder if it's partially socially motivated: things are so bleak that many of us are literally imagining escaping to a fantasy world as our only way out of the mess we're in.

"Caspar D. Luckinbill, What Are You Going to Do?," by Nick Wolven, and "Openness," by Alexander Weinstein, are two stories that would have felt at home in the great Netflix anthology TV series *Black Mirror;* both explore the dark side of technology—how, if we let it, it can take over and rule our lives . . . how (to quote *Fight Club*) the things you own end up owning you (or perhaps, in one of these cases, the things you own end up *pwning* you).

Other selections you'll find here include stories about love, alien visitations, post-climate-change futures, revisionist fairy tales, virtual worlds and corporate malfeasance, and more.

The stories chosen for this anthology were originally published between January 1 and December 31, 2016. The criteria for consideration are (1) original publication in a nationally distributed American or Canadian publication (i.e., periodicals, collections, or anthologies, in print, online, or ebook); (2) publication in English by writers who are American or Canadian, or who have made the United States or Canada their home; (3) publication as text (audiobook, podcast, dramatization, interactive, and other forms of fiction are not considered); (4) original publication as short fiction (excerpts of novels are not knowingly considered); (5) story length of 17,499 words or less; (6) at least loosely categorized as science fiction or fantasy; (7) publication by someone other than the author (self-published works are not eligible); and (8) publication as an original work by the author (i.e., not part of a media tie-in/licensed fiction program).

As series editor, I attempt to read everything I can find that meets these selection criteria. After doing all my reading, I create a list of what I feel are the top eighty stories published in the genre (forty science fiction and forty fantasy). This year those eighty stories were sent to guest editor Charles Yu, who read them and then chose the best twenty (ten science fiction, ten fantasy) for inclusion in the anthology. Charles read all the stories blind, with no bylines attached to them or any information about where a story originally appeared. His selections appear in this volume; the remaining sixty stories are listed in the back of this book as "Notable Science Fiction and Fantasy Stories of 2016."

As usual, in my effort to find the top stories of the year, I scour the field to try to read and consider everything that's published.

Though the bulk of my reading typically comes from periodicals, I always also read dozens of anthologies and single-author collections. Here's just a sampling of the anthologies that published fine work that didn't quite manage to make it into the table of contents or Notable Stories list but are worthwhile just the same: *Dead Letters,* edited by Conrad Williams; *Children of Lovecraft,* edited by Ellen Datlow; *Scary Out There,* edited by Jonathan Maberry; *In the Shadow of Frankenstein,* edited by Stephen Jones; *The Grimm Future,* edited by Erin Underwood; *The Mammoth Book of Cthulhu,* edited by Paula Guran; *A Tyranny of Petticoats,* edited by Jessica Spotswood; *Cyber World,* edited by Jason Heller; *Decision Points,* edited by Bryan Thomas Schmidt; *Clockwork Phoenix 5,* edited by Mike Allen; *Hidden Youth,* edited by Mikki Kendall and Chesya Burke; *Upside Down,* edited by Jaym Gates and Monica Valentinelli; and several others (including the horror anthology *What the #@&% Is That?,* edited by Douglas Cohen and yours truly).

In addition to this, the anthologies *Drowned Worlds,* edited by Jonathan Strahan; *2113: Stories Inspired by the Music of Rush,* edited by Kevin J. Anderson and John McFetridge; and *Summer Days and Summer Nights,* edited by Stephanie Perkins, contain stories represented in the table of contents, and stories on the Notable Stories list appeared in anthologies such as *The Starlit Wood,* edited by Dominik Parisien and Navah Wolfe; *An Alphabet of Embers,* edited by Rose Lemberg; *Bridging Infinity,* edited by Jonathan Strahan; *Unfettered II,* edited by Shawn Speakman; *Humanity 2.0,* edited by Alex Shvartsman; *Genius Loci,* edited by Jaym Gates; *Astro Noise,* edited by Laura Poitras; *Strangers Among Us,* edited by Susan Forest and Lucas K. Law; and *You, Human,* edited by Michael Bailey.

There were fewer eligible single-author collections with original material to consider, but new collections were published by Alexander Weinstein (*Children of the New World*), Caroline M. Yoachim (*Seven Wonders of a Once and Future World and Other Stories*), Patricia A. McKillip (*Dreams of Distant Shores*), Amber Sparks (*The Unfinished World*), Jeffrey Ford (*A Natural History of Hell*), Carlos Hernandez (*The Assimilated Cuban's Guide to Quantum Santeria*), Laird Barron (*Swift to Chase*), Livia Llewellyn (*Furnace*), and Tina Connolly (*On the Eyeball Floor and Other Stories*). Three collections contain stories included on the Notable Stories list: *The Paper Menagerie,* by Ken Liu; *A Collapse of Horses,* by Brian Evenson; and *The Bed Moved,* by Rebecca Schiff. Also of interest, but ineligible because it is made up entirely of reprints, was the debut collection from Carrie Vaughn, *Amaryllis and Other Stories.*

As always, I surveyed more than a hundred different periodicals over the course of the year, paying equal attention to major genre publications like *The Magazine of Fantasy & Science Fiction* and *Asimov's Science Fiction* and to new markets like *Persistent Visions* and *Liminal Stories.* I also do my best to find any genre fiction lurking in the pages of mainstream/literary publications such as *The New Yorker, Tin House,* and *Granta.*

The notable stories on this year's list are drawn from forty-four different publications—twenty-nine periodicals, twelve anthologies, and three single-author collections—from forty-three different editors (counting editorial teams as a unit). The selections themselves are drawn from fourteen different sources—eleven periodicals and three anthologies—from thirteen different editors or editorial teams.

This year marks the first appearance of several periodicals on our table of contents, including *Conjunctions, Fireside Magazine, Beloit Fiction Journal, BuzzFeed READER,* and *The Sun.* Periodicals appearing on the Notable Stories list for the first time this year include *Big Echo, Faerie Magazine, Fairy Tale Review, GigaNotoSaurus, People Holding . . . , The Sun, VQR Online,* and *ZYZZYVA.*

Four of the authors whose work is included in this volume—A. Merc Rustad, Catherynne M. Valente, Dale Bailey, and Nick Wolven—have previously appeared in *BASFF;* thus the remaining fifteen authors (fifteen rather than sixteen because Bailey appears twice) are represented for the first time.

Debbie Urbanski, Brian Evenson, and Ken Liu tied with the most stories in my top eighty this year (three each), and several authors had two each: A. Merc Rustad, Alyssa Wong, Carmen Maria Machado, Caroline M. Yoachim, Dale Bailey, Dominica Phetteplace, N. K. Jemisin, Naomi Novik, Nick Wolven, P. Djèlí Clark, Rich Larson, and Sofia Samatar.

I mentioned above that the *BASFF 2017* stories "This Is Not a Wardrobe Door" and "Welcome to the Medical Clinic at the Interplanetary Relay Station | Hours Since the Last Patient Death: 0" are finalists for the Nebula Award this year. Additionally, "The City Born Great," by N. K. Jemisin, is a Hugo Award finalist. Notable stories that have received award recognition include "Sooner or Later Everything Falls into the Sea," by Sarah Pinsker (Nebula finalist); "You'll Surely Drown Here If You Stay," by Alyssa Wong (Nebula and Hugo finalist); "Seasons of Glass and Iron," by Amal El-Mohtar (Nebula and Hugo finalist); "Things with Beards," by Sam J. Miller (Nebula finalist); "A Fist of Permutations in Lightning and Wildflowers," by Alyssa Wong (Nebula and Hugo finalist); and "The Jupiter Drop," by Josh Malerman (Stoker finalist).

As I've noted in past forewords, I don't log every single story I read throughout the year—I only dutifully log stories that I feel are in the running—so I don't have an exact count of how many stories I reviewed or considered. As in past years, I estimate that it was several thousand stories, perhaps as many as five thousand, altogether.

Naturally, many of the stories I read were perfectly good and enjoyable but didn't stand out enough for me to consider them among the best of the year. I did, however, end up with about a hundred additional stories that were at one point or another under serious consideration, including stories from publications not represented in this anthology, such as *Amazing Stories, The Book Smugglers, Bracken Magazine, Catamaran Literary Reader, Daily Science Fiction, The Dark, Fantastic Stories of the Imagination, Flash Fiction On-*

line, Futuristica, Galaxy's Edge, Intergalactic Medicine Show, Lackington's, Lenny Letter, Liminal Stories, The Lovecraft ezine, Nature Futures, Persistent Visions, and *Slate,* as well as the anthologies and collections named above.

This foreword mentions only a few of the great publications considered for this anthology; see the table of contents and the Notable Stories list to get a more complete overview of the top publications currently available in the field.

Given how many stories I have to consider every year, it's probably obvious that I can do this only with a considerable amount of help. So I'd just like to take a moment to thank and acknowledge my team of first readers, who helped me evaluate various publications that I might not have had time to consider otherwise: Alex Puncekar, Robyn Lupo, Devin Marcus, Sandra Odell, Karen Bovenmyer, and Christie Yant. Thanks also to Tim Mudie at Mariner Books, who keeps everything running smoothly behind the scenes at Best American HQ.

If you've made it this far in the foreword, then maybe you've been introduced to some new publications to look for in the future or been reminded of a few that have fallen off your radar over the years and deserve a second look. Which brings me to one last point I'd like to take the opportunity to drive home.

We're undoubtedly living in a golden age of genre—but not just in literature: also in TV and film. There's more genre entertainment being produced today than any reasonable person would have any hope of keeping up with. That's how it's been with short stories and books for many years; it's one of the reasons volumes like this one are useful and necessary. But now this is increasingly applicable to television and film as well. Though it's probably still possible to keep track of all the genre movies coming out (though any one person is unlikely to do so, because of the quantity and the still wildly varying levels of quality), television is becoming more like publishing in the sense that even if you're a deeply devoted genre fan, you'd basically have to be committed to watching television full-time in order to catch all the genre TV shows being produced. Overall that is a good thing—at least it is if, like me, you love television—even if it makes it harder to have that shared experience anytime you run into a fellow fan; and of course all that film and television (and video game!) entertainment leaves the deeply devoted genre fan with less time to spend on short stories than ever before.

The problem with any form of entertainment is that the more options there are, the harder it is for any one thing to be successful enough to stick around long-term. On television, for example, within the last year the terrific original genre series *BrainDead* and *Incorporated* were both canceled despite brilliant first seasons, and mind-bogglingly good, core genre shows like Syfy's *The Expanse* are doing well enough to get renewed but sort of scraping by. Likewise, the magazines you love today may be gone tomorrow. (And indeed, several seem to have faded away this year—whether it's for good or not, who can say?) Many of them operate on a shoestring, relying on Kickstarter, subscription drives, and support through Patreon.

It all boils down to this: we must support the things we love, whether it's books, television, film, or stories—though I'd say *especially* books and stories! If you like an author or magazine, support it early and often. Word of mouth (including reader reviews at Amazon or Goodreads or the like) can go a long way toward helping an author's career—or a fledgling zine—get off the ground and stay aloft. Short-fiction venues are often labors of love, and they need your support, in the form of readership, subscriptions, and signal-boosting. And it's you readers, who care enough about short fiction to read this book (and this foreword), who are the standard-bearers, so if you love something, say something! Meanwhile, I'll keep doing my part to try to find the best of the best every year, and hey, maybe somehow together, with the help of genre short fiction, we can find a way to transform this dystopian hellscape we're in back into one of those better tomorrows.

Editors, writers, and publishers who would like their work considered for next year's edition, please visit johnjosephadams.com/best-american for instructions on how to submit material for consideration.

— JOHN JOSEPH ADAMS

Introduction

I. *Alternative Realities*

(NOTE: This is true. All of this happened.)

Recently, an anthropologist from another universe showed up at my local coffee shop.

> INTERDIMENSIONAL ANTHROPOLOGIST: I'm an anthropologist from another universe.
>
> ME: Cool.
>
> INTERDIMENSIONAL ANTHROPOLOGIST: I'm from another universe, and that's what you're going to say? Cool? Aren't you wondering how I got here? Don't you think I might have something very important to talk to you about?
>
> ME: [not really interested] Sorry, yeah. You're right.
>
> INTERDIMENSIONAL ANTHROPOLOGIST: Good. I mean, yeesh. We're not off to a great start— [Notices the look on my face . . . or maybe reading my mind] You're zoning me out. Aren't you? You're waiting for me to stop talking so you can go back to your work.
>
> ME: I'm sorry. It's just that I'm under deadline. I'm editing this anthology, and I have to read a whole bunch of short stories—
>
> INTERDIMENSIONAL ANTHROPOLOGIST: It looks like you're browsing pictures of baby pandas.
>
> ME: I suppose you're not leaving this universe until I talk to you.
>
> INTERDIMENSIONAL ANTHROPOLOGIST: Nope.
>
> ME: All right then. What's this about?

The interdimensional anthropologist (who, it turns out, goes by Susan) said she had come here on a Fulbright. Susan had gotten some research money to study our little universe. I asked why ours was worth studying.

SUSAN THE INTERDIMENSIONAL ANTHROPOLOGIST: Not the whole universe. Just a subset.
ME: Oh. I think I know where you're going with this.

Yeah, Susan said. Susan pulled out a manila folder (they have Office Depot in her dimension) and slapped it on the table (we were at Starbucks—like I said, this is all true; you can tell because I'm adding details and also because I'm asserting that it's true).

CASE STUDY IN BIFURCATED REALITY:
AMERICA EARLY 2017

proto-civilization demonstrating multiple indicia of having reached early Phase 2, with satisfaction of the Filbert criterion. Reports and field data suggest there are currently <u>two distinct subrealities coexisting within the same space-time region</u>. Situation highly unstable. Funding granted to enable exploratory investigation. Inquiry will focus on how human inhabitants of this *bifurcated reality* will be affected and whether they will be able to come up with a solution to resolve the problem, or, in the absence of such a solution, what the <u>psychological and emotional consequences will be for these humans (in the event of a negative outcome)</u>.

I took a moment to process this.

ME: I don't like the sound of "negative outcome."
SUSAN THE INTERDIMENSIONAL ANTHROPOLOGIST: Yeah. You shouldn't like it.
ME: So. Okay. What the hell does this all mean?
SUSAN THE INTERDIMENSIONAL ANTHROPOLOGIST: Basically, America in 2017 isn't one reality. It's two separate ones, mostly distinct but with some overlap.
ME: That . . . seems . . . correct. Ridiculous. But correct.
SUSAN THE INTERDIMENSIONAL ANTHROPOLOGIST: You say it's ridiculous, but you have a rich academic literature about this topic already.
ME: We do? I mean, this doesn't sound like science. It sounds like science fiction.
SUSAN THE INTERDIMENSIONAL ANTHROPOLOGIST: Exactly.

Susan handed me a book. I looked at the title page:

The Best American SCIENCE FICTION and FANTASY™ 2017
Edited and with an Introduction by Charles Yu
John Joseph Adams, *Series Editor*

ME: Huh. [then] Is that . . . me?

SUSAN THE INTERDIMENSIONAL ANTHROPOLOGIST: It's one possible you, yeah. You picked these stories?

ME: I guess I did. I mean, I will.

SUSAN THE INTERDIMENSIONAL ANTHROPOLOGIST: Then I have
come to the right place. The humans in this book are demonstrating a kind of technology.

ME: They're writers.

SUSAN THE INTERDIMENSIONAL ANTHROPOLOGIST: Okay. These
human writers are demonstrating a kind of technology.

ME: Stories?

SUSAN THE INTERDIMENSIONAL ANTHROPOLOGIST: Stories.
[scribbling in her interdimensional notepad] Right. That's your
word for it. A narrative technology of a specific kind. Genre stories, science fiction and fantasy. Speculative fiction, some call it.
The ability to create imagined realities.

ME: I'm sorry—hold up, Susan. Are you telling me that science
fiction and fantasy writers caused reality to fragment this way?
Caused America to split into two? That SF/F writers are the root
cause of all of this craziness, with no one knowing what's true? Or,
worse, that we're the reason serious people are starting to have
serious doubts about whether or not there is such a thing as truth
anymore? We're the *problem?*

SUSAN THE INTERDIMENSIONAL ANTHROPOLOGIST: Actually it's
the opposite. Writers of these imaginative realities are not the
problem. They're the solution.

ME: Huh?

SUSAN THE INTERDIMENSIONAL ANTHROPOLOGIST: I will admit,
it's a bit of a contradiction. Or an irony? One of those things—
you humans with your primitive rationality and logic still have
trouble with some of these complexities. [Takes a breath out of
one of her nineteen lungs] Okay, let me try to explain it this way.

Susan took the book and flipped to the table of contents. I
eyed them with great interest, which did not go unnoticed by
Susan.

ME: Would you mind if I . . .

SUSAN THE INTERDIMENSIONAL ANTHROPOLOGIST: Took a picture of the table of contents? Nah. I figured you would.

ME: [grateful] Thanks. It'd just make it so much easier for me to pick the stories if I already knew what I was going to pick. Er, you know what I mean.

SUSAN THE INTERDIMENSIONAL ANTHROPOLOGIST: No prob. Always happy to help form a stable causal loop. [then] Within this book, parallel planes of flattened wood pulp and ink markings, arranged in a particular configuration in this volume of space, are maps, instructions, detailed blueprints of the multiverse.

ME: I mean, sure. But those aren't really . . . real. Are they?

SUSAN THE INTERDIMENSIONAL ANTHROPOLOGIST: Depends on what you mean by real.

ME: Factual. Corresponding to an agreed-upon reality.

SUSAN THE INTERDIMENSIONAL ANTHROPOLOGIST: Given the current state of the American polity, I'm wondering whether you are overestimating the level of agreement. But that's not the point. You're right, they're not real in your universe. But these alternative realities do exist. And they're closer than you think.

ME: [looking around] Close? How close?

SUSAN THE INTERDIMENSIONAL ANTHROPOLOGIST: They are what is known as the adjacent possible. If you can imagine it from this universe, then they must, as a matter of definition, touch your universe.

ME: So all twenty of those stories are actually other possible worlds that border this one.

SUSAN THE INTERDIMENSIONAL ANTHROPOLOGIST: [nodding] You're a quick study. Yes, they not only surround this world, they buttress it. They actually define it.

ME: What do you mean, they define it?

SUSAN THE INTERDIMENSIONAL ANTHROPOLOGIST: Imagine your universe on a map. To the left, an ocean. To the right, mountains. Above and below, other features of the topology.

ME: We're bounded on all sides by our imagination. Leaving us in the middle.

SUSAN THE INTERDIMENSIONAL ANTHROPOLOGIST: Your universe is the negative space defined by these natural boundaries.

ME: Our reality is defined by what we can imagine.

SUSAN THE INTERDIMENSIONAL ANTHROPOLOGIST: All these imaginary worlds are fundamentally grounded in your consensus reality. They depend on it.

ME: So the bigger our imaginations, the richer and more stable our own reality becomes. But then, what about . . .

SUSAN THE INTERDIMENSIONAL ANTHROPOLOGIST: Right. So you can see why this current situation is so dangerous. What's happening now is that the imagination is being challenged. The diversity of viewpoints, the ability to create stories, to have different perspectives, is being systematically destroyed. In its place, a narrative is being decreed.

ME: They're trying to legislate and enforce a single master narrative.

SUSAN THE INTERDIMENSIONAL ANTHROPOLOGIST: And that master narrative is not coherent. It is unconnected from the base reality. It does not depend on consensus. It is an impoverished substitute for reality. The destruction of truth can't go on indefinitely. Reality will continue to fragment, until reality itself loses use as a meaningful term.

ME: This sounds pretty bad. Is it too late?

SUSAN THE INTERDIMENSIONAL ANTHROPOLOGIST: It's not too late. That's where this anthology comes in. The stories, this technology you have invented, they are engineering solutions for structural repair of micro-realities. This is the material science creating an invisible structure that actually strengthens because it depends on the underlying consensus reality. By connecting to the substructure, the foundational reality, it reinforces and delineates, giving a shape to truth. A mosaic, created by the imagination, of independent and pluralistic voices, which form in the aggregate a hidden framework, protecting your world from collapse. They don't assert the truth, they depend upon it. [Checks her interdimensional gadget] Whoops, sorry, I was wrong. Looks like it's too late after all. Bye!

At this, Susan disappeared out of existence.

Turns out the bifurcated reality collapsed, so only one was left. You know what happened next, probably.

The other reality took over. It won. There was just one reality. *This* one.

II. *Alternatives to Reality*

(NOTE: This is also completely true. All of this also happened.)

I was just getting over the whole Susan of it all when another interdimensional being showed up.

ME: Let me guess. Anthropologist.

INTERDIMENSIONAL BEING: Actually, no. I'm a cop. My name is Stan.

ME: This seems bad.

STAN THE INTERDIMENSIONAL COP: I'm not going to lie, sir. It's not good.

ME: Are you going to arrest me?

STAN THE INTERDIMENSIONAL COP: Not you. You're not very important. And anyway, if I were going to arrest someone, it'd be all of you.

ME: So then what are you here for?

STAN THE INTERDIMENSIONAL COP: You people have a lot of explaining to do.

ME: I suppose by "you people" you mean humans.

STAN THE INTERDIMENSIONAL COP: Not all humans. Just Americans. Are you an American?

ME: Please don't talk to me. I don't know anything. Really. You could not have picked a worse person to speak on behalf of humanity. Go talk to that lady over there, with the earbuds, pretending not to notice you. Or maybe that guy with a little bit of cream cheese on the corner of his mouth. Anyone but me.

STAN THE INTERDIMENSIONAL COP: It's good that you're just sort of an average person. A nobody. Someone at random. That way we can be sure we're getting a representative sample.

ME: [gulping] A representative sample for what?

STAN THE INTERDIMENSIONAL COP: This universe is taking up a lot of space. And not producing much in the way of interesting ideas. We're thinking of shutting it down. Plus America seems to have really caused some distortions in reality. The whole place is really just not working out.

ME: Please don't shut down our universe. We like existing. You just caught us at a weird time. Could you maybe come back, like, four years ago? Or maybe a few thousand years from now?

STAN THE INTERDIMENSIONAL COP: [looking around] This is a bad situation.

ME: I know. We know. We know it is.

STAN THE INTERDIMENSIONAL COP: Can you justify your existence? Give me one good reason not to collide this whole place with antimatter and toss it on the junk heap.

I was sort of at a loss for words. I'd never been great under pressure, and this was a little bit above my pay grade. Stan raised his universe-annihilation gadget, set to Total Annihilation. I closed my eyes and said to everyone, *Sorry. I did my best, but I guess my best wasn't good enough.*

And then I realized: I was still holding the book.

I dropped to my knees, pleading for not just my own feeble existence but that of everyone in the cosmos.

ME: If you'd just . . . read this.

STAN THE INTERDIMENSIONAL COP: [holding the book] What am I supposed to do with this?

I hear a deafening noise. I close my eyes, fearing the worst. Nothing.

And then I hear a voice.

VOICE: Read it.

I opened my eyes. Susan!

ME: Susan! I've never been happier to see an interdimensional anthropologist. Why did you come back?

SUSAN THE INTERDIMENSIONAL ANTHROPOLOGIST: To make sure Stan read that book. And also, it'd be bad for my research proposal if he destroyed this place before I published.

STAN THE INTERDIMENSIONAL COP: What's so special about these twenty stories?

SUSAN THE INTERDIMENSIONAL ANTHROPOLOGIST: They represent what the species is capable of. A cross-section in space and time, and look at this. Their actual tech might be primitive, but their conceptual machinery shows promise, shows the potential of what they can do. They investigate selves and others, minds and bodies, differences. Truth and illusion. Universes, large and small, extensive and interior. Slip expertly from their own consciousness into another, inhabiting it. These are empaths, all of them, that I'd put right up there with the Teleflugans.

STAN THE INTERDIMENSIONAL COP: Bullshit. The Teleflugans. Right. Wait . . . really?

SUSAN THE INTERDIMENSIONAL ANTHROPOLOGIST: Really. Just read it, Stan.

Stan pressed it to his cheek for a few milliseconds. Susan watched him expectantly, waiting for his reaction.

SUSAN THE INTERDIMENSIONAL ANTHROPOLOGIST: Well?

STAN THE INTERDIMENSIONAL COP: Well.

Stan started crying. And laughing.

STAN THE INTERDIMENSIONAL COP: Well, shit, Susan. I guess you
    were telling the truth.

Stan turned to me.

STAN THE INTERDIMENSIONAL COP: Human idiot—why didn't
    you tell me you had this technology?
ME: Um, I didn't realize it was so important?
STAN THE INTERDIMENSIONAL COP: That's why you're an idiot.
    You can come up with this and yet not realize how important it is.
ME: Wait a minute. Are you telling me that but for the existence of
    our literature, you would have thought this whole universe was
    worth destroying?
STAN THE INTERDIMENSIONAL COP: Dude, now you're talking
    crazy. The stories won't save the world. But they are evidence of
    something. They are evidence that despite the tenuous grasp on
    reality you all seem to have here, the collapsing of objective truth
    that's going on, and the instability it's causing at this particular
    point in space and time—despite all of that, you still seem to
    have at least a few people interested in imagining better worlds,
    other worlds, the existence of alternative points of view. Based
    on these twenty stories, this narrative speculation, we have . . .
    something to go on. A scrap of hope, for you as a civilization. As
    a species.
ME: So . . . you're not going to annihilate us?
STAN THE INTERDIMENSIONAL COP: Not yet. But you'd better
    keep this up. You're on thin ice. [to Susan] You hungry? I could
    go for a slice of pizza.

And with that, Susan and Stan disappeared from this universe.
For at least another year.
    This is all true. All of this really happened. I mean, to the extent
that "truth" and "reality" still exist.

III. Reality

After the whole thing with Susan and Stan was over, I finished my
coffee. Then I went and got a sandwich. Self-fulfilling timelines
make me hungry. As I ate my sandwich, I dove back into my work,
with renewed vigor and an appreciation for the stakes involved.

Time hardly moved—I must have entered some kind of vortex, as I read the remarkable stories that make up this collection. These stories we tell ourselves, the best of them, they tell us something about what parts of reality we understand well enough to question. About who we are now. And about what we are capable of when we let ourselves imagine the people we could be. These stories, taken together, might be sufficient evidence to persuade the cosmic overlords that despite our shortcomings, we merit an extension pending further consideration. That on some anthropological rubric, we pass a minimum test for proof of civilization. Or better yet, at their very best, they might be (in the words of Stan the Interdimensional Cop) a scrap of hope.

— CHARLES YU

The Best American
SCIENCE FICTION
and FANTASY
2017

LEIGH BARDUGO

Head, Scales, Tongue, Tail

FROM *Summer Days and Summer Nights*

Head

THERE WERE A lot of stories about Annalee Saperstein and why she came to Little Spindle, but Gracie's favorite was the heat wave.

In 1986, New York endured a summer so miserable that anyone who could afford to leave the city did. The pavement went soft with the heat, a man was found dead in his bathtub with an electric fan half submerged in the water next to his hairy knees, and the power grid flickered on and off like a bug light rattling with moths. On the Upper West Side, above the bakeries and delicatessens, the Woolworth's and the Red Apple market, people slept on top of their sheets, sucked on handkerchiefs full of crushed ice, and opened their windows wide, praying for a breeze. That was why, when the Hudson leaped its banks and went looking for trouble on a hot July night, the river found Ruth Blonksy's window wedged open with a dented Candie's shoebox.

Earlier that day Ruth had been in Riverside Park with her friends, eating lemon pucker ices and wearing a persimmon-colored shift that was really a vintage nightgown she'd dyed with two boxes of Rit and mixed success. Rain had been promised for days, but the sky hung heavy over the city, a distended gray belly of cloud that refused to split. Sweat beading over her skin, Ruth had leaned against the park railing to look down at the swaying surface of the river, opaque and nearly black beneath the overcast sky, and had the eerie sense that the water was looking back at her.

Then a drop of lemon ice trickled from the little pink spoon in her hand, startling as a cold tongue lapping at her pulse point, and Marva Allsburg shouted, "We're going to Jaybee's to look at records."

Ruth licked the lemon ice from her wrist and thought no more of the river.

But later that night, when she woke—her sheets soaked through with sweat, a tangle of reeds at the foot of her bed—that sticky trail of sugar was what first came to mind. She'd fallen asleep in her clothes, and her persimmon shift clung wetly to her stomach. Beneath it, her body burned feverish with half-remembered dreams of the river god, a muscular shape that moved through the deep current of sleep, his gray skin speckled blue and green. Her lips felt just kissed, and her head was clouded as if she'd risen too fast from some great depth. It took a long moment for her ears to clear, for her to recognize the moss-and-metal smell of wet concrete, and then to make sense of the sound coming through her open window—rain falling in a steady patter onto the predawn streets below. The heat had broken at last.

Nine months later, Ruth gave birth to a baby with kelp-green eyes and ropes of seaweed hair. When Ruth's father kicked her out of their walkup, calling her names in Polish and English and making angry noises about the Puerto Rican boy who had taken Ruth to her junior prom, Annalee Saperstein took her in, ignoring the neighborhood whispers and clucking. Annalee worked at the twenty-four-hour coin laundry on West Seventy-Ninth. No one was sure when she slept, because whenever you walked past, she always seemed to be sitting at the counter doing her crossword beneath the fluorescent lights, the machines humming and rattling, no matter the hour. Joey Pastan had mouthed off to her once when he ran out of quarters, and he swore the dryers had actually growled at him, so nobody was entirely surprised that Annalee believed Ruth Blonksy. And when, waiting in line at Gitlitz Delicatessen, Annalee smacked Ruth's father in the chest with the half-pound of thinly sliced corned beef she'd just purchased and snapped that river spirits were not to be trusted, no one dared to argue.

Ruth's daughter refused milk. She would only drink salt water and eat pound after pound of oysters, clams, and tiny crayfish, which had to be delivered in crates to Annalee's cramped apartment. But the diet must have agreed with her, because the green-eyed baby grew into a beautiful girl who was spotted by a talent scout while crossing Amsterdam Avenue. She became a famous model, renowned for her full lips and liquid walk, and bought her mother a penthouse on Park Avenue that they decorated with paintings of desert flowers and dry creek beds. They gave Annalee Saperstein a tidy sum that allowed her to quit her job at the coin laundry and move out of the city to Little Spindle, where she opened her Dairy Queen franchise.

At least, that was one of the stories about how Annalee Saperstein came to Little Spindle, and Gracie liked it because she felt it made a kind of sense. Why else would Annalee get copies of French and Italian *Vogue* when all she ever wore were polyester housedresses and Birkenstock sandals with socks?

People said Annalee *knew* things. It was why Donna Bakewell came to see her the summer her terrier got hit by a car and she couldn't seem to stop crying—not even to sleep, or to buy a can of green beans at the Price Chopper, or to answer the phone. People would call her up and just hear her sobbing and hiccupping on the other end. But somehow a chat with Annalee managed what no doctor or pill could and dried Donna's tears right up. It was why, when Jason Mylo couldn't shake the idea that his ex-wife had put a curse on his new Chevy truck, he paid a late-night visit to the DQ to see Annalee. And it was also why, when Gracie Michaux saw something that looked very much like a sea monster breach the waters of Little Spindle Lake, she went looking for Annalee Saperstein.

Gracie had been sitting on the bank of what she considered *her* cove, a rocky crescent on the south side of the lake that no one else seemed to know or care about. It was too shady for sunbathers and devoid of the picnic tables and rope swings that drew vacationers like beacons during the tourist season. She'd been skipping stones, telling herself not to pick the scab on her knee, because she wanted to look good in the jean shorts she'd cut even shorter on her fourteenth birthday, and then doing it anyway, when she heard a splash. One, two, three humps breached the blue surface of the water, a glittering little mountain range, there and then gone, followed by the slap of—Gracie's mind refused to accept it, and at the same time clamored—a *tail*.

Gracie scrabbled backward up the banks to the pines and dragged herself to her feet, heart jackrabbiting in her chest, waiting for the water to part again or for something huge and scaly to haul itself onto the sand, but nothing happened. Her mouth was salty with the taste of blood. She'd bitten her tongue. She spat once, leaped onto her bicycle, and pedaled as hard as she could down the bumpy dirt path to the smooth pavement of the main road, thighs burning as she hurtled through town.

It wasn't much of a hurtle, because Little Spindle wasn't much of a town. There was a mini-mart, a gas station with the town's lone ATM, a veterinary clinic, a string of souvenir shops, and the old Rotary hall, which had become the public library after the library in Greater Spindle flooded ten years before. Little Spindle had never gotten the traffic or the clusters of condos and fancy homes that crowded around Greater Spindle, just a smattering of rental cottages and the Spindrift Inn. Despite the fact that the lake was nearly as big as Greater Spindle and surrounded by perfectly good land, there was something about Little Spindle Lake that put people off.

The lake looked pleasant enough from a distance, glimpsed through the pines in vibrant blue flashes, sunlight spiking off its surface in jewel-bright shards. But as you got closer you started to feel your spirits sink, and by the time you were at its shore, you felt positively mournful. You'd convince yourself to walk down to the beach anyway, maybe swing out on the old tire, but as you let go of the rope, you'd hang for the briefest second above the water and you'd know with absolute certainty that you'd made a horrible mistake, that once you vanished beneath the surface you would never be seen again, that the lake was not a lake but a mouth—hungry, blue, and sullen. Some people seemed impervious to the effects of Little Spindle, but others refused even to put a toe in the water.

The only place that did real business year-round was the Dairy Queen, despite the Stewart's only a few miles away. But why Annalee had chosen to set up shop in Little Spindle instead of Greater Spindle was a mystery to everyone but her.

Gracie didn't head straight for the DQ that day—not at first. In fact, she got all the way home, tossed her bike down in the yard, and had her hand on the screen door before she caught herself. Eric and her mom liked to spend Saturdays in the backyard, just lying next to each other on plastic lounge chairs, snoozing, hands clasped like a couple of otters. They both worked long hours at the hospital in Greater Spindle and hoarded sleep like it was a hobby.

Gracie hovered there at the door, hand outstretched. What could she really say to her mother? Her weary mother who never stopped looking worried, even in sleep? For a moment, at the edge of the lake, Gracie had been a kid again, but she was fourteen. She should know better.

She got back on her bike and pedaled slowly, meditatively, in no direction at all, belief seeping away as if the sun was sweating it out of her. What had she actually seen? A fish maybe? A few fish? But some deeper sense must have been guiding her, because when she got to the Dairy Queen she turned into the half-full parking lot.

Annalee Saperstein was at a table by the window, as she always was, doing her crossword, a Peanut Buster Parfait melting in front of her. Gracie mostly knew Annalee because she liked listening to the stories about her, and because her mom was always sending Gracie to ask Annalee over for dinner.

"She's old and alone," Gracie's mother would say.

"She seems to like it."

Her mom would wave her finger in the air like she was conducting an invisible orchestra. "No one likes being alone."

Gracie tried not to roll her eyes. She tried.

Now she slid into the hard red seat across from Annalee and said, "Do you know anything about Idgy Pidgy?"

"Good afternoon to you too," Annalee grumped, without looking up from her crossword.

"Sorry," Gracie said. She thought of explaining that she'd had a strange start to her day, but instead opted for "How are you?"

"Not dead yet. It would kill you to use a comb?"

"No point." Gracie tried to rope her slick black hair back into its ponytail. "My hair doesn't take well to instruction." She waited, then said, "So . . . the monster in the lake?"

She knew she wasn't the first person to claim she'd seen something in the waters of Little Spindle. There had been a bunch of sightings in the sixties and seventies, though Gracie's mom claimed that was because everyone was on drugs. The town council had even tried to turn it into a tourist draw by dubbing it the Idgy Pidgy—"Little Spindle's Little Monster"—and painting the image of a friendly-looking sea serpent with googly eyes on the WELCOME TO LITTLE SPINDLE sign. It hadn't caught on, but you could still see its outline on the sign, and a few winters back someone had spray-painted a huge phallus onto it. For the three days it took the town council to notice and get someone to paint over it, the sign looked like the Idgy Pidgy was trying to have sex with the *E* at the end of LITTLE SPINDLE.

"You mean like Loch Ness?" Annalee asked, glancing up through her thick glasses. "You got a sunburn."

Gracie shrugged. She was always getting a sunburn, getting over a sunburn, or about to get a sunburn. "I mean like *our* lake monster." It hadn't been like Loch Ness. The shape had been completely different. Kind of like the goofy serpent on the town sign, actually.

"Ask that kid."

"Which kid?"

"I don't know his name. Summer kid. Comes in here every day at four for a cherry dip."

Gracie gagged. "Cherry dip is vile."

Annalee jabbed her pen at Gracie. "Cherry dip sells cones."

"What does he look like?"

"Skinny. Big purple backpack. White hair."

Gracie slid down in the booth, body going limp with disappointment. "Eli?"

Gracie knew most of the summer kids who had been coming to Little Spindle for a while. They pretty much kept to themselves. Their parents invited each other to barbecues, and they moved in rowdy cliques on their dirt bikes, taking over the lakes, making lines at Rottie's Red Hot and the DQ, coming into Youvenirs right before Labor Day to buy a hat or a key chain. But Eli was always on his own. His family's rental had to be somewhere near the north side of the lake, because every May he'd show up walking south on the main road, wearing too-big madras shorts and lugging a purple backpack. He'd slap his way to the library in a pair of faded Vans and spend the entire afternoon there by himself, then pick up his big backpack and trundle back home like some kind of weird blond pillbug, but not before he stopped at the DQ—apparently to order a cherry dip.

"What's wrong with him?" asked Annalee.

It was too hard to explain. Gracie shrugged. "He's a little bit the worst."

"The cherry dip of humans?"

Gracie laughed, then felt bad for laughing when Annalee

peered at her over those thick plastic frames and said, "Because you're the town sweetheart? You could use some more friends."

Gracie tugged at the frayed end of her newly cut shorts. She had friends. Mosey Allen was all right. And Lila Brightman. She had people to eat lunch with, people who waited for her before first bell. But they lived in Greater Spindle, with most of the kids from her school.

"What would Eli Cuddy know about Idgy Pidgy anyway?" Gracie asked.

"Spends all his time in the library, doesn't he?"

Annalee had a point. Gracie tapped her fingers on the table, scraped more of the chipped lilac polish from her thumbnail. She thought of the story of the green-eyed baby and the river god. "So you've never seen anything like Idgy Pidgy?"

"I can barely see the pen in my hand," Annalee said sourly.

"But if a person saw a monster, a real one, not like . . . not a metaphor, that person's probably crazy, right?"

Annalee pushed her glasses up her nose with one gnarled finger. Behind them, her brown eyes had a soft, rheumy sheen. "There are monsters everywhere, *tsigele*," she said. "It's always good to know their names." She took a bite of the puddle that was left of her sundae and smacked her lips. "Your friend is here."

Eli Cuddy was standing at the counter, backpack weighting his shoulders, placing his order. The problem with Eli wasn't just that he liked to be indoors more than outdoors. Gracie was okay with that. It was that he never talked to anyone. And he always looked a little—damp. Like his clothes were clinging to his skinny chest. Like if you touched his skin, he might be *moist*.

Eli planted himself in a two-seater booth and propped a book open on the slope of his backpack so he could read while he ate.

Who eats an ice cream cone like that? Gracie wondered as she watched him take weird, tidy little bites. Then she remembered those shapes moving in the lake. *Sunlight on the water,* her mind protested. *Scales,* her heart insisted.

"What's *tsigele* mean?" she asked Annalee.

"'Little goat,'" said Annalee. "Bleat bleat, little goat. Go on with you."

Why not? Gracie wiped her palms on her shorts and ambled up to the booth. She felt bolder than usual. Maybe because nothing she said to Eli Cuddy mattered. It wasn't like, if she made a fool of herself, he'd have anyone to tell.

"Hey," she said. He blinked up at her. She had no idea what to do with her hands, so she planted them on her hips, then worried she looked like she was about to start a pep routine and dropped them. "You're Eli, right?"

"Yeah."

"I'm Gracie."

"I know. You work at Youvenirs."

"Oh," she said. "Right." Gracie worked summer mornings there, mostly because Henny had taken pity on her and let her show up to dust things for a few dollars an hour. Had Eli come in before?

He was waiting. Gracie wished she'd planned this out better. Saying she believed in monsters felt sort of like showing someone the collection of stuffed animals she kept on her bed, like she was announcing, *I'm still a little kid. I'm still afraid of things that can curl around your leg and drag you under.*

"You know the Loch Ness monster?" she blurted.

Eli's brow creased. "Not personally."

Gracie plunged ahead. "You think it could be real?"

Eli closed his book carefully and studied her with very serious, very blue eyes, the furrow between his eyebrows deepening. His lashes were so blond they were almost silver. "Did you look through my library record?" he asked. "Because that's a federal crime."

"What?" It was Gracie's turn to scrutinize Eli. "No, I didn't spy on you. I just asked you a question."

"Oh. Well. Good. Because I'm not totally sure it's a crime anyway."

"What are you looking at that you're so worried people will see? Porn?"

"Volumes of it," he said, in that same serious voice. "As much porn as I can get. The Little Spindle Library's collection is small but thoughtfully curated."

Gracie snorted, and Eli's mouth tugged up a little.

"Okay, perv. Annalee said you might know something about Idgy Pidgy and that kind of stuff."

"Annalee?"

Gracie bobbed her chin over to the booth by the window, where a nervous-looking man in a Hawaiian shirt had seated himself across from Annalee and was whispering something to her as he tore up a napkin. "This is her place."

"I like cryptozoology," Eli said. Off her blank look, he continued, "Bigfoot. The Loch Ness Monster. Ogopogo."

Gracie hesitated. "You think all of those are real?"

"Not all of them. Statistically. But no one was sure the giant squid was real until they started washing up on beaches in New Zealand."

"Really?"

Eli gave her a businesslike nod. "There's a specimen at the Natural History Museum in London that's twenty-eight feet long. They think that's a small one."

"No shit," Gracie breathed.

Another precise nod. "No. Shit."

This time Gracie laughed outright. "Hold up," she said, "I want a Blizzard. Don't go anywhere."

He didn't.

That summer took on a wavy, loopy, lazing shape for Gracie. Mornings she "worked" at Youvenirs, rearranging knickknacks in the windows and pointing the rare customer toward the register. At noon she'd meet up with Eli and they'd go to the library or ride bikes to her cove, though Eli thought another sighting there was unlikely.

"Why would it come back here?" he asked as they stared out at the sun-dappled water.

"It was here before. Maybe it likes the shade."

"Or maybe it was just passing through."

Most of the time they talked about Idgy Pidgy. Or at least that was where their conversations always started.

"You could have just seen fish," Eli said as they flipped through a book on North American myths, beneath an umbrella at Rottie's Red Hot.

"That would have to be some really big fish."

"Carp can grow to be over forty pounds."

She shook her head. "No. The scales were different." Like jewels. Like a fan of abalone shells. Like clouds moving over water.

"You know, every culture has its own set of megafauna. A giant blue crow has been spotted in Brazil."

"This wasn't a blue crow. And 'megafauna' sounds like a band."

"Not a good band."

"I'd go see them." Then Gracie shook her head. "Why do you eat that way?"

Eli paused. "What way?"

"Like you're going to write an essay about every bite. You're eating a cheeseburger, not defusing a bomb."

But Eli did everything that way—slowly, thoughtfully. He rode his bike that way. He wrote things down in his blue spiral notebook that way. He took what seemed like an hour to pick out something to eat at Rottie's Red Hot when there were only five things on the menu, which never changed. It was weird, no doubt, and Gracie was glad her friends from school spent most of their summers around Greater Spindle so she didn't have to try to explain any of it. But there was also something kind of nice about the way Eli took things so seriously, like he really gave everything his full attention.

They compiled lists of Idgy Pidgy sightings. There had been less than twenty in the town's history, dating back to the 1920s.

"We should cross-reference them with Loch Ness and Ogopogo sightings," said Eli. "See if there's a pattern. Then we can figure out when we should surveil the lake."

"Surveil," Gracie said, doodling a sea serpent in the margin of Eli's list. "Like police. We can set up a perimeter."

"Why would we do that?"

"It's what they do on cop shows. Set up a perimeter. Lock down the perp."

"No TV, remember?" Eli's parents had a "no screens" policy. He used the computers at the library, but at home it was no Internet, no cell phone, no television. Apparently they were vegetarians too, and Eli liked to eat all the meat he could when they left him to his own devices. The closest he got to vegetables was french fries. Gracie sometimes wondered if he was poor in a way that she wasn't. He never seemed short of money for the arcade or hot pretzels, but he always wore the same clothes and always seemed hungry. People with money didn't summer in Little Spindle. But people without money didn't summer at all. Gracie wasn't really sure she wanted to know. She liked that they didn't talk about their parents or school.

Now she picked up Eli's notebook and asked, "How can we surveil if you don't know proper police procedure?"

"All the good detectives are in books."

"Sherlock Holmes?"

"Conan Doyle is too dry. I like Raymond Carver, Ross Macdonald, Walter Mosley. I read every paperback they have here, during my noir phase."

Gracie drew bubbles coming out of Idgy Pidgy's nose. "Eli," she said, without looking at him, "do you actually think I saw something in the lake?"

"Possibly."

She pushed on. "Or are you just humoring me so you have someone to hang out with?" It came out meaner than she'd meant it to, maybe because the answer mattered.

Eli cocked his head to one side, thinking, seeking an honest answer, like he was solving for x. "Maybe a little," he said at last.

Gracie nodded. She liked that he hadn't pretended something different. "I'm okay with that." She hopped down off the table. "You can be the stodgy veteran with a drinking problem, and I'm the loose cannon."

"Can I wear a cheap suit?"

"Do you have a cheap suit?"

"No."

"Then you can wear the same dumb madras shorts you always do."

They rode their bicycles to every place there had ever been an Idgy Pidgy sighting, all the way up to Greater Spindle. Some spots were sunny, some shady, some off beaches, others off narrow spits of rock and sand. There was no pattern. When they got sick of Idgy Pidgy, they'd head over to the Fun Spot to play Skee-Ball or minigolf. Eli was terrible at both, but he seemed perfectly happy to lose to Gracie and to tidily record his miserable scores.

On the Friday before Labor Day, they ate lunch in front of the library—tomato sandwiches and cold corn on the cob that Gracie's mother had made earlier that week. A map of the U.S. and Canada was spread out on the picnic table before them. The sun was heavy on their shoulders and Gracie felt sweaty and dull. She wanted to go to the lake, just to swim, not to look for Idgy Pidgy, but Eli claimed it was too hot to move.

"There's probably a barbecue somewhere," she said, lying on the bench, toes digging in the dead grass beneath the table. "You really want to waste your last school-free Friday just looking at maps in the middle of town?"

"Yeah," he said. "I really do."

Gracie felt herself smiling. Her mother seemed to want to spend all her time with Eric. Mosey and Lila lived practically next door to each other and had been best friends since they were five. It was nice to have someone prefer her company, even if it was Eli Cuddy.

She covered her eyes with her arm to block the sun. "Do we have anything to read?"

"I returned all my books."

"Read me town names off the map."

"Why?"

"You won't go swimming, and I like being read to."

Eli cleared his throat. "Burgheim. Furdale. Saskatoon . . ."

Strung together, they sounded almost like a story.

Gracie thought about inviting Eli when she went to see the end-of-season fireworks up at Okhena Beach the next night, with Lila and Mosey, but she wasn't quite sure how to explain all the time she'd been spending with him, and she thought she should sleep over at Mosey's place. She didn't want to feel completely left out when classes started. It was an investment in the school year. But when Monday came and there was no Eli walking the main road or at the DQ, she felt a little hollow.

"That kid gone?" Annalee asked as Gracie poked at the up-ended cone in her dish. She'd decided to try a cherry dip. It was just as disgusting as she remembered.

"Eli? Yeah. He went back to the city."

"He seems all right," said Annalee, taking the cup of ice cream from Gracie and tossing it in the trash.

"Mom wants you to come for dinner on Friday night," Gracie said.

But she could admit that maybe Eli Cuddy was better than all right.

The next May, right before Memorial Day, Gracie went down to her cove at Little Spindle. She'd been plenty of times over the school year. She'd done her homework there until the air turned too cold for sitting still, then watched ice form on the edges of the water as winter set in. She'd nearly jumped out of her skin when a black birch snapped beneath the weight of the frost on its branches and fell into the shallows with a resigned groan. And on that last Friday in May, she made sure she was on the shore, skipping stones, just in case there was magic in the date or the Idgy Pidgy had a clock keeping time in its heart. Nothing happened.

She went by Youvenirs, but she'd been in the previous day to help Henny get ready for summer, so there was nothing left to do, and eventually she ended up at the Dairy Queen with an order of curly fries she didn't really want.

"Waiting for your friend?" Annalee asked as she sifted through her newspaper for the crossword.

"I'm just eating my fries."

When she saw Eli, Gracie felt an embarrassing rush of relief. He was taller, a lot taller, but just as skinny and damp and serious-looking as ever. Gracie didn't budge, her insides knotted up. Maybe he wouldn't want to hang out again. *That's fine,* she told herself. But he scanned the seats even before he went to the counter, and when he saw her, his pale face lit up like silver sparklers.

Annalee's laugh sounded suspiciously like a cackle.

"Hey!" he said, striding over. His legs seemed to reach all the way to his chin now. "I found something amazing. You want a Blizzard?"

And just like that, it was summer all over again.

Scales

The something amazing was a dusty room in the basement of the library, packed with old vinyl record albums, a turntable, and a pile of headphones tucked into a nest of curly black cords.

"I'm so glad it's still here," Eli said. "I found it right before Labor Day, and I was afraid someone would finally get around to clearing it out over the winter."

Gracie felt a pang of guilt over not spending that last weekend with Eli, but she was also pleased he'd been waiting to show her this. "Does that thing work?" she asked, pointing to the column of stereo gear.

Eli flipped a couple of switches and red lights blinked on. "We are go."

Gracie slid a record from the shelves and read the title: *Jackie*

Gleason: Music, Martinis, and Memories. "What if I only want the music?"

"We could just listen to a third of it."

They made a stack of records, competing to find the one with the weirdest cover—flying toasters, men on fire, barbarian princesses in metal bikinis—and listened to all of them, lying on the floor, big padded headphones hugging their ears. Most of the music was awful, but a few albums were really good. *Bella Donna* had Stevie Nicks on the cover dressed like an angel tree-topper and holding a cockatoo, but they listened to it all the way through, twice, and when "Edge of Seventeen" came on, Gracie imagined herself rising out of the lake in a long white dress, flying through the woods, hair like a black banner behind her.

It wasn't until she was pedaling home, stomach growling for dinner, singing *Ooh baby ooh baby ooh,* that Gracie realized she and Eli hadn't talked about Idgy Pidgy once.

Though Gracie hadn't exactly been keeping Eli a secret from Mosey and Lila, she hadn't mentioned him either. She just wasn't sure they'd get him. But one afternoon, when she and Eli were eating at Rottie's Red Hot, a horn blared from the lot, and when Gracie looked around, there was Mosey in her dad's Corolla, with Lila in the passenger seat.

"Don't you only have a learner's permit?" she asked as Mosey and Lila squeezed in on the round benches.

"My parents don't care, if I'm just coming down to Little Spindle. And it means they don't have to drive me. Where have you been, anyway?" Mosey glanced pointedly at Eli.

"Nowhere. Youvenirs. The usual."

Eli said nothing, just carefully parceled out ketchup into a lopsided steeple by his fries.

They ate. They talked about taking the train into the city to see a concert.

"How come your family doesn't stay at Greater Spindle?" Mosey asked.

Eli cocked his head to one side, giving the question his full consideration. "We've just always come here. I think they like the quiet."

"I like it too," said Lila. "Not the lake so much, but it's nice in the summer, when Greater Spindle gets all crazy."

Mosey popped a fry in her mouth. "The lake is haunted."

"By what?" asked Eli, leaning forward.

"Some lady drowned her kids there."

Lila rolled her eyes. "That's a complete lie."

"La Llorona," said Eli. "The weeping woman. There's legends like that all over the place."

Great, thought Gracie. *We can all start hunting ghosts together.*

She tried to ignore the squirmy feeling in her gut. She'd told herself that she hadn't wanted to introduce Eli to Mosey and Lila because he was so odd, but now she wasn't sure. She loved Mosey and Lila, but she always felt a little alone around them, even when they were sitting together at a bonfire or huddled in the back row of the Spotlight watching a matinee. She didn't want to feel that way around Eli.

When Mosey and Lila headed back to Greater Spindle, Eli gathered up their plastic baskets on a tray and said, "That was fun."

"Yeah," Gracie agreed, a bit too enthusiastically.

"Let's take bikes to Robin Ridge tomorrow."

"Everyone?"

The furrow between Eli's brows appeared. "Well, yeah," he said. "You and me."

Everyone.

Teeth

Gracie couldn't pinpoint the moment Eli dried out, only the moment she noticed. They were lying on the floor of Mosey's bedroom, rain lashing at the windows.

She'd gotten her driver's license that summer, and her mom's boyfriend didn't mind loaning Gracie his truck once in a while so she could drive up to Greater Spindle. Gas money was harder to come by. There were better jobs in Greater Spindle, but none that were guaranteed to correspond with Gracie's mother's shifts, so Gracie was still working at Youvenirs, since she could get there on her bike.

It felt like Little Spindle was closing in on her, like she was standing on a shore that got narrower and narrower as the tide came in. People were talking about SATs and college applications and summer internships. Everything seemed to be speeding up,

and everyone seemed to be gathering momentum, ready to go
shooting off into the future on carefully plotted trajectories, while
Gracie was still struggling to get her bearings.

When Gracie started to get that panicked feeling, she'd find
Eli at the Dairy Queen or the library, and they'd go down to the
"Hall of Records" and line up all the Bowie albums so they could
look at his fragile, mysterious face, or they'd listen to *Emmet Otter's
Jug-Band Christmas* while they tried to decipher all the clues on the
cover of *Sgt. Pepper's*. She didn't know what she was going to do
when the school year started.

They'd driven up to Greater Spindle in Eric's truck without
much of a plan, radio up, windows down to save gas on air conditioning, sweating against the plastic seats, but when the storm had
rolled in they'd holed up at Mosey's to watch movies.

Lila and Mosey were up on the bed painting their toes and picking songs to play for each other, and Gracie was sprawled out on
the carpet with Eli, listening to him read from some boring book
about waterways. Gracie wasn't paying much attention. She was on
her stomach, head on her arms, listening to the rain on the roof
and the murmur of Eli's voice, and feeling okay for the first time
in a while, as if someone had taken the hot knot of tension she
always seemed to be carrying beneath her ribs and dunked it in
cool water.

The thunder had been a near-continuous rumble, and the air
felt thick and electrical outside. Inside, the air conditioning had
raised goose bumps on Gracie's arms, but she was too lazy to get
up to turn it down, or to ask for a sweater.

"Gracie," Eli said, nudging her shoulder with his bare foot.

"Mmm?"

"Gracie." She heard him move around, and when he spoke
again, he had his head near hers and was whispering. "That cove
you like doesn't have a name."

"So?"

"All the little beaches and inlets have names, but not your cove."

"So let's name it," she mumbled.

"Stone . . . Crescent?"

She flopped on her back and looked up at the smattering of
yellow stars stuck to Mosey's ceiling. "That's awful. It sounds like
a housing development or a breakfast roll. How about Gracie's
Archipelago?"

"It's not an archipelago."

"Then something good. Something about Idgy Pidgy. Dragon Scale Cove, or the Serpentine."

"It's not shaped like a serpent."

"Beast Mouth Cove," she said.

"*Beast Mouth?* Are you trying to keep people away?"

"Of course. Always. Silverback Beach."

"Silverbacks are gorillas."

"Silver Scales . . . Something that starts with an *s*."

"Shoal," he said.

"Perfect."

"But it's not a shoal."

"We can call it Eli's Last Stand when I drown you there. You're making this impossible." She flipped back on her stomach and looked up at him. He was propped on his elbows, the book open before him. She'd had another suggestion on her lips, but it vanished like a fish slipping free of the line.

Mosey and Lila were talking in low murmurs, tinny music coming out of Lila's phone. Eli's T-shirt was stretched taut across his shoulders, and the light from the lamp by Mosey's bed had caught around his hair in a halo. She could smell the storm on him, like the lightning had followed him home, like he was made of the same dense rain clouds. His skin didn't look damp. It seemed to gleam. He had one finger on the page, holding his place, and Gracie had the urge to slide her fingers over his knuckles, his wrist, the fine blond hair on his forearm. She reared back slightly, trying to shake the thought from her head.

Eli was looking at her expectantly.

"The name should be accurate," he said, his face serious and determined as always. It was a lovely face, all of that thoughtfulness pushing his jaw forward, making that stern divot between his brows.

Gracie said the first thing that came into her head. "Let's call the cove Chuck."

"Because . . . ?"

"Because you throw things into it." Was she making any sense at all?

He nodded, considering, then broke into a ridiculous, light-filled, hideously beautiful smile. "Perfect."

The ride home was like a kind of punishment—cool air rushing through the windows, the radio turned down low, this strange, unwanted feeling beating a new rhythm in her chest. The dark road spooled out in front of them. She wished she were home. She wished they would never stop driving.

Eli's transformation was a betrayal, a bait and switch. Eli Cuddy was supposed to be safe, and now he felt dangerous. She cast around for someone else to want. She'd had a crush on Mason Lee in the ninth grade, and she made Lila take her up to Okhena Beach, where he was lifeguarding, in the hope that seeing him might jolt some sense into her. Unfortunately, the only amazing thing about Mason was the way he looked with his shirt off. He was like a golden retriever. She understood the appeal, but that didn't mean she wanted to take him home.

Mornings when she knew she was going to see Eli felt suddenly breathless and full of possibility. She bought a new shirt in lush, just-dusk purple, picked out slender silver earrings in the shape of feathers, bought apple-blossom lip gloss because it looked like something magical in its pink-and-gold tin, and when she touched her fingers to her mouth it felt like an incantation. *See me. See me the way I see you.*

Gracie knew she was being stupid. If Eli liked her as more than a friend, he'd never given her any clue. He might even have a girl-friend in the city who he wrote long letters to and made out with between classes. He'd never said he did, but she'd never asked him. It had never mattered before. She didn't want it to matter now.

The summer took on a different shape—a desperate, jagged shape, the rise and fall of a dragon's back. The world felt full of hazards. Every song on every album bristled with portent. She found herself trying to communicate through the records she chose, and interpreting the ones that he chose as code. She forced herself to spend more time with Mosey and Lila, and at Youvenirs, cleaning things that didn't need to be cleaned, battling her new greed for Eli's company. But was it new? From the first, her hours with Eli had been warm sand islands, the refuge that had made the murky swim through the rest of the year bearable.

She was torn between the need to say something, to speak this thing inside her before summer ended, and the conviction that she had to avoid that disastrous course of action at all costs. For the first time, she found herself counting down the days until September. If she could just make it to Labor Day without letting her heart spill out of her lips, she'd have the whole school year to get over this wretched, ridiculous thing that had taken her over.

On the Saturday before Labor Day, Gracie and Eli watched the closing fireworks above Greater Spindle. They sat next to each other on the edge of the truck, knees almost touching, shoulders brushing.

"I wish you had a phone," she said, without meaning to.

"Me too. Sort of."

"Only sort of?"

"I like saving up all the things I want to tell you."

That has to be enough, Gracie told herself, as blue and silver light washed over the sharp gleam of his features. *That should be better than enough.*

It got easier. She missed summer. She missed Eli, but it was a relief to be free of the prospect of seeing him. She went to junior prom with Ned Minnery, who was funny and played trumpet. He loved puns. He wore suspenders and striped pants, and did magic tricks. He was the anti-Eli. There was nothing serious about him. It was a fun night, but Gracie wondered if maybe she wasn't any good at fun. She drank enough peach schnapps to talk herself into kissing Ned, and then got sick by the side of the road.

When Memorial Day came around, she felt ready to see Eli, but she didn't let herself go to the Dairy Queen. She couldn't have that kind of summer again. She wouldn't. She went to Okhena Beach instead, planted herself next to Mosey and Lila on the sand, and stayed there as the sun sank low and the opening weekend bonfire began. When someone brought out a guitar, she found a spot atop a picnic table a little way off, bare feet on the bench, shivering in her sweatshirt. *I'm fine,* she thought, telling herself she'd rejoin the others by the flames in just a minute. *I'm good.* But when she saw Eli walking toward her with those long, loping strides, his hair bright in the firelight, face eager, carrying that stupid backpack, all those months of hard work vanished. How had he even gotten to Greater Spindle? Were his parents letting him use the car now? Longing unfurled inside her, as if it had just been waiting for the warm weather to be aired out.

He sat down beside her and said, "You're not going to believe what I found today. The Hall of Records has a whole collection of spoken-word albums behind the Christmas section. It's amazing."

Gracie made herself laugh. "Can't wait." *Did you miss me? Did you kiss anyone? I did, and it was terrible.*

She couldn't do it. She couldn't spend another summer this way. It would drive her insane. She would make up some excuse—emergency hours at Youvenirs, a cholera outbreak. Whatever it took. She pulled the pot of apple lip balm from her pocket. It was nearly empty, but she hadn't bothered to buy more. It was too embarrassing to remember the things she'd let herself think when she'd paid for it.

Eli snatched it from her palm and hurled it into the darkness, into the lake.

"Hey!" Gracie protested. "Why would you do that?"

He took a deep breath. His shoulders lifted, fell. "Because I've spent nine months thinking of apples."

Silence dropped around them like a curtain. In the distance, Gracie could hear people talking, the lazy strum of guitar chords, but it was all another country, another planet. Eli Cuddy was looking at her with all of his focus, his blue eyes nearly black in the firelight. That hopeless thing in her chest fluttered, became something else, dared to bloom.

Eli's long fingers cupped her face, traced the nape of her neck, kept her still, as if he needed to give her every bit of his attention, as if he could learn her like a language, plot her like a course. Eli kissed Gracie like she was a song and he was determined to hear every note. He kissed her the way he did everything else—seriously.

Now summer was round and full, fruit ready to burst, a sun emerging fat, yellow, and happy from the sea. They kissed behind Youvenirs, in the red velvet seats of the Spotlight, on the floor of the record room—the sound of static filling the headphones around their necks as some song or other reached its end.

"We could go to your house," she suggested.

"We could go to yours."

They stayed where they were.

On afternoons, when they left the DQ, Eli's lips were cold and tasted like cherry. On balmy evenings, when they lay on the banks of the cove named Chuck, his hands were warm and restless. Gracie floated in her sandals. She felt covered in jewels. Her bicycle was a winged horse.

But sometime around the end of July, Gracie heard the drone of the insects turn sorrowful. Despite the heat and the sunburned backs of her thighs and the neon still lit on the main road, she felt summer begin to go.

At night she'd hear her mom and Eric laughing in the living room, the television like gray music, and she'd curl up on her side, that narrow panic settling in. With Eli she could forget she was seventeen. She could forget Little Spindle and what came next. A page out of her mother's life, if she was lucky. A car loan so she could go to community college. Watching the kids from her school leave for other places, better places. She wished Eli had a phone. She wished she could reach out to him in the dark. *We could write letters. I could take the train to New York on the weekends.* At night she thought these things, but by the next afternoon Eli was bright as a coin in the sunlight and all she wanted was to kiss his studious mouth.

Days and nights dissolved, and it wasn't until the Saturday before Labor Day that Gracie said, "Mosey's talking about applying to NYU."

Eli leaned back on his elbows. They were lying on a blanket at the cove named Chuck, the sun making jagged stars through the branches of the oaks and birches. "Will she?" he asked.

"Probably. She's smart enough to get in." Eli said nothing, and Gracie added, "It might be fun to work in the city."

The furrow appeared between Eli's brows. "Sure," he said. "That's a big change, though."

Don't say anything, she told herself. *Leave it be.* But the knife was right there. She had to walk into it. "Do you not want me there?"

Eli shifted forward and tossed a pebble into the lake. "You should go wherever you want."

The hurt that flowered in her chest was a living thing, a plant out of a science fiction movie, all waving tendrils and stinging nettles.

"Sure," she said lightly.

There was nothing wrong with what he'd said. This was a summer thing. Besides, he was right. She should go where she wanted. She didn't need Eli waiting for her to move to the city. She could crash on Mosey's couch until she found a job. Did dorm rooms have couches?

"Gracie—" Eli said, reaching for her hand.

She hopped up. "I've got to go meet Mosey and Lila."

He stood then. Sunlight clung to his hair, his skin. He was almost too bright to look at.

"Let's meet early tomorrow," he said. "I only have one more day to—"

"Yup."

She had her bag on her shoulders and she was on her bike, determined to get away from him before he could see her pride go rolling down her face in big fat tears. She pedaled fast, afraid he'd come after her. Hoping so hard that he would.

She didn't go to work the next day. It wasn't a decision. She just let the minutes drain away. Eli wouldn't come to her house. He'd never seen her room or watched TV on their sofa, just hovered outside in the driveway with his bike while Gracie went to grab a sweater or change her shoes. She'd never even met his parents. Because that was real life and they were something else.

You're being stupid, she told herself. *He'll be gone in two days. Enjoy it while it lasts. Let it be fun.* But Gracie wasn't good at fun, not the kind of fun that other people had. The person she liked best didn't like her enough to want more of her, and she didn't want to pretend that wasn't awful. She was cherry dip cones, all those old paperbacks, records stacked on dusty shelves—something to hold Eli's interest, maybe even something he really liked, but a summer thing, not quite real when the weather turned.

She read. She watched TV. Then the weekend was gone, and she knew Eli was gone with it. That was okay. Next summer she wouldn't be waiting at the Dairy Queen or working at Youvenirs. She'd graduate, and she'd go to New York or Canada or wherever. But she wouldn't be in Little Spindle.

Tail

A week after school started, Gracie went to see Annalee. She hadn't known that she meant to, but she ended up in the fluorescent lights of the Dairy Queen just the same.

She didn't order. She wasn't hungry. She slid into the booth and said, "How do I get better? How do I make this stop hurting?"

Annalee set down her crossword. "You should say goodbye."

"It's too late. He's gone."

"Sometimes it helps to say it anyway."

"Can you tell me . . . Did he ever feel the way I did?"

"Ah, *tsigele*." Annalee tapped her pen gently on Gracie's hand. "Some of us wear our hearts. Some of us carry them."

Gracie sighed. Had she really expected Annalee could make her feel better? This town was full of sham monsters, fake witches, stories that were just stories. But anything was worth a try.

Though the weather was still warm, the main road was quiet, and as she turned onto the narrow dirt path that led to her cove, the woods seemed almost forlorn, as if they were keeping the last watch of summer. She felt guilty. This had been her cove, nameless and comforting before Eli. *Where have you been?* the pine needles whispered.

She leaned her bike against a tree at the clearing and walked down to the shore. It didn't feel like sanctuary anymore. Hadn't Mosey said the lake was haunted? The cove felt full of ghosts she wished she could banish. She had so many good memories with Eli. Did she have to lose all of those too?

That was when Gracie heard it: a single, soft exhalation that might have been a breeze. Then another—a rasping breath. She peered past the shady banks. A body lay slumped in the shallows.

She didn't remember moving, only that one moment she was standing, stunned on the shore, and the next she was on her knees in the water.

"Eli," she cried.

"You came."

"What happened? What is this?" He was so pale he was nearly blue, his veins too close to the surface of his skin.

"I shouldn't have waited. I get three months. That's the rule."

"What rule?"

"I wanted to say goodbye."

"Eli—"

"I was selfish. I didn't want you to go to the city. I needed you to look forward to. I'm sorry. I'm sorry, Gracie. The winters get so long."

"Eli, I have my phone. I can call—"

"I'm dying now, so I can tell you—"

"*You're not dying,*" Gracie shouted. "You're dehydrated, or you have hypothermia." But even as she said it, she realized the water was warmer than it should be.

"It was me that day. You were skipping stones. You'd skinned your knee. I saw you just for a second. It was the last day of May." His eyelids stuttered open, shut. "I shouldn't have kissed you, but I wanted to for so long. It was better than ice cream. It was better than books."

She was crying now. "Eli, please, let me—"

"It's too late."

"Who says? *Who says?*"

He gave the barest shrug. It became a shudder. "The lake. Three months to walk the land. But always I must return to her."

Gracie's mind flew back to that day at the cove, the creature in the water. It was impossible.

"There are no books, below," he said. "No words or language."

No Dairy Queen. No bicycles. No music. It couldn't be.

Gracie blinked, and Eli's form seemed to flicker, ghostly almost, part boy and part something else. She remembered Annalee tapping her hand with the pen. *Some of us wear our hearts. Some of us carry them.*

Gracie's eyes scanned the beach, the tangle of brambles where the woods began. There, a dark little hump in the leaves. She'd never seen him without it—that ugly purple backpack—and in that moment she knew.

She scrambled for it, fell, righted herself, grabbed it open, and split the zipper wide. It gaped like a mouth. It was full of junk. Skee-Ball tickets, minigolf scorecards, a pink-and-gold lip-gloss tin. But there, at the bottom, glinting like a hidden moon . . .

She pulled it from the bag, a long, papery cape of scales that seemed to go on and on, glittering and sharp beneath her fingers, surprising in its weight. She dragged it toward Eli, trailing it behind her, stumbling through the shallows. She pulled his body close and wrapped it around him.

"Here," she sobbed. "Here."

"Three months," he said. "No more."

"It was only a few days—"

"Leave Little Spindle, Gracie. Get free of this place."

"No," she shouted at the lake, at no one at all. "We can make a trade."

Eli's hand gripped her wrist. "Stop."

"You can have me too!"

"Gracie, don't."

The water lapped against her thighs with its own slow pulse, warm as blood, warm as a womb, and she knew what to do. She curled herself into the cloak of scales beside Eli, letting its edges slice into her arms, letting her own blood drip into the water.

"Take me too," she whispered.

"Too late," said Eli. His eyes closed. He smiled. "It was worth it."

Then the hand around her wrist flexed tight, retracted. Gracie watched it stretch and lengthen—a talon, razor-sharp.

Eli's eyes flew open. The smell of rain clouds reached her, then the rumble of thunder, the roar of a river unleashed. The rush of water filled her ears as Eli's body shifted, blurred, shimmered in the fading light. He rose above her, reeling back on the muscular coils of his body, a great snake, a serpent of gleaming white scales, his head like a nodding dragon, his back split by iridescent fins that spread like wings behind him.

"Eli . . ." she tried to say, but the sound that left her mouth wasn't human.

She raised a hand to her throat, but her arms were too short, the wrong shape. She turned and felt her body, strange and strong, thrash through the shallows as her back arched.

In the sunlit water, she glimpsed her reflection, her scales deep gray and alive with rainbows, her fins the bruised violet of twilight, a veil of new stars cast against the darkening sky. She was monstrous. She was lovely.

It was her last human thought. She was diving into the water. She was curled around . . . who was this? Eli. The dim echo of a name, something more ancient and unpronounceable, lived at the base of her brain. It didn't matter. She could feel the slide of his scales over hers as they slipped deeper into the lake, into the pull of the current, together.

Heart

When they found her bicycle leaning against a pine near Little Spindle, Annalee did her best to explain to Gracie's mother. Of course, her mother still called the police. They even sent divers into the lake. The search was fruitless, though one of them claimed that something far too big to be a fish had brushed up against his leg.

Gracie and Eli had summers, three perfect months every year, to feel the grass beneath their feet and the sun on their bare human shoulders. They picked a new city each summer, but they returned most often to Manhattan, where they'd visit with Annalee and Gracie's flummoxed mother in a penthouse on the Upper East Side, and try not to stare at their beautiful host with her running-water skin and river-green eyes.

When fall came, they shed their names with their bodies and traveled the waters of the world. The lake hated to give them up. She threatened to freeze solid and bind them there, but they were two now—sinewy and gleaming—monsters of the deep, with lashing tails and glittering eyes, and the force they created between them smashed old rules and new arguments. They slipped down the Mohawk to the Hudson, past the river god with his sloped gray shoulders, and out into the Atlantic. They met polar bears in the Arctic, frightened manatees near the Florida Keys. They curled together in a knot, watching the dream lights of jellyfish off the coast of Australia.

Sometimes, if they spotted a passenger leaning on the rails of a freighter by himself, they might even let themselves be seen. They'd breach the waves, let the moonlight catch their hides, and the stranger would stand for a moment—mouth agape, heart alive, his loneliness forgotten.

DALE BAILEY

Teenagers from Outer Space

FROM *Clarkesworld Magazine*

THE FIRST ALIENS arrived in Milledgeville, Ohio, when I was
still in diapers. By the time I'd graduated into the frilly pink dresses
my mother put me in for elementary school, you saw them around
occasionally, strolling down Main Street or picnicking by the bandshell in the park. They'd bought into a rundown neighborhood
in the east end of town—primarily Polish and Estonian to that
point, though once the aliens began picking up mortgages over
there, most people just called it Bug Town. This was lazy thinking,
because the aliens didn't look anything like bugs, but what are you
going to do?

I never really had much personal contact with them until their
kids started showing up in my high school classes. There was grumbling, of course. But who was going to tell a hulking seven-foot
alien his kid couldn't come to school? And so I studied *Great Expectations* and home economics in the company of creatures not
of this Earth. Which sounds more dramatic than it really was. We
all got along well enough in class, even if we did keep to our own
sides of the lunchroom.

Which is where it might have ended if it hadn't been for my
best friend, Joan Hayden.

The first thing you have to understand about Joan is that she
had poor taste in boys. Everybody agreed. First there'd been Luke
Jackson, a disaffected former jock who'd been kicked off the football team when he showed up at the homecoming game half in
the bag. After that she'd taken up with a guy named Jimmy Ford,
violating the unspoken divide between the kids in calculus and the
ones in shop. That was about the time Joan got clumsy—started

slipping in the shower and running into doors—so when she worked up the courage to send Jimmy packing, we all agreed that she was well shut of him.

Which brings us to Johnny Fabriano, where this story really gets underway. Johnny looked like a refugee from *The Wild Ones*—black leather jacket, motorcycle boots, and a greasy DA that looked like it hadn't been washed in a week. He'd dropped out of high school the day he'd turned sixteen and had spent the last five years hanging around Red's Billiards Parlor, cadging cigarettes and hustling pool. He was a dead shot, and rumor had it he'd won his car in a hotly contested game of eight-ball with a gearhead from Brookton. The car itself was the envy of every would-be greaser in town—a chopped '49 Mercury coupe painted a glossy midnight purple with stylized tongues of yellow and red flame licking at the hood and fenders.

Joan had already gotten a reputation for being fast—undeserved, I have to put in, and if anyone knew, I did, because Joan confided everything in me. She'd moved in next door when we were both in second grade, and we'd been joined at the hip ever since, sharing every joy and affliction, from scraped knees to first periods, which when Joan's made its debut, I remember how jealous I was—until mine happened along two months later, inflicting such misery upon me that I have never envied anyone anything ever since, or almost never, anyway.

Joan had grown up in a Pentecostal church, daughter to a strict disciplinarian who saw himself as the earthly agent of the Lord. And if at one level Joan rejected all that, at another level she still believed. You never really escape your childhood training, I guess, and it was this division in Joan's personality that ultimately caused all the trouble. For while Johnny Fabriano was a perfect candidate to give her father apoplexy, he was also a young man with an agenda of his own.

You see where this is going, of course, and it's not a happy place. But when the alien got involved, his good intentions only made everything worse. Good intentions usually do.

My name is Nancy Miller, by the way, and it's nice to meet you, I'm sure. If you haven't already figured it out, this story isn't really mine to tell, but my mother always called me Chatty Cathy, so I suppose it's only natural that it should fall to me in the end.

And it's important that you understand that I wasn't always on the scene. Much of what follows is reconstructed from secondhand reports, with all the bias and self-interest inherent in such accounts. In short, these are the facts as I understand them. If you want the truth, you'll have to sort it out for yourself. You always do, I guess.

So cast me in a supporting role: plain-faced confidante and collaborator to the beautiful lead. Joan really *was* beautiful, too, which is to say blond and buxom in the slightly zaftig mold then in fashion. She inspired plenty of interest among the boys at Milledgeville High, but as I've already said, she never returned the affections of the boys who might have brought her happiness, if happiness was even an option for her, and I think it probably wasn't.

Certainly it wasn't with Johnny Fabriano. Like I said, he had an agenda of his own, and if, on Joan's part, he was calculated to infuriate her father, then there's some small irony that had it not been for her father they might never have met in the first place. Sometimes just stopping for gas can change the entire course of your life, and that's exactly what happened when her father decided to swing their old Caddy into Staley's Gulf station one September Sunday after church.

Gas stations were full-service back then—the days of pumping your own fuel were still decades away—and while Mr. Staley fussed with the Caddy's tire pressure, Johnny's '49 Merc roared up to the neighboring pump. Both Joan and her father knew the car, of course—who hadn't seen it around town?—and Joan at least knew its driver by reputation. What she didn't know was what a sweet smile Johnny had. But he did, I can vouch for that myself, and when he turned his head to look at Joan, he passed one to her, like a gift.

Maybe it would have ended there, a shared smile in a gas station parking lot, but Joan's father couldn't help weighing in on the matter. "What a cheap hood," he said, pouring into those two words all the disdain that only those certain of their place in heaven can summon.

That was enough for Joan, of course. As her father wheeled the car out into the street she smiled back at Johnny.

When she told me about it that night, she was almost incandescent with excitement, so I wasn't surprised when she contrived an excuse to walk by Red's Billiards Parlor after school the next day. Johnny's car was parked at the curb outside, and just as we came abreast of the place—I could already see Joan calculating her odds of coaxing me inside—who should appear in the door but Johnny himself, with a cigarette tucked behind his ear and a toothpick in his mouth.

He did a double take, looked Joan up and down, and granted her another smile. It was like the sun coming out from behind a cloud, that smile. I practically melted myself, and he didn't even know I was there.

"Gas station girl," he said, and Joan said, "I'm surprised you remember."

"Remember?" he said. "How could I forget?"

He did some dexterous little trick with his tongue and passed the toothpick from one side of his mouth to the other. "You got a name, Gas Station Girl?"

So she told him her name, and then she said, "You're Johnny Fabriano. I know you."

You could see it pleased him, her knowing his name like that. The way they were looking at each other, it could only go one way, and nowhere good, so I stepped in front of her and held out my hand, hoping to forestall the inevitable. "I'm Nancy," I said.

He ignored the hand and dipped his chin to acknowledge me. "How you doing, Nancy," he said, and then, taking me by the shoulders, he steered me gently to the side. "Where you girls heading?" he asked, but it was really Joan he was speaking to.

"Just walking."

"Not that way. Not unless you're planning to pay Bug Town a visit." Which was true. We'd already reached the end of the line unless we wanted to stop in for drinks at some dive with sawdust on the floor and "Nobody's Lonesome for Me" on the jukebox. Bug Town lay beyond, and Bug Town was forbidden territory. It had been abandoned to the aliens, and those who *did* work up the spit to visit wouldn't say much except that it was "catching strange." It was the "catching" part of that phrase that concerned our parents, for those who spent much time in Bug Town often became odd themselves. They got a faraway look in their eyes, as if they were listening to some distant music that no one else could hear, and drifted into silence. Once in a while you heard about some daring kid making a midnight run through the place, tires screeching, but details were mighty slim on the ground—it was always a friend of a friend of a friend, no one you ever knew—so I figured such after-hours adventures for empty boasts. In short, the aliens walked among us, but we did not walk among the aliens. Which is why, when Johnny asked if we were planning an excursion of our own, I was shocked when Joan shrugged and said, "Sure we are."

Johnny, on the other hand, didn't blink an eye. "Maybe you'd like a ride instead."

"We'll walk," I said, taking Joan's elbow. "Home."

I was wasting my breath.

"Sounds like fun to me," Joan said, prying my fingers loose, and I knew then that it was a lost cause. There was the car, there was the smile, and there was the "cheap hood" himself. Her father already loathed him. So when she said, "You coming, Nance?" I said the only thing I could in response: "No, Joan, and you shouldn't go either."

Like I said, wasting my breath.

A minute later, Johnny keyed the Merc's engine to life and they roared off down Main Street. This time Joan really had gone too far, I thought as I walked home alone—and at the time I had no idea just how far she'd gone.

They really did go all the way to Bug Town, though I wouldn't learn that until later that night, long after the scene that unfolded at the Haydens' when she got home. Any sane girl would have had Johnny drop her off a couple of blocks from her house and manufactured some plausible excuse for her tardiness—an extra hour at the library, a study session that had run too long. Not Joan. That wouldn't have created the intended effect. I was watching from my open bedroom window—the September air still had the glow of summer—when the Merc rumbled up to the curb. Joan's father was waiting at the door. He couldn't have been home long himself. He hadn't even loosened his tie. He was an insurance salesman, though why a man so devoted to the rewards of the afterlife should take such an interest in the perils of this one, I never could understand. But he certainly took an interest in the perils Johnny Fabriano posed to his daughter's eternal soul.

The Merc thundered away before Joan was halfway up the sidewalk. By the time she reached the front porch, the shouting had begun. It continued for the next hour or so, and while I couldn't make out the words, it didn't take a genius to figure out the tenor of the back-and-forth between Joan and her father. Her mother was silent, of course. She knew her place in the biblical hierarchy of the home. Joan, however—well, her father's fury only goaded her to greater histrionics. The entire thing culminated in slammed doors.

He'd locked her into her room, of course. He always did.

It wasn't until after my own dinner that I worked up the courage to call.

"Joan isn't available, Nancy," her father told me, and I could hear the suppressed fury in his voice.

"Thank you, Mr. Hayden," I said. "I guess I'll catch her in school—"

But I never got to finish the phrase.

"How much do you know about this Johnny Fabriano, Nancy?" he said.

"Not much, sir."

"Were you with Joan this afternoon?"

I hesitated a moment too long.

"Well, then," he said. "I'm very disappointed in you, Nancy. In fact, I'd like to speak with your father, if he's available."

He was. My mother shook her head in commiseration when I called him over, and my father winked when he took the phone. He listened patiently to Mr. Hayden and made all the right noises in return, but when he finished the conversation, I didn't get much of a scolding. My father wasn't the scolding type, and besides, we attended the Disciples of Christ Church, which was about as liberal as you could get in Milledgeville, Ohio, in 1955. He bought his insurance from Mr. Hayden, but he didn't have much in the way of personal respect for him.

"Just be a good friend to her, Nance," he said. "God knows she needs one, living in that house."

Around 1 a.m., Joan woke me with a handful of pebbles at my window. This came as no surprise. Sneaking out was routine business to Joan. Just shimmy down the big oak tree outside her window, and clamber back up it whenever she'd accomplished whatever mischief she had to accomplish.

"So what's he like?" I whispered the minute I had her installed in my bedroom, and when she responded, "Dreamy, Nance. He's just dreamy," my heart fell. "Dreamy" was not good. "Dreamy" had the potential for disaster. But what could I do? Discouraging her would merely encourage her, and encouraging her would do the same. It was an impossible hand to play, and I opted then, as I had opted so many times in the past, not to play it at all. I opted for neutrality. It was as close as I could come to fulfilling my father's injunction to be a good friend to Joan.

So what I said was, "Dreamy?"

With conviction: "Dreamy. He's not like other boys, Nancy. He's not like you think."

"What do you mean?"

"Nobody understands him. Everybody thinks he's some . . . cheap hood"—this last she practically spat—"but he's not at all. Why, did you know he takes care of his mother? His father's dead, and she's not well, and he does just everything for her, and nobody understands what a good heart he has. And he's so gentle and soft-spoken and he wants to know all about me. He's really interested in me, not just in, you know—" She broke off, blushing.

Sure, that's what you *think*, I didn't say. What *I* thought was that Johnny was just smoother than the usual high school Lothario who tried to get his hand—or worse—up Joan's skirt. He was twenty-one. He knew how to play the long game. Like I said, he had an agenda of his own. Have you ever known a man who didn't?

"Did you kiss him?"

"Just once. Right before we pulled up to the house. His lips are so soft. You wouldn't think that, the way he looks, would you?"

I wouldn't. But I didn't say that either. Instead I asked where they had gone.

Joan looked down. She was quiet for a long time, and when she met my gaze at last, I saw that she was afraid. "We went to Bug Town," she said.

Which brings me back to the aliens—the bugs, as people called them, though as I said at the beginning of this story, that was just lazy thinking, because they didn't really look anything like bugs. And maybe their appearance isn't all you're curious about. Maybe you want to know where they came from and why and what they planned to do.

But I don't have answers to any of that.

They just started drifting into town by twos and threes and buying up the decaying houses over in the east end. Who can say why?

They were aliens, after all, and their motives were as inscrutable as Joan's were self-evident.

Their appearance, on the other hand—there was no mystery about that. They were monstrous things to look at: olive-green, seven-foot giants, their squarish heads bifurcated by a big, ropy artery that clove their skulls into disproportionate lobes. It wound down between their lidless black eyes—shark-black, and as empty of expression—and split into frills of bony, close-knit flesh that almost looked like baleen. Their mouths, nestled between those frills, were the most disturbing feature of all: three slavering flaps of tissue that dilated open to reveal jagged yellow teeth. All this set atop a massive torso armored in bone, with thick arms and legs and large, three-taloned hands.

And strong.

My freshman year, the first year the aliens showed up at Milledge-ville High, Coach Pack recruited three or four of them for the football team. Where he found uniforms to fit them, I have no idea. Perhaps he had them custom-made. In any case, the aliens were lethally effective on the gridiron, and we would win the state championship two years running, despite the virulent protests of our rivals. Yet the aliens—I won't call them bugs—were essentially gentle creatures, even shy. They kept to themselves and they listened attentively to our teachers. They contributed to class in moist, lisping whispers. They took copious notes.

Their handwriting was beautiful.

But Bug Town? I knew nothing about Bug Town that I haven't already told you. I was as curious as anybody else about the place—but not curious enough to risk "catching strange," so part of me stood in admiration of Joan for daring to go there in the first place. Another part was furious with her, knowing how much she'd risked to defy her father and her father's god.

But whatever her motivations, Joan had little to say about Bug Town.

When I asked her about it, her gaze grew distant, as though she were looking straight through me to some faraway horizon, and when she answered me, her voice was a hollow whisper. I knew then that she'd been touched by strangeness, but I did not yet perceive how deep the wound ran or how unbearable its consequences would be—not merely for her and Johnny Fabriano, but for us all.

I began to get an inkling of that—but nothing more—the next day at school.

There were two aliens in our first-period English class. I can't tell you their real names. I can't reproduce their slobbery, whistling language, and certainly not on the page. But when the aliens moved to Milledgeville, they'd taken human names as well. So you'd see "Jim" at the hardware store, sighting down two-by-fours to make sure they hadn't warped, or "Susan" at the A&P, inquiring about the freshness of the tomatoes. None of them had quite mastered English pronunciation—I expect their weird, dilating mouths precluded mastery—but they could make themselves understood well enough to get along. "Thim" got unbowed two-by-fours, "Thuthan" fresh tomatoes. And the two aliens in our English class, "Eloieth" (Eloise) and "Tham" (Sam—also the star fullback for the Milledgeville Bears), got straight A's. The semester wasn't even two weeks old and they'd already displaced me as Mrs. Guest's favorite student.

Eloieth and Tham—yes I'm going to call them that, not to mock them, but to keep their intrinsic strangeness front and center—were the kind of students who read their assignments days in advance, sat in the front row, and shot their talons up the minute Mrs. Guest asked a question. But Mrs. Guest didn't always call on the kids with their hands up. She had an eye for the doodler and the daydreamer, and just as you were drifting off into some pleasant fantasy or other, she'd bludgeon you with a question—which is what happened to Joan that morning. This in itself wasn't surprising. Joan was an indifferent student at best, if only because her father expected more of her, and she was an inveterate daydreamer. But when Mrs. Guest fired that morning's question in her direction, Joan seemed to have drifted not into some idle fancy but into a deep hypnotic state.

She didn't respond, didn't so much as stir.

Only when Mrs. Guest repeated the question—pointedly, and at volume—did Joan look up, a puzzled look on her face. "I'm sorry, Mrs. Guest."

"What are you sorry for, Miss Hayden?"

"I didn't hear you, that's all. If you could repeat the question, maybe . . ." Joan trailed off into silence.

"Yes, why don't I repeat myself? Surely I have nothing better to do. In stanza nine, Keats writes,

> *And there she lulled me asleep,*
>   *And there I dream'd—Ah! woe betide!*
> *The latest dream I ever dreamt*
>   *On the cold hill's side.*

What do you think he means, Miss Hayden?"

Miss Hayden had no reply on the matter of meaning. The moment stretched. You could hear nothing but the tick of the round schoolroom clock on the wall.

"Miss Hayden?"

But once again Joan had drifted off.

Tham made some weird whistling sound deep in his throat.

"Please, Sam," Mrs. Guest said. "I think we're all expecting to hear from Miss Hayden."

Silence. People stared at their desktops. Joan, however, seemed unfazed. She'd propped her elbow on her desk, her chin on the heel of her hand.

"Perhaps you need to see the nurse, Miss Hayden?"

A subdued ripple of nervous laughter greeted this not-very-funny witticism. Mrs. Guest silenced it with a glare.

"Miss Hayden—" she began, but Tham interrupted her, emitting a long, damp series of clicks and whistles. Joan visibly shook herself in response, and a strange expression—half wonder, half fear—crossed her face. I saw this, I say; I did not imagine it. She shook herself in response and met Mrs. Guest's gaze with an almost physical force. Mrs. Guest shuddered and recoiled. This too I saw; this too I did not imagine.

"The knight has been lulled into sleep, Mrs. Guest," Joan said, firmly, as you might speak to a disobedient child. "He has been enchanted into nightmare by a fairy in the guise of a beautiful woman, and though he may wake upon the cold hill's side, he shall never truly wake again, because one does not wake from a fairy's enchantment."

Eloieth let out a long mournful whistle when Joan finished, and then she and Tham both turned away. Silence gripped the classroom. Mrs. Guest swallowed. "I think that's enough for today," she

said. "If you'll turn to page 74 and answer the discussion questions, we'll take up 'Ode on a Grecian Urn' tomorrow"—and she
retreated to her desk and sat very still and pale until the bell rang
for second period.

I didn't see Joan for the rest of the day—English was the only
class we had together—but when the final bell rang I gathered my
books and ran to meet her for the walk home. She wasn't waiting
for me at the picnic tables on the east side of campus—and she'd
been waiting there every day as long as we'd been in high school.
I didn't stick around. I knew she wouldn't be coming. I knew what
had happened even before I really knew it, if that makes sense, so
I wasn't surprised when I came around the building and saw her
sliding into Johnny's Merc. I called out to her, but she didn't wait.
She didn't even turn around.

The shouting match next door went on longer than usual that
evening, and though I stayed awake until well after midnight, Joan
never showed up at my window. I didn't see her until we walked
to school the next morning—and then only briefly, because we
hadn't gone a block before Johnny's Merc rolled up to the sidewalk and he reached over to crank down the window.

"Anybody want a ride to school?" he asked.

"I do," Joan said brightly, opening the door. The interior of the
car gleamed, every bit as glossy as the exterior—the lavender dash,
the chrome-framed gauges on the instrument panel. The radio
was pumping out Chuck Berry, "Maybellene." Johnny flashed that
reckless grin at Joan. I might as well have been wallpaper. So when
Johnny said, "Coming, Nancy?" I shook my head and turned away.

"I'll walk."

"Suit yourself," Johnny said, and Joan wound up the window
as they pulled away from the curb. She hadn't even said goodbye.

I put my head down and hurried on alone.

By the time we'd moved on to *Idylls of the King* in Mrs. Guest's
class—we were reading the part where Vivien imprisons Merlin in
the tree—that faraway look in Joan's eyes had faded. There were
no more weird incidents with Tham. And she had rededicated herself to infuriating her father by dating Johnny Fabriano.

That was all anyone could talk about. Five years after his premature departure from high school, tales of Johnny's exploits lingered. Among other things, he was said to have raided the school at midnight to steal a carbon copy of Mr. Dunnigan's chem final; fought a legendary bruiser named Otis (now serving time in the state pen) to a blood-spitting draw; and invited Master Sergeant Ashton, the Junior ROTC teacher, who had stormed the beach at Okinawa, to go fuck himself. So every eye was upon her when Joan stepped out of Johnny's flame-bedizened ride. Mr. Hayden soon put a stop to that—he started driving her to school himself—but I knew that Joan was still seeing Johnny on the sly. More than once I woke to the guttural rumble of his car in a neighboring street and knew that she'd availed herself of her arboreal exit.

She certainly wasn't using it to visit me, so I didn't see much of Joan for a while. I walked to school and back alone, we couldn't talk during English, and while she still ate lunch at our table, half a dozen other girls did too. It was hardly the place for confidences. Aside from a chance encounter in the girls' bathroom—and even that was fleeting—we might have been little more than casual acquaintances.

"Do you still think about it?" I asked as we stood in front of the rusty mirrors.

"Think about what?" she said.

"Bug Town."

She didn't answer right away. When she did, she said, "Sometimes it seems like it's the *only* thing I can think about."

Then a gaggle of chattery sophomores burst through the door.

Of course, Joan wasn't the only point of interest that fall. As October deepened, the town turned its attention to high school football. Tham was enjoying a record-breaking season, sometimes piling up more than two hundred yards a game, and his quarterback, an alien kid named Thteven (Steven) who ran a little on the small side at 6'10", was throwing the ball with the kind of pinpoint accuracy you didn't usually see outside the NFL. The Bears often bested their opponents by forty points or more, and they could have doubled those numbers if Coach Pack hadn't routinely pulled Tham and Thteven out of the game at halftime. It didn't seem sporting to keep running up the score, he told the *Milledgeville Courier.*

The aliens attended every game. The adults kept to sections C and D, but their kids stood in the spirit section and stomped in enthusiasm, occasionally ramming a taloned foot right through the metal risers. And you often ran into them at the concession stand. They were especially fond of chili dogs, ordering them by the dozen—with mustard and onions—and sucking them whole into those flappy mouths, like sucking Ping-Pong balls into the nozzle of a vacuum cleaner. Their table manners were generally atrocious, though I always assumed that by their own standards they were probably perfectly acceptable. They wore formfitting knee-length pants—perhaps out of deference to human sensibilities, perhaps not—but otherwise went naked and barefoot.

Their first few days at Milledgeville High they were constantly being sent home for violating the dress code. But when a delegation of alien parents arrived to ask that the principal exempt their children, he capitulated—maybe because he was sitting across his desk from a party of large green monsters from outer space, and maybe because modesty wasn't really an issue, since no one could tell the male and female aliens apart except by their human names, and even then, who could really say for sure? Maybe they had three sexes, or six, or none at all. They were a weird bunch, taken all together. They were aliens.

But they sure had improved Milledgeville's lousy football team. The homecoming game—the usual rout—ended around eight. The dance got underway an hour later. Everybody boogied to "Gum Drop," the aliens in a herky-jerky rhythm that seemed to have nothing to do with that of the song, the humans (most of them) on beat; but when the DJ spun "Take Me Back," the alien kids surrendered the floor to their human counterparts. I heard this all secondhand, of course. I wasn't there—plain old Nancy had no date—just as I wasn't there to see what happened in the parking lot outside. I heard Joan's account that night, and I would later hear Johnny Fabriano's version of events. But I never knew Joan to lie, so I'm confident of that part of the story. My understanding of Tham's motives, on the other hand—to the extent that he had motives and they can be understood—is the product of pure conjecture, and it may be that I'm too rooted in a human perspective to speculate with any accuracy.

What I know for sure is that Joan had been forbidden to attend both the game and the dance. But Joan was not going to be denied the night out. She couldn't attend the game. Some Pentecostal ally of her father would betray her. And she couldn't attend the dance because the chaperones wouldn't admit someone Johnny's age (and especially not Johnny himself). But she could make it a special night, and when she slipped out the window around 8:30, that's just what she intended to do. Apparently Johnny had the same idea. His car was idling a block over, and when she slid in beside him, he had a corsage waiting. They were going to celebrate homecoming on their own, he said, and if his hand lingered when he pinned the flower to her breast, she attributed it to his clumsy fingers.

Johnny'd also bought a couple of bottles of sweet wine. Joan had never tasted the stuff, but she wasn't going to decline another opportunity to defy her father. Besides, it turned out she liked the giddy feeling it gave her, the devil-may-care release from the inhibitions that her Pentecostal childhood had instilled within her. She was pleasantly buzzed by the time they pulled into the school parking lot—a destination Joan had insisted on over Johnny's objections. "Let's go to the dance," she'd said, giggling, and when Johnny pointed out that they couldn't go to the dance, she leaned over and planted a lingering kiss on the tender spot just behind his ear. "We can get close," she whispered, an enticingly ambiguous statement, which is how they wound up parked in the darkest corner of the high school parking lot. The radio was playing the Four Aces, "Melody of Love," when Johnny leaned in to kiss her, and Joan later told me how she remembered the music and the taste of the sweet wine on his lips. It wasn't the first time they had kissed, but it was the first time it really seemed to matter, and she surrendered herself to it.

Johnny slid one hand up Joan's ribs to caress her breast. When she didn't protest, when indeed she seemed to lean into him, he let the other hand drift down to push its way between her thighs.

This wasn't what Joan wanted. It never had been. But Johnny'd been intending to claim this prize for more than a month now, so when Joan protested, murmuring, "No, Johnny," he simply ignored her. He was tugging at her panties when she said it again— *"No, Johnny!"*—and by the time she said it a third time, he'd nearly wormed a finger inside them.

Joan gasped. She tried to thrust Johnny away, but he pushed her back against the seat, bearing down with all his weight. He held her there, panting, and that's when she realized he was fumbling with the buttons on his jeans. That's when she began to scream in earnest.

At the far end of the parking lot, inside the gym, the DJ had just dropped the needle on "See You Later, Alligator." The teenagers from outer space took the floor. Their human peers joined them. The chaperones glanced at their watches—they would be shutting the party down at eleven—and looked out over the dance floor. Nobody was listening for screams from the parking lot, and if they had been, they wouldn't have heard anything over the racket of Bill Haley & His Comets.

Johnny had managed to undo his pants by then.

Joan screamed louder.

And then—this is the part that puzzles me, this the reason that I wish he'd given me his point of view—Tham appeared in the shadows. I still wonder what he was doing out there. None of the aliens smoked, so he hadn't stepped out to sneak a butt. Nor did they drink, so he wasn't outside to sneak one of those either. And he certainly wasn't walking home—Bug Town lay in the opposite direction. Yet there Tham was, and what I keep thinking about, even now, is that time in English when he whistled Joan out of her stupor. Had he communicated the answer to Mrs. Guest's question as well? It certainly wasn't the kind of answer Joan would have provided on her own, after all. Which makes me wonder if there might have been some connection between them, some conduit for alien . . . telepathy, for lack of a better word, that had been laid down during Joan's visit to Bug Town. What I wonder is if he knew that Joan was in distress and came to rescue her.

Good intentions, right? And all the damage they can do.

But the damage didn't come till later. In that moment, there in the dark parking lot, those good intentions paid off in a big way. I'm forever thankful to Tham for what he did next. Joan later told me that she was still fighting, still clawing, still screaming. But Johnny was on the verge of overpowering her. He'd just clamped a hand over her mouth to shut her up when Tham's three massive talons, eight inches each, punctured the roof of Johnny's beloved '49 Merc where it curved down to meet the windshield. Johnny cursed and scrambled back against the steering wheel, tugging at his trousers. Joan shoved herself in the other direction and slammed up against the door.

Tham meanwhile had closed his grip around the metal edge of the roof. He yanked it once, and then a second time, and then—it was like he'd taken hold of the pull tab on a can of peaches—he just peeled back the top of that Merc and flung it to the pavement. In the crashing instant that followed, Joan told me that she was aware of only three things: Johnny screaming in fury, the pale radiance of the moon filling up the car like water, and the monstrous silhouette of Tham's massive, asymmetrical head peering down at her against a field of stars. She reacted instinctively, shrieking as Tham reached inside the passenger cabin, fished her out, and set her gently on her feet beside the car. Johnny meanwhile had exited the driver's-side door, the tire iron he kept under the seat in hand. What he saw as he rounded the hood—a seven-foot-tall monster wearing knee-length trousers and a Milledgeville High letter jacket—stopped him cold. The tire iron clanged to the pavement. He stumbled, grappling for the hood of the car to hold himself upright.

By this time Joan had stopped screaming.

In the stillness, she could hear the thump of "Love Bug" from the high school gym.

Joan reached up and took one of Tham's long talons in her hand.

"This isn't over!" Johnny yelled as they turned away. "This isn't over, you bitch, you hear me!"—but Joan didn't bother looking back. She'd never felt safer in her life. Tham walked her home. Somewhere along the way she unpinned Johnny's crushed corsage and cast it into the shadows beside the sidewalk. And when they reached her house, she marched straight up the walk and rang the bell. Mr. Hayden staggered back into the living room when he opened the door and saw his daughter standing there hand in hand with a towering alien from outer space.

"Hello, Daddy," she said sweetly. "I want you to meet my boyfriend—Sam."

Whether Tham thought he was her boyfriend or not is also a matter of conjecture. But from that night on, there was *something* between them, and the consequences of that relationship would eventually ripple outward to engulf us all. But that was later.

The immediate consequences were more predictable.

Mrs. Hayden, who'd walked to the door behind her husband,

screamed. And when Mr. Hayden started spewing his typical self-righteous bilge, Joan ignored him. She pushed past him, leading Tham by the talon, and introduced him to her mother. "Nithe to meet you, Mthth Hayden," Tham said, flecking her with viscous extraterrestrial spittle. When Mrs. Hayden just blanched by way of reply, her eyes bulging, Joan took him to the kitchen, poured them both a glass of milk, and served up a platter of her mother's homemade chocolate chip cookies. They chatted for fifteen minutes—innocuous gossip about schoolmates and teachers—before Tham took his leave. On his way out, he extended his talons to Joan's father (predictably, Mr. Hayden refused to shake) and nodded to her mother. He probably would have smiled if he could have.

"I'm spending the night with Nancy," Joan said, escorting Tham out to the porch, where she kissed him goodnight.

His kisses were really slobbery, she told me later, and his bony frills posed a considerable challenge. Plus he ate the cookies by sucking them down whole and he slurped his milk.

Otherwise, Tham was pretty close to perfect.

Mr. Hayden showed up at our front door first thing in the morning, demanding that his daughter come home. My father invited him in and left the two of them alone to talk things out, but talking soon led to bellowing and bellowing to the unmistakable sound of a blow. When my father walked back into the room, Joan had one hand to her cheek, but she wasn't crying. She told me later that she was done crying over that man, and as it turned out she was, too. My father quietly suggested that Mr. Hayden might want to go home. Joan was welcome to stay with us until everyone had calmed down, he said.

Mr. Hayden swallowed, but he didn't raise his voice. Mr. Hayden wasn't much more than a bully, and bullies are generally hollow at heart, I think, terrified that the world won't bend to their will. My father certainly wasn't bending. He simply opened the door for Mr. Hayden, who stepped outside. He turned back at the top of the porch steps, seething with humiliation and resentment. His face was white with fury, his fists clenched impotently at his sides.

"I'll have the police here, Dave," he said. "I'll have my daughter home."

"When they arrive I'll be sure to show them that bruise on her face," my father said. "Now get off my porch."

Mr. Hayden walked down the steps and across the yard without looking back. The police never came, though, which is how Joan ended up spending the weekend with us. Come Monday, the bruise had faded to a dull yellow. You had to look close to know it was there at all, and a little blush took care of that. We walked to school together in the bright October morning, chatting amiably about homework and gossiping about the girls at our lunch table. The question of when she would go home did come up in passing ("Never," she said, and she never did). The question of Tham did not.

When the bell rang for first period—we'd moved on to "Goblin Market"—Joan merely smiled at him as she slipped into her desk, and I let myself believe that the "boyfriend" nonsense had passed. Come lunch, I learned that I was wrong.

Joan collected her food and bypassed our table without a word. As she marched toward the corner where the aliens ate, the room gradually grew silent. By the time Tham scooted over to make a place for her at his table, the only sound was the occasional clank of a pot in the kitchen—and then even that stopped, as the staff gathered at the serving window, jaws agape. Joan pulled the whole thing off beautifully, I have to give her that. She never let on that she noticed the silence or the eyes upon her. She just smiled up at Tham and began to eat.

When the final bell rang that afternoon and I walked out to the picnic tables, Joan was waiting. So was Tham. We walked home in companionable silence. Tham carried Joan's books, and shortened his stride periodically so that we could keep up. I half expected to see Johnny's mutilated car idling at some intersection along the way, but if he was there, he hid himself well.

When we reached the house, Joan offered Tham a glass of my mother's lemonade—we'd been neighbors and best friends for so long that she'd practically become a sister, helping herself to whatever she wanted (a privilege I was denied at the Haydens'). Tham declined—"Thankth, but I thould go," he said—and Joan kissed him goodbye right there on the front porch. *She* was on the front porch, anyway. He stood below, to bring their faces into relative proximity. Then he was gone, striding off down the sidewalk while Joan mopped the alien drool off her face with a kitchen towel. Joan's mom watched from her kitchen window. My mom watched too. I caught the telltale twitch of the living room curtain from the corner of my eye. But she didn't say a word when we came in, just smiled and offered us some leftover lemon meringue pie.

Joan and I were puzzling over algebra problems in my room when the phone rang. My mom stuck her head in the door.

"Joan, your mother wants to speak with you."

"I don't have anything to say to her."

"Joan, please, you should—"

Joan looked up. When she spoke she was neither angry nor rude, just matter-of-fact in a way that brooked no argument. "I'm sorry, Mrs. Miller. We don't have anything to say to each other now. If you want me to leave—"

"Of course I don't want you to leave. You're always welcome here, Joan."

Mom gave me a look of mute appeal. But what could I do?

And then Joan said, "Thank you, Mrs. Miller," and turned back to her homework.

But she couldn't stay. We all knew that. Sooner or later—probably sooner—Mr. Hayden really *would* call the police, and in those days there weren't a lot of legal avenues open to a sixteen-year-old girl in conflict with her parents—even if that conflict had culminated in physical abuse. There was much to love about 1955, but like our own or any era, it was anything but perfect. My parents really would have welcomed Joan into our home for the long term. I believe that. But the forces arrayed against them were formidable.

That's what my father said when he came up to my room before dinner.

So I wasn't entirely surprised when Joan didn't come back to my house after school the next day. The problem was, she didn't go home either.

The next day Joan went to Bug Town.

She continued to come to school for a few more days, but she became increasingly distant. She no longer turned in homework, and in class she spent most of her time gazing off into the middle distance, staring at things none of us could see. By the end of the week she was barely speaking at all. But I don't think I realized how entirely lost to us she had become until I gathered my courage to walk across the lunchroom myself on Friday afternoon. I understood then what strength and courage that must have taken on her part. My footsteps echoed in the silence. I could feel the combined gaze of my peers like a leaden cloak upon my shoulders.

The aliens scooted aside so that I could set my tray down across from her.

"Hi, Joan," I said.

She looked up at me and smiled, and I recognized the smile. It was her old, familiar, halfway crooked smile. "Hey, Nance," she said, as she might have said if we'd passed in the hall or she'd picked up the phone to find me on the line. It was that natural and spontaneous, and for a moment, looking at her, I felt like nothing had changed. I think that was the most surprising thing. I expected her to be utterly transformed, tuned to a different wavelength, catching strange. And while there was plenty of that there, she was also just Joan, the Joan I loved and remembered, and I missed her.

"When are you coming home, Joan?"

"I'm not."

I didn't want to be rude, so I glanced nervously at the towering alien kids sitting around us, patiently sucking down the school's indifferent fish sticks and fries, before I leaned forward to whisper, as if they wouldn't hear, "But Joan, they're aliens!"

Joan surveyed the lunchroom. She looked at Luke Jackson, the washed-up jock who'd cared more about booze than he'd cared about her. She looked at Jimmy Ford, who, like her father, had been a bit free with his fists. And if Johnny Fabriano had been there, she would have looked at him too, I'm sure. She looked at them both, and then she turned back to me with a Mona Lisa smile and said, "No worries, Nance. I'm used to it."

I looked down at my own tray of soggy fish sticks and fries. Joan reached out and put her hand over mine where it lay upon the table. "Bug Town is beautiful, Nance," she said, and a wave of sorrow washed through me. "Come with me," she said. "We can be free."

But she was wrong about that. Mostly, anyway.

Johnny showed up at my doorstep Saturday around six. I heard the unmistakable rumble of the Merc's engine as he pulled up to the curb, and when my father—over my objections—sent me to the door to meet him, I saw the car for myself. It might have been a convertible fresh off the assembly line, that's how neatly the thing had been done, but the car had been mutilated all the same.

Shorn of its roof, with its lavender dash laid bare to the October sky and those ridiculous flames licking at the hood and fenders, it had been exposed as a broken toy, the empty vanity of a man who was more boy than man. He didn't even measure up to the title Mr. Hayden had ascribed to him. Johnny Fabriano was no cheap hood. No, Johnny Fabriano was a selfish child whose experience of the world didn't extend much beyond Red's Billiards Parlor, and as he walked up the sidewalk to meet me, he seemed every bit as maimed as his car, stripped of whatever aura of menace he had once possessed, like a kid playing dress-up in his brother's leather jacket and motorcycle boots—a kid who hadn't slept in a week, pale and tired (drawn, my mother would have said), with his trademark duck's ass in disarray.

"How's your mother?" I asked, before he could even start up the stairs.

"My mother?"

"Yeah. You know, your mother. You told Joan about her. How's she doing?"

Johnny hesitated. "She's fine," he said. "I—"

"You what? Hold her hand when she's hurting? Buy her medicine? What?"

Johnny didn't reply.

I sat down on the top step. "I don't doubt that you live with your mother, but I figure the caretaking probably goes in the other direction. She probably gives you spending money. After all, you can't make that much shooting pool." I leaned forward, crossing my arms around my knees. "This is your fault, Johnny. Joan told me what happened in the car."

"Nothing happened," he said. "We were just sitting there talking, and this monster, I don't even know where he comes from, he's just there all of a sudden, and he tears the lid right off the top of my car like that."

"The monster's name is Sam."

"I don't care what his name is. He's a bug, isn't he?" Johnny shrugged. "Maybe he was jealous or something. Who knows what bugs think. I tried to save her, Nance. I came at him with a tire iron, but he was too quick. He just snatched her up and carried her off into the night."

And maybe he believed this. Maybe he thought he was innocent, courageous, whatever. Maybe he'd convinced himself that his

lie was true. People do it all the time. People want to be blameless.
People want to be brave.

Still, I couldn't help laughing—a bitter, joyless laugh. "Not the
way I heard it, Johnny. You're lucky he didn't wrap that tire iron
around your neck." I stood, brushing off my skirt. "This is your
fault. You're the one that tried to rape her." He rocked back a little
at that, like he'd taken a punch. "You're lucky he didn't kill you. I
wish he had. I don't have anything else to say to you."

I was halfway to the door when he said, "I'm going to Bug Town,
Nancy. I'm going to go get her."

I kept my back to him. "Let Mr. Hayden handle it."

Johnny snorted. "That old bastard's not going to do anything."

He was right, of course. Mr. Hayden was done with Joan. She'd
spent a week away from home by then—nights a man of his mind
could interpret in only one way. As far as he was concerned, Joan
had sacrificed her virtue—and when it came to women, virtue was
all that mattered. Joan had shamed him, and if there was anything
Frank Hayden would not abide, it was being shamed. She might as
well have been dead.

"And what are you going to do with her, bring her home?"

"No, Nancy," he said. "You are."

And God help me, I turned around.

I missed her, that's all. She'd been my closest friend—my only
real friend—for almost a decade, and I didn't know how I was
going to go on without her. Aside from my parents, Joan was the
only person I had ever loved. And so, without even talking to my
father, I followed Johnny Fabriano down the walk to his mangled
car. I went to Bug Town with good intentions. I went with love in
my heart. And that was our undoing.

Passing through the outskirts of Bug Town was like passing through
any other dying neighborhood. Worse, maybe. A few human families lingered, but most of the houses stood untenanted, their paint
peeling, weathered FOR SALE signs jutting up from their unkempt
lawns. But as we drove on, the signs dwindled and we began to see
evidence of renovations in progress—skeletal networks of scaffold-
ing, stacks of lumber and cinder block in dusty lawns. Though still
recognizably human, the houses troubled the eye. At first glance,
you couldn't quite say why. At second, you realized that everything

was subtly out of proportion. The lintels of the doors had been jacked up to accommodate seven-foot frames, the rise of each porch stair modified to reflect a lengthier alien stride. Even the angles were almost imperceptibly—disturbingly—out of true. The houses seemed to lean toward the street with an all but sentient vigilance.

We began to see dusky yellow ground cover that you might have mistaken for knee-high weeds had each meaty stalk not sprung to alertness as we passed, and turned watchfully to the street. Pale violet shrubs choked out the familiar autumnal trees, their sinuous branches drifting like seaweed in the still air. Squat, plump cylinders of washed-out orange quickened with breath. Aliens began to appear, striding down sidewalks or rocking in the shade of front porches as the October evening set in. They turned their heads to watch us as we crept by.

With each passing block, the streets became increasingly unearthly. Entire homes had been buried under thick, undulating vines, succulent and smooth. They coiled around windows and doors and slithered out across the lawns to envelop street signs and lampposts. Fleshy, tentacled trees—I have no other word—shouldered up to the sidewalk and intertwined their limbs in a dense, rippling canopy that blocked out the sky. And in that swimming underwater dim, everything pulsed with soft colors—pinks and pale yellows and blues—as if a single heartbeat throbbed in every living molecule. And everything smelled ripe and rich as gardenias just before they go to rot. And everything sang.

I sometimes hear it still, that soft, arrhythmic music, ethereal, and eerie as the tones of a theremin. It got under my skin somehow. It got inside my head, like an itch I couldn't reach to scratch. There was something beautiful about it, and something peaceful, and something utterly cruel. If you listened to it too long, I thought, you might never want to hear anything else again. I wondered if this was what Joan meant when she told me that we could be free, because it didn't sound like freedom to me. It sounded like the worst kind of bondage. It sounded like slavery.

"How come it didn't get you too?" I asked.

Johnny shook his head. "I turned on the radio. I kept my eyes on the road."

"And Joan?"

"Joan looked."

I reached over and switched on the radio, turned it up loud so I couldn't hear that music chiming in my head.

"How are we going to find her?"

"I have no idea," he said.

But in the end it didn't matter. She found us.

She was waiting on the porch of a house—or what had been a house—midway down the next street over. She stood tall and un-afraid at the top step, the one unmoving point in that undulant landscape, her face softly illumined by the slow-pulsing colors. Her hair hung loose around her shoulders, and those succulent vines twined around her calves, like snakes tasting of the air. She looked serene, like a goddess or a saint, indifferent to mere human af-fairs. Yet she smiled when the Merc coasted to a stop at the curb. She smiled when she saw me, and the smile was her old smile, welcoming and warm and faintly mischievous. Just looking at it, I felt a surge of hope that she might yet be saved.

Then Johnny silenced the radio.

That strange, cruel music rang once again inside my head.

"Go get her, Nancy," he said, and when I didn't move, too mes-merized by the terrible beauty of Bug Town, he reached past me to the glovebox and took out a revolver. I gasped—I'd never seen one, not in real life—and I thought once again that he was noth-ing but a fraud, a child play-acting at something he could never be. But the next thing he did made me realize that it was infinitely worse than that. He shoved the muzzle of the gun into my ribs, hissing, "The fucking bug can't have her. Not after what he did to my car," and I saw that Johnny Fabriano was crazy.

Maybe he always had been. Or maybe it was the mutilation of his car that drove him to it—the humiliation of the thing, the exposure of his cowardice, and the consequent fear, jealousy, and fury. Or maybe it was Bug Town itself. Maybe it affected different people in different ways. I can't know for sure. But when he dug the business end of the pistol into my ribs for the second time, I stepped out of the car and started up the walk.

It was the single most terrifying moment of my life. The fleshy yellow stalks of grass bent their attention upon me, and I saw that each one terminated in a black unblinking eye. The snaky vines

coiled around my ankles. I felt the gentle sussurance of the tentacled trees upon my face.

The car door slammed as Johnny scooted out to follow me.
When I looked back, he was maybe five feet behind me, pacing
me, the pistol extended in one shaking hand. His face was strained
and pale, and his eyes were terrified, and as that alien music sang
out inside my head, I felt the full peril of the moment bear down
upon us all.

Then Joan started down the stairs. We met halfway down the
walk, embraced, and stepped away.

"How did you know we were coming?" I asked.

"The music," she said. "Everything sings, and everything speaks.
We all knew you were coming. Don't you feel it?"

And I did. It was like she'd flipped a switch at the base of my
brain. My nerve endings shot out the tips of my fingers, all the way
to the limits of Bug Town, where those first stalks of yellow grass
sprang up from the October earth. A torrent of unfiltered imagery swept me under. I caught flashes of aliens nailing up studs in
those half-renovated houses, of aliens sweeping off porches and
taking dinner out of the oven and changing the oil in their cars,
of aliens—of Eloieth!—bending to their homework and tossing
Frisbees in the dusk. Panic seized me. For a single flailing moment I thought I would drown, and then—"Breathe, Nancy," Joan
said—I got it. It was a matter of focusing the attention, of surf-
ing the wave—and once I mastered it, I came crashing back into
my own moment with a new 360-degree clarity. I saw Johnny at
my back, brandishing his pistol, saw Joan smiling before me, saw
Tham descending the porch steps behind her. He strode down
the walk to stand at her shoulder. The central artery that clove his
skull pulsed with color, pink and blue and yellow, each in turn.
"Hello, Nanthy," he said.

"Hi, Sam," I said. "I came to see if Joan wanted to come home."

"Thath up to Joan."

Joan didn't even hesitate. "No, Nancy," she said. "This is my
home now. I'm free here."

And what I saw then was the most terrible thing of all: Joan had
not been seduced by the aliens. She had chosen them.

Chosen them. Bug Town might have been catching strange, but
our teenage neighbors from outer space had not ensnared her.

The era itself had induced her to seek another path. I understand that now. The '50s weren't an ideal time to be a woman (has there ever been one?). Factor in an abusive father and an oppressive religion, and lots of alternatives might seem preferable. She had made a choice when she'd taken Tham home and introduced him as her boyfriend, when she'd allowed him to walk her back to my house from school, when she'd kissed him goodbye there on my porch. She had chosen Bug Town, and given her particular set of circumstances, who wouldn't have? In striving to escape everything her father represented, she'd run straight into the teeth of a decade that was almost as bad.

Wasn't Bug Town a better option? Wasn't Tham a better man? Who else would have left her to decide her own fate? Not even my father, and he was the most loving man I've ever known. He could see only one path for Joan in the end, and that was to return her to her father's keeping.

"Stay with me," Joan said.

"We would welcome you, Nanthy," Tham said. "Come with uth. Everyone ith welcome." Then, looking at Johnny: "Put athide your weapon. Join uth."

"Never," Johnny said.

"Nanthy?"

Oh, I was tempted. The world had little use for a plain girl like me, even if she did make good grades. What future lay before me? A career as a nurse or a teacher? Or, God help me, a homemaker, a fate worse than death?

But there was that music in my skull, that maddening itch that I could not scratch, that flood of images to be processed. Maybe I'd have gotten used to it in time. I don't know. But in that moment I could not abide that sentient, serpentine world, endlessly interconnected. I was me. I was Nancy and no one else and didn't want to be. I would face whatever was to come alone, no matter the cost.

I was free.

"I can't, Joan," I said.

She nodded. "I'll miss you," she said, reaching out to squeeze my hands.

I never got a chance to reply.

"You can't have her!" Johnny screamed. I staggered away from her, tapping into that network one last time. I saw everything that followed with that same 360-degree clarity, languorous and slow. I saw it all. Saw Johnny swing the gun toward Tham, his hands still shaking. Saw his finger white upon the trigger, saw the hammer fall and the cylinder turn in its casing. I heard the concussion of the shot.

Tham lifted his hand too late. Joan had already hurled herself in front of him. She took the bullet in the stomach. I saw that too. Saw the force of it carry her backward. Saw the blood. There was so much blood.

Tham caught her in one arm. In the same instant, the ropy artery that wound down between his eyes flared red, and a bolt of crimson light erupted from the outstretched talons of his other hand. Johnny never had a chance. A burst of flame engulfed him. The stench of charred flesh filled the air. His blasted bones tumbled to the ground.

Then time kicked back into gear.

Tham had already swung Joan up into his arms. He cradled her like a man carrying his bride across the threshold. "Latht chanth, Nanthy," he said.

I shook my head and stumbled backward toward the car. Tham carried Joan up the porch stairs and through the door of the slithery, vine-grown house. I never saw either one of them again.

The rest of that night is hazy in my memory. I stumbled back to the Merc, I know that, and scrambled across the bench to the wheel. Johnny'd left the key in the ignition, and when I twisted it, the engine roared to life. Johnny—or more likely the Brookton gearhead he'd won the car from—must have modified the engine, because I barely touched the gas and the car lunged forward, like a Doberman breaking its chain.

I nearly lost control on the first corner. On the second one, I did. The car veered across the oncoming lane and careened over the sidewalk. I can still see the fleshy tree it struck. It was stouter than it looked, that tree. The hood of the car folded up like an accordion when I smashed into it. The steering wheel hurtled up to meet me. I remember nothing of the blackness that followed.

When I woke, Bug Town was dying. The slithery vines lashed around as if in agony, and the tentacled trees had begun to droop.

When I crawled out of the car, the stalky yellow grass barely turned to look at me. And in the slow, dimming pulse of colors, I could see that their shark-black eyes had begun to film over.

As for the music, it had died away altogether. There was a profound relief in the silence, and a sadness too, I guess, though the sadness wouldn't really hit until I understood fully the magnitude of our loss. Joan was gone—maybe dead—and the aliens had disappeared. The high school football team's run at the state title had been derailed. The lunchroom seemed strangely empty.

That was later, of course. In the moment, I gave this no thought at all. My brow was tacky with blood, and my head felt as if someone had split it with an ax. It was all I could do to lurch off toward home. I made it maybe half a block before I collapsed in the street. I was still there when the police found me the next morning.

I spent the next night in the hospital, and the morning after that I really was home, headachy and exhausted. My parents couldn't seem to decide whether to baby me or scold me, so they did both by turns, but the babying predominated. Privately, my father even told me that I'd acquitted myself admirably, though I couldn't see much to admire about my complicity, however unintended, in Johnny Fabriano's madness and all the damage it had wrought.

Good intentions, right?

A few days later I felt well enough to go back to school. Everyone was bursting with questions—for a week or so, I was suddenly the most popular girl at Milledgeville High—but Chatty Cathy had fallen silent at last. My grades plummeted that semester. I groped through a fog of guilt and sorrow. The solicitous looks of my teachers were almost unbearable. The last thing I wanted was kindness. I thought of almost nothing but Joan as I had seen her last, cradled in Tham's arms, those strange lights playing on her face. And the blood. So much blood.

I made a comeback in the spring. The fog began to lift, my grades to improve. But Bug Town never recovered. I suppose the bank wrote off the unpaid mortgages. The neighborhood itself fell into ruin.

My father drove me through it—at my insistence and over my mother's objections—a week or so after I went back to school. The place was no longer catching strange. It was hard to believe it ever had been. The yellow stalks of grass lay wilted on the earth, and the ropy vines had withered, leaving houses bearded in brown streamers. In places the streets were virtually impassable. The meaty trees had begun to collapse. We wound through them, crushing limp tentacles beneath our tires. We slipped in silence by the wreckage of Johnny's treasured Merc, its nose crumpled, adding to the indignity Tham had already inflicted upon it. I guess the police must have towed it out of there eventually. I never heard. I *did* hear that all they ever found of Johnny was his bones. His funeral was sparsely attended. I was there. His mother—though she didn't speak to me—looked perfectly healthy.

In retrospect, I suppose that the aliens must have opened some kind of portal from their home world, and that the things that grew there were seeping slowly out into ours. People don't talk about it much these days, but occasionally you'll hear someone speculate that Bug Town was the vanguard of a slow invasion and that its transformation presaged that of the entire planet—that Johnny was a hero who'd saved humanity from the ascension of triumphant alien overlords.

But Johnny Fabriano was no hero. I have no doubt that the aliens were fundamentally benign. I think they'd come to Milledgeville in search of a better life, that in transforming Bug Town they were simply making the neighborhood feel a little more like home. Maybe I'm naive, but I just can't bring myself to believe that you shop at the A&P, picnic in the park, and send your kids to the local high school when you are bent on genocide. If they'd had any interest in crushing us, they could have done so without a second thought. They could open doorways between stars, tear the roofs off cars barehanded, and shoot death rays out of their fingers. Why mess around by taking out mortgages and renovating old houses?

In the end, I believe, they retreated in the face of Johnny's madness. When they slammed that interstellar doorway behind them, they choked off the source of all that catching strange and Bug Town died.

I miss them. Miss Eloieth and Thteven and all the rest of them. I miss Tham, whose good intentions came to naught in the end. I miss Joan most of all. Not a day passes that I don't wonder what happened to her.

I like to think they saved her. I like to think she's free.

HELENA BELL

I've Come to Marry the Princess

FROM *Lightspeed Magazine*

BEFORE JACK CAN apologize to Nancy, she has to believe that dragons exist.

Nancy's mad at him because they were supposed to perform a skit at the talent show and he stood her up. They've been practicing it for two summers. It's called "I've Come to Marry the Princess." When Jack didn't show, Nancy had to go onstage all by herself. He didn't ditch her on purpose; his dragon egg was hatching and he needed to be there. Jack thinks Nancy would forgive him if he told her this, but she hasn't given him the chance.

Nancy said her parents would give him a ride home at the end of camp this year, and he doesn't know if the offer is still good. He hopes it is. It would give him a chance to apologize, the two of them sitting on the gray velvet bench seat of her mother's station wagon, the baby dragon between them.

"I told you dragons were real," Jack would say.

"Dragons eat people, you know."

Jack arrived at camp six years and three weeks ago. His mother dropped him off at his cabin with his trunk, bookbag, and dragon egg. The trunk held three bathing suits, fourteen T-shirts, ten pairs of shorts, white socks, and underwear, each with Jack's name written in black permanent marker in thick block letters. Inside the bookbag were five books from the Craven County Public School recommended summer reading list, a Walkman, various toiletries, an Uno deck, stationery, envelopes, stamps, and four bags of chocolate bars he'd stolen from his older brother, Robert. Robert was going to a different camp, in the mountains, and Jack knew Robert wouldn't notice anything was missing until he got there.

Sometimes Jack still gets letters from Robert. Robert ends each one with a running tally of how many chocolate bars Jack owes him now. It's in the millions. "Because of interest," Robert says.

Jack also gets letters from his parents. They ask him questions about sailing and motorboating and archery and tell him to be good, they'll be there to pick him up at the end of the summer. They never do. Every August Jack drags his belongings to a new cabin and different campers arrive. In the fall they learn to play instruments: harp, violin, piano. In the spring it's always math camp, science camp, or historical reenactment. There are two weeks in the winter when adults fill the cabins. They play soccer and baseball, jump in the river, and stay up all night in the mess hall playing loud music. His counselor says next year they're opening up a space camp, but he's been saying that for a while now. Jack has had the same counselor each summer for seven years; he never remembers Jack's name.

"This your first year?" he asks. "Don't worry. You're going to love it. It can be rough at first, but at the end of four weeks, no one ever wants to leave. You staying for one session or two? Most of us stay for two."

In January and February the camp lets in high schoolers and college students to practice standardized tests: PSAT, LSAT, SAT, DAT, MCAT, PCAT, and VCAT. Jack wasn't very good at them at first, but he's been catching on. Before Nancy stopped talking to him, she lent him her *Cosmo* magazines for their quizzes. Nancy said there's an art to multiple-choice questions. There's always the right answer, the wrong answer that you want to pick anyway, the silly answer, and the answer that leads to the inevitable tragedy of human experience. If you read enough of them, you can figure out which one is which by the way they're phrased, or the way they're ordered. When in doubt, pick *C,* she says. Nancy said she hasn't studied for a history test in three years because she knows exactly how to find out the key result of the Battle of New Orleans just by the way the teacher uses conjunctions. Jack told her there was no result. The war was over before the battle even started. He knew this because he had to pretend to die on a hill, his foot rotting from gangrene. Then the cook got mad at them because they stole too much cheese for special effects and they had to reenact treaty signings the next year. And the year after that and the year after. Jack hated it. All they did was stand around in wool coats and sweat.

Even though he's not very good, Jack has always secretly preferred standardized-test camp. They stay inside and read and take
snack breaks. He also likes the logic puzzles.

A camper with access to the theater hut has six chances to apologize to a
girl. The hut holds the following items: carrots, daffodils, earmuffs, and a
fire extinguisher. The following requirements must be satisfied:
  The girl does not like vegetables.
  The girl does not like flowers.
  The girl's ears are quite warm.
  The girl is not on fire.
Which one of the following could be a complete and accurate list of ways
the boy could be forgiven?

The dragon egg was a gift from his grandmother. She said she'd
found it in the Walmart parking lot, near the cart return. Jack used
to get letters from her, but she died at the end of the first summer.
Jack thinks that's why his parents forgot to come pick him up.

When Jack and his mother first arrived, they drove past the
girls' cabins so they could say hello to one of the counselors. She
was related to Jack, a first cousin, but he'd never met her before
and had a hard time remembering her name. Whenever he saw
her he always nodded and called her "Cuz" because that sounded
like something Robert would say. She nodded back. She could
never remember his name either. "Pleased to meet you, Jeremy."

She introduced him to some of the girls in her cabin, girls who
were about Jack's age. Some of them looked as annoyed to be
there as he was, which was comforting in its own way.

"They seem nice," his mother said.

Jack's cabin was not as nice as the girls' cabin. The screen door
was falling off its hinges and the wood smelled of damp and rot.
Jack's mom kept saying it had "character." The bunk beds were
all different heights and every surface had been written on in
multicolored markers: messages from previous campers and dirty
limericks and crude drawings. Jack thought the messages in the
girls' cabin were probably nicer and more intelligent, with cartoon
hearts and flowers to match their comforters and Laura Ashley
sheets. He was wrong. Nancy told him the girls' cabins were just as
bad-word-filled as the boys', that's just the way camps were.

"But our diagrams are more anatomically correct," she said.

Jack's counselor introduced himself, and then the other boys. Jack watched as the counselor patted each of them on the back and surreptitiously pulled back the collars of their shirts where mothers had written out names like Bob and Timothy and George in the same black permanent marker that Jack's mom used. Jack wondered if the counselor had his name in big block letters somewhere on his clothes too. Just in case he forgot it. Maybe there was a store they all went to that sold prenamed clothing.

When his mother finally left ("Be good," "Okay," "Make friends," "Okay," "Have fun," "Okay," "Don't get eaten by a bear," "Okay"), Jack grabbed his dragon egg and went out into the woods looking for a place to hide it.

This is how I've Come to Marry the Princess goes:

Jack knocks on a pretend door. Nancy answers. She's a guard.

"I've come to marry the princess," Jack says.

"The princess?"

"Yes, the princess."

"Okay. I'll go ask her."

The guard turns around to talk to the king. That's Jack now.

"A knight's at the door. He says he's come to marry the princess."

"The princess?" Jack says.

"Yes, the princess."

"Okay. I'll go ask her."

Then the king tells this to the queen, who finally goes to ask the princess. That's Jack again.

"There's a knight at the door. He says he wants to marry you," Nancy says.

"Marry me?" Jack says.

"Yes. What do you think?"

"No, no, no, a thousand times no."

They rotate again until Jack is the knight and the guard tells him *no, no, no, a thousand times no.*

"Then you must die!" and the knight stabs the guard with a foam sword.

Then he knocks on the door again.

When the egg didn't hatch that first summer, Jack wondered if it was defective. His grandmother had been certain it would hatch, and yet by September it was just as dull and solid as it could be. In the winter he asked one of the men in his cabin to take a look at it. He was a recently divorced ER doctor whose therapist said fresh air and exercise and socialization would do him good. He arrived the first day with a duffel bag full of mass-market paperbacks and refused to speak to anyone else in the cabin except Jack.

Jack asked him if he knew anything about eggs. The man asked if he meant dinosaur eggs. His son used to like dinosaurs.

"It's not a dinosaur egg."

"Robin?"

"No."

"Chicken?"

"No."

"Platypus? Snake? Ostrich?"

Jack pulled the egg out of his backpack and showed him. "Dragon. Don't know what kind."

The ER doctor rolled the egg around on the floor and knocked on its shell. "Looks more like a rock to me."

The doctor suggested that he place it somewhere cool and dry, where it could get plenty of sunlight. Either it would hatch or it wouldn't. No way to tell for sure without cracking it open to see what was actually inside.

Jack met Nancy the second summer. He went to his cousin's cabin on the first day of camp because he knew his mother would want him to. He went early, when he knew there wouldn't be many girls for his cousin to introduce him to. There was a freckled girl named Anna, and Nancy. Nancy didn't talk.

"Don't worry," his cousin told them, "it's his first year too. Isn't it, Justin?"

"Sure," he said.

His cousin told him Nancy never talked to anyone. Her parents were hoping camp would help.

"My parents thought camp would help too," Jack said.

Nancy didn't talk to anyone the first week, nor the second. The boys in Jack's cabin said Nancy had escaped from juvenile prison and was hiding out. Other cabins had their own rumors.

Nancy was a Kennedy.

Nancy had her tongue ripped out by wolves.

Nancy ripped out her own tongue.

Nancy had tattoos.

Nancy had no parents.

Nancy had seventeen parents, the result of a series of divorces, kidnappings, and illegal adoptions.

Nancy was an alien.

Nancy was a witch.

Nancy didn't exist.

Jack thought Nancy had it pretty easy. She could join any group she wanted, do anything she wanted, and no one would stop her because they didn't know what she'd do to them. One time a girl pushed her into the dirt and Nancy got up and then shook the girl's hand. She didn't smile or frown; she gripped the girl's hand in both of hers and then walked away. Later the girl broke her nose after being hit in the face with the boom of a sailboat. Nancy wasn't there, and that's when the witch rumor started. But when the girl with the broken nose came back from the hospital, she told everyone that Nancy was just a nice girl who didn't talk much. And the rumor went away.

"People aren't nearly as mean as other people think," Nancy told him.

The boys in Jack's cabin weren't mean, but there were too many of them and Jack had a hard time keeping them straight. So he divided them into groups. There were the boys who had been coming to camp all their lives and already had all the friends they wanted to make. Jack called them the Jonathans. And the boys who were there for the first time but already knew how to sail or play sports or who had mothers who sent care packages every day filled with candy and *MAD* magazines and soda and other contraband. Those were the Roberts. They were always more popular than the Jonathans, until their newness wore off and they became Jonathans themselves.

"This your first summer?" Jonathan asked Jack. "It must be. I'd remember you. Your parents send you with anything good?"

Jack had three trunks now. Summer, winter, and in-between. The summer trunk held five bathing suits, six shorts, six T-shirts, and twenty pairs of underwear. Every time he sent his laundry out with the other campers', more clothes came back. Sometimes they had other boys' names written in the collars: Barnabus, Crispin, Derrek, and Pierre. Jack never wore these clothes. He was too scared of running into their original owners. Sometimes he wondered if he should take their names too, then maybe people would remember him; maybe another mother would come and pick him up.

That first day, Jack's mother set up an account for him at the camp store. She said he could buy whatever he wanted, within reason. It'd make his father happy if he got some camp clothes: a hat, sweatshirt, maybe even some of those rubber sandals to wear in the river with the Morehead wheel sewn in white thread on the ankle.

By spring of his fourth year Jack had run up a tab of $1,847. He didn't only buy clothes: the store also sold stamps, toiletries, and a stale-tasting candy bar some camper's father invented that no one ever ate. Even the ducks wouldn't touch it. Around Christmas the store sold ornaments, wrapping paper, and better-tasting chocolate. Jack liked the store best in February. They had an entire display case of No. 2 pencils stacked in a giant No. 2 pencil pyramid. You had to ask for help to take one. Jack bought several throughout the day, every day, just hoping it would crumble when the cashier reached over to get him one. It never did.

When the knight knocks on the door the second time, the king answers.

"I've come to marry the princess."

"The princess?"

"Yes, the princess."

"All right, I'll go ask her."

Nancy was the only one who remembered Jack from year to year. "I've got a really good memory," she said. "I'm constantly correcting people when they tell a story wrong. Details are important, unless they're made up."

Nancy told Jack he should try the administrator's office and ask for his paperwork. "You would have to be registered for each session, each camp, otherwise they wouldn't let you stay," she explained. "Bills, medical records, test scores, all of them have to be recorded in the system. Ask for it, any of it, and it'll collapse."

Sometimes Nancy suggested that he just walk out the gate and down the highway. He could steal a horse from the barn, or one of the boats. Jack didn't think those were very feasible, and he didn't have a very good sense of direction.

Why not the bus? she asked. It dropped campers off at the Episcopal church right downtown. Didn't he say he lived on the river?

He could walk from there. If he didn't try, then it was his fault.

"When I was seven years old," Jack said, "I went to a school that put younger students at tables with older students. Lunch was delivered to the head of the table, and it was the job of the older student to pass them out. That year I was at a long table. There were two head students and twelve of us. They passed out eleven plates. I guess each one of them thought the other one had taken care of me. I was reading a book, so I didn't notice until I could hear the scrape of everyone's knives. I waited until someone noticed. No one did. I thought about raising my hand, but I didn't know which one of them to ask. By then it had been so long that I thought I had to think of a reason why I'd waited. They were going to have to ask the kitchen for another plate. One of them would get in trouble. So I kept waiting. I pretended to keep reading, and then I'd have an excuse. Then lunch was over, and I was still hungry, but no one had to be embarrassed about it."

"That's stupid," she said.

"It happened again the next day, and I kept reading. I learned to stuff an apple in my pocket in the morning. I ate bigger breakfasts. Finally, by the third week, I spoke up. 'Excuse me?' I said to the older one, a girl. She seemed nice. 'I don't have a plate.'"

"Did she give you one?"

"It turned out I was at the wrong table. By the time she'd straightened it out, my friend William had eaten his lunch and mine, like he'd been doing every day prior. He was mad at me after that and wouldn't talk to me."

"There are these boys in my school," Nancy said. "They're on the swim team. They're always hungry. After lunch they walk around the cafeteria and go up to any girl who still has fries on her plate, or pizza. 'You really want to eat that?' they say. 'You don't want a paunch, do you?' They always said 'paunch.' We learned it in English class. We all liked the way our lips quivered when we said it. Paunch. 'Come on,' they said. 'We're helping you out.' Some girls, they just hold up their trays when they see those boys coming."

"Why didn't the school do something?"

"No one complained. The girls didn't mind. Some girls, they got extra fries just so they could give them away. Of course, some girls spat on theirs, or brought in extra hot peppers or other things to dice up and put on their pizza, just to see what would happen. One boy got sick; he threw up all during fifth period."

"Did they stop?"

"No. They were stubborn and stupid, like you."

Last summer, Jack did try the bus. It took him all the way into town, where the campers' parents were waiting at the Episcopal church parking lot. Jack could see the top of his house over the trees. The driver wouldn't let him off until a guardian signed for him. They waited all day. Jack asked the driver if he could go inside the church and call his house from the office.

"How do I know you'll call your mother? You could be calling a stranger."

"You could call."

"Camp told me to sit on the bus and wait till all the campers' mothers came and signed for them. Can't leave the bus."

They waited all night, and the next morning the bus driver took him back to camp. A counselor checked his name off on a clipboard.

"You're going to love it here, Jack. What instrument do you play? Did you forget it at home? Don't worry, we have spares."

In June, when he saw Nancy, she sighed. "When I never see you again, I'll know that something good happened."

There's always a reason a boy finds a dragon egg. Jack didn't have a reason. His grandmother gave it to him even though he'd asked for a soccer ball. All the boys at camp would know how to play soccer and he wanted to practice before he went.

"It's an egg," he said.

"A dragon egg," his grandmother said.

"Does that make a difference?"

"You'll be the only one at camp with one, I'm sure," she said.

"Don't dragons eat people?"

"That's just a rumor. Make friends with it."

He thought about telling people it was a soccer ball. A special one. That was heavy. And didn't roll very well. And clinked when you shook it ("Don't do that," his grandmother said, "it'll get mad at you").

The only thing Jack liked about the egg was the thought of having his very own dragon. One that could fly, and speak telepathically, and breathe fire. But after the first summer, and the next, and the next after, he thought maybe his dragon was defective. What kind of dragon would come from a Walmart parking lot?

Jack imagined flying over fields and forests in a dragon-sized silver shopping cart, the balls of his feet balancing on the metal bar as the cart's front end rose and rose, right into the clouds.

"Rawr," he said. "Behold the conquering hero."

When the dragon finally hatched, it was blue. Blue eyes, blue scales, even blue-tinted nails at the end of its delicate blue feet. Its wings were membranous wisps that flapped weakly against the dragon's sides.

"Don't worry," he told the dragon. "You'll grow into them. Then you can take us home."

Jack thought long and hard about a name. Names had power. An evil wizard could ensnare his dragon by guessing its true name.

"Pencil," Jack said. "No one would guess that."

He thought about naming it Nancy, but if anyone in his life were to suddenly turn into an evil wizard, it would be her. Then the name wouldn't be hard to guess at all.

The king asks the queen, who asks the princess, who still says *No, no, no, a thousand times no.* The knight kills the king and then asks the queen, kills her, and finally knocks on the princess's door.

"No, no, no, a thousand times no," she says.

The knight kills the princess, sees what he has done, and says, "Now I must die!" And he does.

Before the audience has a chance to react, Jack and Nancy get up and repeat the skit, but faster.

Then they do it a third time where the knight kills anyone who answers the door.

They practiced it a dozen times, then two dozen. Sometimes they got mixed up and the king was wearing the princess's wig when he told the knight no. Sometimes both Jack and Nancy were the princess, saying no to each other. Sometimes they were both the knight thrusting swords into each other's bellies.

The skit wasn't original. Robert and his friends performed it in the mountains; that's how Jack knows about it. Even though he's never seen it at his camp, Jack fears another cabin will do the skit before they have a chance.

Nancy says it doesn't matter if theirs is the first, last, or thousandth I've Come to Marry the Princess. Theirs will be the best.

*

It is given that an average camp theater stage is 20 feet wide and 14 feet deep.

It is given that Jack suffers from a recurring nightmare in which he forgets to stab Nancy in the stomach and kisses her instead.

Quantity A: The speed Jack can run behind the curtain to vomit in a bucket placed there for just this purpose.

Quantity B: $(x - 2y)(x + 2y) = 4$.

D. The relationship cannot be determined from the information given.

Every Sunday night at summer camp, they have devotions. The counselor reads a passage from something inspirational: the Bible, *Chicken Soup for the Soul,* a favorite novel. It depends a lot on the counselor. Nancy said her counselor liked to read the embarrassing stories from *Seventeen* magazine so all the girls would know that it wasn't just them who passed gas in front of boys or got their first period while wearing white jeans.

"The stories are obviously made up," Nancy said. "They have to be. Each Sunday we've been writing our own entries. Our counselor collects them and mails them off. We're going to see which of us can be the first to get in."

This was Nancy's, published a year after the end of camp:

> One time I fell flat on my face at the talent show. One second I was holding the microphone in one hand and a foam sword in the other, trying to think of a joke to tell, and when the spotlight hit my face, my knees locked, and I fell. As I lay there I could hear a girl in the front row whisper, *Is she dead?* And I said into the microphone, *Not yet.* Everyone clapped and I got up and walked offstage.

Jack looked forward to devotions every week and tried to keep it up the rest of the year. The band counselor played violin and lectured on music theory. In standardized-test camp they read admission essays that "made the difference." In math and science camp they went stargazing.

Adult camp had no counselor, so Jack improvised.

"This is what we do: we each tell a story. It has to be a true story. If you don't have one, maybe just tell us about why you're here. I'll start. I'm here because my parents forgot to pick me up."

"I'm here because my house is being tented for termites."

"I was too cheap to go to Bermuda."

"I went to Bermuda. It's overrated."

"I cut a kid's chest open when he came into the ER. He had bullet holes in his chest, up near the neck. He was practically dead. So I cut his chest open. When the surgeon got there, she looked at me and said, 'What did you do and why did you do it?' I cut his chest open, through the breastplate. I used a saw. 'What did you do?' the surgeon said. Couldn't she see I didn't know? The kid was dying. I'm a doctor. It's what I do. She said he'd had a heartbeat. She wasn't there. She didn't know. 'It's on the chart,' she said. She wouldn't operate. 'You did this,' she said. We scared the nurses. The hospital sent us both to anger management. Later, we got divorced. My therapist thought camp would help."

The doctor left camp the next day. He left Jack his duffel bag full of books. "Sometimes when my wife got called into the ER to do a central line, it wouldn't take too long and she'd be sent home. Only it was too late to go back to sleep and too early to go to the office, so she told me she'd go to Walmart and wander the aisles. She said the nice thing about Walmart was it was always open and no one would talk to you. After the divorce I would drive by the parking lot looking for her car. I figure when I finally know what to say to her, she'll be there."

"What if she isn't?"

"Then I'll say it to somebody else. Hope that egg of yours hatches, Jack."

The morning after the talent show, Jack stole a dozen fish fillets the cook was saving for the end-of-camp banquet. He wrapped them in a dishcloth and brought them out to the woods. He thought they'd help him train Pencil.

"Sit," Jack said. His dragon did nothing.

"Sit," Jack said. And the dragon did nothing.

"Come," Jack said. And the dragon did nothing.

Jack figured that one day he and his dragon would develop telepathy of some sort. He didn't know when that would be.

"Maybe I'll bring you Nancy. You could eat her instead." The dragon bit him.

"You're right, that's not very nice."

When he got back to the cabin, the other boys said Nancy had stopped by to tell him that she'd never forgive him and she hoped he died.

"Your girlfriend was pissed," they said.

"I don't have a girlfriend," Jack said.

"Damn straight," they said.

By lunch everyone was talking about their breakup. About how she'd dumped him. About how she'd thrown bug juice in his face. And how he had cried.

Jack still hadn't seen Nancy. He pictured her throwing bug juice in someone else's face. A pretend Jack: a prop from the theater hut done up in Jack clothes and Jack makeup. He imagined the pretend Jack taking it on the chin. Pretend Jack listened to Nancy's complaints, accepted responsibility, and apologized. Pretend Jack wouldn't have missed the talent show in the first place. He would've left the egg all alone in the woods while he pretended to run a foam sword into Nancy's belly and Nancy pretended to run a foam sword into his. The other campers would remember Pretend Jack the next summer.

"That was a hell of a skit you did last year, Jack," they'd say. "I almost believed you both died up there. I was afraid I'd never see you again."

The dragon grew a little every hour. By dinner it was the size of a large dog. By breakfast the next morning it was the size of a pony. Jack moved the dragon into the theater hut. It was always empty the last week of camp, and Jack didn't want Pencil getting lost in the woods. Jack still didn't know what it ate. He brought it scraps from the mess—spaghetti, meatloaf, scrambled eggs—but Pencil wasn't interested. Maybe dragons didn't need to eat.

Nancy and Jack tried revising I've Come to Marry the Princess to make it their own. They spent every afternoon in the theater hut. Nancy said it was her favorite place at camp. Jack agreed because it was the only building with air conditioning.

In one of Jack and Nancy's made-up versions, the princess said yes. The knight said "Great!" and they proceeded to spend forty-five minutes making wedding preparations, passing messages through the guard, king, and queen. The climax of the story was when the guard misheard "lilies" for "daffodils" and it turned out the knight was allergic and he died from anaphylactic shock. The princess died from grief. Nancy said it was very important that they both die in the skit, otherwise people wouldn't know it was supposed to be funny. If only one of them kicked the bucket, then it'd be a different kind of story entirely.

In another, Nancy and Jack developed an elaborate backstory for the knight and the princess. They wrote it out on cue cards to hold up to the audience to read before the skit so they would know the context.

The knight and princess went on a quest together. They fell in love and the knight has finally returned to marry her as he promised, only the princess is really mad it took him so long to get here.

"What if he had a good reason?" Jack asked. "Maybe he went on another quest."

"Then he should have brought her with him," Nancy said. "That's what you're supposed to do in these situations."

In another, Nancy played all the parts. Jack stayed behind the curtain. Tech crew. This was Jack's favorite version. The only time he appeared onstage was to drag Nancy's body off when she died for the last time. If he wore all black, no one would be able to see him at all.

"Just imagine the entire audience in their underwear," Nancy said. "And remember that no one will remember you anyway."

"They will if I throw up all over the first row."

In another, Nancy answered the door as a dragon, who ate Jack and then the princess.

"Maybe it's a nice dragon," Jack said.

"Don't be stupid. Dragons eat people. It's what they do."

In the end, they decided the original version was best.

"But we can keep practicing until you get over your stage fright," Nancy said. "If you want. I don't mind."

Each evening Jack decides to go to Nancy's cabin first thing in the morning and explain everything. He always chickens out. She'll want to see Pencil. She'll want to know why he didn't tell her about Pencil before. She'll tell his cousin. His cousin will tell the government. The government will take Pencil and perform experiments in Nevada.

Finally Jack writes a letter to his mother. "If it's not too much trouble," he says, "please pick me up early this year. Please come get me on Sunday morning, before everyone else leaves. Before 10 a.m. if possible. I don't like being the last one." He knows when his mother picks him up, she'll ask him why he didn't say anything before. "I didn't feel that way before," he'll say.

After Jack mails the letter, he feels good. Good enough to walk by Nancy's cabin to ask for her address so they can keep in touch. He'll write her a letter when he gets home. "I didn't need you after all." When Pencil is grown, he'll go visit. They can go on quests. They'll be friends again. Pencil won't eat anyone. He won't be that kind of dragon.

His cousin tells him she's not there. "How'd you like your first year at camp, Jonathan? Did you love it? Everyone loves it. This is my twelfth summer, you know. If I had a choice, I'd never leave."

"People with choices always say that." Jack looks for Nancy on the pier. He looks for her at the soccer fields, baseball, the archery and riflery ranges. No one has seen her. She's still mad at him.

"Girls," the boys say. "They get mad and stay mad. It's what they do."

Jack looks for her everywhere and at lunch he waits by the flag-pole as all the cabins stream past him so he can catch her walking in. She never shows.

Jack runs to the theater hut even though he knows everything will be fine. The door is closed and everything is quiet.

Nancy believes (C) that dragons exist. When she meets the dragon, it (C) doesn't eat her. Nancy (C) teaches the dragon tricks. They become (C) good friends. Nancy (C) forgives Jack. (C) Jack's mother picks him up at the end of the summer. (C) Everyone lives happily ever after.

The afternoon before the talent show, Jack and Nancy decided to do the original version of the skit: *I've come to marry the princess. I'll go ask her. No, no, no, a thousand times no.*

"You'll be there, right? You won't chicken out? I'm counting on you. I'll never forgive you if you leave me up there all by myself."

Jack knocks. "I've come to marry the princess," he says.

He knocks again. "I've come to rescue the princess."

He knocks a third time. "I'm going on a quest, and I would like the princess to come with me if she would be so inclined."

Jack knows that Nancy will open the door and forgive him. He believes it with the certainty of choice; there are no other options.

"He's such a sweet dragon," she'll say. "Why didn't you say anything before?"

GENEVIEVE VALENTINE

Everyone from Themis Sends Letters Home

FROM *Clarkesworld Magazine*

THE WATER HERE is never going to make good bread. If I'd known, I would have requested sturdier flour—we'll be waiting six years for the next transport pod. Agosti told me today my bread's good for massaging the gums, like he was trying to focus on the positives. Woods threatened to arrest him anyway, which was nice of him.

But that's really the only thing that makes me sad. Otherwise, I promise, I'm getting along here very well. I miss you too. Every time I'm up late with the dough I imagine you're at the table working, and when I look up it takes me a second to remember. But everyone here is pitching in. Marquez and Perlman and I are figuring out how to cheat an apple tree into producing fruit sooner, and Agosti's building equipment out of our old life-support systems. If it works out, we'll have our own cider in two years. ("We can dip the bread in it," Perlman said, and Woods threatened to arrest her too. Gives him something to do. Imagine being in charge of five people. Good thing he has a knack for building.)

The sun's different than back home—they told us about particles and turbulence on the way over and I was too stupid to understand it and too afraid to tell them, so just pretend I explained and you were really impressed. The planet's locked, so there's really only water on the equator—nothing makes it toward the sun and it's ice by the time you go ten miles further darkside. You're never 100 percent sure what time it even is, except that it's a little more purple in the daylight for the hour we get it, and at sunset it looks like the whole place was attacked by vampires. It's sunset most of the time. That's not too bad if you can just avoid the river; that river never looks right with the dark coming in.

Agosti and Perlman were up until 3:30 shouting about which route will get us over the mountains, which would be more understandable if there were any mountains. But the movie bank's still broken, so it's just as well. I'm betting on Perlman. If anyone could lead us over imaginary mountains, it's her.

My other entertainment is staying up late, trying to fight the water and make bread that will actually rise, and the bird that sings all night. Samara—Perlman—says we're not supposed to assign characteristics from home to the things we find here until they've been observed and documented and whatever else, but—thrush family.

It's most active during our night hours, and we're working on why (trying to make sure it's not drawn to the lights we brought with us, which would be bad news), but in the meantime it seems happy to sit in the trees outside the kitchen and sing. Three little bursts, then a longer one that's so many notes it sounds like showing off, then a little pause to see if anyone's listening, so it's definitely showing off. If I whistle anything, it tries to repeat it, and it's a fairly good mimic, but nothing I do really takes. It knows what it likes.

It has the same woodwind sound as the one back home, the house I lived in when I was young. Hermit thrush? Wood thrush? Something I used to hear all the time and never thought about, of course. Good news is that now it's just me and this one bird and I'll get to start over again with every new animal. This time I'm going to pay better attention.

Perlman will officially name it—they don't ask the cooks how to classify animal species, that's why the company hauled a biologist out here. But Perlman knows I like it, so maybe she'll consult me. I know it best. That should count for something.

All my love.

Proxima Centauri Personnel Status Report: Day 1187
Author: Dr. Samara Perlman

Crew Health: Reiterating that as a biologist, I am not in a position to diagnose or treat any major medical issues, am not sure how I was tasked with this position, and am deeply concerned about how soon we can expect a qualified physician rather than a group of people who had slapdash medic training for three days before they left Earth. That said, all six residents currently seem in good health. Carlos Marquez claims a slight cough, but as the scans came back negative, my money's on allergies. If he dies of tuberculosis next week we'll know I was wrong.

Crew Injuries: Anthony Agosti nursing a minor wrist sprain after having punched a wall. Should he resort to violence again I'll be sending him to Officer Woods for a formal report and some time in the brig. We shouldn't build a new planet with the same problems as the old one.

Crew Mental Health: Marie Roland continues to claim she can't see the mountains to the northwest of Themis. No other signs of psychosis appear, and when questioned or shown pictures of the mountains, Roland becomes distracted and mildly agitated. No tendency to violence. Suspect a minor mental block prevents her from fully acknowledging the terrain—homesickness? For now, as she's still willing to train for the mission, there seems to be no point in forcing the issue; have asked Woods to stop pushing it and will let Marie come to it in her own time.

Crew Mission Training: Expedition prep continues. Entire staff follow regimen of five-kilometer runs on hilly terrain every morning, weightlifting three times a week, rock climbing on nearby hills twice a week. Once the snow melts a little off the pass we'll be able to determine the actual level of dexterity required for the climb and train accordingly. Vigil until then.

to whomever
    there's nothing here left to build and the mountain project is on hold until the thaw and I don't care about sunset please get the movie bank going again before I throw myself in the river full stop
    anthony

to whomever
    there's nothing here left to build and the mountain project is on hold until the thaw and I don't care about sunset please get the movie bank going again before I throw myself in the river full stop
    anthony

*

sorry sent it twice by mistake

wouldn't do that kind of thing if the movie bank worked though probably

anthony

Samara and I did a perimeter walk today, a kilometer out from the camp. I picked almost more plants than I could carry, and I'm fairly sure at least half are edible, which will make meals much more exciting. Samara insisted on running tests for poison, don't worry, but I think if I have to measure one more judicious use of dried black pepper I'm going to scream. I want something that tastes like it grew in the ground.

Samara's amazing. I don't even remember first meeting her; it just feels like I've always known her, which I guess is what close quarters will do to you. We cataloged five species of bird (none of them my bird, so I guess the animals here really can tell day from night and it's something we'll get used to), and she spent a lot more time with insects than I was interested in.

The air here smells just like home. I don't know why—the water's different, so the soil should be different, but it smells exactly like the dirt from my grandmother's garden. It helps stop me from getting lonely, that the soil here might be the same as what we left behind.

Marquez showed us pictures of his children a few nights ago; it's his daughter's birthday. Samara cried, but nobody pushed it. It's strange how much we left behind to be here, and I think no matter how much work you're getting done, sometimes it just hits you how separate you are. We must have really wanted this. I must still.

I know you weren't ready, and you might never be ready. These letters aren't meant to convince you, I promise. It just makes me feel closer to home.

All my love—

Dr. March:

Mixed results, as always. Sunset was a little longer than yesterday, so the seasons function is working. None of the subjects have noticed yet that Vivian and Carlos are interfaces, which bodes well for long-term use of constructed intelligence inside Themis. (Suggest we minimize the rock-climbing training until we can work out the uncanny valley problem in the weight distribution. Can the development team extend the thaw?) But overall, investors should be pleased—let me know if you need any demo footage, I have a clip of everyone working on the gardens that should go over well.

Technical glitch, first incident: Anthony's punch should have broken his hand. I'm not sure if the safety settings are appropriately set or too schoolmarmy. We might need to dial them down and get someone to break their leg as a test run for more realistic game play.

Gigantic fucking technical glitch, ongoing: Marie can't see the mountains. I've checked her equipment, and there's no other potential hardware problems (attached is the most recent server diagnostic for your review, but there's nothing in it that would account for it). Either she has an actual mental block that we can't do anything about, or there's a subjectivity issue somewhere in the code for Themis and we have to find it and fix it. I can't tell which one is more likely, because you made me military instead of medical and I can't just put her in jail until she tells me she sees them. Do we have a timetable for getting security clearance on that or are we going to have to settle for imperfect data?

—Woods

Woods dropped into the chair in Benjamina's cubicle so hard her BIRDS OF MONTANE ECOSYSTEMS reference chart came loose and sank to the floor.

"You gotta fix those mountains," he said.

"My chart, please."

"It's going to break the sim," he said, scooping it up and smoothing a bent edge. "We'll have done four years of work for nothing because Marie has some synapse you can't outsmart."

"The problem's her head, not the software." After a pointed pause, she turned around. He carried some ego out of a Themis session and it took a day or so to wear off; the faster you could remind him that everyone else was actually busy, the better. "You can see the mountains when you're in Themis, and you know they're not there. Sounds like you should take it up with the psych team."

"I'd have thought you wanted to keep her out of all that." He wasn't quite threatening her; he wasn't quite sympathizing. (The reason Woods got chosen for beta-test jobs was how good he could be at Not Quite.)

Benjamina didn't bother to recite any anonymity bullshit.

Woods had been in Themis a long time; they read letters out loud to each other. He knew what she sounded like. "I've been trying."

"They want to test the mountains before we wrap beta."

"We need to look at her file — I can't reverse-engineer a synapse misfire."

"They fixed Agosti's colorblindness."

"That's different," said Benjamina, picking crumbs off her keyboard. She didn't like that fix, for no particular reason. It was productive; it just itched.

"Listen, I like her, but this is going to kill the beta, and you and I will be under the knife."

"Get the psych team to request Marie's file from the warden. Is Perlman at the same place?"

"Nah, Perlman stabbed her husband, she went someplace serious. Roland's just in a prison for fuckups."

"Fine. So get Dr. March to show me the file. I can port into Carlos for eyes on the ground. Then I'll know what I'm dealing with."

"Nobody in this building's willing to talk to the shrinks but me. That should tell you something." Woods stood up, the little bird poster still in his hands. He was holding the very edges, like it was an expensive library book.

One of the things nobody at Othrys talked about was that the longer you spent in Themis, the weirder physical objects were when you came back. Officially, nobody was talking about it because it was just Woods, and no one liked Woods enough to make him for a martyr of motor-skill dissociation. Unofficially, nobody wanted to think Themis came back with you. Benjamina hoped that wore off too.

"How are you doing?"

He was smoothing the edges of the chart with the pads of his fingers as he set it down. He looked up at her like he was surprised.

"I'm going to go eat some decent bread," he said finally, and left.

Benjamina's computer pinged. It was waiting for her letter.

Agosti came back from his walk today and did some very elaborate hand gestures about how much snow is left on the mountain pass and pointing to the northwest, and it took me three minutes to realize it wasn't a buildup to a jerk-off joke. Those fucking mountains. Woods told him to knock it off—very sheriffy thing to do, glad he's finding something to lay down the law about—but still. It gets old.

Samara named that bird *Catharus rolandus*. It's useless to be proud of something that has so little to do with actual contributions from you, but I teared up anyway. Plus that genus is apparently very close to the wood thrush after all! I felt like a scientist! Then I baked a shitty loaf of bread and lost that feeling immediately, because a scientist would know how to outsmart this water.

I loved your letter. Not the markets, though—Themis is really good for reminding you of the value of only knowing a few people. The only thing I miss about the night markets is the two of us wearing those giant sweaters with the huge arms we bought as a joke and ended up needing that whole winter and we had to push the sleeves up before we reached for anything. All the fabrics here are sort of flat. They keep you warm, but it's not the same.

All my love

Mr. Collins:

My name is Dr. Frederick March, and I'm a consulting psychologist for Othrys Games. We've been partnering with your institution to test the latest game from Othrys; I understand you might not have all the details of how the process has gone so far, so first of all, I wanted to thank you, and let you know it's been invaluable. You're assisting us with some truly amazing work about constructed intelligence and full-neuro game play. There are even insights into the human subconscious and stimuli processing that I suspect will have significant implications going forward in other realms of study.

I say all this so you'll understand why I'd so much like to meet to discuss the next steps, since we've had to terminate the study slightly earlier than planned. Your in-house medical team has been exemplary, and we are completely understanding of what happened—immunity to memory suppressants is a risk of repeated exposure and this was discussed prior to beginning. We agree with you that the testing stage has effectively ended—the downside of informed consent.

However, because of this, we would like to work out some visitations with the subjects in question. I understand our team has had some miscommunications with your administration trying to set these up. Let me assure you this is the standard debrief for any long-term player. And in this particular case, I expect that the subjects themselves would benefit from being able to speak with a trained professional about their experience. The amount and type of memories that might be restored have definite in-game applications and are potential data points well within the scope of our contract with your correctional facility. I'm happy to discuss further particulars—please let me know your thoughts.

Sincerely,
Frederick March

Dr. March was already in the VP's office, and Woods wasn't, which meant the worst. Benjamina let the closed-door click echo a moment, trying to decide if looking stoic or penitent would work better. (Women who were too stoic got fired for not caring; women who were too penitent got fired for poor performance.) She forced herself not to ask questions as she sat. Inquisitive women were no better than the other kinds.

"We've had a problem with Themis," the VP said. He looked from one of them to the other. "Frederick knows already."

Of course he did. Benjamina waited.

"It's not the simulation," the VP continued after a moment, as if to put her mind at ease, as if she was concerned that somehow her work wasn't up to par and they would have waited until now to tell her. "In fact, Erytheia—the coders have aliases, it's easier," he explained to Dr. March, "—has our lowest fault rate, and has spent the most time working on individual settings for Roland. I think she could be invaluable to us during the postmortem process."

Benjamina blinked. "Postmortem of what?"

Dr. March turned toward her. "Did you know Ms. Roland was a drug addict?"

"No," she said, and her stomach dropped as she considered why the medical side of the experiment wasn't feasible anymore. "Did she get any memories back when the drugs stopped working, or is it still a fog?"

"She got them back."

Stoic, she thought. Be stoic. No point being penitent now.

"Are Perlman and Agosti still in beta?" If they were, she'd have to talk to their coders about some in-game reason Marie was gone, though she couldn't think of one they would believe. Marie would never leave Themis. She knew it best. Benjamina might have to port in on a simulation and drop dead in front of them.

"No," said the VP. "We decided to stop beta across the board. Dr. March is trying to get the warden to agree to interviews so we can find out how the, uh — the memory process? Is going. It will probably take a few weeks. Woods will go along and observe, obviously — continuity for them — and then he can circle back with you, so we can bring our findings to the team in a way that isn't so . . . clinical. No offense."

"Of course," said Dr. March. He was still looking at Benjamina.

"Let me know when," she said, and that was the last thing anyone needed from her.

She drove home with shaking hands, for no good reason — Marie was a test user, they used to have test users at fucking conventions. She'd liked that better; there were plenty of ways to test what players would believe without lying to them at the beginning. Management wanted to test if the environment could fool the mind, but no one had asked Benjamina. None of this had been her idea. Nothing was her fault.

The night was barely cloudy, and she drove past her turnoff and out until there was nothing but the highway on either side, so when she set up the telescope, she could see a glimpse of Proxima Centauri through the haze of light pollution. It blinked back and forth in the lens, and it was so dim. Light from there would never quite suffice.

No one had said anything to the development team — no one ever did unless something was wrong — but she suspected this game was more than a Virtual Experience market maker. There were private companies prepping long-haul spacecraft with stasis technology; they'd want to train their people in the most realistic conditions possible, and they had money to burn.

Normally she'd write a letter to Marie. *Dear Marie, I was looking up at Proxima tonight and I thought about you. Dear Marie, I got your letter. I programmed the thrush to mimic you a little, and you noticed. When the first astronauts land on Proxima Centauri b, maybe there will really be birds. I've studied everything I can, and there's no telling. It might all be a layer of ice. There might be mountains everywhere. They might try to make a new home in a place that's nothing but poison. Dear Marie, I want you to be happy there.*

Through the lens, the planet slid around the star.

Woods,

After you came and talked to us, Samara found out you hadn't even paid us for our time in Themis. Mistake, by the way—if you'd paid us it would have at least looked like you weren't trying to use us like lab rats and get away with it—and I feel like you should have known better. Not the company, but you. You always seemed like a guy who wanted everything to have a reason.

Samara's got a lawyer, and the company should have papers by now. She told me not to contact you. I'm glad she's suing, because you all deserve it. Go bankrupt.

But I have an offer for whoever's in charge: I can't testify if I'm dead, and I want to go back to Themis permanently. I don't know how long "permanently" is, since the prison refuses to keep people on life support for things like that and you won't want to bring me to a hospital, so just budget accordingly—a person probably starves to death in a week? So, a week. Unless I've built up such a resistance to the meds that it kills me in a few hours, which I assume would be cheaper.

I don't know who actually made Themis. I'm assuming you were involved, because you had the shortest fuse of anybody there, and at the time I thought that's just what being law enforcement did to people, but it makes more sense if you made it. And I don't know who I was writing to, that whole time. In Themis I just thought I had someone I loved, and he was where my letters went. I didn't know I needed to love someone so badly you could lie to me about it for four years—but that's how it worked, the psychologist said. You made Samara write reports because whatever you managed to do with her, there were some things she wouldn't fall for. I was an idiot and I'd been lonely my whole life. You could do anything to me.

It wasn't you, was it? Was it one person writing me back, or did you reply by committee? One of you must have seen the picture of my arrest, since you gave me long hair in Themis. You talked about missing my braids. Whoever it was, go fuck yourself. I didn't even like it, it was too long, but in Themis I kept it long all that time for your sake. I wanted to cut it—it got so humid in the summers

I dreamed of shaving it off, I must have told you, I wrote you so much — but keeping my hair long was like a promise we'd see each other again. So I kept it.

I thought that I couldn't quite picture you because being in stasis on the ship seeped the color out of your dreams. And then it had been a long time, so of course I couldn't really remember you — I looked at your messages and forgot whether you had good posture or not when you typed. I wanted to think you hunched like I did, like that weird pang in the lower back was something we shared 25 trillion miles away. I wondered sometimes why I'd gone to Proxima Centauri if I had someone I loved so much. Not that you can say that to the person you left behind. I never even mentioned it to Samara. But everybody knew Carlos and I had loved ones back home. When there are so few of you, you end up knowing a lot of things that you never talk about.

Carlos isn't real, right? I mean — the doctor told me he wasn't, I know he wasn't. But there wasn't a person pretending to be him? He was just a program that got really excited about apple cider?

I don't even know how to be angry at you — it was the worst hour of my life and I threw up after, but it wasn't you (whoever that is) explaining it, I would have been able to tell. So it still feels like you weren't part of what went wrong, like the program got stuck even after I woke up and you locked me out and I'm still carrying you, someone I love and just forgot —

Anyway, I'm going through withdrawal. The prison definitely doesn't care — they said if I could go through it with the drugs that got me in here I could go through it with whatever they stuck in me to make me forget Themis. But maybe if you read this letter, you still consider me market research and this will be helpful. No appetite, no energy. I have a headache right behind my eyes. I'm always cold, even though Themis was colder than prison so you'd think I wouldn't be. I sleep a lot. I always dream of being back in Themis. Probably good news for you. Sell a million copies. Just give me mine.

And fix the bread. It never worked right, that should be changed.

Let me go home.

Marie

*

Benjamina waited until the office was empty before she crossed the floor to Woods's office. Stoic, not penitent; stoic people didn't skulk over to meet someone they barely liked just to see how interviews had gone with the people they had used.

She'd never been to his office before—he must always have come to her, strange, she'd never even noticed—and it was so blank it startled her into stillness at the threshold.

"Want an invitation?" He was standing, reaching for his coat, like he'd just been waiting for her so they could walk out together. "You look like a vampire."

She didn't say anything, and she didn't move closer; after a second, he cracked a grin. "You're kind of an asshole, Harris."

They walked out in silence, but from the way his thumb brushed the front of his coat lapel over and over, something terrible had happened and they were just waiting to be away from the cameras.

Six blocks later, he said, "It was bad."

She stopped and looked at him.

"She, uh—" He rubbed his hand once, rough, across his forehead. "In Themis she looked fine. Healthy. It was stupid to assume she'd look the same in person, but I didn't expect . . . I didn't expect it. Samara's suing us."

It took her a second too long to catch up, and before she could stop it, it was out: "Because of how Marie looks?"

"No, if Samara knew how Marie looked she'd have just murdered me." His hands had disappeared into his pockets, fists that pulled against the shoulders and ruined the line of his coat. She'd put that into their last game, the noir murder mystery—the private eye yanked on his coat from the inside that same way. She thought she'd invented it; she'd been proud of herself.

The letter he handed her was on paper so thin she hesitated to touch it.

"It's addressed to me, but trust me, it's for you."

She wanted to take it home and read it where she couldn't embarrass herself, but if Woods sat through three interviews she could manage this. She read it in the wide alley garden between two office buildings, where admin staff ate lunch to pretend they'd gotten away from everything. At some point she started shaking; he stood next to her like they were pretending the wind was cold. She read it again. She put it in her pocket. He didn't argue.

"Will you see her again?"

"I could get arrested for passing her company information. We're getting sued."

"I know."

"Fuck it, I'm hungry," he said.

They found a place far enough away they felt all right sitting down. He ate three pieces of bread out of the plastic basket in the first five minutes. Then he tore a napkin into pieces.

"Samara's skin and bones. Anthony's got insomnia. Dr. Asshole said it was just drug interactions. The prison claims the game damages the cortex. They're probably going to sue each other while Samara and Anthony are suing us."

"But not Marie."

He looked at her. His eyes were very dark; they couldn't quite get them to register in Themis—they coded as black, which always looked flat, so anyone who met him in the game thought his eyes were lighter brown. It must have been a surprise for Marie to see him as he really was.

"We can't do that."

"Are you going to see her again?"

"I'm not passing her a letter, Ben."

"Are you allowed to have an assistant with you, for the interviews? Stenography? Someone has to be holding the recorder."

"You're out of your mind."

Her lips pulled tight across each row of teeth. "I have to do something."

"If you're looking to feel less guilty, stop. No such thing."

He blurred underneath the tears that sprang up. She let them go—too late not to be penitent—so her vision would be clearer for what came next. "Then I'll go myself," she said.

"It's more than your job is worth."

There was nothing to say to that; her job had been worth so little there was no point.

Outside it was not quite dark, and just beginning to be cold: the temperature of Themis, decided by a developer so much her senior she'd never met him.

When she turned toward home, he walked with her.

Halfway there, he said, "We have one more interview with her."

Hi Marie,

My handle on the Themis team is Erytheia. It's not my real

name, but it's easier to keep track of who wrote which code this way. Erytheia was one of the daughters of Themis. (I didn't pick it.) When we were getting ready for the dry run they made me your experience specialist so we could concentrate on each user's take on Themis and build as rich a world as possible.

Woods showed me your letter.

I just wanted you to know there wasn't a committee. All your letters came to me, and I read them all. Some of what you told me went into a development memo, like how there weren't enough insects for a landscape with that much standing water and vegetation. But I didn't send my letters to trick you into writing more often, and I didn't discuss anything personal. I answered you because I wanted you to feel like there was a person writing you back. I was the person writing you back.

—E

Hey Marie,

Can you sleep? I can't fucking sleep. My body thinks it's too dark because it's dumb and can only remember one set of things at a time and it's stuck on Themis—like, we were definitely stuck on Themis but you don't have to be such an asshole about it, get used to night and day and let me get some fucking sleep, damn.

And honestly the Themis shit doesn't really bother me. Everything I can remember from there is all of us just doing our best and getting along, so it's not like it was embarrassing. I feel like an idiot for not realizing sooner—now it's so fucking obvious why the movie bank didn't work, because it was too complicated to make it work inside the game or whatever—but actually being there was fine. The part that bothers me is the whole time out here that I thought I was just depressed and dreaming about some random planet is the part that's vanishing, like that's the only part the drugs actually affected once the wall wore off. Can you imagine what we must have looked like to everybody else, hopped up on that stuff?

I'm signing Samara's guy's thing. Are you? You should, they're trying to pay us off but that just means they know they fucked up and want us to keep quiet.

You're not talking to anyone about any of this, right? They told me you're having a rough time and I get that. What wasn't better about Themis than being locked up? But you get killed that way, or they find some reason to extend your sentence twenty years, so zip that shit and just wait for Samara's guy to make us too famous to die.

When we get out we should see if we can get a parole dispensation to cross state lines, it was cool all living together, that was nice. Plus movies work here, that's a reason to stay here. Plus I bet your bread in the real world is amazing.

Keep your cool, Marie. I know you can do this.

—Anthony

Marie,

My attorney heard from Othrys Games that you've been in contact with the company, trying to make a deal to get back to Themis. He wanted to send you a cease-and-desist, but I told him I wanted to talk to you first before we did anything official.

The case we're building downplays the nature of the game as much as possible. It doesn't matter that the game wasn't some battle simulator where we died all the time—it matters that they did it to us without our permission and then hoped people would ignore it because nobody cares about us. If you keep asking to go back in there, they're going to use it as evidence that what they were doing was benign, or helpful, and we're going to have to fight that impression in court, and when the game hits shelves and it's fine, it will look even worse. We're fighting the company—we can't let the game become the thing we're fighting.

This thing is really important—my lawyer says it could be a cornerstone for other cases about prisoners' rights. That's big, Marie. It's bigger than us. Cut it out.

I'm not saying all this to be cruel—I miss it there too. I could do my work and close doors behind me, of course fucking I miss it. But trying to get back to a lie is only going to hurt us. We need to be free again here. This is our shot. What they did to us was wrong—you can't fix that. Let me fight it.

Flush this letter. They can't find it.

Samara

The Othrys lawyers call Benjamina for a deposition, and she sits in a meeting room with no windows with her back to the door—the only other seat, across from the lawyer whose smile is set tight across his face and doesn't get anywhere near his eyes—and tries to ignore that this is all a setup to make her uncomfortable.

She answers fifty questions about the game: its purpose ("Any game's purpose—entertainment"), what game play will be like (it takes ten minutes, and the lawyer's mouth purses the more she talks about how beautiful Themis is), the passage of time ("Four to seven times faster than real time, everybody playing an instance has to agree on the speed if they're playing in the MMORPG rather than single-player," she says, just to watch his jaw tick before he asks for clarification), how long it's been in development (five years), how long the beta test has been going (just over a year), the chance of fatigue ("The same as with any mentally stimulating activity, like a deposition," she says, and the lawyer's lips positively disappear).

"Did you know that Samara Perlman is trying to use the time she spent in Themis as proof of good behavior to reduce her sentence?"

It's an amazing tactic. She keeps her face neutral. "No, I didn't."

"Do you have an opinion on the validity of that?"

"No one who beta-tested Themis ever evidenced any antisocial behavior, and as they believed the simulation was real life, their behavior in Themis would be close to real-world behavior."

"If I play a video game and kill a hundred imaginary people, am I a bad person outside the game?"

"Because of killing the video game people, specifically?"

He takes an even breath in and out. "Miss Harris, if you could answer the question."

"I think there's a line between fantasy and reality, but the three subjects who had Themis beta-tested on them weren't aware that line had even been crossed, so the question is kind of useless."

"Please answer it."

"I did."

He closes his eyes and counts to five this time, which gives her enough time to plant the bug under the table.

She lets the bug run—in for one count of corporate espionage, in for two counts—and siphons out the Othrys talk on her home laptop, with its wallpaper she made from Themis: the view outside the kitchen, where the thrush is singing.

The lawyer hums and taps his pen; in the microphone it sounds like a stone gavel. "Wages we might have to push back on, since I'm not sure we can really count playing video games as 'labor.'"

"Agreed," someone else says. "Plus I see that they're pushing for time served for the passage of time in the game *and* asking for wages for physical hours spent using the game. We can probably use that to shut down this thing at both ends. If they can't decide what was more important, how can we?"

"Good point," the lawyer says. "We should get Warden Collins back in here to talk about labor practices. Give him enough rope to hang himself, we can show the only people using these inmates was the prison."

The next day at work, she comes into Woods's office, closes the door behind her.

"They're going to lose."

"I know."

They stand for a little while not looking at each other. He's put up a panorama of Themis on his office wall. It's the geological survey, before they started the naturalist pass and brought people in; the idea of Themis, before anything really happened. The sun is setting. The sun is always setting.

She waits until they lose the case before she visits Marie.

Marie Roland on Themis is nearly six feet tall, has bakers' arms, covers four feet at a stride. She has lines around her eyes from squinting at the sun; they got deeper on Themis, where the sun is safer to look at. Her voice is deep enough that Benjamina had to program the *Acomys cahirinus* knockoff to startle and bolt when she laughed.

Marie Roland on the other side of the visitation table is some-one who—Benjamina has to accept it all at once, there's no point in doing things with best intentions anymore—Benjamina's driven into the grave.

She sits down. Marie waits a few seconds to look up at her.

"That was you?" she says, and it's with such disdain that Benja-mina almost smiles.

"Yes."

"Have you come to apologize?"

"Yes," she says. "I don't think it will be worth much, but yes."

Marie sits back in her chair. Five seven, maybe five eight; the circles under her eyes are as big as her eyes.

You end up loving the things you make. Benjamina had been

prepared for that—she'd seen it happen in other games, she'd seen it happen to Woods, she had braced herself. But Marie was made already; Benjamina can't look her in the eye.

"Samara got to be a biologist. Anthony was an engineer. Was there a reason I wasn't a scientist? Did my file say I was too stupid?"

Benjamina shrugs. "They assigned you to me. I didn't know enough science to code one."

"You don't know how to bake either," Marie says.

They sit for a moment in quiet. Benjamina leans forward and starts to tell her why she's come, but Marie starts talking, and she freezes.

"I've forgotten a lot of important things," Marie says to the tabletop. "There was—there was a bird, and I know we were trying to make cider but I can't remember how far we got. Was Woods going to arrest us?"

"No. The—uh, the point of the game was to see what people would do with minimal interference."

Marie's gaze is sharp. Benjamina programmed that stare in wholesale, without ever seeing it. In person it feels like a slap.

"So you picked convicts to see what we would do if we thought we could get away with it? Burn in hell."

"I'm wearing a recorder," Benjamina says, "if there's anything you want to get off your chest."

To Penitentiary Staff:

This is a general notice that MARIE ROLAND [ID: 68223-18-0709] should be given a psychiatric evaluation as soon as possible. Recently she has evidenced delusional thinking and bursts of hostility, and a recent visit with a supposed family member left her extremely agitated. All future visits must be approved by the warden's office, and Roland will not be allowed to meet any visitors whatsoever until she has complied with the evaluation and any recommended medication regimen.

Sincerely,

Janet Evanston, on behalf of Christopher Collins, Warden

The following letter to the editor was delivered to our editorial offices by a third party. Upon confirming pertinent facts, the Evening Times *considers the letter worthy of publication.*

When I was in Themis, I caught a fly.

You'll hear about Themis soon, if they aren't already selling it. It's beautiful there. You'll want to stay in it forever. That's not a threat; I just envy you.

When you stand next to the river and think about vampires, know that I was there first. They sent me without telling me it was virtual. I thought I had been selected to be the first inhabitant of a new planet. I should have known better—the game couldn't make me forget who I was, and no one like me gets selected for something like that—but Themis is hard enough to live in that you believe it's real. It never really feels like night or day and your sleep cycle gets messed up and the terrain is rough for vegetables, so you have to fight the soil for eight months to get anything started. It's not easy. The bread there never baked right. I thought it was the water, for a long time.

I'm currently in the [redacted by editors], which is where Othrys tested Themis on us. I didn't volunteer—I was selected for a sleep study, they said, because I had vivid dreams, and it would get me time off for good behavior if I agreed. They never told us about Themis. For a year I lived in two places and I didn't know.

I don't know what they gave me to make me forget, but they gave it to me on each end of Themis, on the way in and after I was out. Eventually my body got used to it—side effect of being an addict, which you think they'd have worried about more, but.

Some things I've forgotten—there was a bird I loved, but I couldn't tell you what it looked or sounded like. It's a bird in a dream. But I remember more of it than I was supposed to.

We tried to sue the game company for experimenting on us without our knowledge or permission. It didn't work; we pushed too hard to have it affect our sentences, I guess.

I'm not writing this because I'm surprised. You're probably not surprised either. Part of me wishes I had it in me to be noble and fight to get us all released because of this—Samara and Anthony deserve their freedom. But I'm writing because I want to live inside Themis until I die, and Othrys says they won't let me.

We lost the lawsuit, so there's no danger in it. It probably looks great to them that I want to go back, anyway. And most people won't live in the same Themis I built. They're making it more interesting for new people. You'll have cities to live in instead of just shipping-crate mess halls; you'll be able to see the mountains. You'll all be dealing with each other.

Samara's lawyer told me the Themis I lived in was a demo they built just for Anthony and Samara and me—it's not the version on the shelves, so I could live inside it and never come into contact with anyone. You'll have a hard time in Themis, but I'll never be the problem.

They developed that game around us, one thing at a time—the daytime got more purple as we went along and we called it the seasons, and the wildlife filled in in bursts because they didn't think we'd remember what had been there the last time. (We did remember—we just thought nature was getting used to us.) Eventually there were plants with briars and fruit flies that would bother me when I was cooking. Real life. Things you believe. I caught one of them late at night, before it could land on some dough I was rolling out for cookies, and I carried it outside because Samara, our team biologist, had told us to be very careful to preserve everything we found so she could catalog all of it.

It's not real, they forced it on us and we were never meant to keep it, I'm not stupid, but I held the fruit fly in the cup of my hand and felt its wings beating. How can they say that's not mine?

Marie Roland

Correction: As the writer of the letter was unavailable for editorial consultation on yesterday's Letter to the Editor, at the advice of legal counsel it has been removed.

"What the fuck did you do?"

Benjamina hands him his coffee. They've told the office they're dating; it explains a lot of time in each other's company.

"I tried to fucking"—she looks around, lowers her volume—"help Marie be someone no one could ignore. That's her best chance."

"Her best chance is a legal appeal by people who know what they're doing, not you on a crusade."

She sits back and looks at him, flat. "You think that this time, for sure, three inmates are going to win against two state prisons and Othrys Games by just quietly doing the right thing."

He leans closer; his hand, flat on the table, almost touches her fist.

"I think if anybody realizes you're the problem, you are going to need help and I am not going to be able to give it. What are you thinking?"

She meets his eye. "I saw Marie."

Review: Themis Is a Whole New World
BY SARAH MCELROY

As a games reviewer, you tend to get jaded about new products. The graphics are increasingly realistic, the plots increasingly dense, and there's a sense that some games are more about one-upsmanship than about providing a transporting experience for players.

Themis is coming to the market nearly three years late, and shrouded in mystery. It was the subject of a lawsuit two years ago, as beta testers complained they hadn't signed on for something as immersive as they got. For normal people, that gives you pause. For gamers, that's the kind of buzz money can't buy. (A one-day-only letter to the editor also appeared in the *Evening Times;* the newspaper didn't respond to requests for comment, so the message-board debate rages on about whether it was a legitimate report from the trenches or genius advertising.)

And if you've been waiting for Themis as long as I have, it's awkward to realize you understand exactly what those beta testers meant.

In terms of practicalities, Themis isn't very much different from half a dozen other VR immersions that have appeared the last few years. You're part of a hardscrabble crew assigned to terraform Themis, the first colony on Proxima Centauri. If you're looking for more plot, you won't find it: the entire hook of Themis is that the world is, quite literally, what you make it.

But what a world. The eternal sunset casts a rosy glow over the camp, the flies hover over any kill you make. And if you think otherwise, trust me, you'll end up making kills—Themis is about moral questions as much as strategy choices, and your team will have to eat something until the potato harvest. Every herbivore on Proxima Centauri is a take on Earth fauna of the taiga, so if you can't look a reindeer in the eye and fire, you're going to go hungry a lot. And you should think quickly; Themis has admirable ambitions about its much-touted real-time settings, but there's no doubt that the optimal game play occurs at about seven times the speed of life, and at that speed, hunger levels are highly responsive. (Given that your larger goal is simply to cross the mountains and make geological observations about the ice on the dark side of the planet, hunger might be the closest you come to emergency action.)

There have been concerns about the complications of MMORPG when everything is quite so unstructured; it's one thing to put up with creeps when they're a mage avatar in your questing party, and another to deal with them in an environment so sharply realized that it might as well be real. I'm honestly not sure how that setting will develop—when we played it in the *Tabula* offices, all was well, but the more you open the encampment to strangers, the greater the risk. It's just as well the game has a Private setting, where you and a handful of AI colleagues split the work and develop the colony in contemplative near-silence. You even get to choose your profession. (Medic is so boring as to be childish; go for Cook. Don't worry—there's no achievement bar. You can mess up bread as much as you want.)

These days, to survive in the marketplace, a game can't just be good and survive. It can't even settle for being impressive. It has to be earthshaking. And for a game that can be explained in a single sentence, Themis really does defy description. I know I'll be seeing copycats for the next ten years; I know none of them will make me feel the way Themis did.

RATING: Must-Have

Hello Sarah,

I saw your piece about Themis in *Tabula*. I am a developer at Othrys who worked on the beta testing for Themis and would love to speak with you further. You can contact me at the email above.

Benjamina Harris

To All Othrys Staff:

Benjamina Harris has been terminated, effective immediately. In the next few days, HR staff may meet with you to ask questions about her performance. We apologize for the inconvenience, and appreciate your cooperation.

Sincerely,

Dan Turpin, CEO

*

It feels so silly, handing Woods a disk—first time she's handled a physical disk in six years, no bigger than her thumbnail, and still passing it over is like handing him a raw egg.

"I told you I can't help you," he says, but she has her hands in her pockets, and after a minute he slips the thing out of sight.

"Thank you," she says. He's furious with her—that she didn't get out before she was fired, that she's had to create a new identity after everyone's already on alert, that she's making him responsible for backup copies of bugged conversations and stolen correspondence that will get her thrown in prison for fifty years. But he's here when he shouldn't be, and that makes him better than some.

"You won't make it out of the country," he says. "Please just hide closer to home. Yosemite's a thousand square miles."

She could. It would be safer. But living alone in a clearing near the river, birds calling out in the dark, mountains to the northwest—she swallows. It would be stealing.

She says, "I hope it's bad enough that someone finds Marie."

She heads south; the sun sets off the red rocks, and there's no one else for a hundred miles, and she sits in the quiet car and compiles a new geography, and realizes she'll never reach the border.

Still, she drives while she can. The footprint of the mesas is so big it never shifts; she moves like someone in a dream, not quite fast enough.

EVENING TIMES

OTHRYS WHISTLEBLOWER TELLS ALL ABOUT SHOCKING MEDICAL EXPERIMENTATION: "THEMIS WASN'T WORTH THE COST"

THE SUNDAY LEDGER

"THE WARDEN KNEW, AND NO ONE STOPPED HIM": HOW "THEMIS" MUST MARK THE END OF THE PRISON INDUSTRIAL COMPLEX

THE NEW YORK STANDARD

THE ORACLE OF OTHRYS: VIDEO-GAME SNITCH BLOWS THE LID OFF VR HORROR

THE LONE CANDLE
THE THEMIS EXPERIMENT: WHY VIRTUAL REALITY MAKES EVERYONE A PRISONER

OWL EYES NEWS
BOSS BATTLE: CHRISTOPHER COLLINS, "THE VIDEO-GAME WARDEN," RETIRES WITH $2 MILLION SEVERANCE

TABULA GAMES
WORLD-CLASS: "THEMIS" BREAKS SALES RECORDS

THE NEW YORK WEEK IN REVIEW
MARIE ROLAND: THE WOMAN WHO CAN NEVER GO HOME

Samara, Anthony,

This is my last letter. I hope this ends up being of some use to you—make no secret of it, if it will help. I'm happy to be anybody's pawn now.

It was an honor building Themis with you. I'm glad you're not coming, but it won't be the same. Marie

Spent today walking downstream a dozen kilometers and recording things. There are more species of cattails in this one stretch than I ever saw on Earth. Saw a lot of teeth marks on them—bodes well for the idea of some Earth-adjacent fauna that have just been scared off by our camp but might eventually be coaxed to come back.

Of course, I shredded my feet and somehow managed to get a giant bruise on my knee without even falling down. (How did they ever let me become a naturalist with a constitution like this?) Listened to a whole chapter of a book while I was soaking in salt water, which is the most salt and the most reading I've gotten since I landed.

You'd think they'd have sent more people, but I guess for a temperate zone you don't really have to. Winters don't kill you here, and it's only a couple of weeks until the pass melts and we can set off for the mountains to do the survey for the second-wave team. (My bet is glacier melt that will sustain a thousand people; Vivian claims there's taiga and we can support twice that. Carlos is holding the money.)

It's winter at home by now, isn't it? I hope all is well with you. I would love to know for sure.

The bread I made today was edible! The bird outside was very proud of me—he sang along with me all night. I threw him crumbs, at the end of it, and he liked them, and it feels like it will even last the night without going stale. This time next year I'll have the hang of it for sure.

That bird really does have a lovely song. They said to be careful assigning old observations to what I find here, but: thrush family. I just know it.

All my love—

E. LILY YU

The Witch of Orion Waste and the Boy Knight

FROM *Uncanny Magazine*

ONCE, ON THE edge of a stony scrub named for a star that fell burning from Orion a hundred years ago, there stood a hut with tin spangles strung from its rafters and ram bones mudded in its walls. Many witches had lived in the hut over the years, fair and foul, dark and light, but only one at any particular time, and sometimes no one lived there at all.

The witch of this story was neither very old nor very young, and she had not been born a witch but had worked, once she was old enough to flee the smashed bowls and shrieks of her home, as a goose girl, a pot scrubber, then a chandler's clerk. On the days when she wheedled the churchwomen into buying rosewater and pomanders, the chandler declared himself fond of her, and on other days, when she asked too many questions, or wept at the abalone beauty of a cloud, or refused to take no for an answer, he loudly wished her back among her geese.

On a Monday like any other, the chandler gave her two inches of onion peel scrawled with an order and precise instructions to avoid being turned into a toad, and shortly thereafter the clerk carried a packet of pins and three vials of lavender oil the three heathery miles from the chandler's shop to the hut on Orion Waste.

The white-haired crone who lived in the hut opened the door, took the basket, and looked the clerk up and down. She spat out a small object and said, "You will do."

"I beg your pardon?"

"I have a proposition for you," the crone said. "It is past time for me to leave this place. There is a city of women many weeks' travel away, and it sings in my mind like a young blue star. Would you like to be a witch?"

Here was something better than liniment for the hurts confided to her, better than candles for warding off nightmares.

"I would," the clerk said.

"Mind, you must not meddle in what is none of your business, nor help unless you are asked."

"Of course," the clerk said, her thoughts full of names.

"Too glib," the crone said. "The forfeit is three years' weeping." She rummaged in her pockets and placed a brass key beside the book on the squat table. "But you won't listen."

The clerk tilted her head. "I heard you clearly."

"Hearing's not listening. You learned to walk by falling, and you'll stir a hornet's nest and see for yourself. I was just as foolish at your age." The crone shook a blackthorn stick under the clerk's nose. "I would teach you to listen, if I had the time. Here is the key. Here is the book. Here is the bell. Be careful who you let through that door."

Grasping the basket and her stick, the crone sneezed twice and strode off into other stories without a backward glance.

And the clerk sat down at the table and leafed through the wormy tome of witchcraft, dislodging mushrooms pressed like bookmarks and white moths that fluttered into the fire. Bent over the book, by sunlight and candlelight, she traced thorny letters with her fingertips and committed the old enchantments, syllable by syllable, to heart.

The villagers who came with bread, apples, mutton, and the black bottles of cherry wine the old witch favored were surprised by news of the crone's departure and doubtful of the woman they knew as goose girl and chandler's clerk. Their doubts lasted only until she compounded the requested charms for luck, for gout, for biting flies, for thick, sweet cream in the pail. For all its forbidding appearance, the Waste provided much of what the book prescribed: gnarled roots that she picked and spread on a sunny cloth, bark peeled in long curls and bottled, snakeskins cast in the shade of boulders and tacked to the rafters.

Certain of her visitors traveled farther, knowing only the hundred-year-old tale of a witch on the Waste. They came stealthily at night and asked for poison, or another's heart, or a death, or a crown, and the witch, longing for the simple low-necked hissing of geese, shut the door in their faces.

A few of these were subtler than the rest, and several lied smoothly. But the crone had left a tongueless bell, forged from cuckoo spit, star iron, and lightning glass, which if warmed in the mouth showed, by signs and symbols, true things. In this way the witch could discern the dagger behind the smile. But the use of it left her sick and shuddering for days, plagued with bad dreams and waking visions, red and purple, and she only resorted to the bell in great confusion.

Three years from when she first parted its covers, the witch turned the last page of the book, read it, and sat back with a sigh. Someone had drawn in the margin a thorny archway, annotated in rusty red ink in a language she did not recognize, but apart from that, she knew all the witchcraft that the book held. The witch felt ponderous with knowledge and elastic with powers.

But because even arcane knowledge and occult powers do not properly substitute for a bar of soap and a bowl of soup, she washed her face and ate.

Loud knocking interrupted her meal. She brushed the crumbs from her lap, wiped the soup from her chin, and opened the door.

A knight stood upon her doorstep, a black horse behind him. A broken lance lay in his arms. He was tall, with a golden beard, and his eyes were as green as ferns.

"Witch," said the knight. "Do you have a spell for dragons?"

"I might," she said.

"What will it cost me? I am sworn to kill dragons, but their fire is too terrible and their strength too great."

"Do you have swan down and sulfur? Those are difficult to find."

"I do not."

"A cartful of firewood?"

"I have no cart and no ax, or I would."

"Then a kiss," the witch said, because she liked the look of him, "and I will spell your shield and your sword, your plate and your soft hair, to cast off fire as a duck's feather casts off rain."

The knight paid her the kiss with alacrity and not, the witch thought, without enjoyment. He sat and watched as she made a paste of salamander tails and serpentine, adding to this a string of ancient words, half hummed and half sung. Then she daubed the mixture over his armor and sword and combed it through his golden hair.

"There you go," she said. "Be on your way."

The knight set his chin upon his fists. "These dragons are formidable," he said. "Larger than churches, with cruel, piercing claws."

"I have never seen one," the witch said, "but I am sure they are."

"I am too tired and bruised to face dragons today. With your permission, I shall sleep outside your house, guard you from whatever creeps in the dark, and set forth in the morning."

"As you wish," the witch said. She shared with him her supper of potatoes, apples, and brookweed and the warmth of her hearth, though the hut was small with him in it, and he told her stories of the court he rode from, of its high bright banners and its king and queen.

In the morning the knight was slow to buckle on his plate. The witch came to the door to bid him farewell, bearing a gift of butternuts knotted in a handkerchief. He raised his shield reluctantly, as if its weight pained him.

"Dragons are horrible in appearance," he said. "Those who see them grow faint and foolish, and are quickly overtaken and torn limb from limb."

"That sounds likely," the witch said.

"They gorge on sheep and children and clean their teeth with men's bones. In their wake they leave gobbets of meat that the crows refuse."

"You have seen dreadful things," the witch said.

"I have." The knight tucked his helmet under his arm and pondered a dandelion growing between his feet. "And the loneliness is worse."

"Perhaps it would be better to have a witch with you."

"Will you come? I carry little money, only promises of royal favor. But I'll give kisses generously and gladly, and swear to serve you and defend you."

"I have never seen a dragon except in books," the witch said. "I would like to."

The knight smiled, a smile so luminous that the sun seemed to rise in his face, and paid her an advance as a show of good faith.

The witch took a warm cloak, the brass key, and at the last

moment, on an impulse, the glass-and-iron bell, then locked the
hut behind her. The knight helped her onto his horse, and together they rode across the Waste and beyond it. Grasshoppers
flew up before them, and quail scattered. Wherever they went, the
witch gazed about her with delight, for she had never traveled far
from her village or the hut on the Waste, and everything she saw
gleamed with newness.

They rode through forests and meadows that had no names
the witch knew, singing and telling stories to pass the time. In the
evenings the witch gathered herbs and dowsed for water, and the
knight set snares for rabbits and doves. The knight had a strong
singing voice and a laugh like a log crumbling in a fire, and the
days passed quickly, unnumbered and sweet.

Before long, however, the land grew parched, and the wind
blew hot and sulfurous. The witch guessed before the knight told
her that they had passed into the country of dragons.

Late one evening they arrived at a deep crater sloped like a
bowl, its edges black and charred. The bitter smoke drifting from
the pit stung their eyes. Down at the center of the crater, something shifted and settled.

"Is that a dragon?" the witch said.

"It is," the knight said, his face long.

"Will you ride into battle?"

"Dragons hunt at night, and their sight is better than a cat's. It
would devour me in two bites before I saw it, then my horse, and
then you."

Clicking his tongue, the knight turned the charger. They rode
until they reached the scant shelter of a dry tree among dry boulders, where they made camp.

The witch scratched together a poor meal of nuts and withered
roots. The knight did not tell stories or sing. At first the witch tried
to sing for the both of them, her voice wavering up through the
darkness. But no matter what she said or sang, the knight stared
into the fire and sighed, and soon she too lapsed into silence.

The next morning the witch said, "Will you fight the dragon
today?"

"It is stronger than me," the knight said, gazing into his reflection on the flat of his sword. "It breathes the fires of hell, and no
jiggery-pokery from a midwife's pestle could endure those flames.
Tomorrow I shall ride back to my king, confess my failure, and

yield my sword. My enemies will rejoice. My mother will curse me and drink."

The witch said nothing to this, but sat and thought.

The sun scratched a fiery path across the sky, hot on the back of her neck, and the air rasped and seethed with the sound of distant dragons.

When it was dark and the knight was sound asleep, the witch drew his sword from its sheath and crept to the black horse. She swung herself up into its saddle, soothing it when it whickered, and with whispers and promises of sugar she coaxed it across the sand to the edge of the crater. There she dismounted and descended in silence.

The dragon waited at the bottom of the pit, its eyes bright as mirrors.

It was not the size of a church, as the knight had said, only about the size of her hut on the Waste, but its teeth were sharp and serrated, its claws long and hooked, and gouts of flame dripped from its gullet as it slithered toward her.

The dragon drew a breath, its sides expanding like a bellows, and the fire in its maw brightened. Sharp shadows skittered over the ashes.

"You are no more frightening than my father," the witch said, with more courage than she felt. "And no less. But I have faced foxes and thumped them, and I shall thump you."

Flames flowered forth from its fangs, and as the witch leaped aside, a third of her hair smoldered and shriveled.

The narrow snout swayed toward her, but the witch shouted two words of binding that sent her staggering backward with their force, and the dragon's jaws clamped shut.

The dragon thrashed its head from side to side, white smoke rising from its nostrils, clawing at its mouth.

Then it charged her, and she ran.

As ashes floated thick around her, and skulls and thighbones broke and scattered under her feet, the witch looked over her shoulder and gasped a word of quenching.

At once the smoke of its breath turned to a noxious steam. The dragon lurched and fell. Although it could not stir, it glared, and its hate was hot on her skin.

The witch lifted the knight's sword, and with tremendous effort, and twelve laborious strokes, she cut off its head.

At dawn she woke the knight, signing because her throat was raw and her lips were cracked, and led him to the scaly black carcass in the crater. The knight stared, then exclaimed and kissed her, and this kiss was sweeter than all that had come before.

"My lovely witch, my darling! With you beside me, why should I fear dragons?"

Although she ached all over, and a tooth felt loose in its socket, the witch blushed and brightened.

They continued into the land of dragons. Water grew more and more elusive, and the pools and damp patches the witch located were brackish and bitter, so when they reached a shallow river, they followed its course. The water was warm and brown, and tadpoles squirmed in it.

One afternoon, as the sun slanted down and strewed diamonds on the river, the witch saw the second dragon. This one was the length of a watchtower and red as dried blood, and it crouched in a muddy wallow, half hidden by dead brush. When she called the knight's attention to it, he wheeled the horse around.

"Are you frightened?" she said.

There was no reply.

"Are you upset?"

He lowered his visor.

"Did I do something wrong?"

His eyes glittered out of his helmet, but he did not say a word.

The witch twined her fingers in the horse's mane and named the birds and burdocks they passed, then prattled about the weather, and still the knight said nothing.

Some hours later, over their supper of frogs, he broke his silence. "This one is viler than the last," he said. "Even you could not vanquish it. Me it would swallow in a snap, sword and all."

"It did not look so terrible," the witch said, lightheaded with relief.

"But it is."

"You are a brave and valiant knight, and I am sure you will succeed."

"Of course you'd say that," the knight said, frowning. "It's not you who will die a nasty death, all teeth and soupy tongue."

"But your sword arm is strong, and your blade is trusty and well kept. Besides, I have enchanted your sword and your armor."

"As you like. I shall challenge it in the morning, and it will eat toasted knight for breakfast. Farewell." The knight turned his back to her, pillowed his head on his hands, and soon was snoring.

The witch had grown fond of the knight, in her way. His fear soured her stomach, and she tossed and turned, unable to sleep for thoughts of his death. In the middle of the night, she arose and sought the dragon.

The reeds were trodden and crushed in a wide swath where it couched, and dead fish and birds lay all about. Its red scales were gray in the dim starlight, and it snuffed and snorted at subtle changes in the wind, finally fixing its eyes upon her. This dragon was heavy and sluggish, unlike the last, but poison dripped in black strings from its jaws. It lifted itself from the muck and lumbered forward.

"You are no more poisonous than my mother," the witch said, swallowing her fear. "And no less. But I have turned biting lye into soap, and I shall render you down as well."

She spoke the words of binding, but the dragon shrugged off her spell like so many flung pebbles. She shouted a word of quenching, and its jaws widened in a mocking grin. As she coughed on the word, her own throat burning, the dragon lunged and snapped.

The mud sucked at her feet as she fled, and marsh vapors wavered and tore as she ran through them. She tried words of severing and words of sickening, tasting blood on her lips, to no avail.

Bit by bit the subtle gases of the dragon's breath slowed and stupefied her. The world spun. Then a root thrusting out of the mire hooked her ankle.

She skidded and slid.

Across the oozy earth the dragon crawled, bubbling and hissing. As its jaws opened to swallow her, the witch, her voice dull, spoke a word of cleansing.

The syllables slipped between scales into the dragon's veins and curdled the deadly blood. The dragon shuddered, its black eyes rolling back. Its snout scraped her leg, and then its long bulk splashed into the mud and lay still.

The witch limped to where the river flowed, languid and wide, and washed off, as best she could, the muck, the rot, the black blood and the red.

The sound of plackart clinking against pauldron woke her in the morning. Her knight—for she was beginning to think of him as hers—was grimly and glumly donning his gear.

No need, the witch wished to say, but her throat hurt as much as if she had swallowed a fistful of pins.

"Wait here," the knight said. "I do not want you to witness my shameful death. When I am crisped and crunched, ride swiftly to the court of Cor Vide and tell them their youngest knight is dead."

He spurred his horse and set off. Within the hour, he returned, his face dark.

"Witch, did you do this?" he said. "Did you kill that dragon while I slept?"

The witch nodded, unable to speak. The knight did not kiss her. He let her clamber onto the horse without offering his arm, and they rode all that day and the next in an ugly silence.

On the third day, when her throat had healed somewhat, the witch rasped, "Are you angry with me?"

"I am never angry, for anger is wicked and poisonous. But what will the court call a knight who lets women slay his dragons?"

"You seemed afraid."

"I wasn't afraid, witch."

"I wanted to help."

"You did more harm than good."

"I am sorry," she said.

"Do not do it again."

The river they were following dwindled to a stream, then to dampness, and then the earth split and cracked, but they continued in the same direction, in hopes that the stream ran underground and sprang up again somewhere.

By and by, their mouths parched, they came to a crooked tower with a broken roof and a great golden serpent wrapped many times around its base. The witch, knight, and horse were the only things that moved upon the barren plain, and they raised a great cloud of dust. While they were still at a distance, the serpent began unwinding itself from the tower.

"Stay, witch," the knight said, looking pale. "My sword is but a lucifer to this creature. Its fire will shrivel me, and the steel of my armor will drip over my bones. I'll die, but I'll die honorably. Remember me. I did love you."

And the witch watched, anxious, as her knight trudged on foot toward the tower, sheets of air around him shimmering with heat.

The serpent's eyes were red jewels, and its forked tongue lashed in and out of its mouth as the knight approached. Rearing up, the serpent spat a feathering jet of fire. The shield rose to meet it. Flames broke on its boss and poured off, harmless.

The knight laughed. His sword flashed.

But its edge rebounded from the scales without cutting, once, twice, and in a trice the serpent had tangled him in its coils and suspended him upside down.

His helmet tumbled off. His sword slipped from his mailed hand. He hung in midair, his golden curls loose, his face exposed.

The serpent squeezed, and he screamed.

The witch screamed too: a word of unraveling. The serpent's loops slackened, and the knight crashed to the ground. She screamed a word of piercing, and the serpent's eyes ran liquid and useless from their sockets. The serpent flailed, blind and enraged, battering the tower. Stones loosened from their mortar and fell. One crushed the knight's shield into splinters.

Finding his footing again, the knight slipped under the thrashing coils and sank his sword into one emptied eye, up to the hilt.

With a roar of agony, and spasms that shook down the upper third of the tower, the dragon expired.

The knight did not stand and savor his triumph. He whirled on the witch.

"I saw you. You goaded it—you spurred it to rage. You were trying to kill me!"

No, the witch would have said, if she were able.

But her lips were blistered and her tongue numb.

She pointed instead, in mute appeal.

A woman had emerged from the tower. She had watched what the witch had done; she could speak to her innocence. Her gown was green, and her smile, which she turned on them, was brilliant as an emerald. Several golden objects on her girdle swung and glittered as she approached, stepping delicately around the pools of smoking blood.

"Did you do this, good knight?" she said. "Have you freed me from this place?"

The knight bowed, then stood taller. "I did, though I did not know you were here. Where shall I bring you? Where will you be safe? You must have friends somewhere."

"Northeast," she said. "A long way."

"However far it is, I will accompany you."

"There is treasure in that tower, if you seek treasure. I stopped

to play with rings, crowns, and necklaces, admiring myself in a
golden glass. I did not realize that it was a dragon's hoard, and that
the possessor would return. He gnawed my palfrey to the hooves
and guarded me greedily from that time on. What I search for is
not there, but that hoard will pay for your time."

"What gold could outshine the copper of your hair? You shall
ride behind me, and this witch shall walk beside. For you look like
a lady, and your feet are too soft for the road."

The lady's eyes danced. "Oh no, the witch shall ride. Both of
us together, if you insist. I have met witches before, and they grow
ugly if spited. This one is quite ugly already, and that smock does
her no favors."

The witch, her breast burning, could not meet the lady's eyes.
She looked instead at her rich green gown, stiff with gilt embroi-
dery. Hanging from her girdle were toys of tin and wood, painted
gold: a carved dog, a jumping acrobat, a wind-up man.

"Let me help you up," the knight said.

"First tie my hands behind me," the lady said. "I am under a
curse. What I touch is mine and ever after shall be."

"A strange curse," the knight said, but obliged. He lifted her
onto the horse in front of the witch. Her red hair blew into the
witch's mouth. For sport, the lady leaned to one side, then the
other, pretending to topple.

"Don't let her fall," the knight said to the witch. "I know you are
jealous and would love nothing better. But if harm comes to her, I
will cut off your head."

They proceeded more slowly after that, the knight leading the
horse, the witch holding the reins, and the strange lady smiling in
the witch's arms. As they rode, the witch wept, but very softly, for
whenever the knight heard, he looked at her with disgust.

"Stop," he said. "Enough. You have no reason to cry."

Then her tears fell hotter and faster into the lady's red hair.

In the lengthening evenings, while the witch foraged, the knight
and lady talked together and laughed. With her hands bound, the
lady could do little for herself, and so the knight fed her, slid her
silken slippers from her feet, and waited on her every wish.

The knight kissed the witch for the food and water she brought
them, briefly and without interest, and apologized to the lady after.
At night the lady nuzzled her head into the crook of the knight's

arm and spread her long hair over them. The witch lay awake, watching the stars until they blurred and ran together.

"Why do you never sing anymore?" the knight said one evening, as the witch turned a rabbit over the fire. "Sing for us."

"He says you have a fine voice, for a witch. Do let me hear it."

"I don't anymore," the witch rasped. The lady grimaced. "I burned it to cinders for him. It hurts to speak."

"You'll heal," the knight said.

"I might, or I might not. The words of power I used were dear, and I am paying."

"You want me to feel guilty," the knight said.

"No, I wanted—"

"I don't want to hear about it." He folded his arms. "There was never any point in talking to you anyway."

The lady laughed and laid her head against his shoulder.

Another evening, as the witch returned with chanterelles and hedgehog mushrooms in her skirt, she heard the knight say, "She's bewitched me, you know. That's why I hunt dragons—for her sport. That's why I kiss her every night—I am forced."

"Such a glorious knight, under the thumb of a lowly thing like her. How awful," the lady said.

"It is awful."

"Why don't you strike her head off while she sleeps?"

"I'm ensorcelled, remember. I cannot kill her. My father, a lord and a haughty man, would have strangled her for her insolence, but I am nothing like him."

"Indeed you are not," the lady said.

"You are kinder than she ever was. I've told you more than I've ever told her. Can you free me, as I have freed you?"

"Say the word, and I shall prick her with poisoned needles while she rides. She will die of that, slowly, unsuspecting, and then you shall be free."

"Do, and I shall follow you faithfully."

"Then pluck the air between the two of you as we go, as if you are pulling petals, and put them in this purse. You'll not see or feel what you gather, as your senses are not so fine, but I shall decoct what is there to a poison."

"I knew it," the knight said. "She has a foul and invisible power over me."

"A strange influence, certainly."

The witch stepped into the firelight, balancing their supper in her muddy skirt, and both the knight and the lady fell quiet and averted their eyes.

The moon waxed and waned, and the witch wearied of weeping. She was sick of holding the lady, sick of suffering her pinpricks, sick of watching the knight play with the lady's russet hair. Her pain had grown tedious and stale, but she was far from home and bewildered, for sometimes, still, the knight smiled at her with swift and sudden fondness, and it was as though he was again the knight she had set forth with, many and many a month ago.

Late one night, as she covered herself with her muddy cloak, she heard a clinking in its folds. In its pocket she found the key to her hut and the tongueless bell, which in her misery she had forgotten about.

The witch put the bell in her mouth, and the world shone.

First she looked upon the sleeping knight. In his place she saw a small boy, much beaten and little loved, his face wet from crying. He writhed in his sleep with fear. Around his limbs wound a silver spell, older than the witch and wrought with greater art than hers, and when the witch strummed the strands of it with a nail, she heard in their hum that they would break and let him grow only when he had slain three dragons by his own hand.

Then the witch saw how she had wronged him by killing the black dragon, the red, and the gold. She would have kissed his forehead and asked forgiveness, but a black asp crept out of his mouth and hissed at her, and she was afraid.

She turned to the lady who slept at his side. A hole gaped in her breast, its torn edges fluttering. The witch stuck her hand in but found nothing: not a bone, not a thread, not corners, nor edges either. It howled with hunger, that hole. The woman who wore it would wander the world, snatching and grasping and thrusting into that aching emptiness everything within reach, forever trying to fill it, and failing.

The witch grieved for her too.

The three of them had camped beside a pool of water, and now the witch knelt on its mossy margin. In the light of the half-moon she saw how her limbs were shriveled and starved for love, her bones riddled with cracks from bearing too much too soon. She sat there for hours, until she knew herself, and the fractures and hollow places within her, and the flame that burned, small and silent, at her core.

And when the witch understood that nothing kept her weeping on the black horse but herself, that the sorcery that had imprisoned her and blinded her was her own, she spat out the bell, dashed her reflection into a million bright slivers, and laughed.

With a whistle, the witch rose into the air, and, whistling, she flew. When she stopped for breath, her feet sank softly to the earth. In this manner she traveled over the country of dragons, through nameless meadows and woods, and across the Orion Waste.

Once in all that time, when her heart gave a sharp pang, the witch put the bell in her mouth and looked back.

Far away, the knight was unknotting the cord around the lady's wrists, first with fingers, and then, when it proved stubborn, with teeth. When her arms were free, he clasped her to his breast and buried his face in her hair.

But in the moment of their embrace, the knight began to shrink. The lady's arms tightened around him. Faster and faster the knight diminished, armor and all, until he was no taller than a chess piece and stiff and still.

The lady caught him between forefinger and thumb. She studied the leaden knight, her expression pleased, then puzzled, then disappointed. At last, shaking her head, she tied him to her girdle between the wooden dog and painted acrobat. Between one knot and the next, she flinched and sucked her finger, as if something had bitten her.

Then she mounted the black horse and rode slowly onward, searching for that which would fill her lack.

After that the witch flew without pause, without eating or drinking, and the wind dried her tears to streaks of salt.

Just as her strength gave out, the hut on Orion Waste rose like a star on the horizon. The witch unlocked the door and collapsed onto her narrow bed. There she remained, shivering with fever, for the better part of a month. One or two people from the village, seeing the light in her window across the scrub, came with eggs and bread and tea, left them silently, and went away again.

One day, in a wave of sweat, the fever broke. The witch crawled to her feet, unlatched the window, and saw the Waste covered in white and yellow wildflowers.

The book of witchcraft lay open on the table, though she was sure no one had touched it. In the margin of the last page, wild roses peppered the tangle of thorns.

A week later, the witch returned to the village, her few belongings in hand, and asked the chandler if he might allow her to mind the shop again. He agreed gladly, for he was old and stiff, and she was quick and could climb the ladder to the highest shelves for him.

There she lived for a year, content, sweeping the floor, mending the shelves, and stirring a little magic into her soaps, so they cleaned better than others, and gave hope besides. She did not speak much, for her voice frightened children, but she listened carefully, and closely, and no one seemed to mind.

And there she would have stayed, growing gray and wise, had not a peddler with a profitable knack for roaming between stories rung the shop bell.

Looking over the wares he had spread on a cloth, all polished and gleaming, the witch and the shopkeeper chose combs, mirrors, scissors, and ribbons to buy. When the silver had been counted out and poured into his hands, and the goods collected, the peddler grinned a gapped grin and dug from his pack a pair of dancing shoes, cut from red leather and pricked all over with an awl.

"For you," he said to the witch. "Secondhand, and a few bloodstains, but pretty, no? *Some* angels don't like to see the poor dance, and the last lass had a heart too clean and Christian to wear them for long, but your heart's spotted, and these are just your size."

"Thank you," the witch said, "but I don't know how to dance. I know how to fly, and slay dragons, and make good soap, but dancing is a mystery."

"Then you should learn," the peddler said.

The shopkeeper sighed, because he could guess what was coming. When the witch approached him three days later, with a request, and a promise, he sent her on her way with a bag containing three cakes of soap, three spools of thread, three needles, a mirror, and a comb, cursing the peddler under his breath.

That night, as the stars glistened overhead, and the frogs and crickets sang a joyful Mass from their secret places, the witch locked up the hut, laced on the red shoes, whistled, and flew.

DEBBIE URBANSKI

When They Came to Us

FROM *The Sun*

They Arrive on a Warm Summer Night with No Breeze

WE WENT TO SLEEP, and in the morning they were here. We saw them on our screens as they emerged from a grove of trees a hundred miles west of us. Their ship had crashed. It was made of a rose-gold metal and looked like a claw with a broken tip. Within hours the government had moved these beings — the "blues," we eventually came to call them — to a holding station outside the nearest city. There we could watch them whenever we wanted, because of the cameras in each room.

We assumed they would have special powers, like mind-reading or levitation, but apparently they couldn't do such things. What they could do was spray a fine white mist from their pores. Although this wasn't what we'd expected, it still seemed amazing to us: White mist! Coming out of an alien's skin! Mostly they just sat there in their rooms. There was a big to-do about how nice their accommodations were: the pricey organic grains they were fed, the high thread count of their sheets, the multiple down pillows, and the room dividers for privacy. The blues spent hours hiding behind those partitions. This became frustrating, because we couldn't see what they were doing; we could only hear them, and the sounds were unrecognizable to us.

They Weren't Supposed to Look Like Us

Science teaches us that creatures adapt to their unique environments. Surely the aliens' home planet must have differed from our own, yet the blues did look almost like us—or like imitations of us. They looked as if they had done their best to look like us. They even began to mimic our speech, though their voices were pitched ridiculously high, higher than a human child's. Their skin, of course, was blue, as were their nails and hair. Mrs. Durand, who has lived here in town for many years, was disappointed. She wanted the blues to look like her dead husband, like in that old sci-fi movie about aliens who took the form of people's deceased loved ones. That was useful, what the aliens in that movie had done.

Grace Madden, Who Also Lives in Our Town, Tells Us About Her Dream

In the dream she went inside the blues' ship. They took her up into the air and welcomed her with circular motions of their arms. They touched her neck and her back and her stomach. The ship's interior was soft and warm and painted with light. The walls seemed to pulse, Mrs. Madden told us, like a heart. That's the picture we had in our minds: an enormous heart going *whoosh, whoosh, whoosh* through space.

Our Town Is Named a Relocation Site, and We React in the Following Ways

Ms. Mueller began the rumors that our water had gone bad. Little Rita Oh refused to sleep, and her mom had to take away her screen at night and lock Rita in her room. Mr. Lucas's hands began trembling. (From fear? Anticipation?) Roger Gibson put on a sandwich board declaring, "The Emperor Has No Clothes!" and he stomped around the train station in a menacing way. Dana Fisher moved up her wedding to Jeff Campbell, even though nobody thought they should get married at a time like this. At their backyard reception Mrs. Fisher laid out somber plates of mashed beans and skewered tomatoes, and a lot of people left early. Young Tom Durand tied a red bandanna over his mouth and stormed into the Pizza Palace waving a water pistol. The Lucases decided to try for another baby, like Mrs. Lucas wanted. Suzie Breton raised her hand in homeroom and let everybody know that she thought the blues were beautiful; they made us less alone in the universe, she said. Somebody kicked in the head of the homeless guy who begged at the interstate on-ramp. Jessica O'Brien complained of cramps. Certain people stopped drinking our town's tap water. Jeff hit his new wife, Dana, in a place where he thought nobody could see it, but we saw it and took note. At our annual summer parade the children dressed up as aliens, or how they imagined aliens should look, wearing grotesque masks and walking around with lurching steps. We were unsure whether this was appropriate. Mr. Lucas forgot his bedroom windows were open, and we heard him tell Mrs. Lucas, "If you just lie there with your legs open, I might as well go fuck a cow. Should I? Should I go fuck a cow?" Many of us felt on edge. Ordinary things appeared unfamiliar or even vulgar.

The Blues Arrive in Buses, and We Stand on the Sidewalks to Greet Them

The whole town came out. All morning we waited, keeping the mood festive and light. Johnny Reynolds strummed his guitar, and Mr. Sullivan gave blue balloon swords to the children, because it was the only shape he could make out of balloons. We drank lemonade and ate popcorn and played word games to pass the time. We wore our best clothing. Our children were well-behaved and patient.

At noon the three school buses appeared in a cloud of diesel exhaust. Dana Campbell threw white confetti left over from her wedding, and the children sang a song about sunshine. We tried to catch a glimpse of the blues, but we couldn't see through the white mist inside the buses. The drivers didn't stop; they continued on to the refugee apartments that had been built east of town, where the blues would live eight to a room. This arrangement was okay because, from what we could tell, the blues enjoyed living close to each other. They were like animals that way. The relocation agency made sure the blues had what they needed: their closets were stocked with used clothes, their pantries filled with donated food. In each apartment hung a video camera.

After their arrival, if we spotted a blue in town—which was rare, as they were skittish in the beginning—we were supposed to treat them kindly. We weren't to call them "aliens," because of the word's connotations.

When We Ask How Far Away Their Home Is, They're Oddly Vague

They said their planet was beautiful, but it didn't sound beautiful. It sounded cold and dark and wet. (The blues themselves smelled like damp wool and spoiled citrus.) They were only one of many tribes on their planet, and none of the tribes were particularly kind to each other. Apparently there were seasons, because at certain times of year heavy fruits hung from the trees, and herds of grunting animals wandered around, offering themselves up for meat. But other times the blues were hungry. Before leaving, they had sold off everything they'd owned, which is why they'd brought nothing with them. "What did you have? What did you sell?" we asked, wanting specifics. They mentioned animals, mainly livestock, and some kind of cloth in which they had wrapped themselves.

Many of the words the blues used to describe where they'd come from we couldn't understand. We shook our heads, and they sketched the object in the dirt: a square box, perhaps, with lines radiating from it. We still had no idea. This is how conversations went with them. We asked if they had been to planets other than ours. The blues said yes, there had been other planets. Honestly they didn't like to talk about it much. If we asked for a story about their home, the blues waved their hands in the air, as if the gesture itself were a story.

Our Children Are Understandably Puzzled

Such a change in what was possible: Aliens! Spaceships! New worlds! It didn't seem healthy for a child's development.

"What color are their penises?" little Jess Mueller asked her mother.

"I'm not sure they have penises," her mother said, blushing. How was she supposed to know? Children should not be thinking about such things. They asked what the blues' poop looked like, how they made their babies, whether they went to hell or heaven when they died, why blue boys were so skinny, and what were those marks on the blue women's faces? We steered the conversation to more suitable topics.

We Don't Tell Our Children That Those Marks Are Bruises, and It Looks Like the Blues Are Starving Their Boys

Once a blue female wandered from their group, shrieking and tearing at her eyes with her nails. Eventually she collapsed, and a blue male strode toward her. We assumed he intended to help her up, but instead he hit her with the back of his hand, then with his fist. We heard the male's fist hitting the female, and her whimpering. The sounds made us sick. "Those fucking barbarians," Ms. Mueller said. We expected the beating to stop, but it went on for a long time. We'd been told not to intervene, out of respect for their culture. If a blue male brought out a leather strap that left welts, we were told not to stare, but also not to avoid looking. We were to act like what they were doing was normal and accept them as they were.

The blues did not hit their children, as far as we knew, but they behaved as if their boys were worthless. At meals, for instance, a blue mother gave each girl an enormous bowl of gruel—seconds if the girl asked for it—along with a chunk of dark bread, while the boys received no bread and were given only a few spoonfuls of the gruel. "They do not get hungry!" a blue female insisted when we asked, though the blue boys looked at us with starving eyes.

To be fair, the blues weren't brutal all the time. They had a playful side to them. Even the adults appeared to enjoy a childish prank. They were known to hide in alleyways and jump out as we walked by. If we feigned surprise—"Oh, my!" or "Look at that!"—they made clicking sounds in their throats, which meant they were satisfied. When they laughed, they sounded like donkeys.

Better to View the Blues from a Distance, We Begin to Think

Through the cameras in their apartments, we could watch the blues on our screens whenever we wanted. We watched how they

ate (with their hands), whether they used the toilets, how they prepared their meals and nuzzled and mated and fought. It was fun
studying them like this. It made us feel like amateur naturalists.
There was none of the usual awkwardness we felt in their presence; we didn't need to worry about what to say or how to act.
Their violence toward each other continued to strike us as bes-
tial—the males biting the females' arms; the females' apparent
pleasure—but we eventually came to expect it. In private, by ourselves in our unmonitored homes, some of us discovered that such
peculiar and brutal scenes held an erotic charge.

Most of all we liked to watch them sleep. They looked the most
like us when they slept, and we felt compassion for them as their
chests rose and fell under the thin blankets.

Despite many such hours of observation, we still had unan-
swered questions. We wished we could understand what kindness
looked like to them, and how they described cruelty, and what they
thought *love* meant.

Our Lives Don't Stop Just Because the Blues Are Here

Winter came, a very mild winter. By February's end the trees were
budding, and there were yellow daffodils in Mrs. Durand's yard.
We were glad for the pretty flowers, no matter when they decided
to come. All around us the trees bloomed spectacularly, fragrant
and white.

In March we put on our spring festival to celebrate the longer
days and shorter nights. As happened every year, we got sick on
Ms. Mueller's fried dough, and we dressed Jeff Campbell up as the
spring maiden and made him dance. Not one blue came. They
could have come—no one was stopping them—but they didn't,
and in a sense it was better that way. Things were as they should be.

Part of the festival is an art contest, and the theme that year
(Mrs. Gorski picked it) was the blues' home planet. A dozen fine
entries came in: paintings of an arctic landscape, an underwater
city, even a terrifying vision of spindly-legged machines that set
trees on fire with their eyes. Only one painting sold, a watercolor
of a monochromic desert purchased by Mrs. Lucas. She hung it in
her family room, then sat on the sofa and stared at that painting

for a long time, entranced by the blowing blue sands and the multiple suns. Perhaps she was trying to imagine herself on the blues' planet.

"What the hell is this?" Mr. Lucas asked when he saw the painting hanging there.

The Blues Decide They Don't Want to Be Watched Anymore, as If It Were Okay for Them to Decide Such a Thing

First they misted up a few of the cameras. The other cameras they covered with their dirty sheets. So Johnny Reynolds marched right into their apartments—he was caretaker of the building, the master keys jangling at his belt—and he wiped the cameras clean and took down the bedsheets. "Don't you touch these again," he scolded.

Within a week the blues had broken every camera. Now that we could no longer watch them, they grew stranger and more savage to us.

They began leaving their apartments more often—*swarming* out of their apartments, is how it felt. We saw them at the bus stops in the morning, and in the afternoons they crowded us out of our parks. We ended their food donations—we had to, because of the shortages—so they dug through restaurant dumpsters and went begging beside the on-ramps. It was unpleasant for us to see all this and also unpleasant for our children, who began asking uncomfortable questions, like why the blues were stuffing rancid food scraps into their mouths. "Run them over," Jeff Campbell said whenever he was in the car and saw a blue beside the road scrounging through a garbage bin. It's not as if Jeff actually ran a blue over; it was just something he said. The point is they weren't trying to act like us, or even to be likable. Though this shouldn't have mattered, privately it did matter: their unpleasant smell, how close they stood to us, those guttural noises they sometimes made in their throats instead of using English. Best to leave them be, we instructed our children. We believed the blues must be going through an adolescent phase from which they'd soon emerge more fully formed and useful to us. Until then, we told our kids, stay away.

To Be Honest, the Blues Have Not Come at the Best Time

The mansions along our once-grand boulevards were falling apart, our children were roaming the streets with their pit bulls, and few of us had jobs—or at least not jobs we wanted. There were deserted retail spaces left over from the boom and also some ruined factories. It wasn't just us. The whole world seemed to be in crisis, with riots and strange weather and war. You know how wars are, even if they're far away: The fiery levels of alert. The panicked glow. The paranoia over everything.

We Advise Each Other Just to Ignore the Blues, but Do All of Us Listen?

Mrs. Madden got it into her head that she could predict the blues' future. She met them in the dimly lit back room of her house, where she sat across from them at a card table. They believed whatever Mrs. Madden said. When she told a blue female, "You hide your pain behind a curtain, but somebody will lift up the curtain," the blue said, "Yes, yes." When Mrs. Madden said to a blue male, "Everything will be okay for you," he nodded, even though things obviously were not okay. She traced the patterns on an older blue's hand and said, "I see darkness up ahead for you, but in your darkness there is a light." Who knew what that meant? We were impressed when Mrs. Madden touched their hands like that. Sometimes in return they gave her a bucket of forest greens or a bowl of ripe tomatoes.

Generally she met with a single blue at a time, but one day she brought a group of them into her back room and said, "I have good news. You thought you were alone here, but you aren't." She said that she saw their deceased loved ones roosting near the ceiling like happy birds, and the blues believed her, as always.

If Mrs. Madden said these things in order to be beloved by someone or something, it worked. She was beloved by the blues. They held her hands. They held each other. They fell onto her soft brown carpet, weeping and squawking. Why not? If believing something makes your life that much better, then by all means go ahead and believe.

We Tell Our Children to Leave the Blues Alone Until They Start Behaving Better, but Do Our Children Listen Either?

Suzie Breton and Rita Oh began bicycling past the blues' apartments before school. The girls stuck out their tongues at the buildings and spit on the blues' lawn—all innocent enough, until one day Suzie and Rita climbed off their bikes and peeked into a first-floor window. (This is what we were reduced to, window peeping, because of what the blues had done to the cameras.) The girls were gazing into a bedroom, which was more nest than room—food scraps on the floor mixed with newspapers and old sheets. On the wall was a photograph of a grove of oak trees. Who knew why it was there?

"I dare you to knock," Rita said.

"No," said Suzie.

Rita made whimpering noises at her. "Are you afraid, you big baby?" She grabbed Suzie's hand and slapped it against the window. Then a blue boy entered the room.

He didn't see them at first. He removed his shirt and faced a mirror on the back of the door. The girls were awed by the deformities of his body: the too-long back, the emaciated legs, the severe angles of his bones. The boy licked the mirror with his tongue. This made Rita giggle.

Suzie jabbed her in the ribs. "He'll hear you."

Rita mimicked the blue boy, sticking her tongue to the window glass.

"Come on. Quit it."

"Dare you to take off your shirt," Rita said.

Suzie blushed and refused.

"God, I knew you wouldn't." Rita pushed Suzie into the window, and the blue boy heard and turned around. Suzie had no idea how to read the expression on his face. Was he sad? Angry? Curious? Pleased?

Rita unbuttoned her shirt to reveal the petite cotton bra her mom had bought her the week before.

"We're late for school," Suzie said.

"As if I care," Rita said, and she flaunted her chest at the blue. The bra had stupid pink flowers along the seams, but Rita showed it off anyway. As the blue boy approached the window, Suzie studied his fingers and the narrow muscles of his shoulders. He raised his hand as if to press it gently to the glass, where she could see her reflection, but instead he slapped his palm against the pane. Both girls stumbled backward. He hit the glass again with his hand. Then he used his head. An animal sound—a goat? a horse?—came out of him as he stared at the girls. He pressed his open mouth against the window, exposing his terrible teeth.

The girls arrived at school that day shaken. They had thought —wrongly, as we all sometimes did—that because the blues had two arms, two legs, and a head, they would act like us. But they were not human. They were something else. So this assumption—we had to keep reminding ourselves—was untrue.

The Blues Force Us to Ponder Some Ethical Questions

Such as: If something is not human, can we expect it to be bound by human laws? Do civil rights apply to these creatures? Do we need search warrants to enter their apartments? Can they be handcuffed and arrested for scaring our children? What does justice mean for a being who often appears more animal than human?

In the winter, when some of the blues began starving due to the continued shortage of food, there was the question of whether we were under any ethical obligation to feed them, especially the children. If something happened to the blue adults—and by this time things were happening to the adults—what were our obligations, exactly, to the children, and how long did these obligations go on? At what point were we allowed to wash our hands of them and focus on the needs of our own families?

We Finally Find a Use for the Blues

They turned out to be trainable. They could wash dishes or drive a truck or clean our houses.

"You can't just *make* them work; you need their permission," Mrs. Gorski told us. "And they'll need wages. They aren't indentured servants. They didn't come here to be our slaves."

For that matter, nobody could think of any good reason why they had come.

They Are Even Entering Our Fantasies

Mrs. Lucas told Ms. Mueller over coffee and danishes that when she closed her eyes in front of that painting she'd bought, "it's like I'm there."

"Like you're where?" Ms. Mueller asked.

"On their planet. And they're all around me."

In Mrs. Lucas's mind, the blues' planet was a desert, like the one in that painting—never mind what the blues had said about their moldy dwellings and their floodplains. And in this desert Mrs. Lucas stood barefoot on the sand, which was similar to the sand here on Earth, only light blue and softer. The sand went on all the way to the horizon, but the landscape didn't feel barren or dead. There were huts to Mrs. Lucas's right: charming and rustic, eight of them in a circle around a dwindling fire. Above hung lovely, fat clouds.

"Also there are two suns," Mrs. Lucas continued. "You'd think it was this lonely place. I mean, I'm in the middle of a desert, all by myself, on a different planet. You'd think I would miss home, but I never miss anything when I'm there."

Next she saw beings approaching in the distance. It was the blues. They were coming toward her carrying baskets of fruits and colorful cloths and flowers, kicking up sand with their feet and singing brightly.

"So you ran away from them, right?" Ms. Mueller said. "Tell me you ran away from them."

"I didn't run. Nobody was afraid."

One of the blue females broke away from the group and brought a cloth to Mrs. Lucas, who touched the fabric—"It was softer than anything I've ever felt"—and the whole time the blue female chattered in her rough, throaty language. She must have been saying something about getting undressed, because she began to unbutton Mrs. Lucas's shirt. The blue female helped Mrs. Lucas out of her clothing with no sense of shame. They laughed together at the scratchy fabrics of her old clothes. Then the blue woman wrapped Mrs. Lucas in the clean new cloth and tied the ends in a knot at her waist.

"This is getting rather wild, Maria," Ms. Mueller said.

It turned out the blues were headed to a lake — a very important lake to them, one of the only lakes on their planet. Mrs. Lucas followed them there. On the way they began to sing again, and though she had no idea what the words meant, she found herself singing them too. When they reached the lake, the blues removed their cloths and leaped naked into the clear water, but Mrs. Lucas remained on the wet sand, waiting to see what would happen next. A blue male began to watch her. He climbed out of the water, dripping, and took the edge of her cloth in his hands and tugged.

"Oh, my God," Ms. Mueller said.

Mrs. Lucas held her cloth tight with both hands, suddenly shy. The blue male slapped her face and neck.

"He did *what?*" Ms. Mueller said.

The blue male let Mrs. Lucas look into his face as long as she needed to until she let go of the cloth. Then he unwrapped her slowly.

Ms. Mueller attempted to change the subject to the ongoing drought. On their screens they'd seen dusty refugees and ranchers standing beside their dead cattle. But Mrs. Lucas returned to the dream, because she wasn't even halfway through it yet. She needed Ms. Mueller to understand the way the blue unwrapped her by forcing her to turn. Soon she was as naked as he was. Then he pushed her into the lake.

"That's enough, Maria, please," Ms. Mueller said, standing suddenly and taking Mrs. Lucas's half-eaten danish to the kitchen.

Things May Get Better, Mrs. Gorski Says, If We Welcome Their Children into Our Schools, So We Try

At the school there was little interaction between the blues and our kids. The blues sat in a far corner of the lunchroom. No one made them sit over there; they just did. And they ate nothing. In classes our children sat as far away as possible from them. The teachers tried their best, even working the blues into their lesson plans: the art of "savage" cultures, for instance, or the physics of space travel, or the portrayal of aliens in fiction. There was a lot of material there. Dana Fisher (she used her maiden name when she taught) asked students in her world-history class to give five-minute presentations on the blues' home planet, drawing on both primary interviews and their imaginations. Suzie Breton went first, standing at the front of the room and describing something like the Amish farms of the past: the horse and buggy, the obedient children and enormous families. Who knew where she'd gotten this idea? Halfway through, a blue boy stood up from his desk and said, "Wrong."

"You sit down," Ms. Fisher ordered.

The blue boy did not sit down.

Suzie Breton began crying, her face red and ugly. "I did my best," she said.

Ms. Fisher told the boy, "Look at what you did. Do I need to write you up?"

The blue boy closed his eyes, and soon his expression, his entire unattractive face, was lost in that infernal mist of theirs.

"You stop that right now," Ms. Fisher demanded.

The mist spread throughout the room. It touched the students. It wrapped itself around Suzie Breton's hair and neck. (It felt, she said, like someone was breathing on her.)

"Get it away from me!" Jessica O'Brien shrieked, grasping at the air, as if that would do any good.

The mist crept up the walls and covered the flags and the model of Monticello on the top shelf. Finally it drifted out the open window and dispersed.

If Mrs. Madden Means the Following as a Warning, the Blues Don't Get It

"I'm not doing this anymore," Mrs. Madden told the blues lounging on her front porch in the sun, waiting their turn to hear her predictions. "Not today, not next week, not next month. Go away. Get out of here! Get! Don't come back!"

Was she having a vision of what we would do before we did it?

The blues shrieked, pounded on her house, tore her flower

beds apart, and uprooted small shrubs with their teeth—their teeth!—but she would not open her door to them again.

We Pull the Blue Children from Our Schools

After months of the blue children sulking in the corners of class-rooms and being bullied—our teachers were not bodyguards; they could not form protective shields around each blue and still be educators—we moved the blues to another building. An old warehouse, actually. To be honest, all the blues had done was dis-tract our kids, and we had our children's futures to consider. Bet-ter to teach those creatures separately, in a special environment where we could focus on topics more vital to them, like how to bathe, or speak clearly, or patch a roof.

You have to understand, none of us hated the blues. We just didn't want to be around them after a certain point. The fact was, we could already imagine them gone. We imagined the sorts of things we might say once they were gone: *Oh, do you remember how they danced? Do you remember those songs we heard drifting out of their apartments at night?* As if we hadn't hated their music and their dancing.

Mr. Lucas Hears About His Wife's Crazy Fantasies

"No human being can fuck you like you need," he said—or rather shouted—to Mrs. Lucas. We think he then tied Mrs. Lucas to the bed. Even with the windows shut we heard them, but we pretended not to hear. It became clear to us that the blues were ruining cer-tain people's lives.

Life Cannot Continue On as It Is, Can It?

Look, we studied the same textbooks as you. We knew all the dark secrets of history, just as you do. When we discussed dark times in the past and the things people had done to each other then, we talked as if such acts had been committed by a different species.

But these were dark times too. And dark things happen in the dark. You don't always have the luxury of sitting there and figuring out who did what to whom. Nobody should walk around acting like they have a golden light inside them, because they don't. The blues were a disappointment to us, and disappointment can breed anger. We wished to be rid of them.

So we got rid of them.

The Morning After, We Wake Up, and It's Over

The whole nasty business seemed like something we had watched, not something we had done. Already the air felt different: lighter, or rather clearer. Something about the sky—though it was still the same sky it had been the previous day—wasn't the same. We opened our windows for the first time in a long while. The charred smell of the fires still burning east of town drifted in, but we soon got used to it. Littered about our lawns and the streets were the rocks and bricks and ropes, looking obscene now in the daylight, like something it was best not to talk about. We got out trash bags and cleaned up. It was not by any means a joyful day. None of us were throwing confetti or kicking our heels together. In fact, we did not look each other in the eye. For the most part we kept to ourselves, raking our yards or organizing canned goods in the kitchen—the sort of tasks you think you'll never have time for, so there is a great satisfaction in doing them. There were a few scenes, a few hysterics, such as Mrs. Lucas running down the street in her bloody dress, which she should have changed out of by that point. Anyone visibly upset was ushered inside and soothed with chamomile tea or something stronger. Though we knew the blues' apartments were empty, Johnny Reynolds went over there just to be sure. He didn't tell us exactly what he'd seen. All he said was that he'd checked every apartment, even looking in the closets and under the mattresses, and there was nothing worth saving.

Toward sunset a few cardinals in the trees of Mrs. Durand's yard began to trill in the most extraordinary way, as if to say that certain things did not have to go on forever, and it was okay that they ended.

Can We Blame Everything Bad That Happens Afterward on the Blues?

Such as Suzie Breton's eventual suicide, or the things Mr. Lucas later did to his wife, or Mr. Sullivan's vodka binges, or the way our children seemed to lack a moral compass?

Take what happened to Donny Mueller. When he disappeared, we didn't worry at first. He was only a sixth grader with chubby legs; how far could he have gone? We searched the schools, the library, the woods. Then we searched the homes and basements of his friends. Finally we found Donny locked up in the Durands' garden shed, a dog collar fastened around his neck. The collar was attached to a chain, which was locked to the floor beside a bowl of water and a pile of rancid meat. The shed smelled of something burned. There were scars. Tom Durand and Donny were in the same grade. Apparently Little Tom had wanted Donny as his pet.

There are other examples, but it's better not to go into them.

We found ourselves wondering: If the blues had never come, would we have been better people?

The Blues Long Gone, We Build Ourselves a River Walk

The river walk has lights that turn on at night to keep us safe. The lights get rid of the shadows, and they're also solar-powered, which people seem to like these days. It shows we care about the planet's resources. Already tourists are strolling along the river, holding hands and buying beverages from the carts, just like we predicted they would. The river walk ends at our town's park, where there are benches under the oak trees and a rose garden and a pond. Autumn is by far the most popular time to visit. The leaves turn orange-red as if they were on fire, though they're obviously not on fire, and after they fall we build enormous leaf piles for children to jump in. At Halloween there are pumpkin-carving contests and a costume parade. The tourists find such traditions charmingly old-fashioned.

Only the rare visitor bothers to ask about the blues. You can spot these people easily. They're the ones walking around with their frowns and notebooks, looking for plaques or some sort of memorial fountain—anywhere they can get down on their knees and make a scene. They're the ones who expect us to look haunted. One woman, clutching an open notebook in which she has thus far written nothing, asks, "You were a relocation site, were you not? Yet it appears you're trying to forget this very fact!" As if forgetting were something to be ashamed of. It's too bad that certain people can look at a town like ours, where nothing is missing anymore, and still see something missing.

When a visitor asks, we don't deny that the blues were among us for a brief time, but there isn't a lot more to say. That was many years ago, and most of us have moved on, because that's what you do. There are only a few people left who'll talk about the blues' time here as if it were important: Mrs. Gorski, Mrs. Madden, Johnny Reynolds, Mrs. Lucas. We feel bad for them, because it means that what followed—i.e., the rest of their lives—must have been a disappointment. Mrs. Gorski will ramble on, if you let her, about what she was wearing the night they came (her fluffy red robe), and the style of her hair (in braids), and what she heard (a whistling in the air), and what she saw in the sky (a burning orb like a small, sad sun). Sure, at first it sounds like a big deal—ooh, beings from another planet, a spaceship landing—until you think about how we hadn't asked them to come. They weren't what we needed.

NISI SHAWL

Vulcanization

FROM *Nightmare Magazine*

*A chemical process for converting natural rubber or related polymers into
more durable materials via the addition of sulfur or equivalent curatives
or accelerators. These additives modify the polymer by forming cross-links
(bridges) between individual polymer chains.*

Brussels, 1898

Another black. A mere illusion, Leopold knew, but he flinched out
of the half-naked nigger's path anyway.

Of course Marie Henriette noticed when he did so. The quick
little taps of the queen's high-heeled slippers echoed faster off the
polished floor as she hastened to draw even with him. "My dearest—Sire—"

Leopold stopped, forcing his entire retinue to stop with him.
"What do you wish, my wife?" He refused to turn around. Once
he had done so, and had seen then no sign of the savage who'd
just the moment before brushed past him—through him—with a
fixed and insolent stare. Not much longer till he would be rid of
his ghosts for good.

The queen reached for his sleeve but held her hand back to
hover above the gold-embroidered cuff. "Are you quite sure you
need to do this? Are you sufficiently well?"

He had wondered whether to tell her about his appointment
with Travert. In the end he hadn't, dreading an increase in court
gossip. "The Museum of the Congo is important to my legacy. We
will not be late for the dedication, Marie," he objected in his usual
mild tone. She said nothing further, and he resumed his progress
down the passage to the palace's exit.

Outside, the sky's silver overcast was brighter than any light Leopold had experienced in more than a month. Perhaps he ought not to have confined himself so long. It didn't seem to have decreased the apparitions. Nigger visions had plagued him night and day. Sometimes they held up their bleeding, handless arms, shaking them accusingly. Gore fountained and dripped from their wounds, yet the carpets over which they passed remained stainless. Illusion only, but it would be a relief to be done with them.

He settled himself comfortably in the royal steam barouche. Marie Henriette hesitated a moment before climbing in beside him. Her fondness for horses was well known, but Leopold had explained patiently the need to show support for the manufacture of rubber and its essential role in modern mechanization. Absently, he patted the reinforced fabric of the seat cushion: water-repellent, elastically resilient, warm to the touch as —

Involuntarily he jerked away. He met the eyes of Driessen, his personal physician, taking the opposite seat. Poorly concealed concern peered back at him. Deliberately, the king set his hand back on the spot from which he'd removed it. When he could turn his head casually, as if taking in a passing prospect, he saw nothing more than a vague cloudiness roiling the air of the steam barouche's interior. Arriving at the site of the museum and disembarking from the machine, he left it behind.

The quiet crunch of the gravel walk comforted him. Climbing granite steps to the half-round portico where he would speak, Leopold threw back his shoulders and gave Driessen and Marie Henriette what he hoped was a reassuring smile. Approaching the podium, he pulled his memorandum pad from his military-style jacket's inner pocket and opened it to the relevant page. He looked out at an audience abruptly filled with hundreds of weeping black faces and with a cry let it fall to the ground.

A stifled gasp came from his queen, counterpoint to the sobs only he could hear. Then the pad was set into his nerveless hand, his fingers bent to curl around and hold it. Driessen. The physician was asking him something. Leopold nodded — he hadn't heard the question clearly, but assumed it concerned his welfare. He would go on with his speech. Noblesse oblige.

"Learned and generous contributors to our great enterprise, the enlightenment of the savage inhabitants of heathen Africa," he began, "it is with joy I invite you today to enter with me the mag-

nificent edifice created to shelter the fruits of our noble laboring."
Continuation became easier with every word. With his mental fac-
ulties fully exercised by the demands of his oratory, Leopold's visions faded till they were virtually invisible. To convince himself
those faint specters were truly immaterial he had only to remind
himself that mere minutes remained now till the appointment.

Travert was sallow-skinned and pitiably slight—also balding and
bespectacled. Perhaps a clandestine Israelite? Quite likely. They
were everywhere, and for the most part harmless. This one waited
on the king in one of the museum's private rooms, which Leopold
found rather plain. Undistinguished paneling, ugly gas lamps affixed to it such as he would never choose. The smell of some crude
cleaning compound troubled his nostrils.

The Jew bowed deeply. "Majesty," he began, "I am mindful of
the great favor you do me in granting me permission to share with
you my new invention. The Variable Pressure Ethereo-Vibrative
Condenser displays the most interesting principles discovered to
date in the field to which I've devoted so much study, so much—"

Marie Henriette wrinkled her pretty brow. "But were you not
hired to oversee the care of the inhabitants of the museum's model
village?" In the confusion following the king's public appearance,
she had shed her attendants and somehow insinuated herself into
the room, taking a seat at Leopold's side. "I'm afraid I see no connection between that and your—Elusively Gyrating—whatever
you may say." Her white shoulders shrugged off their covering of
lace. "The king is busy. He has been ill, overwrought—"

Driessen coughed meaningfully into his fist.

"My queen," said Leopold, "this very illness is the cause of my
curiosity regarding Dr. Travert's investigations. They may perhaps
be of help in curing me"—he swept one shapely hand in the little
Hebrew's direction—"by means he was just about to explain."

"Yes, of course." The bald head ducked in acknowledgment.
"You see, my Condenser renders palpable the vaporous emana-
tions of the spirit world so that they may be, ah, dealt with in a
corporeal manner: jailed, burned, buried, dissected—"

"It is due to evil spirits you've gone on so poorly? You never
told me!" Marie Henriette twisted and leaned toward the king.
Her breasts huddled forward, threatening to spill over the loose

confines of her satin bodice. "Let me bring my confessor to you—tonight, after supper!"

"Why?" demanded Driessen.

Leopold dragged his eyes to where Driessen rocked heel to toe, toe to heel. His brusqueness was to be expected. The royal physician tolerated this latest attempt at reconciliation with Marie Henriette but made no secret of his cynicism in regard to her.

"'Why?'" the queen retorted. "To disavow the guilty sorrows such things find attractive. You will feel much better, dearest, once you've relinquished your burden of sin."

But Leopold had done nothing wrong. The casualties in the Congo were necessary to the extraction of its wealth. He looked at Marie Henriette as blandly as possible. With age, her fascination was shrinking. "Perhaps," he temporized. "However, first we'll try Travert's method." It seemed more certain, more scientific.

Though there was one point about which he felt concern. "You have tested the procedure?" he asked.

"Naturally. With the access to your African subjects you have so kindly granted, I was well able. In fact, I have prepared a demonstration for you to view before your own Condensation. It only remains for me to outline for you the particulars of the apparatus's operation and we'll get started."

It required the full force of Driessen's insistence to make the self-aggrandizing Jew realize he could deliver this outline while simultaneously enacting his far more germane demonstration.

Of Leopold's personal guard only Gagnon, its head, had entered the room with him. In the crowded corridor they rejoined the rest of the detachment, descending thence via unfinished steps to a basement, where the odor of the cleaning compound threatened to overwhelm him, though he couldn't determine if it affected anyone else. After they had negotiated several jogs and branchings, Travert called a halt to the procession and unlocked a large wooden door in the passageway's right-hand wall.

The space they entered held charcoal-colored benches, one covered in a jumble of equipment: glass tubes, snakelike hoses, metal fixtures glittering in the scanty light falling from small windows near the room's bare rafters. Its far end was obscured by a brown velvet curtain. Travert drew that aside to reveal a lectern and, looming behind it, a tall, narrow booth. Or a cage—that might be a better word for it, since bars of brass stretched from its raised floor to a height crowned with a barrel-like tank and some geared apparatuses he couldn't quite descry.

Travert swung the cage's barred door open as they approached. A pale face seemed to coalesce behind it, to shiver and deform itself. Then Leopold realized this was but his own reflection. The bars were backed with smooth panes of leaded crystal, as its inventor explained. At length. They helped to hold in certain vibrations which it was desirable to contain in order to concretize the evanescent portion of the targeted phenomenon. Certain chemicals in combination with steam-driven increases in atmospheric pressure wrought bridging chains of causality between the captive spiritual energy's various potential states and resulted in manifestations tangible to all.

Before the fumes of whatever nauseating substance was so prevalent here bested his control completely, a scuffle at the room's entrance ensued. "Ah! Here is my favorite now—" The Hebrew urged a pair of workingmen forward. In their grip they propelled a struggling nigger woman who slapped and kicked them ineffectually, screeching at them an endless stream of what were doubtless heathen maledictions. Reaching the cage, they flung her inside. Like a wild beast she leaped snarling to her feet and charged the door—but Travert speedily shut and secured it.

Her stink fought strenuously against the chemical scent overlaying everything else. Raising to his nose a cologne-soaked handkerchief he hoped would block these disagreeable odors, Leopold leaned forward to scrutinize the lectern to which Travert now advanced. It had been modified by the addition of a peculiar wheel like a gleaming halo and several switches and levers. Manipulating one of these, the doctor set off a low, heavy-sounding hum. The king looked an inquiry.

"Power from that rank of batteries to your right"—Travert pointed to a row of crates formed of some black, dull-surfaced metal—"primes the mechanism while the generators build up sufficient steam." The nigger wench had ceased her wailing imprecations and sunk to lie sullenly on the cage's bottom. "Much as when the heat and pressure employed in vulcanization collects prior to . . ." Ensorcelled by his own arcane activities, Travert allowed the explanation to trail away. Frowning, he slid a yellow-enameled lever down to a position approximating that of a neighboring blue one.

"Go on," Leopold commanded. His stern tone woke Travert from his trance.

"Whatever manifestations Fifine accords us—"

"'Fifine'?"

The doctor's sallow cheeks blushed like a maiden's. "My name for the subject—I must call her *something*, and her African name is far too outlandish."

With the nipples of her flat dugs aimed at the cage floor like dusky arrowheads, the drab resembled no Fifine Leopold had ever known. And he had known a few. But let the man indulge his fancy. "Very well. What would you tell us about the manifestations of this 'Fifine'?"

"The Condenser will render them visible, palpable, subject to study and measurement. From mere ectoplasmic excrescences they will be focused and solidified—"

"Yes, yes." The soft hum stealing out of the rafters had been growing steadily louder. Leopold pitched his invitation above it. "Driessen, if you will do the honors?" The royal physician laid his hand over the Israelite's and gave the lectern's wheel a swift spin. It connected to the apparatus above the cage by a series of looping belts and toothed cogs, all of which now began to turn. They did not cease to do so when the wheel did.

Brushing his hands together as if to remove invisible soil from his fingers, Driessen released his hold, and Travert deserted his lectern for a new post directly before the cage. He addressed its occupant. "Fifine? You are prepared for a demonstration?"

Leopold was taken aback to hear a reply in French. "How can you ask such a stupid question?" He looked to make sure: yes, it was the nigger herself who answered! "The harm you have caused me with your Condenser has no cure. Haven't I told you? Yet you persist in destroying all that remains to me of those I love."

Travert's cheeks reddened again. "Fifine! Must I gag you? I haven't touched a hair upon your head! What will His Majesty think?" He turned an embarrassed countenance to the king.

"I think that you had better get on with things."

The scientist returned hurriedly to the lectern, ignoring the nigger woman's yammering—as he ought to have done from the first. A red lever was moved to a position paralleling the blue and yellow. Clouds of fog descended from the cage's ceiling, gray and black. The terrible odor increased, forcing Leopold to retreat to lean upon a bench a few feet back. There was naught to see nearer anyway: coiling smoke filled the cage and obscured its contents.

For long moments nothing more happened. Then the laboring noise of the Condenser's growling motors ground slowly down to silence.

Gradually the clouds within the cage cleared, disclosing the slumped form of the black on its still-murky bottom. And—other forms? Smaller shapes were scattered around the large one. Did they stir? Yes! Leopold drew closer. A quiet chirping rewarded him. Ghostly birds hopped and fluttered through the dissipating mist. Like dusty sparrows on some plebian roadway, they pecked at their fellow prisoner, soon rousing her.

An odd expression came over the woman's face. On a white, Leopold would have taken it for a compound of regret and delight. Of course, the lower orders were incapable of such complicated mixtures of emotions. If he hadn't known this for a fact, however, he would have been hard-pressed not to attribute such feelings to her as she petted the hopping, shadow-tinted birds with the most delicate of touches. Under the machine's noise and the twittering the bird things emitted, he caught her whispered murmurs and cooed nonsense.

Travert approached him. "The flock has thinned considerably since our first experiment."

"Indeed?" Leopold imagined the cage busy with the dull-plumed little birds. "What became of them?"

A pursing of his lips made obvious the scientist's Oriental ancestry. "They furnished us with material for several informative experiments. But have you comprehended the procedure so far? The carbon and other additives being linked to the interacting surface of the manifestations and showing us thereby their outlines—"

Would the man never cease droning on? Stifling his exasperation, Leopold glanced significantly toward Driessen, who stepped forward and placed a silencing finger on the Jew's thick lips. "Enough!"

A moment Travert's jaw dropped and hung open; a moment his ungloved hands twitched in the barely breathable air. But then, not being mad, he composed himself and motioned the nigger's escorts to come with him to open up the cage.

Reluctant as she had appeared to enter the brass-and-crystal enclosure, "Fifine" made yet more difficulty about leaving it. One of the doctor's assistants gripped her woolly head, even bringing himself to insert his fingers in her gaping nostrils; the other secured her kicking feet. But they had to call for a third man to grasp her wildly flailing arms before they managed to eject her from the room.

Leopold's eyes followed the disturbance toward the door but came to rest on his queen. The sight of her, almost as green and pale as the walls against which she sought refuge, moved him to hold out a welcoming hand. She ran quickly to catch it up. "I'm so sorry you've been put through such an ordeal, Marie," he apologized. "You need not remain longer if it pains you."

"I could *not* desert you!" Her refusal to leave gratified the king. He caressed her plump wrist, intending to raise it to his lips.

THWACK!

Leopold jumped involuntarily. The doctor reacted to his stare with a guilty shift of his eyes, hefting up the meter stick he carried. "My apologies. I missed my mark," said Travert. "For your convenience, it will naturally be best to clear the Condenser's apparatus immediately, and as we've conducted plenty of trials already with this sort of specimen—" He gave a Levantine hunch of his shoulders and returned to clubbing down the dingy birds shut with him inside the cage. Only four remained active, but they gave the Jew an inordinate amount of trouble, their cries loud and frantic as they flew erratically about. The flat crack of the stick meeting bare metal sounded again and again.

Travert's three assistants reappeared and soon dispatched the last of the vermin in a flurry of high-pitched little shrieks. The Jew then had them shovel out the corpselike refuse.

At last Travert indicated with a bow that the Condenser's cage was ready for Leopold to enter. Driessen walked in before him, examining the situation. "His Majesty will require a chair," the royal physician declared.

Seated upon a velvet-covered, spindle-legged stool, Leopold found the unpleasant odor increased. The cage's door shut, and the heliotrope in which he'd drenched his handkerchief barely

compensated for the intensified smell, which filled the surroundings like a half-live thing. After an interval of building noise above
his head, he heard a subtle hiss and looked up to see the dark,
descending smoke.

Would it affect him, a European, as it had the quasi-animal "Fifine"?

Rotting grayness clogged his eyes, his nose, and, when he tried
breathing through it, his mouth. Stoic determination fled. The
king gagged and fainted.

A cool breeze woke him. Refreshed, he opened his stinging eyes to
gaze upon a little garden planted with tropical trees, bushes, and
flowers—doubtless the produce of his Congolese holdings. He
had designed several such gardens to fill the museum's courtyards.
One of Gagnon's men must have carried him here so he'd more
easily revive. Certainly the fresh air was an improvement, and the
scene that met his eyes far more pleasing than that of the stuffy
cellar: fat stems held nodding blooms of cinnabar, violet, and gold,
and broad leaves, some veined in white or pink, quivered softly on
all sides.

It was proper that the guard, having brought him here, had
departed, but where were Driessen and the queen? Was he actually alone? How odd. No—through the foliage Leopold glimpsed
a young girl approaching him. Comely enough, though her final
steps showed her to be clad in a boy's shirt and trousers.

"Hello. I'm Lily." A frank, open expression sat with habitual
ease upon her healthful features.

Meaning to announce his royal status in a charming yet author-
itative manner, Leopold was suddenly rendered voiceless: the girl's
left leg had that second become a pulpy mess of gore and bone.
His throat filled with vomit. He choked it down.

"Ah. My injury disturbs you. You haven't yet had time to get
used to it as I have." The girl gazed ruefully down at her shattered
limb. "Your soldiers shot me last October, during our rescue of
King Mwenda, and I died that very night. Nearly six months now,
isn't it?"

Leopold gaped at her. He must have looked exceedingly foolish. Chief Mwenda had led a rebellion against the king's Public
Forces. "You are a—a gh-gh-ghost?"

"Isn't it obvious?" She flicked a careless hand at the red ruin on which she stood. Impossibly.

A ghost, then. But she was not black—an English miss, to judge by her accent. A white girl—though perhaps not of Europe? Of Everfair, then, the Fabians' damned infestation of a colony wreaked on lands they'd bought of him? Yes! Had not Minister Vandelaar told him recently of an attempt by those traitors to aid that black brute's escape? Though temporarily successful, it had, so the intelligence minister said, cost the rebels of Everfair an important casualty.

Which would be this Lily. Lily Albin, as he recalled now. Daughter of the rabble's leader, a hoyden suffragette.

Was this to be his sole manifestation?

Where were the sooty multitudes who had haunted him all this while, whose silent groans had pestered him so, bidding fair to drive him mad? As he understood Travert's method, if the nigger ghosts could not be Condensed, they could not be got rid of.

The girl answered as if he'd asked his questions aloud. "Do you think you have any control of who you see?" Her eyes whitened like a blind woman's. "Or how? Or what?"

Rising from beneath the thin scent of the garden's flowers, the mephitic cleaning compound's fumes assaulted him anew. They couldn't have traveled here from the cellar—he must still be inside it! In the Condenser's cage! How could he have forgotten? The stool he sat on was the same. The rest of what he experienced, the vegetation and the building heat, might be nothing more than a hypnotic nightmare induced by that quack Travert.

He swung his head from side to side, peering around the foliage, looking for the Jew or one of his assistants. Shouldn't they be waiting nearby?

The girl Lily laughed. The ivory hollow beneath her neck flexed like the foaming pool below a waterfall. "You thought the Condenser would *cure* you?" She subsided to a low chortle. "Of course you did. Why else submit? But whatever gave you the idea?"

He should humor her. He wiped away a trickle of sweat. His attendants must return soon—or, no, he was asleep and would soon wake. How long had the nigger "Fifine" lain prostrate? Despite his more sensitive and highly evolved nervous system, he surely ought to begin to recover momentarily. He stood up from the stool and thrust aside some obscuring boughs to get a better look around. His entourage remained absent, but a flickering motion just out of sight impelled him forward. A manlike shape, glistening in the patchy sunlight as if made of ebony. He walked swiftly toward it for several meters.

Then he stopped.

The garden was not small. The museum's walls did not enclose it. Nothing did. It was a jungle, not a garden.

Why should this frighten him? Dreams could not hurt or kill him. He would not die.

He reversed his path. Now that he was thinking clearly he realized how stupid he'd been to leave the spot where he first found himself. But when he returned it was to see his seat occupied by the dead girl. "I hope you don't mind? Easier for me than standing." With smiling casualness she gestured again at her mangled leg.

Ever the gentleman, Leopold refrained from pressing the claim of his superior birth, though the oppressive warmth and the burgeoning smell of the cleaning compound threatened to overwhelm his senses. He put a hand out to halt the world's swaying and flinched back from the pricking thorns of the branch he'd grasped. He stared in pain and surprise at the blood welling quickly out of many little wounds—his sacred essence! Wrapping his handkerchief around the cuts seemed to do no good; if anything, they bled more fiercely than before, specks of scarlet growing wider, wetter, joining to make of it one sopping crimson banner.

His Russian cousins could perish as a result of such small injuries. And he?

"Oh, I don't believe you're done for just yet." The ghost Lily gazed up at him with blank eyes. "Though with so much blood you'll be creating many more _____, of greater power. As you will come to find."

He didn't understand the word she had used. "I beg your pardon? More—more—what do you say?"

"_____!" Again she gave her chilling laugh. "The ones you expected to find here instead of me."

The nigger spirits, she meant. He thought she nodded. "Those spawned so far wait with your retinue for you to waken."

The stink and heat and dizzying sway worsened. He fell to his knees. He felt the hot blood soak through his trousers where they sank into its spreading pool. He must rouse himself out of this trance *now,* and then let the Jew's assistants deal with executing whatever this abominable treatment had brought forth. Leopold strove with all his might to wake.

"But no one will be able to do anything to your _____, to even touch them. Except for you."

He was lying on his side. He tried to sit up. What did she mean? "Fifine's" dirty-looking little birds had been easily dispatched.

"Ah, but have you the sort of close and respectful relationship with your dead that she does?" The ghost girl seemed to have lain down next to him, for her face was but centimeters away. "No. You do not."

With those words, her white face sprang suddenly nearer—or did it swell with decay? Tightening like a mask, it slipped rapidly to one side and receded on a tide of blackness. Then that tide too receded.

His eyes were open. Gray clouds parted to reveal the cage's tarnished ceiling. Leopold lay now on his back, looking heavenward. He lifted his wounded hand: no sign of injury remained.

"Your Majesty!" The Jew rushed to his side, Gagnon and Marie Henriette right behind him. The dream was over.

Or was it? A haze of darkness formed above them. Gradually it lowered and interposed itself between the king and his attendants, forming at last into the likeness of a group of soot-skinned savages. Which, as before, no one else appeared to see. Which, it seemed obvious now, no one else ever would.

There were three of them: a handless young buck; a withered old granny with her head staved in; a child with no feet at the ends of her legs. They closed around him, clumsily lifting him from the cage's floor. Leopold's scalp crept as he felt the soft resilience of their nonexistent flesh. He retched convulsively and shoved away the tiny hands, the yielding arms. These newly palpable horrors.

All his life, Leopold had known himself to be as brave and strong as he was good and handsome. All his life till now.

"Sire!" The oily voice of Travert intruded itself into the king's thoughts.

"My dearest!" The queen too sought his attention.

Leopold opened eyes he hadn't realized he'd shut. The ghosts were defiantly visible. But still, always, only to him. Ignoring the phantoms' reproachful gazes, he leaned on the arms his supporters offered, letting them lead him out of the Condenser. As if the weeping niggers reaching to interrupt his passage with their weak and truncated limbs weren't present. As if they made no actual contact. As if the king didn't understand himself doomed till death to feel, over and over, the hideous warmth of their touch.

ALEXANDER WEINSTEIN

Openness

FROM *Beloit Fiction Journal*

BEFORE I DECIDED to finally give up on New York, I subbed classes at a junior high in Brooklyn. A sixth-grade math teacher suffering from downloading anxiety was out for the year, and jobs being what they were, I took any opportunity I could. Subbing math was hardly my dream job; I had a degree in visual art, for which I'd be in debt for the rest of my life. All I had to show for it was my senior collection, a series of paintings of abandoned playgrounds, stored in a U-Pack shed in Ohio. There was a time when I'd imagined I'd become famous, give guest lectures at colleges, and have retrospectives at MoMA. Instead I found myself standing in front of a class of apathetic tweens, trying to teach them how to do long division without accessing their browsers. I handed out pen and paper, so that for once in their lives they'd have a tactile experience, and watched as they texted, their eyes glazed from blinking off message after message. They spent most of the class killing vampires and orcs inside their heads and humoring me by lazily filling out my photocopies.

The city overwhelmed me. Every day I'd walk by hundreds of strangers, compete for space in crowded coffee shops, and stand shoulder to shoulder on packed subway cars. I'd scan profiles, learning that the woman waiting for the N enjoyed thrash-hop and the barista at my local coffee shop loved salted caramel. I'd had a couple fleeting relationships, but mostly I'd spend weekends going to bars and sleeping with people who knew little more than my username. It all made me want to turn off my layers, go back to the old days, and stay disconnected. But you do that and you become another old guy buried in an e-reader, complaining about how no one sends emails anymore.

So I stayed open, shared the most superficial info of my outer layer with the world, and filtered through everyone I passed, hoping to find some connection. Here was citycat5, jersygirl13, m3love. And then one morning there was Katie, sitting across from me on the N. She was lakegirl03, and her hair fell from under her knit cap. The only info I could access was her hometown and that she was single.

"Hi," I winked, and when I realized she had her tunes on, I sent off an invite. She raised her eyes.

"Hi," she winked back.

"You're from Maine? I'm planning a trip there this summer. Any suggestions?"

She leaned forward and warmth spread across my chest from being allowed into her second layer. *"I'm Katie,"* she winked. *"You should visit Bar Harbor, I grew up there."* She gave me access to an image of a lake house with tall silvery pines rising high above the shingled roof. *"Wish I could help more, but this is my stop."* As she stood waiting for the doors to open, I winked a last message. *"Can I invite you for a drink?"* The train hissed, the doors opened, and she looked back at me and smiled before disappearing into the mass of early-morning commuters. It was as the train sped toward work that her contact info appeared in my mind, along with a photo of her swimming in a lake at dusk.

It turned out that Katie had been in the city for a couple years before she'd found a steady job. She taught senior citizens how to successfully navigate their layers. She'd helped a retired doctor upload images of his grandchildren so strangers could congratulate him, and assisted a ninety-three-year-old widow in sharing her mourning with the world. Her main challenge, she said, was getting older folks to understand the value of their layers.

"Every class they ask me why we can't just talk instead," she shared as we lay in bed. Though Katie and I occasionally spoke, it was always accompanied by layers. It was tiring to labor through the sentences needed to explain how you ran into a friend; much easier to share the memory, the friend's name and photo appearing organically.

"At least they still want to speak. My class won't even say hello."

"You remember what it was like before?" she asked. I tried to think back to high school, but it was fuzzy. I was sure we used to talk more, but it seemed like we doled out personal details in hushed tones.

"Not really," I said. "Do you?"

"Sure. My family's cabin is completely out of range. Whenever I go back we can only talk."

"What's *that* like?"

She shared a photo of walking in the woods with her father, the earth covered in snow, and I felt the sharp edge of jealousy. Back where I grew up, there hadn't been any pristine forests to walk through, just abandoned mini-marts, a highway, and trucks heading past our town, which was more a pit stop than a community. The only woods were behind the high school, a small dangerous place where older kids might drag you if you didn't run fast enough. And my parents sure didn't talk. My mother was a clinical depressive who'd spent my childhood either behind the closed door of her bedroom or at the kitchen table, doing crossword puzzles and telling me to be quiet whenever I asked her something. My father had hit me so hard that twice I'd blacked out. My history wasn't the kind of thing I wanted to unlock for anyone, and since leaving Ohio I'd done my best to bury those memories within my layers.

So I spent our first months sharing little of myself. Katie showed me the memories of her best friends and family while I showed her the mundane details of substitute teaching and my favorite bands. I knew Katie could feel the contours of my hidden memories, like stones beneath a bedsheet, but for a while she let me keep the private pain of my unlocked layers.

That summer Katie invited me to spend the weekend with her dad at their cabin. We rented a car and drove up the coast to Maine. We listened to our favorite songs, made pit stops, and finally left I-95 for the local roads. It was late in the afternoon, our car completely shaded by the pines, when our reception started getting spotty. I could feel my connection with Katie going in and out.

"Guess we might as well log off," Katie said. She closed her eyes for a moment, and all of a sudden I felt a chasm open between us.

There was a woman sitting next to me whom I had no access to. "It's okay, babe," she said, and reached out for my hand. "I'm still me." I pressed my palm to hers, closed my eyes, and logged off too.

Her father, Ben, was a big man who wore a puffy green vest that made him appear even larger. "And you're Andy," he said, burying my hand in his. "Let me get those bags for you." He hefted both our suitcases from the trunk, leaving me feeling useless. I followed him into the house, experiencing the quiet Katie had told me about. There were no messages coming from anyone, no buzzposts to read, just the three of us in the cabin and the hum of an ancient refrigerator.

The last time a girlfriend had introduced me to her parents we'd sat at Applebee's making small talk from outer layer info, but with Ben, there were no layers to access. All I knew were the details Katie had shared with me. I knew that her mom had died when she was fourteen, and that her father had spent a year at the cabin grieving, but that didn't seem like anything to bring up. So I stood there, looking out the living room window, trying to remember how people used to talk back in the days when we knew nothing about each other.

"Katie says you've never been to Maine."

"I haven't," I said, the words feeling strange against my tongue.

He walked over to the living room window. The afternoon sun shimmered on the pond, making it look silvery and alive, and the sky was wide and blue, pierced only by the spires of red pines. "Beautiful, isn't it?"

"Yeah," I said. The fridge hummed and from the other room I could hear Katie opening drawers and unpacking. I wasn't sure what else to add. I remembered a detail she had unlocked for me on one of our early dates. "I heard you've caught a lot of fish out there."

"You like fishing?" he asked, placing his hand on my shoulder. "Here, I'll show you something."

Ben retrieved an old tablet from the closet and showed me photos on the screen. There he was with Katie and a string of fish; him scaling a trout in the kitchen sink. We scrolled through the two-dimensional images one by one as people did when I was a kid. Katie came to my rescue. "Come on, I want to show you the lake," she said. "Dad can wow you with his antique technology later."

"One day you'll be happy I kept this," he said. "Katie's baby photos are all on here." He shut down the device and put it back in its case. "Have fun out there. Dinner will be ready in an hour."

Outside, Katie led me on the trails I'd only ever seen in her layers. Here was the gnarled cedar that she'd built a fort beneath, and over there were the rocks she'd chipped mica flakes from in second grade. We climbed down the banks of the trail, holding on to roots that jutted from the earth, and arrived on a stretch of beach speckled with empty clamshells, mussels, and snails that clung to the wet stones. Far down the shore, a rock outcropping rose from the water. A single heron stood on a peak that broke the shoreline.

There was something beautiful about sharing things in the old way—the two of us walking by the shore, the smell of the pine sap, the summer air cooling the late afternoon—and for the first time in years, I wished I had a sketchpad with me. As Katie spoke, her hands moved in ways I hadn't seen people do since childhood, gesturing toward the lake or me when she got excited. I tried to focus on each sentence, sensing my brain's inability to turn her words into pictures. She was talking about the cabin in autumn, logs burning in the fireplace, the smell of smoke, leaves crunching underfoot.

"Are you even listening?" she asked when I didn't respond.

"Sorry," I said. "I'm trying to. It's just that without the *ding* it's hard to know when you're sending . . . I mean *saying* something . . ." I stopped talking, hating the clunkiness of words, and took a deep breath. "I guess I'm just rusty."

Katie softened. "I know. Sometimes when I'm in the city, I can't remember what it looks like up here without accessing my photos. It's kinda messed up, isn't it?"

"Yeah," I agreed, "I guess it is." The heron hunched down and then lifted off, its wide wings flapping as it headed across the lake, away from us.

That night her father fried up the perch he'd caught earlier that day. The herbs and butter filled the small cabin with their scent, and we drank the wine we'd brought. After dinner, Ben brought out a blue cardboard box, and the three of us sat in the living room and played an actual game. I hadn't seen one in over a decade.

"You don't know how to play Boggle?" Katie asked, surprised. The point, she explained, was to make words from the lettered dice and to write them down with pen and paper without accessing other players' thoughts. I sat there trying to figure out what Katie was feeling as she covered her paper with her hand.

"What do you think?" Katie asked after the first round.

"It's fun," I admitted.

"You bet it is," Ben said, and made the dice rattle again.

When Katie and I were in bed, I listened to the crickets outside the screened windows. It'd been a long time since I'd heard the drone of them, each one singing within the chorus.

"So what do you think of it here?"

"It's beautiful. But I can't imagine growing up without connection."

"You don't like the feeling?"

"Not really," I said. Being offline reminded me of my life back home before layers existed, when I'd lived with my parents in Ohio, a miserable time that technology had helped to bury. "Do you?"

"Totally. I could live like this forever." I looked at her in the dark and tried to scan her eyes, but it was just her looking back at me, familiar yet completely different. "What about my dad?"

"I like him," I said, though it was only part of the truth. I was really thinking how different he was from my own father. We'd never sat and ate dinner together or played board games. I'd heat up frozen pizza and eat it in the kitchen while Dad would lie on the couch watching whatever game was on. Eventually he'd get up, clink the bottles into the bin, and that was the sign to shut off the TV. Thinking about it made me feel like Katie and her father were playing a joke on me. There was no way people actually lived like this—without yelling, without fighting.

I felt the warmth of Katie's hand against my chest. "What's the matter?"

"Nothing."

"You can tell me," she said. *"I love you."*

It was the first time she'd actually said the words. At home it was just something we knew. We understood it from the moments we'd stand brushing our teeth together and the feeling would flash through her layers. And sometimes, late at night, right before we'd both fall asleep, we'd reach out and touch each other's hands and feel it.

"I love you too," I managed to get out, and the weight of the words made something shift inside me. I felt the sentences forming in my head, the words lining up as though waiting to be released. Without my layers, there was nothing to keep them from spilling out. "Katie," I said into the darkness. "I want to tell you about my family."

She put her arms around me. "Okay."

And there, in the cabin, feeling Katie's body against mine, I began to speak. I didn't stop myself, but leaned into my voice and the comfort of hearing my words disappearing into the air with only Katie and the crickets as witnesses.

It was that night in the cabin that helped us grow closer. Shortly after we returned, I unlocked more layers for her and showed her the pictures of my father and mother—the few I'd kept. There was my high school graduation: my mother's sunken eyes staring at the camera, my father with his hands in his pockets, and me in between, none of us happy. I showed her the dirty vinyl-sided house and the denuded lawn, blasted by cold winters and the perpetual dripping oil from my father's truck. And she showed me her own hidden layers: her mother's funeral in a small church in Maine, her father escaping to the cabin afterward, learning to cook dinner for herself. Having unlocked the bad memories, I also uncovered the few good ones I'd hidden: a snowy day, my father, in a moment of tenderness, pulling me on a sled through the town; my mother emerging from her room shortly before she died to give me a hug as I left for school.

Feeling the closeness that sharing our layers brought, Katie suggested we give total openness a shot. It meant offering our most painful wounds as a gift to one another, a testament that there was no corner of the soul so ugly as to remain unshared. It'd become increasingly common to see the couples in Brooklyn, a simple *O* tattooed around their fingers announcing the radical honesty of their relationship to the world. They went to Open House parties, held in abandoned meatpacking plants, where partiers let down all their layers and displayed the infinite gradations of pain and joy to strangers while DJs played Breaknoise directly into their heads. I resented the couples, imagining them to be suburban hipsters who'd grown up with loving parents, regular allowances, and easy histories to share.

Total openness seemed premature, I told Katie, not just for us but for everyone. Our culture was still figuring out the technology.

A decade after linking in, I'd find drinking episodes that had migrated to my work layer or, worse yet, porn clips that I had to flush back down into the darkness of my hidden layers.

"I'm not going to judge you," she promised as we lay in bed. She put her leg over mine. "You do realize how hot it'll be to know each other's fantasies, right?" There were dozens of buzz-posts about it — the benefits of total intimacy, how there were no more fumbling mistakes, no guessing, just a personal database of kinks that could be accessed by your partner.

"What about the darker layers?"

"We need to uncover those too," Katie said. "That's what love is: seeing all the horrible stuff and still loving each other."

I thought I understood it then, and though my heart was in my throat, my terror so palpable that my body had gone cold, I was willing to believe that total openness wasn't the opposite of safety but the only true guarantee of finding it. So late that summer evening, Katie and I sat on the bed, gazing into one another's eyes, and we gave each other total access.

I've spent a lot of time thinking about what went wrong, whether total openness was to blame or not. Some days I think it was, that there's no way to share the totality of yourself and still be loved, that secrets are the glue that holds relationships together. Other times I think Katie and I weren't meant to be a couple for the long haul; total openness just helped us find the end more quickly. Maybe it was nothing more than the limits of the software. We were the first generation to grow up with layers, a group of kids who'd produced thousands of tutorials on blocking unwanted users but not a single one on empathy.

There were certainly good things that came from openness. Like how, after finding my paintings, Katie surprised me with a sketchpad and a set of drawing pencils. Or the nights when I'd come home from a frustrating day of substitute teaching and she'd have accessed my mood long before I saw her. She'd lay me down on the bed and give me a massage without us even winking one another. But all too often it was the things we didn't need to share that pierced our love: sexual histories that left Katie stewing for weeks; fleeting attractions to waiters and waitresses when we'd go out to dinner; momentary annoyances that would have been best left unshared. Letting someone into every secret gave access to our dark corners, and rather than feeling sympathy for each other's failings, we blamed each other for nearsightedness, and soon layers of resentment were dredged up. There was a night at the bar when I watched Katie struggling to speak loudly enough for the bartender to hear, and I suddenly realized his face resembled the schoolyard bully of her childhood. *"You have to get over that already,"* I blinked angrily. Soon after, while watching a film I wasn't enjoying, she tapped into layers I hadn't yet registered. *"He's just a fictional character, not your father."*

And then there was the final New Year's Eve party at her friend's place out in Bay Ridge. The party was Y2K-themed, and guests were expected to actually speak to one another. A bunch of partygoers were sporting Bluetooth headsets into which they yelled loudly. We listened to Jamiroquai on a boom box and watched Teletubbies on a salvaged flat-screen. Katie was enjoying herself. She danced to the songs and barely winked anyone, happy to be talking again. I tried to be sociable, but I was shut down, giving access to only my most superficial layers as everyone got drunk and sloppy with theirs.

We stood talking to a guy wearing an ironic trucker's cap as he pretended we were in 1999. "So you think the computers are going to blow up at midnight?" he asked us.

Katie laughed.

"No," I said.

"Come on," Katie blinked. *"Loosen up."*

"I'm not into the kitsch," I blinked back.

"Mostly I'm just excited about faxing things," the guy in the trucker's cap joked, and Katie laughed again.

"You know faxing was the early nineties, right?" I said, and then blinked to Katie, *"Are you flirting with this guy?"*

"All I'm saying is check out this Bluetooth. Can you believe folks wore these?"

"I know, that's crazy," Katie said. *"No, I'm not flirting. I'm talking. How about you try it for a change?"*

"I told you, I don't like talking."

"Great, so you're never going to want to talk, then?"

"Did you guys make any New Year's resolutions?" the guy asked us.

"Yeah," Katie said, looking at me, "to talk more." In her annoyance an image from a deeper layer flashed into clear resolution. It was a glimpse of a future she'd imagined for herself, and I saw us canoeing in Maine, singing songs with our kids. Even though we'd discussed how I never wanted children, there they were, and while I hadn't sung aloud since grade school, there was a projection of me singing. Only then did I see the other incongruities. My eyes were blue not brown, my voice buoyant, my physique way more buff than I ever planned to become. And though I shared similarities with the man in the canoe, as if Katie had tried to fit me into his mold, the differences were clear. There in the canoe was the family Katie wanted, and the man with her wasn't me.

"What the fuck?" I said aloud.

"It's just a question," the guy said. "If it's personal, you don't have to share. I'm giving up gluten."

"Excuse us for a minute," I said, and I blinked for Katie to follow me. We found a quiet spot by the side of the flat-screen TV.

"Who the hell is that in your future?" I whispered.

"I'm really sorry," she said, looking at me. "I do love you."

"But I'm not the guy you want to spend your life with?"

"Ten . . . nine . . . eight," the partiers around us counted as they streamed the feed from Times Square.

"That's not true," Katie said. "You're almost everything I want."

There was no conscious choice about what happened next, just an instinctive recoiling of our bodies, the goose bumps rising against my skin as our layers closed to each other. I couldn't access the lake house anymore or the photos of her father; her childhood dog was gone, followed by the first boyfriend and her college years, until all that was left were my own private memories, trapped deep within my layers, and the pale tint of her skin in the television's light. We were strangers again, and we stood there, looking at each other, while all around us the party counted down the last seconds of the old year.

I logged off for long periods after we broke up. I gave up on trying to convince my students to have real-life experiences. When they complained that reading the "I Have a Dream" speech was too boring, I let them stream a thrash-hop version instead, and I sat looking out the window thinking about Katie. I walked to my station alone every day and sat on the train with my sketchpad, drawing the details I remembered from our trip to Maine: the shoreline with its broken shells and sunlight, the heron before it took flight,

Katie's face in the summer darkness. It's the intangible details that I remember the clearest, the ones that there's no way to draw. The taste of the perch as we sat around the table; how a cricket had slipped through the screened windows and jumped around our bed that night; how, after we'd gotten it out, the coolness of the lake made us draw the blankets around us; and how Katie, her father, and I had sat together in the warm light of the living room and played a game, the lettered dice clattering as her father shook the plastic container.

"All right, Andy, you ready?" he'd asked me, holding his hand over the lid.

And I'd thought I was.

JEREMIAH TOLBERT

Not by Wardrobe, Tornado, or Looking Glass

FROM *Lightspeed Magazine*

THE SCENT OF fresh lilacs and the boom of a cannon shot muffled by distance prefaced the arrival of the rabbit hole. Louisa jerked upright in her seat, and her book fell from her lap to slap against the cold pavement of the station floor. Dropping a book would normally cause her to cringe, but instead she allowed herself a spark of excitement as a metal maintenance door creaked open on rusty hinges. Golden light spilled out onto dazed commuters. Was this it? Was this *finally* it?

The silhouette of a centaur beckoned toward the gathering crowd from within the rabbit hole. In a melodious voice, she called out, "Richard! Come quickly. Without your aid, the Inkies destroy everything that is beautiful and good in our world!"

A middle-aged man in a gray business suit laughed and ran forward, the crowd begrudgingly parting before him. "Never fear," he shouted, stepped through the hole, and pulled the door shut behind him. The lighting in the station returned to normal. The smell of flowers was replaced with the usual smell of stale urine, newsprint, and body odor. A train rumbled in the distance, perhaps soon to arrive, or perhaps not.

Louisa bent down to pick up her book. The front cover was creased on the corner, but otherwise it was fine. The other commuters returned to those things commuters do to keep their mind off the boredom of travel: phones, newspapers, iPads, crossword puzzles.

Still not her turn. Not this time. To work in the mundane world, then.

*

The agency had placed Louisa with Dewey, Putnam, and Low, a small but venerable legal office downtown. The interview had been very brief, as temps were harder to find since rabbit holes. In the past six months, the calls had gotten more frequent; Louisa had developed a good reputation for dependability. She had little else to do with her time since the cancer had finished its relentless march through her mother's bones.

"Do you have one?" asked the office supervisor, a stern-sounding woman named Catherine (absolutely never, *ever* to be called "Cathy," she had instructed). Her name and voice conjured pictures of Catherine the Great, but in person she was considerably shorter, wider, and balder than the Russian leader.

"No."

"The last girl we hired never bothered to come in. And the young man before that showed for three days. I'm sure it's wonderful, frolicking with elves in the forest, but we here in the *real world* have work to do." She said "real world" with a degree of bitterness that evoked considerable sympathy in Louisa. Perhaps she too had been passed over.

"I am dedicated to my work, don't worry. What would you like me to do?" Of course, she didn't say that if her rabbit hole did arrive, she wouldn't be coming back. She still had to pay rent for the time being, after all.

Catherine waved at the paperwork threatening to topple from the side of her desk. "File these, to start." Catherine dismissed Louisa by simply ignoring her in favor of the computer. It took a long moment before Louisa realized she was supposed to leave. She could appreciate a supervisor who didn't expect her to spend hours chitchatting about television or current events, two things that held no interest for Louisa, unless you counted the rabbit holes as current events.

Louisa gathered up the paperwork and wandered in search of the filing room. Most of the offices were dark and empty. The few people she saw looked frazzled and weary, like people for whom sleep had dropped a few levels on the hierarchy of needs—kindred spirits, those. She had seen that exhaustion many times in the mirror during her mother's long decline.

Many of the lawyers were nearly hidden behind stacks of paperwork as large as the one she was attempting to file, which, if nothing else, signaled job security. One young man looked up as she stopped to stare. He gave her a half-smile, raised an immaculately sculpted eyebrow.

Louisa blushed. "Um . . . which way to the filing room?"

He pointed down the hall. He opened his mouth to speak, but she turned and fast-walked away before he could make a sound. She didn't know how to talk to attractive young men anymore, if she ever had. Best to avoid it as much as possible.

Instead she went to work in the small, dimly lit room down the hall. The system was a standard though slightly antiquated one, as promised. The room itself would have been unremarkable but for one of the ceiling-high wooden cabinets; it was padlocked with two fist-sized chrome locks and a heavy steel chain. A sticky note indicated that T to Th had been moved to the neighboring cabinet indefinitely, and pointed with a marker-drawn arrow to the right. When Louisa pressed her ear to the drawer, harp music whispered from within.

Louisa rooted through her pockets for her notebook, flipped to the end of her list of "Types of Rabbit Holes," and wrote "FILING CABINETS" in neat letters. She snapped it shut, tucked it away, and began to work.

The first week passed in silent drudgery, which was just fine for her. Jobs like this with clearly defined tasks, ones that involved a minimum of interaction with other people, were her specialty. The thing that interested her most was the locked rabbit hole in the cabinet, which at first Catherine had no interest in explaining.

Each day Louisa ate her lunch at 12:30 exactly, methodically and quickly, without interest. The food was secondary to the book she hoped to read.

In this one, a teenage boy fell through the ice of a lake and woke up in a cold land ruled by witches made of curdled frost and coal-stained snow. Giant fish wove paths of light through the sky, drifting silently overhead like grand zeppelins. She had already written "ICY LAKE" in her notebook.

The writing was pedestrian, not that she could do better. But it passed the time. Some of the imagery carried her away for a few moments, but since the rabbit holes, even her old favorites felt hollow; new works, untouched by the pixie dust of childhood nostalgia, couldn't begin to compare to tantalizing new-reality.

The shuffle of footsteps on ragged carpet drew Louisa's attention from the story, and Catherine walked past, pausing for a moment as if debating whether or not to make conversation, but continued to the microwave. She placed a plastic bowl of half-frozen soup inside and set the timer.

"How are you finding the work?"

"I don't mind filing," Louisa said carefully.

"Good. We have plenty for you." Catherine chuckled halfheartedly, and the microwave beeped. She removed the soup, only the tips of her fingers touching the bowl, and carried it to sit across from Louisa. She lowered her head and pursed her lips and blew across the surface. Tiny ripples shimmered across the yellowish liquid.

"So," Catherine said, stirring now with a plastic spoon. "You . . . you really don't have one at all?"

Louisa shook her head.

Catherine smiled. "You're so lucky."

Louisa forced a smile.

"Have you noticed how much emptier the streets are now? How many of the shops have closed?" Catherine asked. She took a tentative bite of soup, held her mouth half open for a moment, and exhaled sharply. Finally she swallowed. "It's one of the things we're working on here."

"Really?" Louisa had wondered what sort of work would keep lawyers so busy now. Crime was falling steadily, from what she'd read. Why would anyone steal anything when they could go to a world where their every desire would be met? The poor became kings. The rich, they got whatever it was *they* wanted. Everyone was happier down their rabbit holes.

"So much abandoned property." Catherine shrugged. "It's a tricky area to sort out. There are interested buyers, but it's a bit of a gray area. The buyers, I mean."

"I should get back to work," Louisa said. "Like you said, there's a lot of filing."

"Can you hear the music still?" Catherine asked, her voice softening.

"Yes," Louisa said, suspicions now confirmed.

"I always loved the harp." Catherine stared at the wall just over Louisa's shoulder, staring really at nothing at all that could be seen. "Such a beautiful instrument. My mother made me learn the violin. Said the harp wasn't a respectable instrument. Too expensive. Not *practical*..." She trailed off, mindlessly stirring the last of her soup.

Not sure if Catherine expected her to say anything else at all, Louisa decided it was safer to remain silent. After a few minutes she gave a quiet wave, stood, and returned to the filing room. Catherine didn't seem to notice.

Around the work for the law firm, Louisa finished three more fantasy novels and added two more rabbit holes to her notebook. The coming drought of books loomed heavily in her thoughts during her increasingly deserted commute to DPL's offices. New books were harder to come by. Few were being written, and even fewer were published. The writers had been some of the first to disappear.

Friday evening, a dumpster in the alley beside her apartment building expelled a man in a golden-feathered headdress riding a six-legged brown stallion. He shook a spear at the sky and shouted something in a language Louisa didn't understand. He smiled at her; his white teeth stood out sharply against his deeply tanned skin. Then he nudged the horse into a trot and down the street. He turned the corner at the mini-mart and disappeared into the evening.

By the time Louisa made it to the dumpster, the glow was gone. She added it to her list in quick, angry letters.

It was only later that she realized it was the first time she'd seen anything leave a rabbit hole other than herself.

Louisa had *entered* someone else's rabbit hole twice.

The first had been a manhole cover that led to a strange world of talking mushrooms and brick architecture that gleamed red under cloudless blue skies. It hadn't been what she expected. But of course it hadn't. It wasn't *hers*. After a day, she took a warp pipe home, and the gleaming gold coins she had collected turned into dust when she returned.

The second time was after Annabelle had stopped calling, something she had done twice weekly ever since their mother had become ill and Louisa had volunteered to come home from college and take care of her.

The calls had followed a simple script: three to four minutes of banal pleasantries, five minutes about their mother's declining health, and then an awkward few minutes about how Louisa was coping with it all. The calls hadn't stopped after their mother's death, only gotten shorter, which had only served to confirm Louisa's suspicions that the calls were not about what they seemed to be about. They were tailored to make Annabelle feel better for not being there, for staying at Stanford and finishing *her* degree.

She resented the calls, but it wasn't until they ended that she realized how much she needed them to anchor herself in the world.

Three months into the rabbit holes situation, Louisa took the train to Annabelle's house out in Napierville. The house was empty. The doors and windows were all open, and the curtains billowed outward in the breeze. Anna's husband had moved out the year before, but Louisa didn't know the details. She searched the yard first; even the dog was missing. Whether down a rabbit hole of its own or with Annabelle, Louisa didn't know. Maybe Anna's husband had taken the dog.

She obsessed about that for weeks afterward. Did even animals have their own worlds? Did every living thing *but* Louisa have a secret world of its own out there?

Louisa closed all the windows and swept the house. She called in sick to her temp job and waited a week, in case her sister had gone on a business trip and forgotten to tell her. She stayed in the guest bedroom, even though the bed in her sister's room looked more comfortable. Somehow, to sleep in there would have been acknowledging the truth too much.

On the last day, she searched the house for clues, finally discarding any notion that she was violating Anna's privacy. The rabbit hole was in the attic. An old steamer trunk opened onto a tropical island where statues as large as skyscrapers had been built in Annabelle's likeness. Pirate ships were moored off the white sand beaches, their guns silent but ominous. A volcano puffed gray smoke overhead, and a deep, masculine chanting echoed through the jungle. Louisa had called out her sister's name, but there was no way Annabelle could have heard her over the riot of noise. The rabbit hole pinched closed a moment after she stepped back home.

If she had just taken a little longer, she might have been trapped there in someone else's secret world. What would have happened to her? Would it have been any worse than being stranded in the "real" world?

She didn't know the answer to that question. Didn't want to know. Louisa gave up on other people's rabbit holes, confident that none of them would ever be quite right if it wasn't meant exactly for her.

One month after she began working at Dewey, Putnam, and Low, she walked to the corner newsstand. She was out of library books and thought perhaps she would try her hand at the crossword puzzle in the *Tribune*. She was terrible at crossword puzzles, but the Monday puzzle was usually within her abilities.

The man behind the counter was no longer a man at all, strictly speaking. He had a human body and wore a large white button-up shirt with the sleeves rolled up around massive elbows, but he possessed the head of a buffalo, round and shaggy with black-brown fur. His placid eyes watched Louisa as she tried to make a selection from the papers; they were days out of date. Her hands shook as she picked up a copy of the *Times* from the past Monday, then handed a five-dollar bill to the buffalo-headed man. He reached below the counter and retrieved her change without taking his eyes off her.

"What happened to Vincent?" she asked suddenly, the words escaping quickly before she could stomp them back down.

The bisontaur shrugged. "Gone over," he said in a soft, almost feminine voice. If it wasn't for the heavy horns above his ears, Louisa might have revised her estimation of his sex.

"He sold you his stand?" she asked.

His large eyes narrowed. "I paid for the stand. It is mine."

Louisa didn't know what that meant, but she decided not to ask any further questions, and hurried to catch the train. It was twelve minutes late anyway, and arrived empty.

Catherine was not waiting at the front desk when Louisa arrived. Louisa had been mentally preparing for her boss's tirade; she'd received real blistering monologues from bosses in the past, and felt deflated and hollow when she had no one to deliver her excuses to.

Louisa gathered up a stack of filing that was waiting. Half again as many offices were empty today as the day when she started. She wondered what a lawyer wanted in a rabbit hole. She pictured some kind of Court World where the opponents were buffoonish cartoon characters, the moronic jury easily swayed by proper human logic. The clients were . . . wealthy royalty? The judge presiding over it all a sphinx, lion's tail lashing in time to the arguments. Or perhaps not. What little Louisa knew about the fantasy lives of normal people she found bland and unimpressive.

In the filing room, the old cabinet T–TH was open. Paperwork blew around the room, and the harpsong was louder than ever. The chains, lock, and a heavy red bolt cutter lay on the floor like the weapons at a crime scene in a television forensic drama.

Louisa closed the cabinet and allowed herself a good cry. In some ways, Catherine had been the best boss she had ever had.

Paychecks stopped coming, and Louisa stopped going in. She believed the office would be empty by now, and for some reason she could not explain, she did not want to see it in that state. She preferred to picture it struggling along valiantly, dealing with the legal matters that remained, a handful of dedicated lawyers keeping civilization together.

Out of things to read, she passed time flipping through TV channels. Most of them were blank. On a few she saw shows, but not put on by humans. A talk show hosted by a gorgon. The camera cut to a pan across an audience full of giant snakes. A game-show host that looked like a living statue, asking questions to a panel of a hobbit, a brown bear wearing hipster glasses, and a thin vapor mist that just barely took the outline of a woman.

It reminded her of traveling to another country, where the culture is completely foreign and the language is one you had tried to take in high school but you had forgotten most of since. Traveling there and turning on a television in a hotel room. The shows were just like that. Alienating.

Louisa rang her temp agency, hoping for anything better to do. She got a disconnect message.

Louisa took a late-night walk through the city. The streets were not as empty now. Traffic was lighter, mostly made up of chariots drawn by lions or Victorian carriages drawn by giant-sized mice. There was the occasional steam-powered tank, but the drivers were generally nice enough to take the main avenues.

Louisa stopped and watched an ogre wearing a policeman's uniform buy a hot dog from a cart operated by a ghost in a burial shroud.

She wanted to ask them questions, but the thought of talking to either of them terrified her. So far, the city's new residents had ignored her. It seemed best not to draw attention to herself.

In the park she was chased by leering goblins. They shouted obscenities at her in accents she didn't recognize, but the meaning of the words was clear enough. *Stay off our turf.*

She ran home and locked her door. She turned on the TV again. A local channel was airing a roundtable discussion between a badger, a toad, a weasel, and a beaver. They were debating upcoming mayoral elections in crisp English accents. Louisa turned off the television and went to bed.

"Rent's due," said the satyr standing in her doorway. He wore half a dozen gold chains around his neck, and his great mane of hair had been slicked down with Palmolive.

Louisa blinked, went to her purse at the counter, and began to write the check. The satyr laughed.

"Can't accept that," he said. "Rent's one hundred crowns a month or one thousand dollars cash. No checks."

"What's a crown?"

"It's, uh, a gold coin. About this big." He made a circle between his thumb and forefinger the size of a quarter.

"Where am I supposed to get those?" Louisa asked.

"Not my problem. You can have a couple of days, because I like you. After that, you're out on the street." He turned on his hooves and left before she could argue. "Plenty of Others looking for a place," he said over his shoulder. Something in the way he said the word made it clear that *Others* was what they called themselves.

She thought about robbing a bank or maybe the museum. In her imagination, banks were full of gold bars, but that couldn't be true, could it? She remembered reading that the gold standard had gone out years ago and there was hardly any gold in the money system at all.

She found a rare coins dealer on Milwaukee. The proprietor was human — tall, thin, with graying hair. He shook his head sadly at her before she even spoke.

"I've traded away everything even *resembling* gold," he said.

"To who?" she asked. "People like me?"

He laughed. "No, no. Them. The Others. I've gotten such marvelous things in return. Do you need a singing sword? Or a kite that can fly when there is no wind?"

"Could I pay my rent with any of those?" she asked. He shrugged.

"Why are you still here?" she asked. Speaking at all felt like a talent that had grown rusty with disuse.

He looked surprised at the question. "Business is better than ever," he said. "Sorry I couldn't help you." With that, he disappeared into his back room. She browsed the displays, hoping he had overlooked something gold, but he had not.

What else could she do? That night she packed all of her belongings, starting with the books.

In the morning she bought a train ticket to the suburbs from the automated ticket machine, which luckily still accepted her debit card. She took only a suitcase with her for now. She would send for her things later. Somehow. Surprisingly, the train was on time. It even had passengers. A few looked somewhat human. They all wore business dress, and when the train stopped, they hurried off and into the street like any other group of commuters. The only difference was that they were smiling. Louisa shivered.

Annabelle's house had been painted, and the doors had new locks. The yard had been mowed. The doghouse out back was gone. A square patch of dead earth was the only sign that it had ever been there. It was the patch that convinced Louisa she hadn't somehow come to the wrong home, gotten off at the wrong stop and wandered confused in a foreign neighborhood that looked just enough like her sister's to stretch the deception.

She entered the yard, climbed the handful of steps, and rang the doorbell.

A moment later it opened. A woman wearing a blue dress and a yellow apron tied around her waist answered. Giant swan's wings folded away as she dusted her hands off on the apron.

"Yes? Can I help you?"

"Who are you? This is my sister's home."

The swan woman's eyes softened. "Poor thing, left behind? What a shame. I'm sorry, but this is not your sister's home anymore. My mate and I paid for it fairly."

"I don't believe you," Louisa says, raising her voice. "You have to get out!"

The soft gaze hardened and the woman hissed. "Take it up with our attorneys at Dewey, Putnam, and Low."

The words came as a blow to her, and Louisa turned and walked away in a daze. So now she knew whom the law firm had been working for and who had been purchasing the abandoned property all along. The strange family living inside Anna's home weren't squatters. They had paid for it. They had paid for everything in equal trade. One world for another, and more.

She took the next train back to the city, fuming. If anyone still worked for Dewey, Putnam, and Low, they would answer her questions, or she would burn the place to the ground.

Yellow light spilled out into the darkened hallway of the law firm from a single office. Louisa had been surprised that her keys still worked, but after all, what would anyone want with the contents of the last working human law firm in the city?

Inside was the young man who had given her directions on her first day. He looked as impossibly tired as before, but he still smiled at her when she stood in the doorway.

"I don't suppose you've come back to help with the filing," he said.

She shook her head. The anger had burned up on the long ride here. She bit her lip to keep from crying again; she had cried entirely too much recently.

"Too bad." He sighed. "Nobody has been answering my classified ads lately. You know, I think you're the only human I've seen this week. Sometimes, with the Others, it can be hard to tell, though."

"Which one are you?" she asked. The sting had returned to her tone, and she was thankful.

"I'm Langford Putnam, but I wasn't even a junior partner yet. My father was Howard Putnam. That's his name on the masthead," he said. "So what can I do for you?"

"You helped a family of Others take my sister's home."

"We do a lot of that. Where?"

She gave him the address.

He began to poke and prod the stacks, lifting an edge here and there. He finally pulled one thick folder out of the middle of a pile. "Ah, here we go." The rest of the paperwork toppled to the floor, scattering. He paid it no mind.

He opened the folder and began to read, muttering to himself. "Did your sister have a will?"

Louisa shook her head. "Not that I know of."

"Too bad," he said. "She might have left you the property in that, and it would give us some leverage. Unfortunately, the couple that moved in there have a legally binding contract transferring ownership. Signed by your sister, even."

"They do?" She blinked. "How is that possible?"

Langford Putnam shrugged. "How is any of this possible? You could probably challenge it in court, but who knows who or what you would get for a judge."

"Are you helping me?" she asked.

"Of course I am. There aren't a lot of us left. We should probably stick together," he said, smiling that smile that made her stomach twist into knots.

"Isn't that a conflict of interest?"

He shrugged again. "The Others have settled in enough that I think they only keep me employed as a novelty. I'm not sure they would care."

"Why are *you* still here?" she asked. The boldness from before was slipping away. She did her best to cling to it.

"I could ask you the same question," he said, grinning, and her resolve crumbled. Louisa sobbed.

He jumped up from his chair, knocking over further paperwork, and put an arm around her shoulder, ushering her to his spare chair. He kicked off another stack and helped her sit.

"Hey, sorry, touched a nerve, huh?"

"All my life! All my life I've read stories about fantasy worlds. I used to *dream* about being whisked away to my real parents, to where I *really* belonged." Langford offered a tissue, and she daubed at her tears with it. "When the rabbit holes opened, I thought it was only a matter of time. I looked everywhere, but I couldn't find *mine.*"

She shouted it, didn't care who heard her now: "IT'S! NOT! FAIR!"

He nodded, let her cry for a moment, and then said quietly, "I bet that made you feel like a real Susan Pevensie."

"Exactly! What did I do to deserve being left behind? At first it was about escape. It's all I ever dreamed about, you know? But now it's about—"

"Feeling abandoned."

"Yes."

"First of all, I don't think you ever did anything wrong! It's actually probably quite the opposite. Working with the Others, I've picked up hints here and there about how it all works. Nothing concrete, but what if you've got it all backward?"

She sniffed. "What do you mean?"

"First of all, you're not the only one left. I'm here. So you're not alone. The thing is, the rabbit holes are tailor-made for each person, right? The perfect escape. But have you wondered, with all those stories you've read since you were a kid, exactly what your rabbit hole would look like?"

"Of course," she snapped. "It would be beautiful. Full of danger and adventure. I would be needed, needed really for the first time since my mother . . . well, since a long time ago. I would be *important*."

"Would you be the queen?"

"At least! Or an empress."

"Of what?"

She paused. "Of everything?"

"Where are the specifics? Are we talking a standard European fantasy world with dragons and all that? Miévillian weird city? Satirical rabbits and playing cards?"

She said nothing. When she tried to picture her perfect rabbit hole, all she had was a feeling.

Langford continued: "You've traveled to a thousand worlds in your books. Think about how much you've seen."

She frowned. "You think that no *one* rabbit hole world would satisfy me?"

He nodded furiously. "That's exactly it! How do you tailor the perfect escape for a serial escapist? It can't be done. Just about anything would have bored you eventually. Mine sure bored the hell out of *me*."

"Yours? You had a rabbit hole?" she asked.

"I still do." He pulled a watch on a long silver chain from his pocket and opened it. Dazzling light spilled from the clock face, and birds sang inside.

"I did the save-the-world thing, and it was *easy*. What's going on

back here is a lot more interesting. So I came back. I visit sometimes when I need to relax." He closed the watch face, and the
light vanished. "I may have read a little too much myself. When I
was younger."

"You can come and go?"

He nodded. "They're rabbit holes, not prisons. It's not a matter of 'can' so much as a matter of 'want.' Heck, I can even take
visitors if . . ." He blushed. "Sorry, I probably sound like I'm brag-
ging."

Louisa shook her head. "It's okay . . ."

"My guess is, whatever powers are behind the Others and all of
this, they knew they couldn't tempt you. Not really."

He stood and went to the window, pulling open the shade, and
beckoned to Louisa. She joined him, looking out across the city.

Enormous, sinuous feathered shapes weaved between the buildings, some of which were crawling with stone-skinned workers re-
making skyscrapers into castlelike edifices. Ghostly ships drifted
on the lake, their shimmering sails iridescent in the fading sunlight. And below them, countless varied shapes moved in traffic,
armors, scales, and slick skins glinting under flickering streetlamps
and neon signs.

"I don't know," Langford said. "I've always loved this city, but
I spent the first half of my life wishing I could live anywhere else
at all. It took me some travel, extraordinary and mundane, and a
lot of thinking, but eventually I came to see its truth. This place is
home, and in its own way, it's—"

"Beautiful," she whispered. Could that be it? All this time, she
hadn't been looking at it right? Now that she was elevated above
her problems, literally, she could see the world for what it was
becoming—something stranger than whatever could be on the
other side of a single rabbit hole.

Why *would* she want to leave this?

"Thank you," she said.

"Don't thank me yet. I haven't even started to solve your housing problem."

"You'll help me? Why?"

"Secret reasons," he said with a sly smile.

That was a puzzling thread to unravel, but for now she was content to stare out at the city with renewed wonder. How had she
missed it? It was almost if *this* world was being made just for her. It

was beautiful; it was dangerous and probably full of adventure; and just maybe it needed *her*.

She rummaged through coat pockets, retrieved her notebook, and flipped past the lists of rabbit holes to a blank page.

"Can I borrow a pen?"

Langford fumbled in his pockets, then offered a nice heavy steel-capped pen.

"Those flying things? Would you call those dragons?"

Langford stared out the window for a moment, then said, "I can't think of a better word to describe them, can you?"

"I'll accept that challenge," Louisa said, and began a new list.

CATHERYNNE M. VALENTE

The Future Is Blue

FROM *Drowned Worlds*

1. Nihilist

MY NAME IS Tetley Abednego and I am the most hated girl in Garbagetown. I am nineteen years old. I live alone in Candle Hole, where I was born, and have no friends except for a deformed gannet bird I've named Grape Crush and a motherless elephant seal cub I've named Big Bargains, and also the hibiscus flower that has recently decided to grow out of my roof, but I haven't named it anything yet. I love encyclopedias, a cassette I found when I was eight that says *Madeline Brix's Superboss Mixtape '97* on it in very nice handwriting, plays by Mr. Shakespeare or Mr. Webster or Mr. Beckett, lipstick, Garbagetown, and my twin brother Maruchan. Maruchan is the only thing that loves me back, but he's my twin, so it doesn't really count. We couldn't stop loving each other any more than the sea could stop being so greedy and give us back China or drive-time radio or polar bears.

But he doesn't visit anymore.

When we were little, Maruchan and I always asked each other the same question before bed. Every night we crawled into the Us-Fort together—an impregnable stronghold of a bed which we had nailed up ourselves out of the carcasses of several hacked-apart bassinets, prams, and cradles. It took up the whole of our bedroom. No one could see us in there once we closed the porthole (a manhole cover I swiped from Scrapmetal Abbey stamped with stars, a crescent moon, and the magic words *New Orleans Water Meter*), and we felt certain no one could hear us either. We lay together under our canopy of moldy green lace and shredded buggy hoods and mobiles with only one shattered fairy fish remaining. Sometimes I asked first and sometimes he did, but we never gave the same answer twice.

"Maruchan, what do you want to be when you grow up?"

He would give it a serious think. Once, I remember, he whispered, "When I grow up I want to be the Thames!"

"Whatever for?" I giggled.

"Because the Thames got so big and so bossy and so strong that it ate London all up in one go! Nobody tells a Thames what to do or who to eat. A Thames tells *you*. Imagine having a whole city to eat and not having to share any! Also there were millions of eels in the Thames and I only get to eat eels at Easter, which isn't fair when I want to eat them all the time."

And he pretended to bite me and eat me all up. "Very well, you shall be the Thames and I shall be the Mississippi and together we shall eat up the whole world."

Then we'd go to sleep and dream the same dream. We always dreamed the same dreams, which was like living twice.

After that, whenever we were hungry, which was always all the time and forever, we'd say *We're bound for London-town!* until we drove our parents so mad that they forbade the word *London* in the house, but you can't forbid a word, so there.

Every morning I wake up to find words painted on my door like toadstools popping up in the night.

Today it says NIHILIST in big black letters. That's not so bad! It's almost sweet! Big Bargains flumps toward me on her fat seal-belly while I light the wicks on my beeswax door and we watch them burn together until the word melts away.

"I don't think I'm a nihilist, Big Bargains. Do you?"

She rolled over onto my matchbox stash so that I would rub her stomach. Rubbing a seal's stomach is the opposite of nihilism.

Yesterday an old man hobbled up over a ridge of rusted bicycles and punched me so hard he broke my nose. By law, I had to let him. I had to say, *Thank you, Grandfather, for my instruction*. I had to stand there and wait in case he wanted to do something else to me. Anything but kill me, those were his rights. But he didn't want more, he just wanted to cry and ask me why I did it and the law doesn't say I have to answer that, so I just stared at him until he went away. Once a gang of schoolgirls shaved off all my hair and wrote CUNT in blue marker on the back of my skull. *Thank you, sisters, for my instruction.* The schoolboys do worse. After graduation they come round and eat my food and hold me down and try to make me cry, which I never do. It's their rite of passage. *Thank you, brothers, for my instruction.*

But other than that, I'm really a very happy person! I'm awfully lucky when you think about it. Garbagetown is the most wonderful place anybody has ever lived in the history of the world, even if you count the pyramids and New York City and Camelot. I have Grape Crush and Big Bargains and my hibiscus flower and I can fish like I've got bait for a heart so I hardly ever go hungry and once I found a ruby ring *and* a New Mexico license plate inside a bluefin tuna. Everyone says they only hate me because I annihilated hope and butchered our future, but I know better, and anyway, it's a lie. Some people are just born to be despised. The Loathing of Tetley began small and grew bigger and bigger, like the Thames, until it swallowed me whole.

Maruchan and I were born fifty years after the Great Sorting, which is another lucky thing that's happened to me. After all, I could have been born a Fuckwit and gotten drowned with all the rest of them, or I could have grown up on a Misery Boat, sailing around hopelessly looking for land, or one of the first to realize people could live on a patch of garbage in the Pacific Ocean the size of the place that used to be called Texas, or I could have been a Sorter and spent my whole life moving rubbish from one end of the patch to the other so that a pile of crap could turn into a country and babies could be born in places like Candle Hole or Scrapmetal Abbey or Pill Hill or Toyside or Teagate.

Candle Hole is the most beautiful place in Garbagetown, which is the most beautiful place in the world. All the stubs of candles the Fuckwits threw out piled up into hills and mountains and caverns and dells, votive candles and taper candles and tea lights and birthday candles and big fat colorful pillar candles, stacked and somewhat melted into a great crumbling gorgeous warren of wicks and wax. All the houses are little cozy honeycombs melted into the hillside, with smooth round windows and low golden ceilings. At night, from far away, Candle Hole looks like a firefly palace. When the wind blows, it smells like cinnamon, and freesia, and cranberries, and lavender, and Fresh Linen Scent and New Car Smell.

2. The Terrible Power of Fuckwit Cake

Our parents' names are Life and Time. Time lay down on her Fresh
Linen Scent wax bed and I came out of her first, then Maruchan.
But even though I got here first, I came out blue as the ocean, not
breathing, with the umbilical cord wrapped round my neck and
Maruchan wailing, still squeezing onto my noose with his tiny fist,
like he was trying to get me free. Doctor Pimms unstrangled and
unblued me and put me in a Hawaiian Fantasies–scented wax hollow in our living room. I lay there alone, too startled by living to
cry, until the sun came up and Life and Time remembered I had
survived. Maruchan was so healthy and sweet-natured and strong,
and even though Garbagetown is the most beautiful place in the
world, many children don't live past a year or two. We don't even
get names until we turn ten. (Before that, we answer happily to
Girl or Boy or Child or Darling.) Better to focus on the one that
will grow up rather than get attached to the sickly poor beast who
hasn't got a chance.

I was born already a ghost. But I was a very noisy ghost. I
screamed and wept at all hours while Life and Time waited for
me to die. I only nursed when my brother was full, I only played
with toys he forgot, I only spoke after he had spoken. Maruchan
said his first word at the supper table: *please*. What a lovely, polite
word for a lovely, polite child! After they finished cooing over him,
I very calmly turned to my mother and said, *Mama, may I have a
scoop of mackerel roe? It is my favorite.* I thought they would be so
proud! After all, I made twelve more words than my brother. This
was my moment, the wonderful moment when they would realize
that they did love me and I wasn't going to die and I was special
and good. But everyone got very quiet. They were not happy that
the ghost could talk. I had been able to for ages, but everything in
my world said to wait for my brother before I could do anything at
all. *No, you may not have mackerel roe, because you are a deceitful wicked
little show-off child.*

When we turned ten, we went to fetch our names. This is just
the most terribly exciting thing for a Garbagetown kid. At ten, you
are a real person. At ten, people want to know you. At ten, you will
probably live for a good while yet. This is how you catch a name:
wake up to the fabulous new world of being ten and greet your

birthday Frankencake (a hodgepodge of well-preserved Fuckwit snack cakes filled with various creams and jellies). Choose a slice, with much fanfare. Inside, your adoring and/or neglectful mother will have hidden various small objects—an aluminum pull tab, a medicine bottle cap, a broken earring, a coffee bean, a wee striped capacitor, a tiny plastic rocking horse, maybe a postage stamp. Remove item from your mouth without cutting yourself or eating it. Now, walk in the direction of your prize. Toward Aluminumopolis or Pill Hill or Spanglestoke or Teagate or Electric City or Toyside or Lost Post Gulch. Walk and walk and walk. Never once brush yourself off or wash in the ocean, even after camping on a pile of magazines or wishbones or pregnancy tests or wrapping paper with glitter reindeer on it. Walk until nobody knows you. When, finally, a stranger hollers at you to get out of the way or go back where you came from or stop stealing the good rubbish, they will, without even realizing, call you by your true name, and you can begin to pick and stumble your way home.

My brother grabbed a chocolate snack cake with a curlicue of white icing on it. I chose a pink-and-red tigery-striped hunk of cake filled with gooshy creme de something. The sugar hit our brains like twin tsunamis. He spat out a little gold earring with the post broken off. I felt a smooth, hard gelcap lozenge in my mouth. Pill Hill it was then, and the great mountain of Fuckwit anxiety medication. But when I carefully pulled the thing out, it was a little beige capacitor with red stripes instead. Electric City! I'd never been half so far. Richies lived in Electric City. Richies and brightboys and dazzlegirls and kerosene kings. My brother was off in the opposite direction, toward Spanglestoke and the desert of engagement rings.

Maybe none of it would have happened if I'd gone to Spanglestoke for my name instead. If I'd never seen the gasoline gardens of Engine Row. If I'd gone home straightaway after finding my name. If I'd never met Goodnight Moon in the brambles of Hazmat Heath with all the garbage stars rotting gorgeously overhead. Such is the terrible power of Fuckwit Cake.

I walked cheerfully out of Candle Hole with my St. Oscar backpack strapped on tight and didn't look back once. Why should I? St. Oscar had my back. I'm not really that religious nowadays. But everyone's religious when they're ten. St. Oscar was a fuzzy green Fuckwit man who lived in a garbage can just like me, and frowned a lot just like me. He understood me and loved me and knew how to bring civilization out of trash, and I loved him back even though he was a Fuckwit. Nobody chooses how they get born. Not even Oscar.

So I scrambled up over the wax ridges of my home and into the world with Oscar on my back. The Matchbox Forest rose up around me: towers of EZ Strike matchbooks and boxes from impossible, magical places like the Coronado Hotel, Becky's Diner, the Fox and Hound Pub. Garbagetowners picked through heaps and cairns of blackened, used matchsticks looking for the precious ones that still had their red-and-blue heads intact. But I knew all those pickers. They couldn't give me a name. I waved at the hot-heads. I climbed up Flintwheel Hill, my feet slipping and sliding on the mountain of spent butane lighters, until I could see out over all of Garbagetown just as the broiling cough-drop-red sun was setting over Far Boozeaway, hitting the crystal bluffs of stock-piled whiskey and gin bottles and exploding into a billion billion rubies tumbling down into the hungry sea.

I sang a song from school to the sun and the matchsticks. It's an ask-and-answer song, so I had to sing both parts myself, which feels very odd when you have always had a twin to do the asking or the answering, but I didn't mind.

> Who liked it hot and hated snow?
> The Fuckwits did! The Fuckwits did!
> Who ate up every thing that grows?
> The Fuckwits did! The Fuckwits did!
> Who drowned the world in oceans blue?
> The Fuckwits did! The Fuckwits did!
> Who took the land from me and you?
> The Fuckwits did, we know it's true!
> Are you Fuckwits, children dear?
> We're GARBAGETOWNERS, free and clear!
> But who made the garbage, rich and rank?
> The Fuckwits did, and we give thanks.

The Lawn stretched out below me, full of the grass clippings and autumn leaves and fallen branches and banana peels and weeds and gnawed bones and eggshells of the fertile Fuckwit world, slowly turning into the gold of Garbagetown: soil. Real earth. Terra bloody firma. We can already grow rice in the dells.

And here and there big, blowsy flowers bang up out of the rot: hibiscus, African tulips, bitter gourds, a couple of purple lotuses floating in the damp mucky bits. I slept next to a blue-and-white orchid that looked like my brother's face.

"Orchid, what do you want to be when you grow up?" I whispered to it. In real life, it didn't say anything back. It just fluttered a little in the moonlight and the seawind. But when I got around to dreaming, I dreamed about the orchid, and it said: *a farm.*

3. Murdercunt

In Garbagetown, you think real hard about what you're gonna eat next, where the fresh water's at, and where you're gonna sleep. Once all that's settled you can whack your mind on nicer stuff, like gannets and elephant seals and what to write next on the Bitch of Candle Hole's door. (This morning I melted MURDERCUNT off the back wall of my house. Big Bargains flopped down next to me and watched the blocky red painted letters swirl and fade into the Buttercream Birthday Cake wax. Maybe I'll name my hibiscus flower Murdercunt. It has a nice big sound.)

When I remember hunting my name, I mostly remember the places I slept. It's a real dog to find good spots. Someplace sheltered from the wind, without too much seawater seep, where no one'll yell at you for wastreling on their patch or try to stick it in you in the middle of the night just because you're all alone and it looks like you probably don't have a knife.

I always have a knife.

So I slept with St. Oscar the Grouch for my pillow, in the shadow of a mountain of black chess pieces in Gamegrange, under a thicket of tabloids and *Wall Street Journals* and remaindered novels with their covers torn off in Bookbury, snuggled into a spaghetti pile of unspooled cassette ribbon on the outskirts of the Sound Downs, on the lee side of a little soggy Earl Grey hillock in Teagate. In the morning I sucked on a few of the teabags, and the dew on them tasted like the loveliest cuppa any Fuckwit ever poured his stupid self. I said my prayers on beds of old microwaves and moldy photographs of girls with perfect hair kissing at the camera. *St. Oscar, keep your mighty lid closed over me. Look grouchily but*

*kindly upon me and protect me as I travel through the infinite trashcan of
your world. Show me the beautiful usefulness of your Blessed Rubbish. Let
me not be Taken Out before I find my destiny.*

But my destiny didn't seem to want to find me. As far as I
walked, I still saw people I knew. Mr. Zhu raking his mushroom
garden, nestled in a windbreak of broken milk bottles. Miss Aman-
charia gave me one of the coconut crabs out of her nets, which was
very nice of her, but hardly a name. Even as far away as Teagate,
I saw Tropicana Sita welding a refrigerator door to a hull-metal
shack. She flipped up her mask and waved at me. Dammit! She
was Allsorts Sita's cousin, and Allsorts drank with my mother every
Thursday at the Black Wick.

By the time I walked out of Teagate I'd been gone eight days. I
was getting pretty ripe. Bits and pieces of Garbagetown were stuck
all over my clothes, but no tidying up. Them's the rules. I could
see the blue crackle of Electric City sparkling up out of the richie-
rich Coffee Bean 'Burbs. Teetering towers of batteries rose up like
desert hoodoo spires—AA, AAA, 12-volt, DD, car, solar, lithium,
anything you like. Parrots and pelicans screamed down the battery
canyons, their talons kicking off sprays of AAAs that tumbled down
the heights like rockslides. Sleepy banks of generators rumbled
pleasantly along a river of wires and extension cords and HDMI
cables. Fields of delicate light bulbs windchimed in the breeze.
Anything that had a working engine lived here. Anything that still
had *juice*. If Garbagetown had a heart, it was Electric City. Electric
City pumped power. Power and privilege.

In Electric City, the lights of the Fuckwit world were still on.

4. Goodnight Garbagetown

"Oi, Tetley! Fuck off back home to your darkhole! We're full up
on little cunts here!"

And that's how I got my name. Barely past the battery spires of
Electric City, a fat gas-huffing fucksack voltage jockey called me a
little cunt. But he also called me Tetley. He brayed it down from
a pyramid of telephones and his friends all laughed and drank
homebrew out of a glass jug and went back to not working. I
looked down—among the many scraps of rubbish clinging to my
shirt and pants and backpack and hair was a bright-blue teabag

wrapper with TETLEY CLASSIC BLEND BLACK TEA written on it in cheerful white letters, clinging to my chest.

I tried to feel the power of my new name. The *me*-ness of it. I tried to imagine my mother and father when they were young, waking up with some torn-out page of *Life* or *Time* magazine stuck to their rears, not even noticing until someone barked out their whole lives for a laugh. But I couldn't feel anything while the volt-humpers kept on staring at me like I was nothing but a used-up potato battery. I didn't even know then that the worst swear word in Electric City was *dark*. I didn't know they were waiting to see how mad I'd get 'cause they called my home a darkhole. I didn't care. They were wrong and stupid. Except for the hole part. Candle Hole never met a dark it couldn't burn down.

Maybe I should have gone home right then. I had my name! Time to hoof it back over the river and through the woods, girl. But I'd never seen Electric City and it was morning and if I stayed gone a while longer maybe they'd miss me. Maybe they'd worry. And maybe now they'd love me, now that I was a person with a name. Maybe I could even filch a couple of batteries or a cup of gasoline and turn up at my parents' door in turbo-powered triumph. I'd tell my brother all my adventures and he'd look at me like I was magic on a stick and everything would be good forever and ever amen.

So I wandered. I gawped. It was like being in school and learning the Fuckwit song, only I was walking around *inside* the Fuckwit song and it was all still happening right now everywhere. Electric City burbled and bubbled and clanged and belched and smoked just like the bad old world before it all turned blue. Everyone had such fine things! I saw a girl wearing a ballgown out of a fairy book, green and glitter and miles of ruffles, and she wasn't even *going* anywhere. She was just tending her gasoline garden out the back of her little cottage, which wasn't made out of candles or picture-books or cat-food cans but real cottage parts! Mostly doors and shutters and really rather a lot of windows, but they fit together like they never even needed the other parts of a house in the first place. And the girl in her greenglitter dress carried a big red watering can around her garden, sprinkling fuel stabilizer into her tidy rows of petrol barrels and gas cans with their graceful spouts pointed toward the sun. Why not wear that dress all the time? Just a wineglass full of what she was growing in her garden would buy almost anything else in Garbagetown. She smiled shyly at me. I hated her. And I wanted to be her.

By afternoon I was bound for London-town, so hungry I could've slurped up every eel the Thames ever had. There's no food lying around in Electric City. In Candle Hole I could've grabbed candy or a rice ball or jerky off any old midden heap. But here everybody owned their piece and kept it real neat, *mercilessly* neat, and they didn't share. I sat down on a rusty Toyota transmission and fished around in my backpack for crumbs. My engine sat on one side of a huge cyclone fence. I'd never seen one all put together before. Sure, you find torn-off shreds of wire fences, but this one was all grown up, with proper locks and chain wire all over it. It meant to Keep You Out. Inside, like hungry dogs, endless barrels and freezers and cylinders and vats went on and on, with angry writing on them that said HAZMAT or BIOHAZARD or RADIOACTIVE or WARNING or DANGER or CLASSIFIED.

"Got anything good in there?" said a boy's voice. I looked round and saw a kid my own age, with wavy black hair and big brown eyes and three little moles on his forehead. He was wearing the nicest clothes I ever saw on a boy—a blue suit that almost, *almost* fit him. With a *tie*.

"Naw," I answered. "Just a dry sweater, an empty can of Cheez Whiz, and *Madeline Brix's Superboss Mixtape '97*. It's my good-luck charm." I showed him my beloved mixtape. Madeline Brix made all the dots on her *i*'s into hearts. It was a totally Fuckwit thing to do and I loved her for it even though she was dead and didn't care if I loved her or not.

"*Cool,*" the boy said, and I could tell he meant it. He didn't even call me a little cunt or anything. He pushed his thick hair out of his face. "Listen, you really shouldn't be here. No one's gonna say anything because you're not Electrified, but it's so completely dangerous. They put all that stuff in one place so it couldn't get out and hurt anyone."

"Electrified?"

"One of us. Local." He had the decency to look embarrassed. "Anyway, I saw you and I thought that if some crazy darkgirl is gonna have a picnic on Hazmat Heath, I could at least help her not die while she's doing it."

The boy held out his hand. He was holding a gas mask. He

showed me how to fasten it under my hair. The sun started to set rosily behind a tangled briar of motherboards. Everything turned pink and gold and slow and sleepy. I climbed down from my engine tuffet and lay under the fence next to the boy in the suit. He'd brought a mask for himself too. We looked at each other through the eyeholes.

"My name's Goodnight Moon," he said.

"Mine's . . ." And I did feel my new name swirling up inside me then, like good tea, like cream and sugar cubes, like the most essential me. "Tetley."

"I'm sorry I called you a darkgirl, Tetley."

"Why?"

"It's not a nice thing to call someone."

"I like it. It sounds pretty."

"It isn't. I promise. Do you forgive me?"

I tugged on the hose of my gas mask. The air coming through tasted like nickels. "Sure. I'm aces at forgiving. Been practicing all my life. Besides . . ." My turn to go red in the face. "At the Black Wick they'd probably call you a brightboy, and that's not as pretty as it sounds either."

Goodnight Moon's brown eyes stared out at me from behind thick glass. It was the closest I'd ever been to a boy who wasn't my twin. Goodnight Moon didn't feel like a twin. He felt like the opposite of a twin. We never shared a womb, but on the other end of it all, we might still share a grave. His tie was burgundy with green swirls in it. He hadn't tied it very well, so I could see the skin of his throat, which was very clean and probably very soft.

"Hey," he said, "do you want to hear your tape?"

"What do you mean *hear* it? It's not for hearing, it's for luck."

Goodnight Moon laughed. His laugh burst all over me like butterfly bombs. He reached into his suit jacket and pulled out a thick black rectangle. I handed him *Madeline Brix's Superboss Mixtape '97* and he hit a button on the side of the rectangle. It popped open; Goodnight Moon slotted in my tape and handed me one end of a long wire.

"Put it in your ear," he said, and I did.

A man's voice filled up my head from my jawbone up to the plates of my skull. The most beautiful and saddest voice that ever was. A voice like Candle Hole all lit up at twilight. A voice like the

whole old world calling up from the bottom of the sea. The man
on Madeline Brix's tape was saying he was happy, and he hoped I
was happy too.

Goodnight Moon reached out to hold my hand just as the sky
went black and starry. I was crying. He was too. Our tears dripped
out of our gas masks onto the rusty road of Electric City.

When the tape ended, I dug in my backpack for a match and a
stump of candle: dark red, Holiday Memories scent. I lit it at the
same moment that Goodnight Moon pulled a little flashlight out
of his pocket and turned it on. We held our glowings between us.
We were the same.

5. Brightbitch

Allsorts Sita came to visit me today. Clicked my knocker early in
the morning, early enough that I could be sure she'd never slept
in the first place. I opened for her, as I am required to do. She
looked up at me with eyes like bullet holes, leaning on my waxy
hinges, against the T in BRIGHTBITCH, thoughtfully scrawled
in what appeared to be human shit across the front of my hut.
BRIGHTBITCH smelled, but Allsorts Sita smelled worse. Her
breath punched me in the nose before she did. I got a lungful
of what Diet Sprite down at the Black Wick optimistically called
"cognac": the thick pinkish booze you could get by extracting the
fragrance oil and preservatives out of candles and mixing it with
wood alcohol the kids over in Furnitureford boiled out of dining
sets and china cabinets. Smells like flowers vomited all over a New
Car and then killed a badger in the back seat. Allsorts Sita looked
like she'd drunk so much cognac you could light one strand of her
hair and she'd burn for eight days.

"You fucking whore," she slurred.

"Thank you, Auntie, for my instruction," I answered quietly.

I have a place I go to in my mind when I have visitors who aren't
seals or gannet birds or hibiscus flowers. A little house made all
of doors and windows, where I wear a greenglitter dress every day
and water my gas-can garden and read by electric light.

"I hate you. I hate you. How could you do it? We raised you and
fed you and this is how you repay it all. You ungrateful bitch."

"Thank you, Auntie, for my instruction."

In my head I ran my fingers along a cyclone fence and all the barrels on the other side read LIFE and LOVE and FORGIVENESS and UNDERSTANDING.

"You've killed us all," Allsorts Sita moaned. She puked up magenta cognac on my stoop. When she was done puking she hit me over and over with closed fists. It didn't hurt too much. Allsorts is a small woman. But it hurt when she clawed my face and my breasts with her fingernails. Blood came up like wax spilling and when she finished she passed out cold, halfway in my house, halfway out.

"Thank you, Auntie, for my instruction," I said to her sleeping body. My blood dripped onto her, but in my head I was lying on my roof made of two big church doors in a gas mask listening to a man sing to me that he's never done bad things and he hopes I'm happy, he hopes I'm happy, he hopes I'm happy.

Big Bargains moaned mournfully and the lovely roof melted away like words on a door. My elephant seal friend flopped and fretted. When they've gone for my face she can't quite recognize me and it troubles her seal-soul something awful. Grape Crush, my gannet bird, never worries about silly things like facial wounds. He just brings me fish and pretty rocks. When I found him, he had a plastic six-pack round his neck with one can still stuck in the thing, dragging along behind him like a ball and chain. Big Bargains was choking on an ad insert. She'd probably smelled some ancient fish and chips grease lurking in the headlines. They only love me because I saved them. That doesn't always work. I saved everyone else too, and all I got back was blood and shit and loneliness.

6. *Revlon Super Lustrous 919: Red Ruin*

I went home with my new name fastened on tight. Darkgirls can't stay in Electric City. Can't live there unless you're born there, and I was only ten anyway. Goodnight Moon kissed me before I left. He still had his gas mask on so mainly our breathing hoses wound around each other like gentle elephants, but I still call it a kiss. He smelled like scorched ozone and metal and paraffin and hope.

A few months later, Electric City put up a fence around the whole place. Hung up an old rusty shop sign that said EXCUSE

OUR MESS WHILE WE RENOVATE. No one could go in or out except to trade, and that had to get itself done on the dark side of the fence.

My mother and father didn't start loving me when I got back, even though I brought six AA batteries out of the back of Goodnight Moon's tape player. My brother had got a ramen flavor packet stuck in his hair somewhere outside the Grocery Isle and was every inch of him Maruchan. A few years later I heard Life and Time telling some cousin how their marvelous and industrious and thoughtful boy had gone out in search of a name and brought back six silver batteries, enough to power anything they could dream of. What a child! What a son! So fuck them, I guess.

But Maruchan did bring something back. It just wasn't for our parents. When we crawled into the Us-Fort that first night back, we lay uncomfortably against each other. We were the same, but we weren't. We'd had separate adventures for the first time, and Maruchan could never understand why I wanted to sleep with a gas mask on now.

"Tetley, what do you want to be when you grow up?" Maruchan whispered in the dark of our pram-maze.

"Electrified," I whispered back. "What do you want to be?"

"Safe," he said. Things had happened to Maruchan too, and I couldn't share them any more than he could hear Madeline Brix's songs.

My twin pulled something out of his pocket and pushed it into my hand till my fingers closed round it reflexively. It was hard and plastic and warm.

"I love you, Tetley. Happy birthday."

I opened my fist. Maruchan had stolen lipstick for me. Revlon Super Lustrous 919: Red Ruin, worn almost all the way down to the nub by some dead woman's lips.

After that, a lot of years went by but they weren't anything special.

7. If God Turned Up for Supper

I was seventeen years old when Brighton Pier came to Garbagetown. I was tall and my hair was the color of an oil spill; I sang pretty good and did figures in my head and I could make a candle out of damn near anything. People wanted to marry me here and there, but I didn't want to marry them back so they thought I was stuck up. Who wouldn't want to get hitched to handsome Candyland Ocampo and ditch Candle Hole for a clean, fresh life in Soapthorpe, where bubbles popped all day long like diamonds in your hair? Well, I didn't, because he had never kissed me with a gas mask on and he smelled like pine-fresh cleaning solutions and not like scorched ozone at all.

Life and Time turned into little kids right in front of us. They giggled and whispered and Mum washed her hair in the sea about nine times and then soaked it in oil until it shone. Papa tucked a candle stump that had melted just right and looked like a perfect rose into her big no-fancy hairdo and then, like it was a completely normal thing to do, put on a cloak sewn out of about a hundred different neckties. They looked like a prince and a princess.

"Brighton Pier came last when I was a girl, before I even had my name," Time told us, still giggling and blushing like she wasn't anyone's mother. "It's the most wonderful thing that can ever happen in the world."

"If God turned up for supper and brought all the dry land back for dessert, it wouldn't be half as good as one day on Brighton Pier," Life crowed. He picked me up in his arms and twirled me around in the air. He'd never done that before, not once, and he had his heart strapped on so tight he didn't even stop and realize what he'd done and go vacant-eyed and find something else to look at for a long while. He just squeezed me and kissed me like I came from somewhere, and I didn't know what the hell a Brighton Pier was but I loved it already.

"What is it? What is it?" Maruchan and I squealed, because you can catch happiness like a plague.

"It's better the first time if you don't know," Mum assured us. "It's meant to dock in Electric City on Friday."

"So it's a ship, then?" Maruchan said. But Papa just twinkled his eyes at us and put his finger over his lips to keep the secret in.

The Pier meant to dock in Electric City. My heart fell into my stomach, got all digested up, and sizzled out into the rest of me all at once. Of course, of course it would, Electric City had the best docks, the sturdiest, the prettiest. But it seemed to me like life was happening to me on purpose, and Electric City couldn't keep a darkgirl out anymore. They had to share like the rest of us.

"What do you want to be when you grow up, Maruchan?" I said to my twin in the dark the night before we set off to see what was better than God. Maruchan's eyes gleamed with the Christmas thrill of it all.

"Brighton Pier," he whispered.

"Me too," I sighed, and we both dreamed we were beautiful Fuckwits running through a forest of real pines, laughing and stopping to eat apples and running again and only right before we woke up did we notice that something was chasing us, something huge and electric and bound for London-town.

8. Citizens of Mutation Nation

I looked for Goodnight Moon everywhere from the moment we crossed into Electric City. The fence had gone and Garbagetown poured in and nothing was different than it had been when I got my name off the battery spires, even though the sign had said for so long that Electric City was renovating. I played a terrible game with every person that shoved past, every face in a window, every shadow juddering down an alley, and the game was *Are you him?* But I lost all the hands. The only time I stopped playing was when I first saw Brighton Pier.

I couldn't get my eyes around it. It was a terrible, gorgeous whale of light and colors and music and otherness. All along a boardwalk jugglers danced and singers sang and horns horned and accordions squeezed and under it all some demonic engine screamed and wheezed. Great glass domes and towers and flags and tents glowed in the sunset, but Brighton Pier made the sunset look plain-faced and unlovable. A huge wheel full of pink and emerald electric lights turned slowly in the warm wind but went nowhere. People leaped and turned somersaults and stood on each other's shoulders and they all wore such soft, vivid costumes, like they'd all been cut out of a picturebook too fine for anyone like me to read. The tumblers lashed the pier to the Electric City docks and cut the engines, and after that it was nothing but music so thick and good you could eat it out of the air.

Life and Time hugged Maruchan and cheered with the rest of Garbagetown. Tears ran down their faces. Everyone's faces.

"When the ice melted and the rivers revolted and the Fuckwit world went under the seas," Papa whispered through his weeping, "a great mob hacked Brighton Pier off of Brighton and strapped engines to it and set sail across the blue. They've been going ever since. They go around the world and around again, to the places where there's still people, and trade their beauty for food and fuel. There's a place on Brighton Pier where if you look just right, it's like nothing ever drowned."

A beautiful man wearing a hat of every color and several bells stepped up on a pedestal and held a long pale cone to his mouth. The mayor of Electric City embraced him with two meaty arms and asked his terrible, stupid, unforgivable question: "Have you seen dry land?"

And the beautiful man answered him: "With my own eyes."

A roar went up like angels dying. I covered my ears. The mayor covered his mouth with his hands, speechless, weeping. The beautiful man patted him awkwardly on the back. Then he turned to us.

"Hello, Garbagetown!" he cried out, and his voice sounded like everyone's most secret heart.

We screamed so loud every bird in Garbagetown fled to the heavens and we clapped like mad and some people fell onto the ground and buried their face in old batteries.

"My name is Emperor William Shakespeare the Eleventh and I am the Master of Brighton Pier! We will be performing *Twelfth Night* in the great stage tonight at seven o'clock, followed by *The Duchess of Malfi* at ten (which has werewolves) and a midnight acrobatic display! Come one, come all! Let Madame Limelight tell your FORTUNE! TEST your strength with the Hammer of the Witches! SEE the wonders of the Fuckwit World in our Memory Palace! Get letters and news from the LAST HUMAN OUTPOSTS around the globe! GASP at the citizens of Mutation Nation in the Freak Tent! Sample a FULL MINUTE of real television, still high-definition after all these years! Concerts begin in the Crystal Courtyard in fifteen minutes! Our Peep Shows feature only the FINEST actresses reading aloud from GENUINE Fuckwit historical records! Garbagetown, we are here to DAZZLE you!"

A groan went up from the crowds like each Garbagetowner was just then bedding their own great lost love and they heaved toward the lights, the colors, the horns and the voices, the silk and the electricity and the life floating down there, knotted to the edge of our little pile of trash.

Someone grabbed my hand and held me back while my parents, my twin, my world streamed away from me down to the Pier. No one looked back.

"Are you her?" said Goodnight Moon. He looked longer and leaner but not really older. He had on his tie.

"Yes," I said, and nothing was different than it had been when I got my name except now neither of us had masks and our kisses weren't like gentle elephants but like a boy and a girl and I forgot all about my strength and my fortune and the wonderful wheel of light turning around and around and going nowhere.

9. Terrorwhore

Actors are liars. Writers too. The whole lot of them, even the horn players and the fortunetellers and the freaks and the strongmen. Even the ladies with rings in their noses and high heels on their feet playing violins all along the pier, and the lie they are all singing and dancing and saying is, *We can get the old world back again.*

My door said TERRORWHORE this morning. I looked after my potato plants and my hibiscus and thought about whether or not I would ever get to have sex again. Seemed unlikely. Big Bargains concurred.

Goodnight Moon and I lost our virginities in the Peep Show tent while a lady in green fishnet stockings and a lavender garter read to us from the dinner menu of the Dorchester Hotel circa 2005.

"Whole Berkshire roasted chicken stuffed with black truffles, walnuts, duck confit, and dauphinoise potatoes," the lady purred. Goodnight Moon devoured my throat with kisses, bites, need. "Drizzled with a balsamic reduction and rosemary honey."

"What's honey?" I gasped. We could see her but she couldn't see us, which was for the best. The glass in the window only went one way.

"Beats me, kid," she shrugged, recrossing her legs the other way. "Something you drizzle." She went on. "Sticky toffee pudding with lashings of cream and salted caramel, passionfruit soufflé topped with orbs of pistachio ice cream . . ."

Goodnight Moon smelled just as I remembered. Scorched ozone and metal and paraffin and hope, and when he was inside me it was like hearing my name for the first time. I couldn't escape the *me*-ness of it, the *us*-ness of it, the sound and the shape of ourselves turning into our future.

"I can't believe you're here," he whispered into my breast. "I can't believe this is us."

The lady's voice drifted over my head. "Lamb cutlets on a bed of spiced butternut squash, wilted greens, and delicate hand-harvested mushrooms served with goat cheese in clouds of pastry . . ."

Goodnight Moon kissed my hair, my ears, my eyelids. "And now that the land's come back, Electric City's gonna save us all. We can go home together, you and me, and build a house and we'll have a candle in every window so you always feel at home . . ."

The Dorchester dinner menu stopped abruptly. The lady dropped to her fishnetted knees and peered at us through the glass, her brilliant glossy red hair tumbling down, her spangled eyes searching for us beyond the glass.

"Whoa, sweetie, slow down," she said. "You're liable to scare a girl off that way."

All I could see in the world was Goodnight Moon's brown eyes and the sweat drying on his brown chest. Brown like the earth and all its promises. "I don't care," he said. "You scared, Tetley?" I shook my head. "Nothing can scare us now. Emperor Shakespeare said he's seen land, real dry land, and we have a plan and we're gonna get everything back again and be fat happy Fuckwits like we were always supposed to be."

The Peep Show girl's glittering eyes filled up with tears. She put her hand on the glass. "Oh . . . oh, baby . . . that's just something we say. We always say it. To everyone. It's our best show. Gives people hope, you know? But there's nothing out there, sugar. Nothing but ocean and more ocean and a handful of drifty lifeboat cities like yours circling the world like horses on a broken-down carousel. Nothing but blue."

10. We Are So Lucky

It would be nice for me if you could just say you understand. I want to hear that just once. Goodnight Moon didn't. He didn't believe her and he didn't believe me and he sold me out in the end in spite of gas masks and kissing and Madeline Brix and the man crooning in our ears that he was happy, because all he could hear was Emperor William Shakespeare the Eleventh singing out his big lie. *Resurrection! Redemption! Revivification! Land Ho!*

"No, because, see," my sweetheart wept on the boardwalk while the wheel spun dizzily behind his head like an electric candy crown, "we have a plan. We've worked so hard. It *has* to happen. The mayor said as soon as we had news of dry land, the minute we knew, we'd turn it on and we'd get there first and the continents would be ours, Garbagetowners, we'd inherit the Earth. He's gonna tell everyone when the Pier leaves. At the farewell party."

"Turn what on?"

Resurrection. Redemption. Renovation. All those years behind the fence Electric City had been so busy. Disassembling all those engines they hoarded so they could make a bigger one, the biggest one. Pooling fuel in great vast stills. Practicing ignition sequences. Carving up a countryside they'd never even seen between the brightboys and brightgirls, and we could have some too if we were good.

"You want to turn Garbagetown into a Misery Boat," I told him. "So we can just steam on ahead into nothing and go mad and use up all the gas and batteries that could keep us happy in mixtapes for another century here in one hot minute."

"The Emperor said . . ."

"He said his name was Duke Orsino of Illyria too. And then Roderigo when they did the werewolf play. Do you believe that? If they'd found land, don't you think they'd have stayed there?"

But he couldn't hear me. Neither could Maruchan when I tried to tell him the truth in the Peep Show. All they could see was green. Green leafy trees and green grass and green ivy in some park that was lying at the bottom of the sea. We dreamed different dreams now, my brother and I, and all my dreams were burning.

Say you understand. I had to. I'm not a nihilist or a murdercunt or a terrorwhore. They were gonna use up every last drop of Garbagetown's power to go nowhere and do nothing, and instead of measuring out teaspoons of good honest gas, so that it lasts and we last all together, no single thing on the patch would ever turn on again, and we'd go dark, *really* dark, forever. Dark like the bottom of a hole. They had no right. *They* don't understand. This is *it*. This is the future. Garbagetown and the sea. We can't go back, not ever, not even for a minute. We are so lucky. Life is so good. We're going on and being alive and being shitty sometimes and lovely sometimes just the same as we always have, and only a Fuckwit couldn't see that.

I waited until Brighton Pier cast off, headed to the next rickety harbor of floating foolboats, filled with players and horns and glittering wheels and Dorchester menus and fresh mountains of letters we wouldn't read the answers to for another twenty years. I waited until everyone was sleeping so nobody would get hurt except the awful engine growling and panting to deliver us into the dark salt nothing of an empty hellpromise.

It isn't hard to build a bomb in Electric City. It's all just lying around behind that fence where a boy held my hand for the first time. All you need is a match.

11. *What You Came For*

It's such a beautiful day out. My hibiscus is just gigantic, red as the hair on a peep-show dancer. If you want to wait, Big Bargains will be round later for her afternoon nap. Grape Crush usually brings a herring by in the evening. But I understand if you've got other places to be.

It's okay. You can hit me now. If you want to. It's what you came for. I barely feel it anymore.

Thank you for my instruction.

A. MERC RUSTAD

This Is Not a Wardrobe Door

FROM *Fireside Magazine*

DEAR GATEKEEPER,

Hi my name is Ellie and I'm six years old and my closet door is broken. My best friend Zera lives in your world and I visited her all the time, and sometimes I got older but turned six again when I came back, but that's okay. Can you please fix the door so I can play with Zera?

Love,

Ellie

Zera packs lightly for her journey: rose-petal rope and dewdrop boots, a jacket spun from bee song and buttoned with industrial-strength cricket clicks. She secures her belt (spun from the cloud memories, of course) and picks up her satchel. It has food for her and oil for Misu.

Her best friend is missing and she must find out why.

Misu, the palm-sized mechanical microraptor, perches on her seaweed braids, its glossy raindrop-colored feathers ruffled in concern.

Misu says, *But what if the door is locked?*

Zera smiles. "I'll find a key."

But secretly she's worried. What if there isn't one?

Dear Gatekeeper,

I hope you got my last couple letters. I haven't heard back from you yet, and the closet door still doesn't work. Mommy says I'm wasting paper when I use too much crayon, so I'm using markers this time. Is Zera okay? Tell her I miss playing with the sea monsters and flying to the moon on the dragons most of all.

Please open the door again.

—Ellie, age 7

Zera leaves the treehouse and climbs up the one thousand five hundred three rungs of the polka-dot ladder, each step a perfect note in a symphony. When she reaches the falcon aerie above, she bows to the Falcon Queen and asks if she may have a ride to the Land of Doors.

The Falcon Queen tilts her magnificent head. "Have you not heard?" the queen asks in a voice like spring lightning and winter calm. "All the doors have gone quiet. There is a disease rotting wood and rusting hinges, and no one can find a cure."

Misu shivers on Zera's shoulder. *It is like the dreams,* Misu says. *When everything is silent.*

Zera frowns. "Hasn't the empress sent scientists to investigate?"

The Falcon Queen nods. "They haven't returned. I dare not send my people into the cursed air until we know what is happening."

Zera squares her shoulders. She needs answers, and quickly. Time passes differently (faster) on Ellie's home planet, because their worlds are so far apart, and a lag develops in the space-time continuum.

"Then I will speak to the Forgotten Book," Zera says, hiding the tremor in her voice.

The falcons ruffle their feathers in anxiety. Not even the empress sends envoys without the Forgotten Book's approval.

"You are always brave," says the Falcon Queen. "Very well, then, I will take you as far as the Island of Stars."

Hi Gatekeeper,

Are you even there? It's been almost a year for me and still nothing. Did the ice elves get you? I hope not. Zera and I trapped them in the core of the passing comet so they'd go away, but you never know.

Why can't I get through anymore? I'm not too old, I promise. That was those Narnia books that had that rule (and they were stupid, we read them in class).

Please say something,
—Ellie, age 8

Zera hops off the Falcon Queen's back and looks at the Island of
Stars. It glows from the dim silver bubbles that thicken in the air
like tapioca pudding.

She sets off through the jungle of broken wire bed frames and
abandoned armchairs; she steps around rusting toys and rotting
books. There are memories curled everywhere—sad and lonely
things, falling to pieces at the seams.

She looks around in horror. "What happened?"

Misu points with a tiny claw. *Look.*

In the middle of the island stands the Forgotten Book, its glass
case shattered and anger radiating off its pages.

LEAVE, says the book. BEFORE MY CURSE DEVOURS YOU.

Gatekeeper,
    I tried to tell Mom we can't move, but she won't listen. So now
I'm three hundred miles away and I don't know anybody and all I
want to do is scream and punch things, but I don't want Mom to
get upset. This isn't the same closet door. Zera explained that the
physical location wasn't as fixed as normal doors in our world, but
I'm still freaking out.

    I found my other letters. Stacks of notebook paper scribbled
in crayon and marker and fingerpaint—all stacked in a box in
Mom's bedroom.

    "What are you doing with this?" I screamed at Mom, and she
had tears in her eyes. "Why did you take the letters? They were
supposed to get to Zera!"

    Mom said she was sorry, she didn't want to tell me to stop since
it seemed so important, but she kept finding them in her closet.

    I said I'd never put them there, but she didn't believe me.

    "We can't go there again," Mom said. "No one ever gets to go
back!" And she stomped out of the kitchen and into the rain.

    Has my mom been there? Why didn't she ever tell me? Why did
you banish her too?

    What did we do so wrong we can't come back?
    —Ellie

*

Zera's knees feel about to shatter.

"Why are you doing this?" Zera grips an old, warped rocking chair. "You've blacked out the Land of Doors, haven't you?"

YES, says the Book. ALL WHO GO THERE WILL SLEEP, UN-DREAMING, UNTIL THE END.

Zera blinks hard, her head dizzy from the pressure in the air. "You can't take away everyone's happiness like this."

NO? says the Book. WHY NOT? NO ONE EVER REMEMBERS US THERE. THEY FORGET AND GROW OLD AND ABANDON US.

"That's not true," Zera says. "Ellie remembers. There are others." Misu nods.

Zera pushes through the heavy air, reaching out a hand to the Book. "They tell stories of us there," Zera says, because Ellie used to bring stacks of novels with her instead of PBJ sandwiches in her backpack. "There are people who believe. But there won't be if we close all the doors. Stories in their world will dry up. We'll start to forget them too."

WE MEAN NOTHING TO THEM.

Zera shakes her head. "That's not true. I don't want my best friend to disappear forever."

Gatekeeper,

I don't know why I bother anymore. You're not listening. I don't even know if you exist.

It's been a while, huh? Life got busy for me. High school, mostly. Mom got a better job and now we won't have to move again. Also I met this awesome girl named LaShawna and we've been dating for a month. God, I'm so in love with her. She's funny and smart and tough and kind—and she really gets me.

Sometimes she reminds me of Zera.

I asked Mom why she kept my letters.

She didn't avoid me this time. "I had a door when I was younger," she said, and she looked so awfully sad. "I was your age. I met the person I wanted to stay with forever." She let out her breath in a whoosh. "But then the door just . . . it broke, or something. I tried dating here. Met your father, but it just wasn't the same. Then he ran off and it was like losing it all again."

I told LaShawna about Zera's world. She said she didn't want to talk about it. I think maybe she had a door too.

I was so angry growing up, feeling trapped. You know the best thing about Zera? She *got* me. I could be a girl, I could be a boy, and I could be neither—because that's how I feel a lot of the time. Shifting around between genders. I want that to be okay, but here? I don't know.

The thing is, I don't want to live in Zera's world forever. I love things here too. I want to be able to go back and forth and have friends everywhere, and date LaShawna and get my degree and just *live*.

This will be my last letter to you, Gatekeeper.

If there was one thing Zera and I learned, it's that you have to build your own doors sometimes.

So I'm going to make my own. I'll construct it out of salvaged lumber; I'll take a metalworking class and forge my own hinges. I'll paper it with all my letters and all my memories. I'll set it up somewhere safe, and here's the thing—I'll make sure it never locks.

My door will be open for anyone who needs it: my mom, LaShawna, myself.

—Ell

The Book is silent.

"Please," Zera says. "Remove the curse. Let us all try again."

And she lays her hand gently on the Forgotten Book and lets the Book see all the happy memories she shared with Ellie once, and how Ellie's mom Loraine once came here and met Vasha, who has waited by the door since the curse fell, and Misu, who befriended the lonely girl LaShawna and longs to see her again—and so many, many others that Zera has collected, her heart overfilled with joy and loss and grief and hope.

In return, she sees through space and time, right into Ell's world, where Ell has built a door and has her hand on the knob.

"Ell," Zera calls.

Ell looks up, eyes wide. "Zera?"

"Yes," Zera says, and knows her voice will sound dull behind the door. "I'm here."

Ell grins. "I can see your reflection in the door! Is that the Book with you?"

The Book trembles. SHE REMEMBERS.

Zera nods. The air is thinning, easing in her lungs. "I told you. Not everyone forgets."

I would like to see LaShawna again, says Misu.

VERY WELL, says the Book. THE CURSE WILL BE REMOVED.

Ell turns the handle.

Bright light beams into the Island of Stars, and Ell stands there in a doorway, arms spread wide. Zera leaps forward and hugs her best friend.

"You came back," Zera says.

"I brought some people with me too," Ell says, and waves behind her, where two other women wait.

Loraine steps through the light with tears in her eyes. "I never thought I could come back . . ."

Misu squeaks in delight and flies to LaShawna.

Zera smiles at her friends. Things will be all right.

"We have a lot of work to do to repair this place," Zera says. She clasps Ell's hands. "The curse is gone, but we have to fix the doors and wake the sleepers. Are you ready?"

Ell grins and waves her mom and girlfriend to join her. "Yes. Let's do this."

On the Fringes of the Fractal

FROM *2113: Stories Inspired by the Music of Rush*

I WAS WORKING the squirt station on the breakfast shift at Peevs Burgers when I learned that my best friend's life was over.

The squirt guns were connected by hoses to tanks, each tank containing a different slew formula. Orders appeared in lime-green letters on my screen, and I squirted accordingly. Two Sausage Peev Sandwiches took two squirts from the sausage slew gun. An order of Waffle Peev Sticks was three small dabs of waffle slew. The slew warmed and hardened on the congealer table, and because I'd paid attention during the twenty-minute training course and applied myself, I knew just when the slew was ready. I was a slew expert.

Sherman was the other squirter on duty that morning. The orders were coming in fast and he was already wheezing on account of his exercise-induced asthma. His raspy breaths interfered with my ability to concentrate. You really have to concentrate because after four hours of standing and squirting there's the danger of letting your mind wander, and once you do that you can lose control of the squirts and end up spraying food slew all over the kitchen like a fire hose.

"Wasted slew reflects badly on you," said one of the inspirational posters in the employee restroom.

"What's eating you, Sherman?" I asked, squirting eggs.

He squirted out twelve strips of bacon. "Nothing. Don't worry about it. Not your problem."

I'd known Sherman for a long time. We'd grown up as next-door neighbors, had gone to the same schools, had the same teachers. This year we were both taking Twenty-Five Places That Will Blow Your Mind (geography) and Six Equations You Won't Believe (precollege math) and You'll Have Itchy Eyes After Reading These Heartbreaking Stories (AP English). We did everything together, and even though he was a little higher stat than I was, he never made me feel weird about it.

"C'mon, Sherman. Don't just stand there squirting in silent pain. Tell your pal Deni what's wrong."

He wheezed a while longer, really laboring. Then, like a miserable little volcano, he let it out: "My family lost stat yesterday."

The cold hand of dread fondled my knee. "How much stat?"

"All of it. Every last little bit. We got zeroed out."

Startled, I impulse squirted and missed the congealer entirely. Biscuit slew landed on the floor.

"My mom lost her job," he explained. "And my dad gained nine pounds. My sister got more zits. The swimming pool water was yellow when the Stat Commission came to audit. It was a bunch of stuff. Just a perfect storm of bad stat presentation." He rubbed his forearm across his nose. "I might as well be dead."

I could only agree with him.

Stat was determined by a complicated algorithm that factored in wealth, race, genealogy, fat-to-muscle ratio, dentition, and dozens of other variables from femur length to facial symmetry to skull contours. It was determined by the attractiveness of one's house. The suitability of one's car. You could lose stat from a bad haircut. You could lose it by showing up to school with food slew on your blouse. I had done that once during freshman year and never gained it back.

Stat was the cornerstone of our great meritocracy.

In olden days, one of the worst punishments society could exact upon you was outlawing. It meant you were literally outside the law. You had no privileges, no protections, no rights. Anyone could just up and kill you without consequence. Being declared no-stat was a lot like that. Without stat, Sherman's family would lose everything. Their house. The right to wear current fashions. To see the latest movies. To vote. And I could lose stat of my own just by being friends with a no-stat person.

My heart felt like a clammy potato. What was happening to my friend was worse than death. It was erasure.

I scraped congealed slew off the congealer, dumped it into various containers, and sent it down the slew chute to the drive-thru window.

"I just don't know what to do," Sherman said, squirting and wheezing.

I felt something surging within me like high-pressure burger slew through a lunch rush gun. This was a new feeling. A powerful feeling. The feeling that I could do something to break the patterns of my life and take Sherman along with me. The feeling that I could make a difference.

I was such an idiot.

"I'll tell you what we're going to do," I declared. Sherman looked up from his station. Doubt and hope warred on his face. "We're going to save your life."

The next morning the alarm nagged me awake before dawn. It was early enough to hear the drones arrive, their rotors hurling morning birds from their paths. Delivery portals in the rooftops opened like flower petals and the drones dropped statpacks from their bomb bays. All over the division, people rushed to see what they'd been supplied with. I was usually in no hurry, but I needed to get an early start, so I gathered my share of my family's package and brought it to my room.

My stat was pretty low, so as usual it was knockoff-brand shoes, last month's cutoff jeans, and a shirt the exact same brown as my skin. I could already hear the kids in the school halls calling me Miss Monochrome. There were keys for the day's new music releases from Top Three Radio, and some movies I didn't really want to see and nobody else did either.

But I was lucky. It could have been worse. This morning, for the first time since he was born, Sherman would get nothing.

I said goodbye to my family: my mom and dad and sister, just noises and voices behind closed bathroom doors. Showers. Hair dryers. Giggles and high jinks from *Morning Hard News*. I wondered if I'd ever hear them again. Swallowing the lump in my throat, I went next door to collect Sherman.

He was something of a demoralized wreck. My clothes were low-stat fashion, but he was literally wearing the same thing he wore yesterday. His hair was literally the same old parrot yellow. Yesterday's color. The sight of him only steeled my resolve. I could not let him live like this.

We loaded ourselves into my scuffed-up three-wheel grandma car and set out down the long, curving roads of our division.

We passed Cedar Grove Lane and Cedar Grove Court and Cedar Grove Place and Cedar Grove Way and made our way out to Cedar Grove Avenue.

We drove by Peevs Drugs, and Peevs Market, and Peevs Quik Oil and Tune-up, and Peevs 24-Hour Whatevers, and I didn't even slow down at Peevs Burgers.

"Don't you have breakfast shift in an hour?" Sherman said.

Sherman no longer worked at Peevs. They'd scrapped him when he lost his stat.

"I called in sick. This is more important."

I grinned, thinking Sherman would thank me, but he only looked at me with something between wonder and disgust.

"You have no idea what you're doing, do you?"

I continued past the little circle of bricks and the water feature and the grass you weren't allowed to picnic on that marked the border of our division. "Taking a hit for a friend is never a mistake." That was a line from *Bomm and Gunn,* the first movie Sherman and I ever saw together at the Peevs Cinnecle. Bomm says it to Gunn, and then they both get shot to death by a gang of mutant cool kids. They go down with their middle fingers raised. Slow motion and everything.

It's pretty romantic.

Sherman just sighed from the passenger seat. "You're a pal," he said. Which were Gunn's last words, spoken through a dazzling arterial mist.

What I remember more than the movie was the popcorn. I couldn't afford any and Sherman could, so Sherman sprang for a big tub and shared it with me. That's the kind of thing that makes friends for life.

Sherman inserted my stereo key into the stereo and futilely searched the Top Three stations for anything other than the top three hits. "So what's the plan?"

"We're going to go see Miss Spotty Pants."

"Your . . . dog?"

"Miss Spotty Pants will know how to help us," I said, ignoring

Sherman's tone of disbelief. There is little room for disbelief on a quest, I feel.

Sherman shook his head and made wheezy sounds of exasperation. "Then this isn't really about me and my stat. This is about you and your dog."

"It's about both of us, okay?"

Sherman stayed quiet a long time, thinking it over. "Okay, Deni," he said at last. "Okay. I fully support you in your misguided effort to redress injustices perpetrated against us."

I glanced at him. "Really?"

He shrugged. "Sure, why not? I'm no-stat. What have I got to lose?"

And so, after going past another Peevs Drugs and Peevs 24-Hour Whatevers, we arrived at Miss Spotty Pants's house.

She lived in a very nice house. There were eight bushes in the front yard, whereas my house had only four. Pillars supported a little roof thing over the door, which I suppose protected people from rain and birds. The fake stones in the lower outside walls were more three-dimensional than my house's fake stones.

The doorbell played some Bach or Beethoven or Boston or one of those other classical guys whose name starts with a B, and Miss Spotty Pants's new owner opened the door.

"Oh," said Mrs. Godfrey, with an uncomfortable smile. "It's you kids."

The Godfreys used to live across the street from me and Sherman, but their stat had gone up high enough after work promotions that they were able to upgrade to a better division. Mrs. Godfrey looked quite different than I remembered. Her hair was bouncier and her teeth more symmetrical. But what really struck me were her pants. They changed length right before our eyes, rising above the ankles, charging halfway up her calves, then plunging back down and flaring out like trombone bells.

"Hey, Mrs. Godfrey," Sherman said. "What's going on?"

"Well, actually, this is a busy time—" she said, eager to get rid of us.

"No, I mean your pants. What's going on with your pants?"

She stood a little taller, a little prouder. "They're smart pants. They interface with the fashion channels and adjust themselves moment to moment as tastes evolve."

Tastes were evolving really fast.

"I was hoping we could see Miss Spotty Pants," I said.

"Oh, I . . . Well, as I said, this is a very busy time—"

"Is that Deni?" came a familiar voice from inside the house. There was a scrabbling and a galloping and then there she was, my old Dalmatian. She leaped through the doorway and almost knocked me off my feet. Standing on her hind legs with her paws on my chest, her butt wiggled so fast I thought her tail would fly right off and break a window. I scratched her behind her ears, which did nothing to kill her enthusiasm. I had to wipe my watering eyes.

When the Godfreys moved, they put in an application to take Miss Spotty Pants with them, even though she'd been my dog since she was a puppy. She was a shelter dog, and you never know what you're getting with a shelter dog. But once her mods kicked in at about seven months old and she started talking and her extra spots came in, the Godfreys decided she was a really cool dog. And since the Godfreys had higher stat, they got their way.

Mrs. Godfrey didn't want to let us in, but when Miss Spotty Pants bared her teeth, she relented. Mrs. Godfrey even got Sherman and me a couple of Peevs Colas and left us alone in the living room with Miss Spotty Pants. The inside of the Godfreys' house wasn't all that different from the inside of my house, only better in every way. We sat on their better couch and drank their Peevs from their better refrigerator. After some more obligatory petting and scritching, Miss Spotty Pants curled up at my feet and asked me what had brought me and Sherman. We told her about how Sherman's family had been declared no-stat, and that we hoped she could help us.

She'd spent the first few months of her life in the pound, and she'd heard things from the other strays and rejects. Some of them came from far away, redolent with exotic, faraway scents, with odd dialects and strange ideas, and tales from distant lands. And when she came to our house, getting me up every two hours to pee, she spoke to me about what she'd learned in the concrete kennels.

She told me of lights and wonders. There was a city, she told me. And I asked her what a city was, and she wasn't sure. All she knew was that it was different than the divisions. She told me of towers that scraped the skies, and grand parks and boulevards teeming with people, a place of variety and a million smells and a million sounds and of things one could barely imagine.

"Miss Spotty Pants," I said, "how'd you like to go for a ride?"

She glanced around the Godfreys' living room, with its better TV and better sofa and better cola. And before I could ask again, she was out the door and in my car, panting with irrepressible glee.

Things got weird once we left our familiar divisions behind. So weird that at one point Sherman shouted for me to stop and pull over, and the three of us got out and stood on the sidewalk.

"Did you know this was here?" I asked Miss Spotty Pants.

"I never even imagined," she said, her voice a gruff whisper.

There, at the intersection of Spring Brook Falls Avenue and Brook Falls Spring Avenue, were a burger place, a drugstore, a supermarket, and a convenience store.

Not a single one of them was a Peevs.

They were all something called a Wiggins.

Wiggins Burgers.

Wiggins Drugs.

Wiggins 24-Hour Whatevers.

We stared in wonder for what seemed like hours.

"No matter what happens from this point on," I said, "I will never forget this moment."

We went inside the 24-Hour Whatevers to buy fruit film snacks.

They were the same fruit film snacks you could get at Peevs.

We drove for days, taking turns sleeping in the back seat and subsisting on the fruit film. I wondered if my family missed my voice through their bathroom doors. After so many days on the road my brain began to change and time lost meaning. When we got out to pee at gas stations my feet felt disconnected from the ground. The car's odometer said we had driven hundreds of miles, yet, paradoxically, the farther we drove, the less distance we seemed to cover. Sherman and Miss Spotty Pants said they felt the same way.

"It's the fractal," said Sherman from the passenger seat. He stared ahead with red-rimmed eyes as if he was looking at something horrible and he couldn't look away, like maybe a ghost or a dead brown lawn.

I remembered something about fractals. We'd covered them in Twelve Amazing Mathematical Concepts Everyone Should Know Before Eleventh Grade. A fractal is a pattern that repeats itself. Magnify it, and you'll see the same pattern as if you'd reduced it.

Yes, we were in a fractal. The little streets curving out from bigger streets like the bent legs of a millipede. The regularity and spacing of the houses, the stores, the divisions. It had become like a fever dream where you keep repeating the same bit of the dream until you feel your brain contract, squeezing your thoughts down into a hot little cage.

"We are stains," Sherman said. "And we are glorious." He had a weird glow in his eye, like the time he drank green milkshake slew from the back of the walk-in freezer seven months after St. Patrick's Day.

Miss Spotty Pants stretched her jaws in a great big yawn. "What are you talking about?"

"We are stains. And stains are glorious, because a stain is a variation in the fractal. A stain doesn't repeat itself endlessly. A stain is unique." He was gaining boldness as he spoke, becoming more alive. "Being a stain shouldn't be a cause for humiliation and stat reduction. It should be celebrated."

Sherman was saying dangerous, subversive stuff. The kind of stuff that could cost you stat. But like he'd said, he had nothing more to lose.

It was exciting and made me want to speed through the streets and do doughnuts in the cul-de-sacs.

We kept on until Miss Spotty Pants spied a dim glow on the horizon, and I aimed the car toward it. As the hours and days piled on, the light grew brighter.

"It's the city," she said. "It must be."

It turned out that she was right. Only the city turned out not to be what we'd hoped.

It was Sherman's turn behind the wheel, and he'd fallen asleep and bumped into a fire hydrant at three miles an hour, waking me and my dog. We all got out of the car. Miss Spotty Pants peed on the hydrant while Sherman and I stared up at towers stained by rain and wind rising from fields of concrete like accusatory fingers, their windows covered with moss and lichen. The buildings were constructed from a dizzying array of materials. Glass and concrete and brick and marble. Back home, all was stucco. Stucco was the only element in the periodic table.

Weeds grew thick in the fissured, unnavigable streets, and we had no choice but to leave the car behind. We picked our way along the jumbled sidewalks, our voices hushed in fear and reverence. Miss Spotty Pants's ears pricked at the scrabbling and scratching sounds that came from the shadows in the fallen buildings. When something meowed I held on to her collar to prevent her from racing off on her own. But the only living thing we saw was a coyote down an alley. It carried a pink mannequin hand in its jaws and looked at us with its head cocked in curiosity before deciding we were bad news and trotting deeper into the shadows.

The city was a sad place, a lost place, a haunted place. But that didn't mean it was a bad place. If I closed my eyes, I could almost imagine what it might have been, alive with millions of people hurrying to jobs, or singing, or dancing, arguing, loving, fighting. A population as varied as the building materials, all smashing together like atoms and creating energy. Here, I sensed possibility. Squandered possibility, maybe, but possibility nonetheless. Cracked and crumbling, dust and destruction, but a place that inspired dreams instead of just processing desires.

"Dudes," I said, "the divisions suck."

Sherman and Miss Spotty Pants agreed that they did.

No matter what, we would not go back.

The city became less appealing when the bombing began.

With an eerie electronic *vorp* from the sky, a green spike of light struck the street. Bits of torn-up road sprayed everywhere, pelting us with gravel. We shrieked and ran like chickens with ignited BBQ lighters up their cloacas and scrambled toward the ruins of a pizza restaurant that was neither a Peevs nor a Wiggins but a Tonys, which might have been the name of an actual human being, when a bomb struck the roof. The windows blew out and felled the three of us with hot wind.

"Split up!" Sherman screeched, choking on black smoke.

"No, stay together!" I screamed back.

"Let's find a bank," Miss Spotty Pants suggested, a little more calmly.

"I don't even know where my ATM card is!"

I was a tiny bit traumatized by now.

"Banks used to be more than ATMs," Miss Spotty Pants said with an impatient bark. "They used to have inside parts too, and they kept the money in vaults. We can shelter in one."

Purple sky machines with complex geometries sent down more

laser spikes. Blooms of white and red fell everywhere, blasting the structures to bits. Glowing red crablike mechanisms descended upon the towers, crawling over them and eating their way down to the steel beams. Shards of glass fell, just glittering white flakes from this distance, like fairy dandruff, and we watched in open-mouthed fascination as the tower sank into itself with storm clouds of billowing debris.

Sherman and I saw the merits in Miss Spotty Pants's suggestion. We chicken-ran until we found a solid-looking ruin with the word BANK carved into a slab of concrete above the missing doors. Stumbling as the earth beneath our feet trembled, we scrambled through ivy and fallen ceiling until we found the vault.

We huddled there, shaking and crying and clutching one another as the machine tempest continued to obliterate the city.

At last the bombardment ended.

Leaving our shelter, we blinked at the sunlit sky like gophers peering out from their holes with hawks circling overhead. The bombs had finished the ancient towers, and even the debris-strewn streets and sidewalks had been reduced to little more than fine powder drifting against charred weeds.

We wandered along the red sediment that had once been bricks, trying to find my car. Miss Spotty Pants claimed she'd located where we'd parked it by smell, and I suppose it's possible that the blackened slab of half-melted blobby stuff had once been my car.

Sherman began to dig through the wreckage with his hands.

"What are you looking for?" I asked him, numb.

"Fruit film snacks," he said.

I shrugged and joined him, though when the best-case scenario is you get to eat another fruit film snack, you've really lowered your expectations in life.

Sherman started laughing a little.

"What's so funny?"

He scooped handfuls of dust and gravel. "We're the highest-stat people who live here," he said. "We're the cool kids."

"That's not a bad way of looking at it," I said, and I laughed too.

Miss Spotty Pants called us idiots and bit both of us.

We weren't alone for much longer. More machines arrived.

First came the vacuums, some of them as big as the buildings the bombs had destroyed. They rolled in on massive treads and sucked up the dust. Through some internal process, they formed new bricks and slabs that they expelled through their rear ends. Giant metal octopi trailed behind them and arranged the recycled building materials into shapes that soon became familiar. Colossal devices rolled through and left bands of pristine green grass in their paths, like reverse lawn mowers. Other machines built roads, and swarms of little helicopters sprayed all the buildings with stucco.

The whole process took slightly more than six hours.

The final thing to go up was a billboard. It read *Oakview Springs, Good Living for Good Families, A Peevs Community*. Within a day there was a Peevs Drugs and a Peevs Burgers and a Peevs 24-Hour Whatevers.

We chose a street at random, Meadowlark Avenue, and followed it to Meadowlark Way and turned down Meadowlark Lane. There was a still-empty house at the end of the cul-de-sac. Miss Spotty Pants pushed through the pet door and let us inside.

You have to live somewhere, after all.

After a few weeks, a family moved in. We never saw them, because the house had more bedrooms and bathrooms than it had people, so it wasn't hard to hide. We subsisted on pilfered cereal and instant waffles and, of course, more fruit snacks. The family bought everything in massive quantities at Peevs BulkCo and didn't notice the small amounts that went missing.

One morning I awoke to the sound of drones. Neither I nor Sherman nor Miss Spotty Pants was due statpacks because we weren't on the division's stat registry. But I wanted to go out and see the delivery anyway. Maybe out of nostalgia. Or maybe to remind myself that I'd accomplished what I set out to do, which was save Sherman from no-stat shame. I suppose that was even true if you squinted. The unexamined life was not worth living, wrote Socrates according to the Greek philosophy unit in Eight Ideas That Will Astonish You class. But then Socrates got to live in a real city.

So we tiptoed down the hallway, past shut bathroom doors. I heard the sounds of showers and hair dryers and chortles from *Morning Hard News*. It was almost like living with my own family. Maybe it even was my own family. Behind closed doors we are all the same.

Outside, we watched the drone swarm approach. The rooftop delivery ports opened like blossoms greeting the dawn, and the drones pollinated them with products.

"What do you think we look like to them?" Miss Spotty Pants said, squatting to pee.

Sherman pursed his lips, thinking about it. "We must look like stains."

I hoped we did look like stains. Like glorious stains without status, marring the perfection of the endless sprawl.

PETER S. BEAGLE

The Story of Kao Yu

FROM *Tor.com*

THERE WAS A judge once in south China, a long time ago — during
the reign of the Emperor Yao, it was — named Kao Yu. He was stern
in his rulings, but fair and patient, and all but legendary for his
honesty; it would have been a foolish criminal — or, yes, even a
misguided emperor — who attempted to bribe or coerce Kao Yu.
Of early middle years, he was stocky and wide-shouldered, if a little
plump, and the features of his face were strong and striking, even
if his hairline was retreating just a trifle. He was respected by all,
and feared by those who should have feared him — what more can
one ask from a judge even now? But this is a story about a case in
which he came to feel — rightly or no — that *he* was the one on trial.

Kao Yu's own wisdom and long experience generally governed
his considerations in court, and his eventual rulings. But he was
uniquely different from all other judges in all of China, in that
when a problem came down to a matter of good versus evil — in
a murder case, most often, or arson, or rape (which Kao Yu particularly despised) — he would often submit that problem to the
judgment of a unicorn.

Now the *chi-lin*, the Chinese unicorn, is not only an altogether
different species from the white European variety or the menacing
Persian karkadann; it is also a different *matter* in its essence from
either one. Apart from its singular physical appearance — indeed,
there are scholars who claim that the *chi-lin* is no unicorn at all,
but some sort of mystical dragon-horse, given its multicolored coat
and the curious configuration of its head and body — this marvelous being is considered one of the Four Superior Animals of Good
Omen, the others being the phoenix, the turtle, and the dragon it-

self. It is the rarest of the unicorns, appearing as a rule only during the reign of a benign emperor enjoying the Mandate of Heaven. As a result, China has often gone generation after weary generation without so much as a glimpse of a *chi-lin*. This has contributed greatly to making the Chinese the patient, enduring people they are. It has also toppled thrones.

But in the days of Judge Kao Yu, at least one *chi-lin* was so far from being invisible as to appear in his court from time to time, to aid him in arriving at certain decisions. Why he should have been chosen—and that at the very beginning of his career—he could never understand, for he was a deeply humble person, and would have regarded himself as blessed far beyond his deserving merely to have seen a *chi-lin* at a great distance. Yet so it was; and, further, the enchanted creature always seemed to know when he was facing a distinctly troublesome problem. It is well known that the *chi-lin,* while wondrously gentle, will suffer no least dishonesty in its presence, and will instantly gore to death anyone whom it knows to be guilty. Judge Kao Yu, it must be said, always found himself a little nervous when the sudden smell of a golden summer meadow announced unmistakably the approach of the unicorn. As righteous a man as he was, even he had a certain difficulty in looking directly into the clear dark eyes of the *chi-lin.*

More than once—and the memories often returned to him on sleepless nights—he had pleaded with the criminal slouching before him, "If you have any hope of surviving this moment, do not lie to me. If you have some smallest vision of yet changing your life—even if you have lied with every breath from your first—tell the truth *now.*" But few there—tragically few—were able to break the habit of a lifetime; and Judge Kao Yu would once again see the dragonlike horned head go down, and would lower his own head and close his eyes, praying this time not to hear the soft-footed rush across the courtroom and the terrible scream of despair that followed. But he always did.

China being as huge and remarkably varied a land as it is, the judge who could afford to spend all his time in one town and one court was in those days very nearly as rare as a unicorn himself. Like every jurist of his acquaintance, Kao Yu traveled the country round a good half of the year: his usual route, beginning every spring, taking him through every village of any size from Guangzhou to Yinchuan. He traveled always with a retinue of three: his burly lieutenant, whose name was Wang Da; his secretary, Chou Qingshan; and Hu Longwei, who was both cook and porter—and, as such, treated with even more courtesy by Kao Yu than were his two other assistants. For he believed, judge or no, that the more lowly placed the person, the more respect he or she deserved. This made him much beloved in rather odd places, but not nearly as wealthy as he should have been.

The *chi-lin*, naturally, did not accompany him on his judicial rounds; rather, it appeared when it chose, most often when his puzzlement over a case was at its height and his need of wisdom greatest. Nor did it ever stay long in the courtroom, but simply delivered its silent judgment and was gone. Chou Qingshan commented—Kao Yu's other two assistants, having more than once seen that judgment executed, were too frightened of the unicorn ever to speak of it at all—that its presence did frequently shorten the time spent on a hearing, since many criminals tended to be even more frightened than they, and often blurted out the truth at first sight. On the other hand, the judge just as often went months without a visit from the *chi-lin*, and was forced to depend entirely on his own wit and his own sensibilities. Which, as he told his assistants, was a very good thing indeed.

"Because if it were my choice," he said to them, "I would leave as many decisions as I was permitted at the feet of this creature out of heaven, this being so much wiser than I. I would then be no sort of judge, but a mindless, unreasoning acolyte, and I would not like that in the least." After a thoughtful moment, he added, "Nor would the *chi-lin* like it either, I believe."

Now it happened that in a certain town, where he had been asked on very short notice to come miles out of his way to substitute for a judge who had fallen ill, Kao Yu was asked to pass judgment on an imprisoned pickpocket. The matter was so far below his rank—it would have been more suited for a novice in training—that even such an unusually egalitarian person as Kao Yu bridled at the effrontery of the request. But the judge he was replacing, one Fang An, happened to be an esteemed former teacher of his, so there was really nothing for it but that he take the case. Kao Yu shrugged in his robes, bowed, assented, arranged to remain another night at the wagoners' inn—the only lodging the town could offer—and made the best of things.

The pickpocket, as it turned out, was a young woman of surpassing, almost shocking beauty: small and slender, with eyes and hair and skin to match that of any court lady Kao Yu had ever seen, all belying her undeniable peasant origins. She moved with a gracious air that set him marveling, *What is she doing before me, in this grubby little courtroom? She ought to be on a tapestry in some noble's palace, and I . . . I should be in that tapestry as well, kneeling before* her, *rather than this other way around.* And no such thought had ever passed through the mind of Judge Kao Yu in his entirely honorable and blameless life.

To the criminal in the dock he said, with remarkable gentleness that did not go unnoticed by either his lieutenant or his secretary, "Well, what have you to say for yourself, young woman? What is your name, and how have you managed to place yourself into such a disgraceful situation?" Wang Da thought he sounded much more like the girl's father than her judge.

With a shy bow—and a smile that set even the chill blood of the secretary Chou Qingshan racing—the pickpocket replied humbly, "Oh, most honorable lord, I am most often called Snow Ermine by the evil companions who lured me into this shameful life—but my true name is Lanying." She offered no family surname, and when Kao Yu requested it, she replied, "Lord, I have vowed never to speak that name again in this life, so low have I brought it by my contemptible actions." A single delicate tear spilled from the corner of her left eye and left its track down the side of her equally delicate nose.

Kao Yu, known for leaving his own courtroom in favor of another judge if he suspected that he was being in some way charmed or cozened by a prisoner, was deeply touched by her manner and her obvious repentance. He cleared his suddenly hoarse throat and addressed her thus: "Lanying . . . ah, young woman . . . this being your first offense, I am of a mind to be lenient with you. I therefore sentence you, first, to return every single *liang* that you have been convicted of stealing from the following citizens—" and he nodded to Chou Qingshan to read off the list of the young pickpocket's victims. "In addition, you are hereby condemned"—he saw Lanying's graceful body stiffen—"to spend a full fortnight working with the night soil collectors of this community, so that those pretty hands may remember always that even the lowest, filthiest civic occupation is preferable to the dishonorable use in which they have hitherto been employed. Take her away."

To himself he sounded like a prating, pompous old man, but everyone else seemed suitably impressed. This included the girl Lanying, who bowed deeply in submission and turned to be led off by two sturdy officers of the court. She seemed so small and fragile between them that Kao Yu could not help ordering Chou Qingshan, in a louder voice than was strictly necessary, "Make that a week—a week, not a whole fortnight. Do you hear me?"

Chou Qingshan nodded and obeyed, his expression unchanged, his thoughts his own. But Lanying, walking between the two men, turned her head and responded to this commutation of her sentence with a smile that flew so straight to Judge Kao Yu's heart that he could only cough and look away, and be grateful to see her gone when he raised his eyes again.

To his assistants he said, "That is the last of my master Fang An's cases, so let us dine and go to rest early, that we may be on our way at sunrise." And both Wang Da and Chou Qingshan agreed heartily with him, for each had seen how stricken he had been by a thief's beauty and charm; and each felt that the sooner he was away from this wretched little town, the better for all of them. Indeed, neither Kao Yu's lieutenant nor his secretary slept well that night, for each had the same thought: *He is a man who has been much alone—he will dream of her tonight, and there will be nothing we can do about that.*

And in this they were entirely correct, for Kao Yu did indeed dream of Lanying the pickpocket, not only that night but for many nights thereafter, to the point where, even to his cook, Hu Longwei, who was old enough to notice only what he was ordered to notice, he appeared like one whom a lamia or succubus is visiting in his sleep, being increasingly pale, gaunt, and exhausted, as well as notably short-tempered and—for the first time in his career—impatient and erratic in his legal decisions. He snapped at Wang Da, rudely corrected Chou Qingshan's records and transcriptions of his trials, rejected even his longtime favorites of Hu Longwei's dishes, and regularly warned them all that they could easily be replaced by more accomplished and respectful servants, which was a term he had never employed in reference to any of them. Then, plainly distraught with chagrin, he would apologize to each man in turn and try once again to evict that maddening young body and captivating smile from his nights. He was never successful at this.

During all this time, the *chi-lin* made not a single appearance in his various courtrooms, which even his retinue, as much as they feared it, found highly unusual, and probably a very bad omen. Having none but each other to discuss the matter with, often clustered together in one more inn, one more drovers' hostel, quite frequently within earshot of Kao Yu tossing and mumbling in his bed, Chou Qingshan would say, "Our master has certainly lost the favor of heaven due to his obsession with that thieving slut. For the life of me, I cannot understand it—she was pretty enough, in a coarse way, but hardly one to cost *me* so much as an hour of sleep."

To which Wang Da would invariably respond, "Well, nothing in this world would do *that* but searching under your bed for a lost coin." They were old friends, and, like many such, not particularly fond of each other.

But Hu Longwei—in many ways the wisest of the three—when off duty would quiet the other two by saying, "If you both spent a little more time considering our master's troubles and a little less on your own grievances, we might be of some actual use to him in this crisis. He is not the first man to spend less than an hour in some woman's company and then be ridden sleepless by an unresolved fantasy, however absurd. Do not interrupt me, Wang. I am older than both of you, and I know a few things. The way to rid Kao Yu of these dreams of his is to return to that same town—I cannot even remember what it was called—and arrange for him to spend a single night with that little pickpocket. Believe me, there is nothing that clears away such a dream faster than its fulfillment. Think on it—and keep out of my cooking wine, Chou, or I may find another use for my cleaver."

The lieutenant and the secretary took these words more to heart than Hu Longwei might have expected, the result being that somehow, on the return leg of their regular route, Wang Da developed a relative in poor health living in a village within easy walking distance of the town where Lanying the pickpocket resided—employed now, all hoped, in some more respectable profession. Kao Yu's servants never mentioned her name when they went together to the judge to implore a single night's detour on the long way home. Nor, when he agreed to this, did Kao Yu.

It cannot be said that his mental or emotional condition improved greatly with the knowledge that he was soon to see Snow Ermine again. He seemed to sleep no better, nor was he any less gruff with Wang, Chou, and Hu, even when they were at last bound on the homeward journey. The one significant difference in his behavior was that he regained his calm, unhurried court-room demeanor, as firmly decisive as always, but paying the strict-est attention to the merits of the cases he dealt with, whether in a town, a mere village, or even a scattering of huts and fields that could barely be called a hamlet. It was as though he was in some way preparing himself for the next time the beautiful pickpocket was brought before him, knowing that there *would* be a next time, as surely as sunrise. But what he was actually thinking on the road to that sunrise . . . that no one could have said, except perhaps the *chi-lin*. And there is no account anywhere of any *chi-lin* ever speak-ing in words to a human being.

The town fathers were greatly startled to see them again, since there had been no request for their return and no messages to announce it. But they welcomed the judge and his entourage all the same, and put them up without charge at the wagoners' inn for a second time. And that evening, without notifying his mas-ter, Wang Da slipped away quietly and eventually located Lanying the pickpocket in the muddy alley where she lived with a number of the people who called her "Snow Ermine." When he informed her that he came from Judge Kao Yu, who would be pleased to honor her with an invitation to dinner, Lanying favored him with the same magically rapturous smile, and vanished into the hovel to put on her most respectable robe, perfectly suitable for dining with a man who had sentenced her to collect and dispose of her neighbors' night soil. Wang Da waited outside for her, giving ear-nest thanks for his own long marriage, his five children, and his truly imposing ugliness.

On their way to the inn, Lanying—for all that she skipped along beside him like a child on her way to a puppet show or a party—shrewdly asked Wang Da, not why Kao Yu had sent for her, but what he could tell her about the man himself. Wang Da, nor-mally a taciturn man, except when taunting Chou Qingshan, re-plied cautiously, wary of her cleverness, saying as little as he could in courtesy. But he did let her know that there had never been a woman of any sort in Kao Yu's life, not as long as he had worked for him—and he did disclose the truth of the judge's *chi-lin*. It is perhaps the heart of this tale that Lanying chose to believe one of these truths and to disdain the other.

Kao Yu had, naturally, been given the finest room at the inn, which was no great improvement over any other room, but did have facilities for the judge to entertain a guest in privacy. Lanying fell to her knees and kowtowed—knocked head—the moment she entered, Wang Da having simply left her at the door. But Kao Yu raised her to her feet and served her Dragon in the Clouds tea, and after that *huangjiu* wine, which is made from wheat. By the time these beverages had been consumed—time spent largely in silence and smiles—the dinner had been prepared and brought to them by Hu Longwei himself, who had pronounced the inn's cook "a northern barbarian who should be permitted to serve none but monkeys and foreigners." He set the trays down carefully on the low table, peered long and rudely into Lanying's face, and departed.

"Your servants do not like me," Lanying said with a small, unhappy sigh. "Why should they, after all?"

Kao Yu answered, bluntly but kindly, "They have no way of knowing whether you have changed your life. Nor did I make you promise to do so when I pronounced sentence." Without further word he fed her a bit of their roast pork appetizer, and then asked quietly, "Have you done so? Or are you still Lanying the Pickpocket?"

Lanying sighed again, and smiled wryly at him. "No, my lord, these days I am Lanying the Seamstress. I am not very good at it, in truth, but I work cheaply. Sometimes I am Lanying the Cowherd—Lanying the Pig Girl—Lanying the Sweeper at the market." She nibbled daintily at her dish, plainly trying to conceal her hunger. "But the pickpocket, no, nor the thief, nor . . ." And here she looked directly into Kao Yu's eyes, and he noticed with something of a shock that her own were not brown, as he had remembered them, but closer to a kind of dark hazel, with flecks of green coming and going. "Nor have I yet been Lanying the Girl on the market, though it has been a close run once or twice. But I have kept the word I did not give you"—she lowered her eyes then—"perhaps out of pride, perhaps out of gratitude . . . perhaps . . ." She let the words trail away unfinished, and they dined without speaking for some while, until Lanying was able to regard Kao Yu again without blushing.

Then it was Kao Yu's turn to feel his cheeks grow hot, as he said, "Lanying, you must understand that I have not been much in the society of women. At home I dine alone in my rooms, always; when I am traveling I am more or less constantly in the company of my assistants Wang, Chou, and Hu, whom I have known for many years. But since we met, however unfortunately, I have not been able to stop thinking of you, and imagining such an evening as we are enjoying. I am certain that this is wrong, unquestionably wrong for a judge, but when I look at you I cannot breathe, and I cannot feel my heart beating at all. I am too old for you, and you are too beautiful for me, and I think you should probably leave after we finish our meal. I do."

Lanying began to speak, but Kao Yu took her wrists in his hands, and she—who had some experience in these matters—felt his grip like manacles. He said, "Because if you never make away with another purse in your life, Lanying the Pickpocket is still there in the back of those lovely eyes. I see her there even now, because although I am surely a great fool, I am also a judge."

He released his hold on her then, and they sat staring at one another—for how long Kao Yu could never say or remember. Lanying finally whispered, "Your man Wang told me that a unicorn, a *chi-lin*, sometimes helps you to arrive at your decisions. What do you think it would advise you if it were here now?"

Nor was Kao Yu ever sure how many minutes or hours went by before he was finally able to say, "The *chi-lin* is not here." And outside the door, Chou Qingshan held out his open palm and Wang Da and Hu Longwei each grudgingly slapped a coin into it as the three of them tiptoed away.

Lanying was gone when Kao Yu woke in the morning, which was, as it turned out, rather a fortunate thing. He was almost finished tidying up the remains of their meal—several items had been crushed and somewhat scattered, and one plate was actually broken—when Wang Da entered to tell him that his dinner guest had stopped long enough while departing the inn in the deep night to empty the landlord's money box, leaving an impudent note of thanks before vanishing. And vanish she certainly had: the search that Kao Yu organized and led himself turned up no trace of her, neither in her usual haunts nor in areas where she claimed to have worked or was known to have friends. Snow Ermine had disappeared as completely as though she had never been. Which, in a sense, she never had.

Kao Yu, being who he was, compensated the landlord in full—over the advice of all three of his assistants—and they continued on the road home. No one spoke for the first three days.

Finally, in a town in Hunan Province, where the four of them were having their evening meal together, Kao Yu broke his silence, saying, "Every one of you is at complete liberty to call me a stupid, ridiculous old fool. You will only be understating the case. I beg pardon of you all." And he actually kowtowed—knocked head—in front of his own servants.

Naturally, Chou, Wang, and Hu were properly horrified at this, and upset their own dishes rushing to raise Kao Yu to his feet. They assured him over and over that the robbery at the inn could not in any way be blamed on him, even though he *had* invited the thief to dinner there, and she *had* spent the night in his bed, taking fullest advantage of his favor . . . The more they attempted to excuse him of the responsibility, the more guilty he felt, and the angrier at himself for, even now, dreaming every night of the embraces of that same thief. He let his three true friends comfort him, but all he could think of was that he would never again be able to return the gaze of the unicorn in his courtroom with the same pride and honesty. The *chi-lin* would know the truth, even of his dreams. The *chi-lin* always knew.

When they returned without further incident to the large southern city that was home to all four of them, Kao Yu allowed himself only two days to rest, and then flung himself back into his occupation with a savage vengeance aimed at himself and no one else. He remained as patient as ever with his assistants—and, for the most part, with the accused brought to him for judgment. Indeed, as culpable as his dreams kept telling him he was, he sympathized more with these petty, illiterate, drink-sodden, hopeless, useless offscourings of decent society than he ever had in his career—in his life. Whether the useless offscourings themselves ever recognized this is not known.

Wang Da, Chou Qingshan, and Hu Longwei all hoped that time and work would gradually free his mind of Snow Ermine—which was the only way they spoke of her from then on—and at first, because they wanted it so much to be true, they believed that it must be. And while they were at home in the city, living the life of a busy city judge and his aides, dining with other officials, advising on various legal matters, speaking publicly to certain conferences, and generally filling their days with lawyers and the law, this did indeed seem to be so. Further, to their vast relief, Kao Yu's unicorn paid him no visits during that time; in fact, it had not been seen for more than a year. In private, he himself regarded this as a judgment in its own right, but he said nothing about that, considering it his own harsh concern. So all appeared to be going along in a proper and tranquil manner, as had been the case before the mischance that called him to an all-but-nameless town to deal with the insignificant matter of that wretched—and nameless—pickpocket.

Consequently, when it came the season for them to take to the long road once more, the judge's assistants each had every reason to hope that he would show himself completely recovered from his entanglement with that same wretched pickpocket. Particularly since this time they would have no reason to pass anywhere near that town where she plied her trade, and where Kao Yu might just conceivably be called upon again to pass sentence upon her. It was noted as they set out not only that the weather was superb, but that their master was singing to himself: very quietly, true—almost wordlessly, almost in a whisper—but even so. The three looked at each other and dared to smile; and if smiles made any sound, that one would have been a whisper too.

At first the journey went well, barring the condition of the spring roads, which were muddy, as always, and sucked tiresomely at the feet of their horses. But there were fewer criminal cases than usual for Kao Yu to deal with, and most of those were run-of-the-mill affairs: a donkey or a few chickens stolen here, a dispute over fishing rights or a right of way there, a wife assaulting her husband—for excellent reasons—over there. Such dull daily issues might be uninteresting to any but the participants, but they had the distinct advantage of taking up comparatively little time; as a rule Kao Yu and his retinue never needed to spend more than a day and a night in any given town. On the rare occasions when they stayed longer, it was always to rest the horses, never themselves. But that suited all four of them, especially Wang Da, who, for all his familial responsibilities, remained as passionately devoted to his wife as any new bridegroom and was beginning to allow himself sweet visions of returning home earlier than expected. The others teased him rudely that he might well surprise the greengrocer or the fishmonger in his bed, but Kao Yu reproved them sharply, saying, "True happiness is as delicate as a dragonfly's wing, and it is not to be made sport of." And he patted Wang Da's shoulder, as he had never done before, and rode on, still singing to himself, a very little.

But once they reached the province where the girl called Snow Ermine lived—even though, as has been said, their route had been planned to take them as far as possible from her home—then the singing stopped, and Kao Yu grew day by day more silent and morose. He drew apart from his companions, both in traveling and in their various lodgings; and while he continued to take his cases, even the most trifling, as seriously as ever, his entire court-room manner had become as dry and sour as that of a much older judge. This impressed very favorably most of the local officials he dealt with, but his assistants knew what unhappiness it covered, and pitied him greatly.

Chou Qingshan predicted that he would return to his old self once they were clear of the province that had brought him to such shame and confusion; and to some degree that was true as they rode on from town to village, village to town. But the soft singing never did come again, which in time caused the cook, Hu Long-wei, to say, "He is like a vase or a pot that has been shattered into small bits, and then restored, glued back together, fragment by fragment. It will look as good as new, if the work is done right, but you have to be careful with it. *We* will have to be careful."

Nevertheless, their progress was so remarkable that they were almost two weeks ahead of schedule when they reached Yinchuan, where they were accustomed to rest and resupply themselves for a few days before starting home. But within a day of their arrival Kao Yu had been approached by both the mayor of the town and the provincial governor as well, both asking him if he would be kind enough to preside over a particular case for them tomorrow. A Yinchuan judge had already been chosen, of course, and would doubtless do an excellent job; but like every judge available, he had no experience handling such a matter as murder, and it was well known that Kao Yu—

Kao Yu said, "Murder? This is truly a murder case you are asking me to deal with?"

The mayor nodded miserably. "We know that you have come a long journey, and have a long journey yet before you . . . but the victim was an important man, a merchant all the way from Harbin, and his family is applying a great deal of pressure on the entire city administration, not me alone. A judge of your stature agreeing to take over . . . it might calm them somewhat, reassure them that something is being done . . ."

"Tell me about the case," Kao Yu interrupted brusquely. Hu Longwei groaned quietly, but Chou and Wang were immediately excited, though they properly made every effort not to seem so. An illegally established tollgate, a neighbor poaching rabbits on a neighbor's land—what was that compared to a real murder? With Kao Yu they learned that the merchant—young, handsome, vigorous, and with, as even his family admitted, far more money than sense—had wandered into the wrong part of town and struck up several unwise friendships, most particularly one with a young woman—

"A pickpocket?" Kao Yu's voice had suddenly grown tight and rasping.

No, apparently not a pickpocket. Apparently her talents lay elsewhere—

"Was she called . . . Snow Ermine?"

"That name has not been mentioned. When she was taken into custody, she gave the name 'Spring Lamb.' Undoubtedly an alias, or a nickname—"

"Undoubtedly. Describe her." But then Kao Yu seemed to change his mind, saying, "No . . . no, do not describe her to me. Have all the evidence in the matter promptly delivered to our inn, and let me decide then whether or not I will agree to sit on the case. You will have my answer tonight, if the evidence reaches the inn before we do."

It did, as Kao Yu's assistants knew it would; but all three of them agreed that they had never seen their master so reluctant even to handle the evidence pertaining to a legal matter. There was plenty of it, certainly, from the sworn statements of half a dozen citizens swearing to having seen the victim in the company of the accused; to the proprietor of a particularly disreputable wine shop, who had sold the pair enough liquor, jar on jar, to float a river barge; let alone the silent witness of the young merchant's slit-open purse, and of the slim silver knife still buried to the hilt in his side when he was discovered in a trash-strewn alley with dogs sniffing at his body. There was even—when his rigor-stiffened left hand was pried open—a crushed rag of a white flower. Judge Kao Yu's lamp burned all night in his room at the inn.

But in the morning, when Wang Da came to fetch him, he was awake and clear-eyed, and had already breakfasted, though only on green tea and sweetened congee. He was silent as they walked to the building set aside for trials of all sorts, where Hu Long-wei and Chou Qingshan awaited them, except to remark that they would be starting home on the day after tomorrow, distinctly earlier than their usual practice. He said nothing further until they reached the courtroom.

There were two minor cases to be disposed of before the matter of the young merchant's murder: one a suit over a breach of contract, the other having to do with a long-unpaid family debt. Kao Yu settled these swiftly, and then—a little pale, his words a bit slower, but his voice quiet and steady—signaled for the accused murderer to be brought into court.

It was Lanying, as he had known in his heart that it would be, from the very first mention of the case. Alone in his room, he had not even bothered to hope that the evidence would prove her innocent, or at very least raise some small doubt as to her guilt. He had gone through it all quickly enough and spent the rest of the night sitting very still, with his hands clasped in his lap, looking toward the door, as though expecting her to come to him then and there, of her own will, instead of waiting until morning for her trial. From time to time, in the silence of the room, he spoke her name.

Now, as the two constables who had led her to his high bench stepped away, he looked into her calmly defiant eyes and said only, "We meet again."

"So we do," Lanying replied equably. She was dressed rakishly, having been seized before she had time to change into garments suitable for a court appearance; but as ever she carried herself with the pride and poise of a great lady. She said to Kao Yu, "I hoped you might be the one."

"Why is that? Because I let you off lightly the first time? Because I . . . because it was so easy for you to make a fool of me the next time?" Kao Yu was almost whispering. "Do you imagine that I will be quite as much of a mark today?"

"No. But I did wish to apologize."

"Apologize?" Kao Yu stared at her. "*Apologize?*"

Lanying bowed her head, but she looked up at him from under her long dark eyelashes. "Lord, I am a thief. I have been a thief all my life. A thief steals. I knew the prestige of your invitation to dine would give me a chance at the inn's money box, and I accepted it accordingly, because that is what a thief does. It had nothing to do with you, with my . . . liking for you. I am what I am."

Kao Yu's voice was thick in his throat. "You are what you have become, which is something more than a mere thief and pickpocket. Now you are a murderer."

The word had not been at all hard to get out when he was discussing it with the mayor, and with his three assistants, but now it felt like a thornbush in his throat. Lanying's eyes grew wide with fear and protest. "*I?* Never! I had *nothing* to do with that poor man's death!"

"The knife is yours," Kao Yu said tonelessly. "It is the same one I noticed at your waist when you dined with me. Nor have I ever seen you without a white flower in your hair. Do not bother lying to me any further, Lanying."

"But I am not lying!" she cried out. "I took his money, yes—he was stupid with wine, and that is what I do—but killing is no part of it. The knife was stolen from me, I swear it! Think as little of me as you like—I have given you reason enough—but I am no killer, you *must* know that!" She lowered her voice, to keep the words that followed from the constables. "Our bodies tell the truth, if our mouths do not. My lord, my judge, you know as much truth of me as anyone does. Can you tell me again that I am a murderer?"

Kao Yu did not answer her. They looked at each other for a long time, the judge and the lifelong thief, and it seemed to Chou Qingshan that there had come a vast weariness on Kao Yu, and that he might never speak again to anyone. But then Kao Yu lifted his head in wonder and fear as the scent of a summer meadow drifted into the room, filling it with the warm, slow presence of wild ginger, hibiscus, lilacs, and lilies—and the *chi-lin.* The two constables fell to their knees and pressed their faces to the floor, as did his three assistants, none of them daring even to look up. The unicorn stood motionless at the back of the courtroom, and Kao Yu could no more read its eyes than he ever could. But in that moment he knew Lanying's terrible danger for his own.

Very quietly he said to her, "Snow Ermine, Spring Lamb, thief of my foolish, foolish old heart . . . nameless queen born a criminal . . . and, yes, murderer—I am begging you now for both our lives. Speak the truth, if you never do so again, because otherwise you die here, and so do I. Do you hear me, Lanying?"

Just for an instant, looking into Lanying's beautiful eyes, he knew that she understood exactly what he was telling her, and, further, that neither he nor the *chi-lin* was in any doubt that she had slain the merchant she robbed. But she was, as she had told him, what she was; and even with full knowledge of the justice waiting, she repeated, spacing the words carefully, and giving precise value to each, "Believe what you will. I am no killer."

Then the judge Kao Yu rose from his bench and placed himself between Lanying and the unicorn, and he said in a clear, strong voice, "You are not to harm her. Everything she says is a lie, and always will be, and still you are not to harm her." In the silence that followed, his voice shook a little as he added, "Please."

The *chi-lin* took a step forward—then another—and Lanying closed her eyes. But it did not charge; rather, it paced across the courtroom to face Kao Yu, until they were standing closer than ever they had before, in all the years of their strange and wordless partnership. And what passed between them then will never be known, save to say that the *chi-lin* turned away and was swiftly gone—never having once glanced at Lanying—and that Kao Yu sat down again and began to weep, without ever making a sound.

When he could speak, he directed the trembling constables to take Lanying away, saying that he would pass sentence the next day. She went, this time, without a backward glance, as proudly as ever, and Kao Yu did not look after her but walked away alone. Wang Da and Chou Qingshan would have followed him, but Hu Longwei took them both by the arms and shook his head.

Kao Yu spent the night alone in his room, where he could be heard pacing constantly, sometimes talking to himself in ragged, incomprehensible tatters of language. Whatever it signified, it eliminated him as a suspect in Lanying's escape from custody that same evening. She was never recaptured, reported, or heard of again—at least, not under that name, nor in that region of China—and if each of Kao Yu's three friends regarded the other two skeptically for a long time thereafter, no one accused anyone of anything, even in private. Indeed, none of them ever spoke of Lanying, the pickpocket, thief, and murderer for whom their master had given up what they knew he had given up. They had no words for it, but they knew.

For the *chi-lin* never came again, and Kao Yu never spoke of that separation either. The one exception came on their silent road home, when darkness caught them between towns, obliging them to make camp in a forest, as they were not unaccustomed to doing. They gathered wood together, and Hu Longwei improvised an excellent dinner over their fire, after which they chatted and bantered as well as they could to cheer their master, so silent now for so many days. It was then that Kao Yu announced his decision to retire from the bench, which shocked and dismayed them all, and set each man entreating him to change his mind. In this they were unsuccessful, though they argued and pleaded with him most of the night. It was nearer to dawn than to midnight, and the flames were dwindling because everyone had forgotten to feed them, when Chou Qingshan remarked bitterly, "So much for justice, then. With you gone, so much for justice between Guangzhou and Yinchuan."

But Kao Yu shook his head and responded, "You misunderstand, old friend. I am only a judge, and judges can always be found. The *chi-lin* . . . the *chi-lin* is justice. There is a great difference."

He did indeed retire, as he had said, and little is known of the rest of his life, except that he traveled no more, but stayed in his house, writing learned commentaries on curious aspects of common law and, on rare occasions, lecturing to small audiences at the local university. His three assistants, of necessity, attached themselves to other circuit-riding judges, and saw less of one another than they did of Kao Yu, whom they never failed to visit on returning from their journeys. But there was less and less to say each time, and each admitted—though only to himself—a kind of guilt-stricken relief when he died quietly at home, from what his doctors termed a sorrow of the soul. China is one of the few countries where sadness has always been medically recognized.

There is a legend that after the handful of mourners at his funeral had gone home, a *chi-lin* kept silent watch at his grave all that night. But that is all it is, of course—a legend.

Smear

FROM *Conjunctions: 67, Other Aliens*

1.

AKSEL COULD SEE a smear, something just inside the vessel's skin. He blinked, rubbed his eyes. It was still there.

"Query," he asked. "What am I seeing?"

The voice responded, *I cannot know what you are seeing. I can only know what you are looking at.*

"All right," he said. "What am I looking at?"

The voice did not respond. Why did the voice not respond? Surely it knew what he meant. And then he remembered.

"*Query,*" he said. "What am I looking at?"

The voice responded immediately, *Bulkhead.*

"No," he said. "There's something there, something more."

The voice in his head responded, *Interior of your faceplate.*

"No," he said. "Not that either." He called on the vessel to remove his helmet, which it did by extruding a chrome claw from a bulkhead and plucking it deftly off his head. *Why did it do that?* he wondered. *It could have done it just as easily by deploying a focused magnetic field.* Was the vessel trying to unsettle him?

He looked again. The smear was still there, just in front of the bulkhead, a few inches away from it, over his head, perhaps a meter long, a half meter wide. He reached up and tried to touch it, but, strapped down as he was, couldn't reach. "Query," he repeated. "What am I looking at?"

Bulkhead, the voice insisted.

"No," he said. "Between myself and the bulkhead."

For a long time the voice said nothing. Had he gotten the form wrong? He didn't need to say *query* again, did he? But then, finally, hesitantly, the voice spoke.

Are you looking at the object properly? Is your gaze centered upon it? If your gaze is not centered upon it, you are no longer looking at it, but merely remembering it.

He instructed the vessel to reposition his chair until the smear was centered in his vision. He focused his eyes on it. He held his gaze steady, unblinking.

"Query," he repeated. "What am I looking at?"

Bulkhead, the voice said.

"No," he replied, irritated. "In front of the bulkhead."

There is nothing between your eyes and the bulkhead.

But it was there, he could see it. A smear, semitransparent but certainly present. He was sure he could see it. What was he seeing?

I can tell you what you are looking at, the voice said, unbidden, *but not what you are seeing.* Which made him wonder if the voice had burrowed deeper into his head than he had realized and could hear what he was thinking.

2.

Apart from the vessel, apart from the voice, he had been alone for a very long time. He had been strapped into the vessel and then the vessel had been accelerated to an extraordinary rate, but very gradually, over the course of days, so as not to kill him.

The chair had been made so that he would never have to leave it until he left the vessel for good. The chair was now so integrated with his body that it was hard for him to remember where body stopped and chair began. When he awoke, he felt as if he didn't have a body. It was a tremendous effort to move a digit, let alone a limb.

When he awoke, the vessel displayed on the inside of his faceplate a countdown of the months, days, minutes, and seconds before deceleration would begin.

Off, he whispered, and the vessel reduced the countdown to a red pixel.

Why was he awake? Was he meant to be awake? He was still groggy, still woozy. Maybe he wasn't awake at all but only dreaming. He wasn't meant to be awake in the vessel, ever.

Why am I awake? he whispered, and suddenly there were words in front of his eyes, as if the faceplate had been written on. It was the vessel, responding.

Unexpected failure in storage system, the words read.

What failure? he asked.

Storage system component 3/9aOxV.

Excuse me? he said. Upon which the vessel displayed a series of schematics that made no sense to him at all.

So he would remain unstored for the rest of the trip. Would he die? The vessel indicated he would not die: it would feed him intravenously through the chair, converting the molecules of extraneous portions of itself into nourishment. Would he waste away sitting in the chair? The vessel indicated no, that it would continue the stimulation of muscles and nerves that it had been conducting while he was in storage. Which meant that his body was constantly twitching, his muscles bunching and releasing, but that he was not the one doing it. It was being done to him.

He asked the vessel for a distraction. It opened a feed to his faceplate and showed him space around itself, mostly black, a few specks of light. He asked if it couldn't provide music or some sort of teleplay, but as it turned out, no, it couldn't. He was never meant to be awake—nobody was ever meant to be awake on the vessel. The vessel could show him space. The vessel could show him schematics.

Perhaps if he told it stories, he hoped, it could learn to tell them back.

Indeed, it did tell them back: verbatim each time. When instructed to construct its own stories, it offered a mishmash of what he'd already told it, but in a way that made little sense.

And so instead he regarded schematics, examined a representation of space on the inside of his faceplate, traced the curve of the bulkhead with his eyes. He slept, woke, slept. He never ate, but, fed intravenously, was never hungry. At least not at first. He watched his body grow lean, hardly an ounce of fat left. His suit draped loosely on him.

Are you sure I'm being fed enough to survive? he asked.

Technically speaking, the vessel responded, *you are being fed enough to survive.*

The voice manifested after several weeks of his being awake, alone. At first he sensed it more than heard it, had a strange inkling that something was there, speaking to him—or, rather, trying to speak to him. Was it the vessel? At first he thought, yes, it was the vessel. But they didn't talk quite alike. And when he asked the vessel about the voice, it seemed baffled.

For some time—days, even weeks—he just listened. He taught himself to filter out the noise of the vessel around him and just wait, listen. It was as if the voice was there, slightly beyond a frequency he could hear, making his eardrums throb slightly but not in a way that conveyed sense. He spoke to it, tried to coax it to speak back, until suddenly, to his surprise, it did.

It had rules, formulae that must be followed, patterns of speech it seemed prone to respond to. He had stumbled onto them only slowly and gradually. It would not always tell him what he wanted to know. There was still much he didn't know.

3.

Vessel, he whispered, *please replace my helmet.*

The same chrome claw on a long pale arm plucked the helmet from the floor with surprising delicacy and pushed it back onto his head. When it was affixed, he looked again for the smear through the faceplate. It was still there, still visible. It didn't matter what the voice claimed.

He asked the vessel about the smear.

There is nothing there, the voice said again, despite his not following discourse protocol. *I already told you.*

"I wasn't speaking to you," Aksel said. "I was speaking to the vessel."

But the vessel did not respond. The faceplate in front of his eyes remained blank.

"Have you disabled my interface?" he asked.

There was no response, either from vessel or from voice.

"Query, have you disabled my interface?" he asked.

Query, the voice responded. *What is an interface?*

Interface, interface. What an odd word, he told himself. *Intraface* would mean inside the face, within the face, which made sense. But *interface* would mean between the face. What did that even mean: between the face?

"Query," he began, but the voice immediately cut him off. *Don't ask,* it said.

It had a tone now . . . did it have a tone? Had it had that mocking tone before? What was the voice? What did it have to do with him? Why was he willing to listen to it? Why hadn't he panicked?

But no matter how he tried to work himself up, he couldn't bring himself to panic. Maybe the voice was doing that to him too.

His arm was little more than a stick wrapped in skin. Looking at it, it didn't look like an arm that could possibly belong to him. In fact, the more he looked at it, the less it looked like an arm at all.

But when had he taken his suit off? Why was he looking at a bare arm at all? And why, if he wasn't wearing his suit, was he wearing his helmet?

Or wait. *Was* he wearing his helmet?

His gaze slowly slid to the smear, then slid away. If he looked at it out of the corner of his eye, it almost made sense, almost looked familiar. He tried to look at it and not look at it at the same time, but, like the voice had been at first, it felt like he could almost sense something but not quite. As if whatever it was was impinging on this world by accident, was only being seen because of an anomaly.

What if that anomaly is me? he wondered.

Or was that the voice wondering it?

Perhaps, if he got closer. Perhaps, if he regarded it from one side, at an oblique angle.

Vessel, he whispered, *move the chair forward.*

But the chair didn't move. The vessel was paying him no heed. Perhaps, as with the smear, it no longer realized he was there.

*

He kept looking, kept staring. Part of him felt the smear was staring back. Watching him. Was it staring back? No. It was just a smear, a smear couldn't stare.

If he could only get closer, move a little nearer, then he'd see it clearly, he was sure. Almost sure.

Time went by. Years maybe, or what felt like years. When he regarded his arm again, it still didn't look like an arm. When he lifted the claw on the end of it and touched the release and kept pushing until the belts restraining him actually parted, it looked even less like an arm.

It took immense effort to free himself from the chair. And more effort still to crawl across the deck. Still more to turn and look upward, to regard the smear.

Was it still there? Yes, it was still there, but differently distended from this angle. It was, almost, a face. It was, almost, a human face. He crawled a little closer, looked up again. Still smeared, still distorted, but anamorphically transformed. Yes, a face. Maybe. He crawled until his head was touching the skin of the bulkhead and then looked up again. Yes, a face, a face very much like his own—his own face, in fact. He stared into it, filled with wonder.

After a moment the face smiled, tightly, in a way that bared its teeth.

Or would have bared them if what was inside the mouth was teeth.

4.

They scanned the small craft. Nothing harmful detected, no extraordinary presences, nothing to give pause. Out of caution they kept the craft quarantined, alone at its dock, for several weeks before finally sending a team in.

The man was out of his chair, eyes wide open, staring up at the upper portion of the vessel's bulkhead. He had been torn free of the chair and his legs were tangled with a snarl of tubes and wires, many of which were still attached to his body. A discolored spill of dried fluid spread in a trail behind him. His neck was bent impossibly upward, his body desiccated and bloodless.

"Where's his suit?" asked one of the technicians.

The other shrugged. "I don't know," he said.

"What's with his arm?"

"Arm?" said the other. "Is that what that is?"

It was contorted, and little more than bone. He reached out and pushed down on the arm with his boot. The body yawed to one side, hollow or nearly so. When he drew his boot back, the body rocked back and forth, slowly settling onto the floor.

He grunted. "What do we do with him?"

"Incinerate him," said the other.

"And the craft?"

There was a long moment before the other responded. "No reason to destroy that," he finally said. "We can salvage it."

But he wasn't looking at the other technician as he said it. Instead he seemed to be looking at a spot high up the bulkhead, near the curve where wall became ceiling. He took a step forward and reached his hand out through the air, as if to touch something. Then he drew back and stared at his gloved hand.

"What is it?" asked the other.

"Nothing," he said, confused. "I thought I saw something. My . . . faceplate must be dirty."

The other nodded. He started for the airlock. When he realized the first wasn't following, he stopped, looked back.

"Coming?" he asked.

"Just a moment," said the first. He had pulled one arm from its sleeve and back into his suit and now had it pressed between the suit and his chest. He worked the fingers up past where the suit joined the helmet, trying to rub at the faceplate from the inside.

"Come on," the other pressed.

"You go ahead," the first managed to say. "I'll follow you out in just a moment."

All alone, he just stood there, hand caught between his throat and the rim of the helmet, waiting. He had seen something, he was sure. Or almost. A swath, a fluttering, something almost visible.

What was it? he wondered.

Or not quite that: *Query: what was it?* he wondered. Yes, that was what the thought had been. What a strange way to think.

He wriggled his fingers, swallowed.

The City Born Great

FROM *Tor.com*

I SING THE CITY.

Fucking city. I stand on the rooftop of a building I don't live in and spread my arms and tighten my middle and yell nonsense ululations at the construction site that blocks my view. I'm really singing to the cityscape beyond. The city'll figure it out.

It's dawn. The damp of it makes my jeans feel slimy, or maybe that's 'cause they haven't been washed in weeks. Got change for a wash-and-dry, just not another pair of pants to wear till they're done. Maybe I'll spend it on more pants at the Goodwill down the street instead . . . but not yet. Not till I've finished going *AAAAaaaaAAAAaaaa* (breath) *aaaaAAAAaaaaaaa* and listening to the syllable echo back at me from every nearby building face. In my head, there's an orchestra playing "Ode to Joy" with a Busta Rhymes backbeat. My voice is just tying it all together.

Shut your fucking mouth! someone yells, so I take a bow and exit the stage.

But with my hand on the knob of the rooftop door, I stop and turn back and frown and listen, 'cause for a moment I hear something both distant and intimate singing back at me, basso-deep. Sort of coy.

And from even farther, I hear something else: a dissonant, gathering growl. Or maybe those are the rumblers of police sirens? Nothing I like the sound of, either way. I leave.

"There's a way these things are supposed to work," says Paulo. He's smoking again, nasty bastard. I've never seen him eat. All he uses his mouth for is smoking, drinking coffee, and talking. Shame; it's a nice mouth otherwise.

We're sitting in a café. I'm sitting with him because he bought me breakfast. The people in the café are eyeballing him because he's something not-white by their standards, but they can't tell what. They're eyeballing me because I'm definitively black, and because the holes in my clothes aren't the fashionable kind. I don't stink, but these people can smell anybody without a trust fund from a mile away.

"Right," I say, biting into the egg sandwich and damn near wetting myself. Actual egg! Swiss cheese! It's so much better than that McDonald's shit.

Guy likes hearing himself talk. I like his accent; it's sort of nasal and sibilant, nothing like a Spanish-speaker's. His eyes are huge, and I think, *I could get away with so much shit if I had permanent puppy eyes like that.* But he seems older than he looks—way, way older. There's only a tinge of gray at his temples, nice and distinguished, but he feels, like, a hundred.

He's also eyeballing me, and not in the way I'm used to. "Are you listening?" he asks. "This is important."

"Yeah," I say, and take another bite of my sandwich.

He sits forward. "I didn't believe it either, at first. Hong had to drag me to one of the sewers, down into the reeking dark, and show me the growing roots, the budding teeth. I'd been hearing breathing all my life. I thought everyone could." He pauses. "Have you heard it yet?"

"Heard what?" I ask, which is the wrong answer. It isn't that I'm not listening. I just don't give a shit.

He sighs. "Listen."

"I *am* listening!"

"No. I mean, listen, but not to me." He gets up, tosses a twenty onto the table—which isn't necessary, because he paid for the sandwich and the coffee at the counter, and this café doesn't do table service. "Meet me back here on Thursday."

I pick up the twenty, finger it, pocket it. Would've done him for the sandwich, or because I like his eyes, but whatever. "You got a place?"

He blinks, then actually looks annoyed. "*Listen,*" he commands again, and leaves.

I sit there for as long as I can, making the sandwich last, sipping his leftover coffee, savoring the fantasy of being normal. I people-watch, judge other patrons' appearances; on the fly I make up a poem about being a rich white girl who notices a poor black boy in her coffee shop and has an existential crisis. I imagine Paulo being impressed by my sophistication and admiring me, instead of thinking I'm just some dumb street kid who doesn't listen. I visualize myself going back to a nice apartment with a soft bed, and a fridge stuffed full of food.

Then a cop comes in, fat florid guy buying hipster joe for himself and his partner in the car, and his flat eyes skim the shop. I imagine mirrors around my head, a rotating cylinder of them that causes his gaze to bounce away. There's no real power in this—it's just something I do to try to make myself less afraid when the monsters are near. For the first time, though, it sort of works: the cop looks around, but doesn't ping on the lone black face. Lucky. I escape.

I paint the city. Back when I was in school, there was an artist who came in on Fridays to give us free lessons in perspective and lighting and other shit that white people go to art school to learn. Except this guy had done that, and he was black. I'd never seen a black artist before. For a minute I thought I could maybe be one too.

I can be, sometimes. Deep in the night, on a rooftop in Chinatown, with a spray can for each hand and a bucket of drywall paint that somebody left outside after doing up their living room in lilac, I move in scuttling, crablike swirls. The drywall stuff I can't use too much of; it'll start flaking off after a couple of rains. Spray paint's better for everything, but I like the contrast of the two textures—liquid black on rough lilac, red edging the black. I'm painting a hole. It's like a throat that doesn't start with a mouth or end in lungs: a thing that breathes and swallows endlessly, never filling. No one will see it except people in planes angling toward LaGuardia from the southwest, a few tourists who take helicopter tours, and NYPD aerial surveillance. I don't care what they see. It's not for them.

It's real late. I didn't have anywhere to sleep for the night, so this is what I'm doing to stay awake. If it wasn't the end of the month, I'd get on the subway, but the cops who haven't met their quota would fuck with me. Gotta be careful here; there's a lot of dumb-fuck Chinese kids west of Chrystie Street who wanna pretend to be a gang, protecting their territory, so I keep low. I'm skinny, dark; that helps too. All I want to do is paint, man, because it's in me and I need to get it out. I need to open up this throat. I need to, I need to . . . yeah. Yeah.

There's a soft, strange sound as I lay down the last streak of black. I pause and look around, confused for a moment—and then the throat sighs behind me. A big, heavy gust of moist air tickles the hairs on my skin. I'm not scared. This is why I did it, though I didn't realize that when I started. Not sure how I know now. But when I turn back, it's still just paint on a rooftop.

Paulo wasn't shitting me. Huh. Or maybe my mama was right, and I ain't never been right in the head.

I jump into the air and whoop for joy, and I don't even know why.

I spend the next two days going all over the city, drawing breathing holes everywhere, till my paint runs out.

I'm so tired on the day I meet Paulo again that I stumble and nearly fall through the café's plate-glass window. He catches my elbow and drags me over to a bench meant for customers. "You're hearing it," he says. He sounds pleased.

"I'm hearing coffee," I suggest, not bothering to stifle a yawn. A cop car rolls by. I'm not too tired to imagine myself as nothing, beneath notice, not even worth beating for pleasure. It works again; they roll on.

Paulo ignores my suggestion. He sits down beside me and his gaze goes strange and unfocused for a moment. "Yes. The city is breathing easier," he says. "You're doing a good job, even without training."

"I try."

He looks amused. "I can't tell if you don't believe me or if you just don't care."

I shrug. "I believe you." I also don't care, not much, because I'm hungry. My stomach growls. I've still got that twenty he gave me, but I'll take it to that church-plate sale I heard about over on Prospect, get chicken and rice and greens and cornbread for less than the cost of a free-trade small-batch-roasted latte.

He glances down at my stomach when it growls. Huh. I pretend to stretch and scratch above my abs, making sure to pull up my shirt a little. The artist guy brought a model for us to draw once, and pointed to this little ridge of muscle above the hips called Apollo's belt. Paulo's gaze goes right to it. *Come on, come on, fishy fishy. I need somewhere to sleep.*

Then his eyes narrow and focus on mine again. "I had forgotten," he says, in a faint wondering tone. "I almost . . . It's been so long. Once, though, I was a boy of the *favelas*."

"Not a lot of Mexican food in New York," I reply.

He blinks and looks amused again. Then he sobers. "This city will die," he says. He doesn't raise his voice, but he doesn't have to. I'm paying attention now. Food, living: these things have meaning to me. "If you do not learn the things I have to teach you. If you do not help. The time will come and you will fail, and this city will join Pompeii and Atlantis and a dozen others whose names no one remembers, even though hundreds of thousands of people died with them. Or perhaps there will be a stillbirth—the shell of the city surviving to possibly grow again in the future but its vital spark snuffed for now, like New Orleans—but that will still kill *you*, either way. You are the catalyst, whether of strength or destruction."

He's been talking like this since he showed up—places that never were, things that can't be, omens and portents. I figure it's bullshit because he's telling it to *me*, a kid whose own mama kicked him out and prays for him to die every day and probably hates me. *God* hates me. And I fucking hate God back, so why would he choose me for anything? But that's really why I start paying attention: because of God. I don't have to believe in something for it to fuck up my life.

"Tell me what to do," I say.

Paulo nods, looking smug. Thinks he's got my number. "Ah. You don't want to die."

I stand up, stretch, feel the streets around me grow longer and more pliable in the rising heat of day. (Is that really happening, or am I imagining it, or is it happening *and* I'm imagining that it's connected to me somehow?) "Fuck you. That ain't it."

"Then you don't even care about that." He makes it a question with the tone of his voice.

"Ain't about being alive." I'll starve to death someday, or freeze some winter night, or catch something that rots me away until the hospitals have to take me, even without money or an address. But

I'll sing and paint and dance and fuck and cry the city before I'm done, because it's mine. It's fucking *mine.* That's why.

"It's about *living*," I finish. And then I turn to glare at him. He can kiss my ass if he doesn't understand. "Tell me what to do."

Something changes in Paulo's face. He's listening now. To me. So he gets to his feet and leads me away for my first real lesson.

This is the lesson: great cities are like any other living things, being born and maturing and wearying and dying in their turn.

Duh, right? Everyone who's visited a real city feels that, one way or another. All those rural people who hate cities are afraid of something legit; cities really are *different.* They make a weight on the world, a tear in the fabric of reality, like . . . like black holes, maybe. Yeah. (I go to museums sometimes. They're cool inside, and Neil deGrasse Tyson is hot.) As more and more people come in and deposit their strangeness and leave and get replaced by others, the tear widens. Eventually it gets so deep that it forms a pocket, connected only by the thinnest thread of . . . something to . . . something. Whatever cities are made of.

But the separation starts a process, and in that pocket the many parts of the city begin to multiply and differentiate. Its sewers extend into places where there is no need for water. Its slums grow teeth, its art centers claws. Ordinary things within it, traffic and construction and stuff like that, start to have a rhythm like a heartbeat, if you record their sounds and play them back fast. The city . . . quickens.

Not all cities make it this far. There used to be a couple of great cities on this continent, but that was before Columbus fucked the Indians' shit up, so we had to start over. New Orleans failed, like Paulo said, but it survived, and that's something. It can try again. Mexico City's well on its way. But New York is the first American city to reach this point.

The gestation can take twenty years or two hundred or two thousand, but eventually the time will come. The cord is cut and the city becomes a thing of its own, able to stand on wobbly legs and do . . . well, whatever the fuck a living, thinking entity shaped like a big-ass city wants to do.

And just as in any other part of nature, there are things lying in wait for this moment, hoping to chase down the sweet new life and swallow its guts while it screams.

That's why Paulo's here to teach me. That's why I can clear the city's breathing and stretch and massage its asphalt limbs. I'm the midwife, see.

I run the city. I run it every fucking day.

Paulo takes me home. It's just somebody's summer sublet in the Lower East Side, but it feels like a home. I use his shower and eat some of the food in his fridge without asking, just to see what he'll do. He doesn't do shit except smoke a cigarette, I think to piss me off. I can hear sirens on the streets of the neighborhood—frequent, close. I wonder, for some reason, if they're looking for me. I don't say it aloud, but Paulo sees me twitching. He says, "The harbingers of the enemy will hide among the city's parasites. Beware of them."

He's always saying cryptic shit like this. Some of it makes sense, like when he speculates that maybe there's a *purpose* to all of it, some reason for the great cities and the process that makes them. What the enemy has been doing—attacking at the moment of vulnerability, crimes of opportunity—might just be the warm-up for something bigger. But Paulo's full of shit too, like when he says I should consider meditation to better attune myself to the city's needs. Like I'mma get through this on white-girl yoga.

"White-girl yoga," Paulo says, nodding. "Indian man yoga. Stockbroker racquetball and schoolboy handball, ballet and merengue, union halls and SoHo galleries. You will embody a city of millions. You need not *be* them, but know that they are part of you."

I laugh. "Racquetball? That shit ain't no part of me, chico."

"The city chose you, out of all," Paulo says. "Their lives depend on you."

Maybe. But I'm still hungry and tired all the time, scared all the time, never safe. What good does it do to be valuable if nobody values you?

He can tell I don't wanna talk anymore, so he gets up and goes to bed. I flop on the couch and I'm dead to the world. Dead.

Dreaming, dead dreaming, of a dark place beneath heavy cold waves where something stirs with a slithery sound and uncoils and turns toward the mouth of the Hudson, where it empties into the sea. Toward *me*. And I am too weak, too helpless, too immobilized by fear, to do anything but twitch beneath its predatory gaze.

Something comes from far to the south, somehow. (None of

this is quite real. Everything rides along the thin tether that connects the city's reality to that of the world. The *effect* happens in the world, Paulo has said. The *cause* centers around me.) It moves between me, wherever I am, and the uncurling thing, wherever it is. An immensity protects me, just this once, just in this place—though from a great distance I feel others hemming and grumbling and raising themselves to readiness. Warning the enemy that it must adhere to the rules of engagement that have always governed this ancient battle. It's not allowed to come at me too soon.

My protector, in this unreal space of dream, is a sprawling jewel with filth-crusted facets, a thing that stinks of dark coffee and the bruised grass of a *futebol* pitch and traffic noise and familiar cigarette smoke. Its threat display of saber-shaped girders lasts for only a moment, but that is enough. The uncurling thing flinches back into its cold cave, resentfully. But it will be back. That too is tradition.

I wake with sunlight warming half my face. Just a dream? I stumble into the room where Paulo is sleeping. "*São* Paulo," I whisper, but he does not wake. I wiggle under his covers. When he wakes he doesn't reach for me, but he doesn't push me away either. I let him know I'm grateful and give him a reason to let me back in, later. The rest'll have to wait till I get condoms and he brushes his ashy-ass mouth. After that, I use his shower again, put on the clothes I washed in his sink, and head out while he's still snoring.

Libraries are safe places. They're warm, in the winter. Nobody cares if you stay all day as long as you're not eyeballing the kids' corner or trying to hit up porn on the computers. The one at Forty-Second—the one with the lions—isn't that kind of library. It doesn't lend out books. Still, it has a library's safety, so I sit in a corner and read everything within reach: municipal tax law, *Birds of the Hudson Valley, What to Expect When You're Expecting a City Baby: NYC Edition*. See, Paulo? I told you I was listening.

It gets to be late afternoon and I head outside. People cover the steps, laughing, chatting, mugging with selfie sticks. There're cops in body armor over by the subway entrance, showing off their guns to the tourists so they'll feel safe from New York. I get a Polish sausage and eat it at the feet of one of the lions. Fortitude, not Patience. I know my strengths.

I'm full of meat and relaxed and thinking about stuff that ain't actually important—like how long Paulo will let me stay and whether I can use his address to apply for stuff—so I'm not watching the street. Until cold prickles skitter over my side. I know what it is before I react, but I'm careless again because I *turn to look* . . . Stupid, stupid, I fucking know better; cops down in Baltimore broke a man's spine for making eye contact. But as I spot these two on the corner opposite the library steps—short pale man and tall dark woman both in blue like black—I notice something that actually breaks my fear because it's so strange.

It's a bright, clear day, not a cloud in the sky. People walking past the cops leave short, stark afternoon shadows, barely there at all. But around these two, the shadows pool and curl as if they stand beneath their own private, roiling thundercloud. And as I watch, the shorter one begins to . . . *stretch,* sort of, his shape warping ever so slightly, until one eye is twice the circumference of the other. His right shoulder slowly develops a bulge that suggests a dislocated joint. His companion doesn't seem to notice.

Yooooo, nope. I get up and start picking my way through the crowd on the steps. I'm doing that thing I do, trying to shunt off their gaze—but it feels different this time. Sticky, sort of, threads of cheap-shit gum fucking up my mirrors. I *feel* them start following me, something immense and wrong shifting in my direction.

Even then I'm not sure—a lot of real cops drip and pulse sadism in the same way—but I ain't taking chances. My city is helpless, unborn as yet, and Paulo ain't here to protect me. I gotta look out for self, same as always.

I play casual till I reach the corner and book it, or try. Fucking tourists! They idle along the wrong side of the sidewalk, stopping to look at maps and take pictures of shit nobody else gives a fuck about. I'm so busy cussing them out in my head that I forget they can also be dangerous: somebody yells and grabs my arm as I Heisman past, and I hear a man yell out, "He tried to take her purse!" as I wrench away. *Bitch, I ain't took shit,* I think, but it's too late. I see another tourist reaching for her phone to call 911. Every cop in the area will be gunning for every black male aged whatever now.

I gotta get out of the area.

Grand Central's right there, sweet subway promise, but I see three cops hanging out in the entrance, so I swerve right to take Forty-First. The crowds thin out past Lex, but where can I go? I sprint across Third despite the traffic; there are enough gaps.

But I'm getting tired, 'cause I'm a scrawny dude who doesn't get enough to eat, not a track star.

I keep going, though, even through the burn in my side. I can feel *those* cops, the *harbingers of the enemy,* not far behind me. The ground shakes with their lumpen footfalls.

I hear a siren about a block away, closing. Shit, the UN's coming up; I don't need the Secret Service or whatever on me too. I jag left through an alley and trip over a wooden pallet. Lucky again—a cop car rolls by the alley entrance just as I go down, and they don't see me. I stay down and try to catch my breath till I hear the car's engine fading into the distance. Then, when I think it's safe, I push up. Look back, because the city is squirming around me, the concrete is jittering and heaving, everything from the bedrock to the rooftop bars is trying its damnedest to tell me to go. Go. *Go.*

Crowding the alley behind me is . . . is . . . the shit? I don't have words for it. Too many arms, too many legs, too many eyes, and all of them fixed on me. Somewhere in the mass I glimpse curls of dark hair and a scalp of pale blond, and I understand suddenly that these are—this is—my two cops. One real monstrosity. The walls of the alley crack as it oozes its way into the narrow space.

"Oh. Fuck. No," I gasp.

I claw my way to my feet and haul ass. A patrol car comes around the corner from Second Avenue and I don't see it in time to duck out of sight. The car's loudspeaker blares something unintelligible, probably *I'm gonna kill you,* and I'm actually amazed. Do they not see the thing behind me? Or do they just not give a shit because they can't shake it down for city revenue? Let them fucking shoot me. Better than whatever that thing will do.

I hook left onto Second Avenue. The cop car can't come after me against the traffic, but it's not like that'll stop some doubled-cop monster. Forty-Fifth. Forty-Seventh and my legs are molten granite. Fiftieth and I think I'm going to die. Heart attack far too young; poor kid, should've eaten more organic; should've taken it easy and not been so angry; the world can't hurt you if you just ignore everything that's wrong with it; well, not until it kills you anyway.

I cross the street and risk a look back and see something roll onto the sidewalk on at least eight legs, using three or four arms to push itself off a building as it careens a little . . . before coming straight after me again. It's the Mega Cop, and it's gaining. *Oh shit oh shit oh shit please no.*

Only one choice.

Swing right. Fifty-Third, against the traffic. An old folks' home, a park, a promenade . . . fuck those. Pedestrian bridge? Fuck that. I head straight for the six lanes of utter batshittery and potholes that is FDR Drive, do not pass Go, do not try to cross on foot unless you want to be smeared halfway to Brooklyn. Beyond it? The East River, if I survive. I'm even freaked out enough to try swimming in that fucking sewage. But I'm probably gonna collapse in the third lane and get run over fifty times before anybody thinks to put on brakes.

Behind me, the Mega Cop utters a wet, tumid *hough,* like it's clearing its throat for swallowing. I go

over the barrier and through the grass into fucking hell I go one lane silver car two lanes horns horns horns three lanes SEMI WHAT'S A FUCKING SEMI DOING ON THE FDR IT'S TOO TALL YOU STUPID UPSTATE HICK screaming four lanes GREEN TAXI screaming Smart Car hahaha cute five lanes moving truck six lanes and the blue Lexus actually brushes up against my clothes as it blares past screaming screaming screaming

screaming

screaming metal and tires as reality stretches, and nothing stops for the Mega Cop; it does not belong here and the FDR is an artery, vital with the movement of nutrients and strength and attitude and adrenaline, the cars are white blood cells and the thing is an irritant, an infection, an invader to whom the city gives no consideration and no quarter

screaming, as the Mega Cop is torn to pieces by the semi and the taxi and the Lexus and even that adorable Smart Car, which actually swerves a little to run over an extra-wiggly piece. I collapse onto a square of grass, breathless, shaking, wheezing, and can only stare as a dozen limbs are crushed, two dozen eyes squashed flat, a mouth that is mostly gums riven from jaw to palate. The pieces flicker like a monitor with an AV cable short, translucent to solid and back again—but FDR don't stop for shit except a presidential motorcade or a Knicks game, and this thing sure as hell ain't Carmelo Anthony. Pretty soon there's nothing left of it but half-real smears on the asphalt.

I'm alive. Oh, God.

I cry for a little while. Mama's boyfriend ain't here to slap me and say I'm not a man for it. Daddy would've said it was okay—tears mean you're alive—but Daddy's dead. And I'm alive.

With limbs burning and weak, I drag myself up, then fall again. Everything hurts. Is this that heart attack? I feel sick. Everything is shaking, blurring. Maybe it's a stroke. You don't have to be old for that to happen, do you? I stumble over to a garbage can and think about throwing up into it. There's an old guy lying on the bench—me in twenty years, if I make it that far. He opens one eye as I stand there gagging and purses his lips in a judgy way, like he could do better dry heaves in his sleep.

He says, "It's time," and rolls over to put his back to me.

Time. Suddenly I have to move. Sick or not, exhausted or not, something is . . . pulling me. West, toward the city's center. I push away from the can and hug myself as I shiver and stumble toward the pedestrian bridge. As I walk over the lanes I previously ran across, I look down onto flickering fragments of the dead Mega Cop, now ground into the asphalt by a hundred car wheels. Some globules of it are still twitching, and I don't like that. Infection, intrusion. I want it gone.

We want it gone. Yes. It's time.

I blink and suddenly I'm in Central Park. How the fuck did I get here? Disoriented, I realize only as I see their black shoes that I'm passing another pair of cops, but these two don't bother me. They should—skinny kid shivering like he's cold on a June day; even if all they do is drag me off somewhere to shove a plunger up my ass, they should *react* to me. Instead it's like I'm not there. Miracles exist, Ralph Ellison was right, any NYPD you can walk away from, hallelujah.

The Lake. Bow Bridge: a place of transition. I stop here, stand here, and I know . . . everything.

Everything Paulo's told me: it's true. Somewhere beyond the city, the Enemy is awakening. It sent forth its harbingers and they have failed, but its taint is in the city now, spreading with every car that passes over every now-microscopic iota of the Mega Cop's substance, and this creates a foothold. The Enemy uses this anchor to drag itself up from the dark toward the world, toward the warmth and light, toward the defiance that is *me*, toward the burgeoning wholeness that is *my city*. This attack is not all of it, of course. What comes is only the smallest fraction of the Enemy's old, old evil — but that should be more than enough to slaughter one lowly, worn-out kid who doesn't even have a real city to protect him.

Not yet. It's time. *In* time? We'll see.

On Second, Sixth, and Eighth Avenues, my water breaks. Mains, I mean. Water mains. Terrible mess, gonna fuck up the evening commute. I shut my eyes and I am seeing what no one else sees. I am feeling the flex and rhythm of reality, the contractions of possibility. I reach out and grip the railing of the bridge before me and feel the steady, strong pulse that runs through it. *You're doing good, baby. Doing great.*

Something begins to shift. I grow bigger, encompassing. I feel myself upon the firmament, heavy as the foundations of a city. There are others here with me, looming, watching — my ancestors' bones under Wall Street, my predecessors' blood ground into the benches of Christopher Park. No, *new* others, of my new people, heavy imprints upon the fabric of time and space. São Paulo squats nearest, its roots stretching all the way to the bones of dead Machu Picchu, watching sagely and twitching a little with the memory of its own relatively recent traumatic birth. Paris observes with distant disinterest, mildly offended that any city of our tasteless upstart land has managed this transition; Lagos exults to see a new fellow who knows the hustle, the hype, the fight. And more, many more, all of them watching, waiting to see if their numbers increase. Or not. If nothing else, they will bear witness that I, we, were great for one shining moment.

"We'll make it," I say, squeezing the railing and feeling the city contract. All over the city, people's ears pop, and they look around in confusion. "Just a little more. Come on." I'm scared, but there's no rushing this. *Lo que pasa, pasa* — damn, now that song is in my head, *in me* like the rest of New York. It's all here, just like Paulo said. There's no gap between me and the city anymore.

And as the firmament ripples, slides, tears, the Enemy writhes up from the deeps with a reality-bridging roar —

But it is too late. The tether is cut and we are here. We become! We stand, whole and hale and independent, and our legs don't even wobble. We got this. Don't sleep on the city that never sleeps, son, and don't fucking bring your squamous eldritch bullshit here.

I raise my arms and avenues leap. (It's real but it's not. The ground jolts and people think, *Huh, subway's really shaky today.*) I brace my feet and they are girders, anchors, bedrock. The beast of the deeps shrieks and I laugh, giddy with postpartum endorphins. *Bring it.* And when it comes at me I hip-check it with the BQE, backhand it with Inwood Park, drop the South Bronx on it like an elbow. (On the evening news that night, ten construction sites will report wrecking-ball collapses. City safety regulations are so lax; terrible, terrible.) The Enemy tries some kind of fucked-up wiggly shit—it's all tentacles—and I snarl and bite into it 'cause New Yorkers eat damn near as much sushi as Tokyo, mercury and all.

Oh, now you're crying! Now you wanna run? Nah, son. You came to the wrong town. I curb-stomp it with the full might of Queens and something inside the beast breaks and bleeds iridescence all over creation. This is a shock, for it has not been truly hurt in centuries. It lashes back in a fury, faster than I can block, and from a place that most of the city cannot see, a skyscraper-long tentacle curls out of nowhere to smash into New York Harbor. I scream and fall, I can *hear* my ribs crack, and—no!—a major earthquake shakes Brooklyn for the first time in decades. The Williamsburg Bridge twists and snaps apart like kindling; the Manhattan groans and splinters, though thankfully it does not give way. I feel every death as if it is my own.

Fucking kill you for that, bitch, I'm not-thinking. The fury and grief have driven me into a vengeful fugue. The pain is nothing; this ain't my first rodeo. Through the groan of my ribs I drag myself upright and brace my legs in a pissing-off-the-platform stance. Then I shower the Enemy with a one-two punch of Long Island radiation and Gowanus toxic waste, which burn it like acid. It screams again in pain and disgust, but *Fuck you, you don't belong here, this city is mine, get out!* To drive this lesson home I cut the bitch with LIRR traffic, long vicious honking lines; and to stretch out its pain I salt these wounds with the memory of a bus ride to LaGuardia and back.

And just to add insult to injury? I backhand its ass with Hoboken, raining the drunk rage of ten thousand dudebros down on it like the hammer of God. Port Authority makes it honorary New York, motherfucker; you just got Jerseyed.

The Enemy is as quintessential to nature as any city. We cannot be stopped from becoming, and the Enemy cannot be made to end. I hurt only a small part of it—but I know damn well I sent that part back broken. Good. Time ever comes for that final confrontation, it'll think twice about taking me on again.

Me. *Us.* Yes.

When I relax my hands and open my eyes to see Paulo striding along the bridge toward me with another goddamned cigarette between his lips, I fleetingly see him for what he is again: the sprawling thing from my dream, all sparkling spires and reeking slums and stolen rhythms made over with genteel cruelty. I know that he glimpses what I am too, all the bright light and bluster of me. Maybe he's always seen it, but there is *admiration* in his gaze now, and I like it. He comes to help support me with his shoulder, and he says, "Congratulations," and I grin.

I live the city. It thrives and it is mine. I am its worthy avatar, and together? We will never be afraid again.

Fifty years later.

I sit in a car, watching the sunset from Mulholland Drive. The car is mine; I'm rich now. The city is not mine, but that's all right. The person is coming who will make it live and stand and thrive in the ancient way . . . or not. I know my duty, respect the traditions. Each city must emerge on its own or die trying. We elders merely guide, encourage. Stand witness.

There: a dip in the firmament near the Sunset Strip. I can feel the upwelling of loneliness in the soul I seek. Poor, empty baby. Won't be long now, though. Soon—if she survives—she'll never be alone again.

I reach for my city, so far away, so inseverable from myself. *Ready?* I ask New York.

Fuck yeah, it answers, filthy and fierce.

We go forth to find this city's singer, and hopefully to hear the greatness of its birthing song.

CAROLINE M. YOACHIM

Welcome to the Medical Clinic at the Interplanetary Relay Station | Hours Since the Last Patient Death: 0

FROM *Lightspeed Magazine*

A. You take a shortcut through the hydroponics bay on your way to work and notice that the tomato plants are covered in tiny crawling insects that look like miniature beetles. One of the insects skitters up your leg, so you reach down and brush it off. It bites your hand. The area around the bite turns purple and swollen.

You run down a long metal hallway to the Medical Clinic, grateful for the artificially generated gravity that defies the laws of physics and yet is surprisingly common in fictional space stations. The sign on the clinic door says HOURS SINCE THE LAST PATIENT DEATH: The number currently posted on the sign is zero. If you enter the clinic anyway, go to C. If you seek medical care elsewhere, go to B.

B. You are in a relay station in orbit halfway between Saturn and Uranus. There is no other medical care available. Proceed to C.

Why are you still reading this? You're supposed to go to C. Are you sure you won't go into the clinic? No? Fine. You return to your quarters and search the station's database to find a cure for the raised purple scabs that are now spreading up your arm. Most of the database entries recommend amputation. The rash looks pretty serious, and you probably ought to go to C, but if you absolutely refuse to go to the clinic, go to Z and die a horrible, painful death.

*

C. Inside the clinic, a message plays over the loudspeakers: "Welcome to the Medical Clinic at the Interplanetary Relay Station, please sign your name on the clipboard. Patients will be seen in the order that they arrive. If this is an emergency, we're sorry—you're probably screwed. The current wait time is six hours." The message is on endless repeat, cycling through dozens of different languages.

The clipboard is covered in green mucus, probably from a Saturnian slug-monkey. They are exceedingly rude creatures, always hungry and extremely temperamental. You wipe away the slime with the sleeve of your shirt and enter your information. The clipboard chirps in a cheerful voice, "You are number 283. If you leave the waiting room, you will be moved to the end of the queue. If your physiology is incompatible with long waiting-room stays, you may request a mobile tracker and wait in one of our satellite rooms. The current wait for a mobile tracker is four hours."

If you decide to wait in the waiting room, go to D. If you request a mobile tracker, go to D anyway, because there is no chance you will get one.

D. You hand the clipboard to the patient behind you, a Tarmandian Spacemite from the mining colonies. As you hand it off, you realize the clipboard is printing a receipt. The sound of the printer triggers the spacemite's predatory response, and it eats the clipboard.

"Attention patients, the clipboard has been lost. Patients will be seen in the order they arrived. Please line up using the number listed on your receipt. If you do not have a receipt, you will need to wait and sign in when a new clipboard is assembled."

If you wait for the new clipboard, go back to C. If you are smart enough to recognize that going back to C will result in a loop that does not advance the story, proceed to E.

E. Instead of waiting in line, you take advantage of the waiting-room chaos to go to the nurses' station and demand treatment. There are two nurses at the station, a tired-looking human and a Uranian Doodoo. The Doodoo is approximately twice your size, covered in dark brown fur, and speaks a language that only contains the letters *d, t, b, p,* and *o.* If you talk to the human nurse, go to F. If you talk to the big brown Doodoo from Uranus, go to G. Also, stop snickering. The planet is pronounced "urine iss," not "your anus."

F. The human nurse sees the nasty purple rash on your arm and demands that you quarantine yourself in your quarters. If you accept this advice, go back to B. Have you noticed all the loops in this story? The loops simulate the ultimate futility of attempting to get medical care. What are you still doing here? Go back to B. Next time you get to the nurses' station, remember to pick the nonhuman nurse.

G. You approach the Uranian nurse and babble a bunch of words that end in *oo,* which is your best approximation of Doodoo language. Honestly, the attempt is kind of offensive. The Doodoos are a civilization older than humankind, with a nuanced language steeped in a complex alien culture. Why would you expect a random assortment of words ending in *oo* to communicate something meaningful?

Thankfully, the nurse does not respond to your blatant mockery of its language, so you hold out your arm and point to the purple rash. In a single bite, it eats your entire arm, cauterizing the wound with its highly acidic saliva. The rash is gone. If you consider yourself cured, proceed to Y. If you stay at the clinic in hopes of getting a prosthetic arm, go to H.

H. You approach the human nurse and ask about the availability of prosthetic limbs. He hands you a stack of twenty-four forms to fill out. The Doodoo nurse has eaten the hand you usually write with. If you fill out all the forms with your remaining hand, go to I. If you fill out only the top form and leave the rest blank, hoping that no one will notice, go to I.

I. The nurse takes your paperwork and shoves it into a folder. He leads you down a hallway to an exam room filled with an assortment of syringes and dissection tools. "Take off all your clothes and put on this gown," the nurse instructs, "and someone will be in to see you soon." If you do what the nurse says, go to J. If you keep your clothes on, go to K.

*

J. The exam room is cold and the gown is three sizes too small and paper-thin. You sit down, only to notice that the tissue paper that covers the exam table hasn't been changed and is covered in tiny crawling insects that look like miniature beetles. Sitting down is a decision that has literally come back to bite you in the ass. If you leap up screaming and brush the insects off your bare skin, go to L. If you calmly brush the insects away and then yell for someone to come in and clean the room, go to L.

K. Three hours later, the doctor arrives. You are relieved to see that she is human. You ask her if she can issue you a prosthetic limb. She says no, mumbles something about resource allocation forms, and leaves. If you accept her refusal and decide to consider yourself cured, go to Y. If you scream down the hall at the departing doctor that you must have a new arm, go to L.

L. A security officer comes, attracted by the sound of your screams. Clinic security is handled by a six-foot-tall Tarmandian Spacemite with poisonous venom, sharp teeth, and a fondness for U.S. tax law. If you run, go to M. If you are secretly a trained warrior and decide to kill the Tarmandian Spacemite with your bare hands so you can eat its head, go to N. If you sit very still and hope the Tarmandian Spacemite goes away, go to O.

M. Running triggers the predatory instincts of the Tarmandian Spacemite. Go to Z.

N. You use your completely unforeshadowed (but useful!) fighting skills to overpower the security officer. The head of the Tarmandian Spacemite is a delicious delicacy, salty and crunchy and full of delightful worms that squiggle all the way down your throat. Unfortunately, you forgot to remove the venomous fangs. Go to Z.

O. You sit perfectly still on the exam table, and tiny insects that resemble miniature beetles crawl into your pants and bite you repeatedly, leaving a clump of purple bumps that look suspiciously similar to the scabby rash you had on your arm when you arrived at the clinic. When you're sure the Tarmandian Spacemite is gone, go to P.

*

P. You have lost an arm and the lower half of your torso is covered in a purple rash. If you decide to cut your losses and consider yourself cured, go to R. If you rummage through the cabinets in the exam room, go to S.

Q. There is nothing in the story that directs you to this section, so if you are reading this, you have failed to follow instructions. Go directly to Z and die your horrible, painful death. Or skip to somewhere else, since you clearly aren't playing by the rules anyway.

R. You sneak out of the clinic and return to your quarters. You search the station database for treatments for your beetle-induced purple rash. There is no known cure, although some patients have had luck with amputation of the affected areas. Sadly, you are incapable of amputating your own ass. Even if you go back to the clinic, the rash is now too widespread to be treated. Go to Z. Or, if you want to see what would have happened if you'd opted to search through the exam room cabinets, go to S. But remember, going to S is only to see what hypothetically would have happened. Your true fate is Z.

S. You rummage through the cabinets and find an assortment of ointments and lotions. If you read the instructions on all the bottles, go to T. If you select a few bottles at random and slather them on your rash, go to T. Have you noticed how often you end up in the same place no matter what you chose? In the clinic, as in life, decisions that seem important are often ultimately meaningless. In the end, all of us will die and none of this will matter. Now seriously, go to T.

T. None of the ointments or lotions do anything for your rash. The Uranian nurse comes in to clean the room and discovers you. If you pretend to work at the clinic, go to U. If you ask for help with your rash, go to V. If you run away, go to W.

(There is no U, much as there is no hope for patients of the clinic. The nurse would have recognized you anyway. Go to V.)

V. The Doodoo from Uranus (seriously, are you in third grade? Stop pronouncing the planet as "your anus") examines your rash and amputates the affected areas by eating them, neatly cauterizing the wound with the acid in its saliva. You are now a head with approximately half a torso. If you consider yourself cured, go to X. Otherwise, go to Z.

W. You flee from the Uranian nurse but slip on a puddle of slimy green mucus excreted by another patient, probably that idiot slug-monkey that slimed the clipboard. You crash into the wall, and before you can get back up, the Uranian nurse amputates the areas affected by the rash by eating them, neatly cauterizing the wound with the acid in its saliva. You are now a head with approximately half a torso. If you consider yourself cured, go to X. Otherwise go to Z.

X. You are not cured. You are a head with half a torso, and missing several internal organs. Go to Z.

Y. Congratulations, you have survived your trip to the Medical Clinic at the Interplanetary Relay Station! All you have to do now is fill out your discharge papers. You start filling out the forms with your one remaining hand, but you accidentally drop the pen onto the oozing foot of the Saturnian slug-monkey waiting in line behind you. This is undoubtedly the idiot that slimed the sign-in clipboard. You cuss the slug-monkey out with some choice words in French. Choice words because it was rude to leave slime all over the clipboard. French because you know better than to make a slug-monkey angry. You've watched enough education vids to know that slug-monkeys are always hungry, which makes them temperamental.

Unfortunately for you, Saturnian slug-monkeys are far better educated than arrogant humans give them credit for. This one is fluent in several languages, including French. It eats you. Go to Z.

Z. You die a horrible, painful death. But at least you won't have to deal with your insurance company!

ALICE SOLA KIM

Successor, Usurper, Replacement

FROM *BuzzFeed READER*

THERE WAS NO question of going home that night. The streets
below Lee's high-rise apartment had flooded, and everyone had
received an alert that the beast had been sighted near their area.
If they went out, their safety could not be guaranteed. The word-
ing of the alert troubled everyone, even though of course this was
always the case — the non-guarantee of anyone's safety ever — but
still the warnings were alarmingly pushy and made your phone
buzz and compelled you to look immediately at the message from
the city telling you hi, just a reminder that we're all going to die
someday, especially you, and it might even happen sooner than
expected. Hiiiiiiiii!

When Wong had lifted his phone to check if it had been dam-
aged by the rain, it buzzed with the alert; then each of theirs did,
one after another. Lee ran to the windows and drew the blinds
shut. It was superstition, she knew, but they had all heard rumors
that even seeing the beast could be dangerous. That night, half of
the group was missing, having canceled earlier with many excla-
mation points. Sick! Headache! Forgot! In utter terror of going
outside! Only Huynh, Kim, and Wong had made it. Not everyone
in the group was Asian, but only the Asians were present tonight,
which made them feel a little self-conscious.

Lee was glad to see them. The group was not small enough to
feel awkward, like that time when it was only Lee and someone
else facing Kim like a parent and a principal as they were going
to town on his writing. As was customary, Lee was hosting, since
her writing was up for discussion by the group tonight. Another
custom: the consumption of alcohol.

Huynh had brought a box of pinot grigio that had a picture of an actual bottle of wine on the front, which seemed like an unintuitive marketing choice, to remind you so baldly of what you weren't getting. But Huynh didn't care if something was gross, as long as there was a lot of it. She ate like she'd recently emerged from a nuclear bunker.

Kim had brought a six-pack of gruesomely hoppy IPA, which gave one's tongue a post-diarrhea sensation, desiccated and sour. Lee still had three bottles in her fridge from the last time the group had met at her place, about five rounds ago.

Finally, Wong had brought a bottle of whiskey less than half full, an extremely irritating offering which would only be appreciated later in the evening.

The restaurants in the area had stopped delivering, so Lee set a pot of pasta bubbling on the stove. Everyone kept glancing at it resentfully, knowing that it would make them feel fat immediately and ravenous half an hour later. They still wanted it, very much.

Wong tried to call couch for the night and Huynh smiled at him. "You can try," she said.

Lee dragged a dusty air mattress from the closet and told Wong and Kim they could sleep on it tonight. This was a cursed air mattress; those who lay upon it were flush with the floor before dawn and beset with prehistorically brutal colds by morning, but no one had to know that.

Though their friendships were no less potent across genders, something old-fashioned and unchill, an Asian, nonhuggy thing, kept them from sharing physical boy-girl space too closely. Huynh, in fact, was terrible at physical contact in general; Huynh hugged like a haunted porcelain doll that had come to life. One summer during college, Lee, Wong, and Kim had sublet an apartment in the city together, and without any argument or question Lee had taken the king bed in the master bedroom, while Wong and Kim had shared the tiny guest bedroom and its twin floor mattress, where essentially Kim slept curled by Wong's feet every night, sprawled half on the mattress and half on a pile of clothes on the floor.

Of course, no one had thought to give Lee the tiny guest bedroom. But that was usual: Lee got things, occasionally (it seemed like) more things than any one person deserved, but she worked hard enough to deserve many of them. Like her apartment. She made enough money to buy everything that the store had told her went with the items she had picked out; her home was beautiful in a way that wouldn't necessarily make you compliment the owner, since it was clear that some giant hand with impeccable corporate catalog taste had set down each element in her home like a chess piece, only letting go when everything was just right. But her friends were hers, and her friends she surveyed in satisfaction, draped over her furniture, pinned in here for the night. Everyone, the older they got, slipped away, was harder to hold to real plans or, once the plans were made and honored, harder to keep for long enough, as if death and the way objects got colder and spun out further and further from each other was a process that began long, long, long before the actual dying and heat loss, so subtly that no one knew to be scared enough to stop it.

Lee loved her friends, and she loved that they couldn't leave tonight. Could there be something like taxidermy but without anything dying? she wondered. If she could do something like killing her friends (but not killing, of course not killing) but a kind of killing of their lives and outside worlds that would force them to stay here and have fun, except they wouldn't even know they were being forced, it's just that staying here and having fun would be all that they wanted to do and could imagine doing, would she do it?

The intercom beeped. Lee was startled, for no one else had been expected. On the intercom she saw a long-haired girl standing still, head hanging, blurred by the rain. It was—well, Lee had forgotten the girl's name, but she did know that the girl was a new member of the group, a person someone else had invited.

Lee buzzed her in. She heard the distant *shunk* of the elevator below, then the doors slid open. The elevator opened directly into Lee's apartment, as it did for every unit in the building, which was supposed to be a fancy amenity but felt more like having a giant hole that led right into your guts. Not that kind of hole.

So right away the girl was in Lee's apartment. No time to think about whether it was the right choice or not to let her in, although why wouldn't it be? The rain had reduced the girl to the purest essence of herself, hair plasticked to her head, clothes and even skin seeming to adhere more tightly to her skeleton. She had long, thick bangs. Although the rain had separated them into chunks, the bangs covered her eyes so perfectly that you only knew she had eyes because you assumed she had eyes, why wouldn't she have eyes, but—

—did she have eyes?

The girl swiped at her forehead with the back of her hand like a cat, revealing her eyes, which of course she did have. They were small and very white and very black like dominoes. "Sorry I'm late!" she said.

"Sorry you got caught out there," said Lee. "Did you get the alert?"

The girl shook her head. "I don't have a phone."

Lee reminded herself that lots and lots and lots of people didn't have phones. Among the people she knew, how many of them did not have a phone? Even if the answer was zero, it didn't mean it was wrong to not have a phone.

The girl did not have a phone, and it did not look like she brought alcohol. She only brought her wet hair and disappearing eyes. Lee brought her a clean towel from the bathroom and the girl accepted it, smiling. Everyone said hi with disturbing and transparent vigor to make up for the fact that no one knew her name. Still, they found her familiar, and each knew for certain that one of them had invited the girl into the group.

Of course, no one had invited the girl here, at least not on purpose. This was one of those things that someone else, perhaps some unseen observer, could figure out in two seconds, but it would take everyone who was in the room much longer, which was really too bad.

"Thanks for having me, guys," said the girl. She sat down and twisted her legs together, the towel draped over her shoulders.

They ate the pasta with butter, salt, soy sauce, hot sauce, peanut butter, back-of-the-fridge Parmesan that had gone the texture of Comet, and anchovy paste. Many of those ingredients were on the list only because of Huynh. Outside the sky boomed and the rain sounded swarming and continuous, which made the food taste better. The girl wasn't eating. Instead she sipped a beer and asked everyone questions about themselves. People new to the group were either shy and watchful, embarrassed to admit what they didn't know, or they were loud and bossy about it, forcing others to explain themselves in the simplest terms possible. Basically, did they see the world from the orientation *I am new to you,* or were they more of a *you are new to me* person? The girl was very much the latter.

What are you working on right now? And you and you and you and you?

Where did you all meet? How did you all meet? How come you all like each other?

What are you doing in this city?

It was nice enough, certainly, to be asked questions, until it was clear she was being an avid robot debutante of an interrogator who despite not seeming super-interested in the answers would not quit with the goddamn questions, which was much worse than someone just talking a lot and being boring, because this way it turned you into the boring one, it shanghaied you into boringosity and from inside the prison of your voice brayed autobiographically on and on as you were helpless to stop it.

Lee, who was working on a gruesome fantasy trilogy, watched Kim's (short stories featuring a guy much like himself, also named Kim, always) nascent sexual interest in the girl wither and die, while Wong's (boarding-school memoir full of lies) nonsexual interest in the girl as a potential subject of later shit-talking grew, his spare body leaning ever closer to her. Wong gave Lee a look so blankly innocent that it was obviously horrifically rude, and Lee was glad the girl hadn't noticed. Huynh (long short stories often about people grappling with philosophical conundrums who inevitably ended up committing sudden acts of violence) looked up from her phone.

"Guess whose birthday it is today," she said.

"Who?" said Kim.

"It's mine," said Huynh.

"Your birthday! How old are you, exactly?" said Wong. They'd been friends with Huynh for years, maybe three, but since they hadn't gone to college with her, they weren't clear on her exact age. They only knew that she existed in the same category of melty sameishness which they had all descended into after college.

"2_!" Huynh smiled rectangularly, all teeth, no eyes, and let out a cute, strangled scream. "Aaagh!"

2_! Quite an age. The age to start getting serious. A nasty-ass terrifying age. If they were honest, it was the age to already be a little serious, so you could be ready to have your life be perfect by

the time you were 3_ or thereabouts, right? Huynh was not serious. She wore hoodies that had draggy ape-arm sleeves and scissor
holes for her thumbs. For the past year and a half she had been
living on an insurance payout from a car accident she'd been in.
Unfortunately, Huynh had not grown up with money and so was
unable to do anything with hers but lose it quickly and clumsily.
She only ate bad impulse delivery—franchise pizzas and gummy
Thai—and was always rebuying headphones and power cords and
ordering unrealistic dresses she'd neither wear nor return and always, always paying the late fees on anything capable of accruing
them. Though she either seemed horny or had the ability to become so, Huynh had never dated anyone, as far as they knew. Of
Huynh but never, ever to Huynh, Wong said that he wished he
could hire her a life coach, or even be her life coach, because her
life was such a mess that you could make a huge difference in it
just by telling her to eat one vegetable a week or to write down her
appointments somewhere.

That said, the rest of them were also 2_ or about to be, and if
you looked past the relationships, the good jobs, the minor artistic
plaudits and encouragements, it wasn't like they were doing so hot
either.

"So young," said the girl.

"Really?" said Kim. He looked at her, age indeterminate à la
one of their people: Girlish bangs. Pink tank top. Pale, springy
cheeks that could look resplendent with baby fat or slack and jowly
depending on how tired she was or how much water she'd drunk.
A long, long, very long, too long neck trisected by deep horizon-
tal wrinkles. Sometimes people got those from reading too much.
Even kids.

"Of course very young," she said. "Happy birthday, Huynh."

Then Lee, Kim, and Wong remembered to shout "Happy birthday!" at Huynh. They had been friends for so long that it was too
easy for strangers to outpolite them. "I wish we had a cake for
you," said the girl, smiling at Huynh.

Hmm! Mighty presumptuous, what with the girl having just met
Huynh and the rest of them. Although, then again, the girl was
here because she was supposed to know one of them. And now
the girl had learned too much about them, and they nothing at all
about her. Of course, at this point it would be completely impossible for them to ask her for her name.

Joke was on the girl. Lee had a slice of cake in the freezer. It was too bad, she had just managed to successfully forget that the cake was in her fridge, but at least she would immediately be able to get rid of it. She microwaved the cake for a few minutes, imagining wiggly rays—invisible on this wavelength but blaring red and deadly merely one level over—shooting into and through her guts.

When she brought the cake over to Huynh, they screamed. Wong hovered his hands above the cake, a movement that landed somewhere between doing Reiki and preparing to strangle someone.

"Are you sure?" said Huynh.

"I want to get rid of it," said Lee. "It's a cursed cake. But you eating it on your birthday will reverse the curse."

"Reverse the curse," said the girl.

"It was her wedding cake," said Wong. "You can tell because the frosting looks like a couch."

"And now it's passing into another state of matter," said Kim. "Moment of silence, please."

Huynh put a fist delicately over her mouth. "I— *mmplgh!* I declare the curse reversed."

"Yeah," said Kim. "Fuck that guy."

They were quiet for a moment. Then, as the girl said, "Why don't we get started," the power blinked out.

At first all was chaos and panic; at first it was as if without their noticing the outside had bled and dripped into the inside until the inside had been fully painted over by the outside and now the beast was here with them, the inside that was the outside; the lights in the street and the surrounding buildings had gone out too, and all was darkness as the girl sat there smiling, which no one could see.

Then everyone remembered that they had their phones and one by one they appeared in the dark as busts glowing delicately blue in a far-future museum, the unspecified museum they were trying to make it into with their writing, as stupid as that sounded and whether they admitted it to themselves or not, because it wasn't as if their jobs or families or stations in life or beauty or kindness or cruelty would get them there. They were investing their current happiness against future gain, except the cause-and-effect was screwy and some of them weren't doing this on purpose—some of them were very, very unhappy, so their main consolation was that their eventual glorious future would stretch backward in time. So they dug in, burrowed tight foxholes where they could be surrounded by their unhappiness, nurtured sweet little gardens made up of and inside their unhappiness.

Hey! Holy fuck. Are we still alive or are we dead right now? Oh my god. Hiiiiiiii! they said to each other, laughing. Kim took a photo of everyone in their tiny blue islands. Lee found a flashlight, and the girl produced candles and a bottle from a backpack they hadn't noticed.

"They said there would be a storm tonight," she said, laughing as she laid out the candles for Lee to light. "I came prepared!" Her teeth glinted. Lee noticed that her hair hadn't dried at all, not one bit. Dark ropes of it clung to her shoulders and chest, and a few strands were wrapped around her throat; Lee had the urge to brush them out of the way.

The girl said, "I want you guys to be happy."

"We've been talking a lot," said Lee. "What about you? What do you write? What are you doing in the city?"

"Look, I brought alcohol," said the girl. "Bourbon." She sprang up and scampered to Lee's kitchen, where she pulled out the first cuplike objects her hands touched—mugs, a highball glass, a soup bowl. "You guys drink bourbon, right? Writers. All you writers. Bourbon is a thing writers are supposed to drink. Drink up." They felt both flirted with and completely humiliated.

Somehow they had ended up in a circle sitting on the floor. It felt safer that way. Once the lights went out, it was best to preemptively cut your ties to other so-called necessities, like furniture.

"Let's do shots," said the girl.

They drank. The girl's arm snaked out, long and white, and poured more. "Another!" she shouted. That was certainly a kind of person, the person who demanded that everyone do shots. Or, given that you couldn't always predict who would get that antic gleam, who would yell for more shots the way a child might scream for another story and would literally not stop with the shots until something bad and un-fun happened—the shots monster was more like a demon that roamed bars and colleges and worked holiday parties to possess the susceptible.

Lee's face never got red, but too much alcohol still begrimed her on a cellular level; her drunks felt dark and deeply allergic, but at least they didn't fuck up her countenance. Unlike Kim, whose eyes always went an itchy highlighter-pink in the presence of even a drop of a beer, though there was something manly and endearing and almost bruised-looking about his inflamed face.

"You're being so guarded around me," the girl whispered sadly.

When are we going to talk about my writing? Lee wanted to say but didn't. Who cared, anyway. It was a particularly gnarly excerpt from book two of her fantasy trilogy, the kind of piece that would drag the group into unhelpful arguments about blood-spatter patterns and what kinds of plausible damage could be done to a person via broadsword, unicorn horn, mace. They did not respect her. *Just wait,* she thought. *I will be rich and respected. I will not have to choose, the way you all think you're choosing.*

The shots monster changed form and the girl lit up. "I know!" she said. "Drinking game!"

The girl made everyone write down nouns on little scraps of paper torn from a small notebook she produced from her backpack. The paper scraps were folded and piled in the middle of the circle. The girl took a die out of her pocket and told them that when it was your turn, you would pick a scrap of paper before rolling the die—making sure no one else could see the number you got.

If you got an even number, you had to tell a true story that involved the thing that was written on the paper scrap you picked. If the number was odd, you would make a story up. Then everyone would go around the circle and guess if the story was true or false. Whoever is wrong drinks. For each person who guesses right, the storyteller has to take a drink.

"Because you're all writers," said the girl. They felt embarrassed again.

Kim said, "Let's do this." He selected a piece of paper and turned away from the circle and rolled. "Okay," he said. "I can work with this."

The paper said NAME.

"My last name—there's a shit-ton of us," Kim said. "But my first name is less common." The first time he got a story published, he thought about changing things up, maybe throwing in a middle name. But he decided to use his regular name, as is, since he wanted all the glory and acclaim ("such as there was") for himself, the normal everyday self with whom he was already familiar. Why should some artificial new construct—some guy who hadn't even been there through the hard work—take all the credit?

Years passed, he got a few more things published, and one day something strange happened. Kim received an email from a prestigious literary journal accepting a short story of his. Great! Except Kim didn't recognize the title of the story, because he hadn't written it. He let the journal know that they had gotten him mixed up with someone else. Now, if it had ended there, it would have been a funny little blip, a cute story he could tell about the time he got something he really wanted but it turned out to have been a terrible mistake and was thus immediately wrested from him, talk about impostor syndrome, I'll tell you about impostor syndrome.

But that incident begat others, in which he started receiving both acceptances and rejections for things he hadn't written. "A lose-lose situation. The acceptances didn't feel good and the rejections still felt terrible." Kim started thinking again about using another name, except now he'd racked up a few publications and it would be a giant ass-pain to start all over again. But nor could he let the current situation stand. What to do?

Just the other day, the other Kim contacted Kim. The other Kim's email was neutral in tone, very direct. He stated that he had been getting mistaken for Kim off and on over the past few years and surmised that this must also be happening to Kim in the other direction. So he made a proposal: since it was apparent that they both worked slowly, why not pool their resources and combine themselves into one Kim? The other Kim wrote, "I have read your work and though it is quite different from my own, I believe we would complement each other well. Please also keep in mind that half of something is better than all of—as it stands right now, for both of us—absolutely nothing."

"We complete each other," said Kim. This whole time, he had kept himself from reading the other Kim's stories. He had this irrational idea that if he were to do so, something awful would happen—he might learn something it would be much better for him not to know. So he hadn't decided yet. Although of course he was definitely going to say no.

"True," said Wong.

"False," said Lee.

"False," said Huynh.

"True," said the girl.

Kim pointed at Lee and Huynh. "Drink," he said.

"Why would you never tell us this?" said Huynh.

Kim shrugged. "It just happened."

"No, dick, I know you said the other Kim just wrote to you, but I'm talking about the earlier stuff."

"I didn't know you then."

Huynh glowered at him. The girl threw her head back and laughed. "Love it. I'm getting so much out of this. I'm so glad we're doing this." She refilled their cups. The level of liquid in the bottle appeared unchanged.

Wong was next. The paper said SCHOOLBOY. He blanched.

"I got a bad one," Wong said, making a face. He thought for a moment, then began.

When Wong talked at length, he was hypnotic. Which could be bad at times, since his clipped accent, the precision of his speech, and the rich perverted sweet-rot depth of his voice all combined to make it sound like he really meant everything he said. One learned very quickly that this was not the case, but when confronted with that voice, one had a little trouble remembering that, now didn't one. He could be intimidating, especially for Huynh, who was already continually shoulder-chipped by the fact that she hadn't gone to the same fancy college as the rest of them. He hurt feelings often, but he didn't mean to—a dumb joke from another person would sound like a blithe yet piercing condemnation from the president of the 1 percent from Wong. That voice!

Wong told of a friendship he had had while in boarding school in Switzerland. This was a close friendship, childish because it was so obsessive, but adult because they seemingly saw each other clearly; they were fully mutually admiring of each other. Though Wong and the friend resembled each other physically and had similar tastes and personalities and aptitudes for school and sport, they treasured in the other the things that were different: Wong's easy, conversational manner with teachers and fellow students alike; the friend's single-minded ability to complete a paper or problem set from start to finish without interruption; one's thick, fashionable glasses; the other's adorably decorative smattering of acne. "It was very gay, as I can see you thinking, but my friend was not gay. Or perhaps a little, just for me. There was this one time in Paris—

"Anyway, I was extremely popular," Wong said, as only Wong

could say. But this friend gave Wong something no other friend could. Wong, who had been orphaned when he was a small child, knew no one else and was known by no one else to such a comforting extent. The friend knew Wong so well partially because they were so similar, which then made the differences all the more apparent, something to be mapped and delineated and treasured.

One winter break, they lied to various parties and spent break unsupervised in one of the Wong family properties in Paris. Toward the end of break the friend received news that his parents had been killed in an accident. And after the funeral, the friend would be moved to another school, closer to his relatives.

The friend did not want to go to a strange new school, to leave Wong and his other friends behind. So they came up with a plan. Wong would go to the new school in his friend's stead, while the friend would stay at their school, where he could impersonate both Wong and himself. "When you feel bad, be me," Wong had told him. It would help. And if the friend missed himself, felt the need for a small pocket of space-time in which to grieve, then he could always return to himself. It was only supposed to be temporary. So it was that Wong left their school in his friend's place.

"For a whole season I pretended to be him," said Wong. He blinked slow and smoothed his hair back. "The end," he said.

Kim made a farting noise. "When did you guys switch back again?" he asked.

"Yeah, what happened? Did anyone ever find out?" said Huynh.

Wong said, "Time's up. Make your guesses."

"False," said Lee.

"False," said Huynh.

"True," said the girl.

"Falsest horseshit I've ever heard," said Kim.

"You'll all have to drink," said Wong. "All of you!" As the rest of them complained, he cackled and drained his glass.

"I'll allow it," said the girl. She and Wong clinked glasses.

It was Lee's turn. The paper said SUCCESSOR. "Pass," said Lee.

The next slip of paper said USURPER. Well, if she didn't want SUCCESSOR, she definitely didn't want USURPER. "Pass on this too," said Lee.

The next slip said REPLACEMENT.

Lee yelled, "I'm not doing any of these, you assholes," and against her will she remembered finding the pictures of her ex-husband's old girlfriends, the new girlfriend who had usurped Lee's position, the one who had replaced that one, and the other one, or was it two, after—it was hard to remember exactly, because the photos had been in some kind of circular book with no covers, no clear end or beginning, you could easily have flipped through all the women and gone back around to the beginning without even noticing; that was what they looked like.

Huynh was looking at her calmly. Lee remembered how perfect Huynh had been, matter-of-fact yet merciless. "Don't dwell. Just another yellow-fever cracker-ass white guy," Huynh had said. "Throw him back."

Huynh pushed a square of paper toward Lee. "Here, try one more." Her face was unreadable.

Lee unfolded the paper. Printed on it in tiny block letters was the word SHART. She hung her head, then began to shake with laughter—something about the careful, meek handwriting, more than the word itself even. "Noooooo," she moaned. "That does it. I'm skipping my turn." Huynh raised her glass to Lee. Wong and Kim looked relieved and drank. The girl refilled everyone's cups. The bottle remained nearly full.

"You humans," murmured the girl. She grinned at them, tilting her head. "I mean, us. Us humans. We're just such a blast."

Huynh got MATTRESS. She nodded as though she had been expecting it. Years ago, before all of them had met, Huynh had been going through a rough time. There was no money. She was living in an expensive city but was too poor and depressed to move anywhere else and could not stomach the thought of going back home—her dad was mentally ill and homeless, and her mom had left for Vietnam a while back. "I guess with all the people over the years telling her to go back to her own country, she was finally like, 'Huh, you know what, that's actually like not a bad idea!'" said Huynh. "You fuckers."

Huynh had signed up with a temp agency, who immediately found her an assignment with amazingly inconvenient hours that paid terribly, but she took it, afraid that if she turned this one down she would not be placed elsewhere. During the final days before she had to move out of her current apartment, she searched through the classifieds and found exactly two apartments she could afford. One was so affordable because it was free—she would only have one roommate and would have to refrain from wearing clothing while in the apartment ("no sex no touching," the ad had said, "i'm not some CREEP").

Huynh took the other apartment. It was a room in a two-bed-room apartment, clean and empty except for a mattress and a suitcase. She had a roommate who she would never see. The roommate slept on the mattress from about 10 p.m. to 6 a.m. Nor-mal-people stuff. Huynh slept on the mattress during the day. At night she worked as an admin in a warehouse where they made and sent out copies of X-rays to hospitals. The schedule did not feel so good. She slept when she was supposed to, and presumably for the right number of hours, but waking up always felt cruel, as if she had just closed her eyes and hours passed in seconds, an evil trick.

Her roommate communicated with her through notes. Like: *Please wash the sheets. I did it last time. We will trade off on this. I hope you understand. Best, A.M.* Huynh wrote back: *No problem! Thank you. Best, P.M.*

This could not go on forever, but it went on for a while, until the night that Huynh, racked with a flu and three canker sores, slept through her two alarms, slept through the sinking of the sun and the rising of the sun, and sat up midday, horrified that she had stolen her roommate's bed time. Huynh lay back down, sweaty and weak, figuring that when her roommate came back she could apologize. Maybe the roommate would take pity on her when she saw how ill she was, since she seemed very reasonable in her notes.

But the roommate never returned. No notes, no nothing. Huynh stayed in bed for three melty days, alternately dozing off and listening fearfully for the turn of the doorknob. And then: "Then I got in that accident and became the woman you see be-fore you today," said Huynh.

"True," everyone said in unison. Huynh nodded again and drank once, twice, thrice, four times. She didn't seem drunk. Lee wondered just what was in the bottle that the girl had brought.

"My turn," said the girl. She leaned forward and plucked one of the slips of paper out of the pile. Her hair, still soaking wet, spattered the floor.

BARGAIN, it said on the paper. The girl sat up straight. She sud-denly seemed very tall, and not only tall but big.

"I really liked hearing your stories," she said. "I really like that kind of thing. I had a good feeling about you guys. Not just the one who drew me here—all of you. Such great need." She stood in one swift motion, unswiveling herself from the ground like a ballerina, walked over to the window, and yanked the blinds open. Lee shouted.

The girl said, "Don't worry. There's something I want you to see. It can't hurt you."

The slight emphasis on *it* clearly bothered everyone, but they got up and stood next to the girl by the window.

Outside, it was still raining, though not as hard as before. Some people must have had generators, because they could see scattered lights on in some of the apartments across the way and in the bodega on the corner. There was the beast, ambling down the street. It raised its arm and waved at the girl. The girl waved back. "You see?" she said gently, not looking away from the beast. As quietly as possible, Huynh puked up the wedding cake. Finally the girl glanced behind her, annoyed, and snapped her fingers. The candles went out.

In the dark, they ran scared and huddled together in a corner. Lee thought, *I let it in. I let it in!*

No: somebody called it here. And, also, this is true: we all kept it here.

Their knees buckled; they all became sleepy at once. "Shh," said the girl somewhere in the dark, and they slowly slumped to the ground. "Let's end it nice," she said. "Like a slumber party. We'll lie down and just talk until we sleep. In the morning I'll be gone and you won't remember a thing. Won't that be nice? Doesn't that make you less scared now?"

They had spread out around the living room, lying flat and exhausted and finding themselves already drifting off to sleep, despite the hard wooden floors and the fears that one of them would encounter Huynh's puke puddle. Each of them felt the girl pressing against them, her body huge and warm and firm, snaking and coiling around the room.

"It's a bad time for you," the girl said. "There's so much water, but it's bad. Sour. You're running out of time to be noticed even though it's all you've ever wanted. Your lives are running out, the world's life running out—" She sounded like she was about to cry. "I wish I could help you all."

The girl's coils wrapped around Lee, Huynh, Kim, and Wong and tightened ferociously. "I can't. You know it can only be one," she said. Her eyes were the size of books, laptops, pillows, getting larger by the second. For a moment they welled up again. She wanted to console them by letting them know that the one who had called her here—well, that person just wanted it more, didn't they? But all of them wanted it! They wanted the face that would be their face and theirs only; they all were so tired of appearing and immediately receding like a finger painting made in the sea, they wanted to be carved as stone into the minds of their friends and family and loved ones and hated ones and people worldwide who'd never meet them in the flesh, whether they were the one who was obsessed, or the one who didn't feel good about anything else, or the one who was naturally talented and too lazy to find praise elsewhere, or the one who wanted to be famous and loved in a way that didn't require talking or looking good. It was too bad! The girl lifted her face to the ceiling in a silent cry and wept for a minute. Then she bent her head and ate.

In the morning, they woke up jolly and hungover. Three of them less than they used to be, but they would not ever know it. Nor would the one who had become more, who had received some crucial bump in talent or desire or perseverance or pure idiot luck, and who would be famous, in a way, years later. We don't need to talk about that. Better to think about what the fame did to the others—how the sheer proximity of awardpartymoviesbookstravelhotelcruditésgraduationspeeches made success feel actually possible, maybe even attainable, while at other times inducing in them a fresh, keening despair, inscribing behind their eyelids shining golden letters like:

H E R E I S Y O U R L I F E then a sickly, disorienting leap over hundreds of millions of miles of alien terrain over to T H E R E I S T H E I R L I F E

These lands were on the same planet only technically. In one direction they were so far away from each other on the globe that in another direction they almost touched. But they never touched. Years later, one was famous, and meanwhile, the others would hope to be, almost be, and finally never be. There were so many tiny little steps between each stage that each one felt much like the last, and thus the letdown was gentle, merciful—barely noticeable, even.

NICK WOLVEN

Caspar D. Luckinbill, What Are You Going to Do?

FROM *The Magazine of Fantasy & Science Fiction*

I

I'M ON MY way to work when the terrorists strike. The first attack nearly kills me. It's my fault, partly. I'm jaywalking at the time.

There I am, in the middle of Sixth Avenue, an ad truck bearing down in the rightmost lane. I feel a buzz in my pocket and take out my phone. I assume it's Lisa, calling about the TV. I put it to my ear and hear a scream.

There are screams, and there are screams. This is the real deal. It's a scream that ripples. It's a scream that rings. It's a scream like a mile-high waterfall of glass, like a drill bit in the heart, like a thousand breaking stars.

I stand shaking in the street. The ad truck advances, blowing paint and air, leaving a strip of toothpaste ads in its wake. I have enough presence of mind to step back as the truck chuffs by. I look down and see a smile on my toes: three perfect spray-painted teeth on each new shoe.

When I get to the curb, the screaming has stopped, and a man is speaking from my phone.

"Caspar D. Luckinbill! Attention, Caspar D. Luckinbill! What you just heard were the screams of Ko Nam, recorded as he was tortured and killed by means of vibrational liquefaction. Men like Ko Nam are murdered every day in the FRF. Caspar D. Luckinbill, what are you going to do?"

What am I going to do? What am I supposed to do? I stand on

the curb staring at my phone. I have no idea who Ko Nam is. I have no idea what the FRF is. And what in God's name is vibrational liquefaction?

I give it a second's thought, trying my best to be a good, conscientious, well-informed citizen of the world. But it's 9:15 and I have teeth on my shoes, and I'm already late for work.

My employer is the contractor for the external relations department of the financial branch of a marketing subsidiary of a worldwide conglomerate that makes NVC-recognition software. NVC: nonverbal communication. The way you walk. The way you move. Our programs can pick you out of a crowd, from behind, at eighty paces, just by the way you swing your arms. Every move you make, every breath you take. Recognizing faces is so old school.

We claim to be the company that launched ubiquitous computing. Every company claims that, of course. That's what makes it so ubiquitous.

Recognition software is not a technology. Recognition software is an idea. The idea is this: You are the world. Every teeny-weeny-tiny thing you do ripples out and out in cascades of expanding influence. Existence is personal. Anonymity is a lie. It's time we started seeing the faces for the crowd.

I believe that's true because I wrote it. I wrote it for a pamphlet that was sent to investors in the financial branch of the marketing subsidiary by whose ER department I'm employed. I don't think they used it.

For eight years running I've worked in this office, which is probably a record here in the soi-disant capital del mundo. My wife, Lisa, says I'm wasting my time. She says that someone with my smarts ought to be out there changing the world. I tell her I am changing the world. After all, every teeny-weeny-tiny thing I do ripples out and out in cascades of expanding influence. Lisa says it's obvious I've sold my soul.

Really, the corporate culture here is quite friendly. The front door greets me by name when I enter. The lobby fixes me coffee, and it knows just how I like it. Seventy percent pan-equator blend, thirty percent biodome-grown Icelandic, roasted charcoal-dark, with twenty milliliters of lactose-reduced Andean free-range llama milk and just a squirt of Sri Lankan cardamom sweetener, timed to be ready the moment I arrive.

It's a classy workplace. The bathroom stalls are noise-canceling. The lobby plays light jazz all day long.

Today when I go in, the jazz isn't playing. Today there is silence. Then a crackle. A hum.

And then the screaming begins.

This time there are words. A woman is sobbing. I can't make out the language. Some of it sounds like English. All of it sounds very, very sad.

The receptionist listens from behind his desk. It seems to me that his eyes are disapproving.

The sobbing goes on for several seconds. Then a man begins to speak.

"Caspar D. Luckinbill!" the man says. "What you just heard were the cries of Kim Pai as her husband was taken away by government agents. People like Kim Pai's husband are abducted every day in the FRF. Caspar D. Luckinbill, what are you going to do?"

The voice cuts off. The light jazz resumes.

"Abducted!" says the receptionist, looking at the speakers.

"It's . . . something." I try to explain. "It's a wrong number. It's a crossed wire. I don't know what it is."

"The FRF!" the receptionist says, looking at me as if I've fallen out of the sky.

I hurry to my desk.

My desk chair sees me coming and rolls out to welcome me. My desk is already on. As I sit down, the desk reads me three urgent messages from my supervisor. Then it plays an ad for eye-widening surgery. "Nothing signals respectful attention to an employer, a teacher, or a lover quite like a tastefully widened eye!" Then it plays a video of a man being killed with a table saw.

I jump out of my chair. I avert my face. When I look back, there's no more man and no more saw, and the screen is vibrant with blood.

"Caspar D. Luckinbill!" blares the computer. "Caspar D. Luckinbill, do you know what you just saw? Steve Miklos came to the FRF to teach math to learning-disabled children. Because of his promotion of contraceptives, he was afflicted with acute segmentation by supporters of the HAP. Caspar D. Luckinbill, how can you possibly allow such atrocities to continue? Will you sit idly by while innocent people are slaughtered? Caspar D. Luckinbill, what are you going to do?"

I know exactly what I'm going to do. I call my friend Armando.

"Armando," I say, "I have a computer problem."

Armando is the kind of friend everyone needs to have. Armando is my friend who knows about computers.

I tell Armando about the phone call this morning. I tell him about the sobbing in the lobby. I hold out my phone and show him what my desk is doing.

"You've got a problem," Armando says.

"I can see that," I say. "I can hear it too, everywhere and all the time. How do I make it go away?"

"You don't understand," Armando says. "This isn't an IT problem. This is a real problem. You've been targeted, Caspar. You've been chosen."

"What is it, some kind of spam?"

"Worse," Armando says. "Much worse. It's mediaterrorism."

Mediaterrorism. The term is not familiar.

"You mean like leaking classified information?"

"I mean," Armando says, "that you're being terrorized. Don't you feel terrorized?"

"I feel confused. I feel perplexed. I feel a certain degree of angst."

"Exactly," Armando says.

"I feel bad for the people of the FRF. Where exactly is the FRF?"

"I think it's somewhere in Africa."

"The names of the victims don't sound African. The names of the victims sound Asian."

"There are Asians in Africa," Armando says. "There are Africans in Asia. Don't be so racist."

I look at my desk, where people are dying and children are starving and Wendy's franchises are exploding in blooms of shocking light.

"But why did they pick me? What do I have to do with the FRF? Why do they keep using my name?"

"The answer to all those questions," Armando says, "is, Who knows? It's all essentially random. It's done by computer."

"That doesn't explain anything."

"Computers don't need explanations," Armando says. "Computers just do what they do."

"Should I send them some money? What should I do?"

Armando clutches his head. "What's the matter with you, Caspar? Send them money! Don't you have principles?"

"I'd send them some money if I knew where they were. The FRF. It sounds postcolonial."

"Can't you see?" says Armando. "This is what they want. This is what terrorists do. They get into your head. It's not about what you do, Caspar. It's about how you feel." He points through the screen. "I'll tell you what you need to do. You need to get off the grid. Before this spreads."

"Spreads? Do you mean —?"

But I have to end the call. My supervisor, Sheila, is coming through the cubicles.

"Caspar," Sheila says, "can I ask you something? Can I ask you why people are being butchered in your name?"

I see that she has a sheet of printout in her hand.

"I've been trying to figure that out myself," I say.

Sheila looks at my desk, which currently displays a smoking pile of severed feet.

"I don't want this to be awkward," Sheila says. "But I just talked to Danny, out in the lobby. He says he heard screaming when you came in. He says it began the moment you entered. He says it was a pretty awful way to start the morning."

The severed feet are gone. My desk now shows a picture of a sobbing baby sitting in a pile of bloody soda cans.

"You don't need to tell me," I say.

"The thing I want to say," Sheila says, "is that we're a very modern office. You know that. We're more than just coworkers here. We're cosharers. We're like thirty people, all ordering and sharing one big pizza. And if one person orders anchovies . . ."

The desk shows a falling building. The concrete cracks and showers into a blossom of dust-colored cloud. I can't stop looking at the printout in Sheila's hand.

"I didn't order anything," I say. "The anchovies just found me."

Sheila holds out the printout. I take it and read:

Caspar D. Luckinbill, do you know what you have done?

You have been complicit in the deaths of thousands.

Payments made in your name, Caspar D. Luckinbill, have contributed, directly or indirectly, to supporting the murderous HAP party of the FRF. With your direct or indirect financial assistance, thugs and warlords have hurled this once-peaceful region into anarchy.

Over two hundred thousand people, Caspar, have been tortured, killed, or imprisoned without trial.

One hundred new children a week are recruited into the sex trade, and twice that many are injured in unsafe and illegal working environments.

While you sit idly by, Caspar, a woman is attacked in the FRF every eighteen minutes. An acre of old-growth forest is destroyed every fifty-seven seconds, and every half second, sixty-eight liters of industrial runoff enter the regional watershed. Every sixteen days a new law targeting vulnerable groups is passed by dictatorial fiat, and for every seventeen dollars added annually to the PPP of a person in the upper quintile of your city, Caspar, an estimated eighty and a half times that person's yearly spending power is subtracted monthly from the FRF's GDP.

Caspar D. Luckinbill, YOU have enabled this. YOU have helped to bring about these atrocities.

YOU have heard the cries of women in agony.

YOU have learned the names of murdered men.

YOU have seen the faces of suffering children.

Caspar D. Luckinbill, what are you going to do?

"This was posted to the company news feed," Sheila says. "It went to my account. It went to everybody's account. It appeared on our public announcement board. There were pictures. Horrible pictures."

"Aren't there filters?" I say. "Aren't there moderators?"

"It got through the filters," Sheila says. "It got past the moderators."

"Someone should do something about that."

"Indeed," Sheila says, and looks at me very frowningly.

"It's not my problem," I say. "It's like spam. It's a technical thing. It's mediaterrorism."

"I understand," Sheila says. "I understand everything you're saying. What I also understand is that we're a very modern office, and we're all in this together. And right now, some of us who are in this are being made to feel very unproductive."

"I'll see what I can do," I say, and turn back to my desk.

I spend the rest of the morning looking up the FRF. There are no sovereign nations by that name, none that I can find, not in the world at this time. There are several militias, two major urban areas, five disputed microstates, seven hundred and eighty-two minor political entities, ninety NGOs, most of them defunct, over a thousand corporate entities, over ten thousand documented fictional entities, and a few hundred thousand miscellaneous uses of the acronym.

I check news stories. An island off the coast of the former state of Greece once claimed independence under the name FRF, but it's now known as the ADP and is considered part of the new Caliphate of Istanbul.

I spend my lunch break obsessing about a phrase. *Payments made in my name.* What payments in my name? I don't make donations to murderous regimes. I give to charity. I eat foreign food. I buy clothes from China and rugs from Azerbaijan. Tin-pot dictators? Not my profile.

I call my bank. I call my credit card companies. Money circulates. Money gets around. The buck never stops, not really, not for long. Is it all a big bluff? What payments in my name?

No one can tell me.

I obsess about another phrase: *directly or indirectly.* It strikes me that the word *indirect* is itself, in this context, extremely indirect.

I spend the afternoon looking up mediaterrorism. Armando's right. It's a thing. It can come out of nowhere, strike at any time. Once you've been targeted, it's hard to shake. It's like identity theft, one article says—"except what they steal is your moral complacency."

I call the company IT department. They say the problem is with my CloudSpace provider. I call my CloudSpace provider. They say the problem is with my UbiKey account. I call my UbiKey account. They say it sounds like a criminal issue. The woman on the line gets nervous. She isn't allowed to talk about criminal issues. There are people listening. There are secret agreements. It's all very murky. It's a government thing.

I call the government. They thank me for my interest. I call the police. They just laugh.

While I make my calls, I see the mutilated bodies of eighteen torture victims, watch tearful interviews with five assault survivors, and peer into the charnel-laden depths of three mass graves.

Children's faces stare from my screen. They are pixelated and human. Their eyes seem unnaturally wide.

At the end of the day, I call Armando. "I'm getting nowhere," I say. "I've been researching all day."

Armando looks confused.

"My problem," I remind him. "My mediaterrorism."

"Aha. Right. Well, at least you're keeping busy."

"I'm going in circles, buddy. I don't know what to do."

"I'll tell you what to do," Armando says. "Go home. Watch TV. Break out the Maker's Mark. Get in bed with your lovely wife. Put everything to do with the FRF out of your mind. Your mission now, Caspar, is to be a happy man. If you're not happy, the bastards win."

I'm almost home when I remember.

Lisa! The new TV!

I run the last two blocks, slapping the pavement with my toothy shoes, nearly crashing into the ad-drone that's painting a half-naked woman on our building.

This week my wife and I decided to take the plunge. We're plunging together into the blissful depths of immersive domestic entertainment. We're getting Ubervision.

A day came when Lisa and I could no longer duck the question. Here we were with a videoscreen in the living room, a videoscreen in the bedroom, a videoscreen in the kitchen, videoscreens on our phones, videoscreens on our desks, videoscreens in our books. Why not take the next big leap? Why not have videoscreens everywhere?

Sometimes I would like to read the news in bed without having to prop my head up. Wouldn't it be nice if there were screens on the ceiling? Sometimes I would like my floor to be a carpet of roses. Wouldn't it be nice if the floor could do that? Call me lazy, call me self-indulgent, but sometimes I would like to use the bathroom, or see what's in the fridge, without necessarily looking away from my TV show. Wouldn't it be nice if I could point at any surface in my home, anytime I wanted, and turn it into a full-spectrum screen?

Lisa and I went to school for fifty years between us. We work sixty-hour weeks. Who would deny us life's little pleasures? And what pleasure could be littler than a TV across from the toilet?

After all, it's not just about entertainment. Ubervision is smart. Ubervision gets to know you. It learns your habits; it picks up your tastes. It knows what you want to watch before you do. Ubervision tells you when you're getting fat, promotes local food, reminds you where your wife goes on Wednesdays. Ubervision's a key component of the wisely wired life.

I read that in an advertisement painted on the bottom of a swimming pool. Maybe I had chlorine in my eyes. What the advertisement didn't appear to mention is that Ubervision is also a real pain in the *Allerwertesten* to install. Lisa's been taking off to watch the technicians work. They have to coat every wall, replace every door. This is invasive home surgery.

Normally Lisa works longer hours than I do. She's a contractor for the auditing department of the fundraising department of the remote offices of the Malaysian branch of a group that does something with endangered animals. Either they put them in zoos or they take them out of zoos; I can never remember.

Today's the big day. When I get home, Lisa's lying in her teak sensochair, eating Singaporean vacuum-food, wearing a sleep mask.

"Is it done?" I say.

The sleep mask looks at me. "Check this out," says Lisa.

I shout. I wave. I try to warn her.

It's too late.

Ubervision has activated.

I know exactly what's going to happen.

When the first wave of screams has died away, Lisa sits up and takes off her sleep mask. "This isn't what I expected," she says, looking at the bleeding and shrieking walls. "Why is every channel playing the same show? And why is that show so incredibly terrible?"

I feel like a person who's confused his laundry drone with his dogwalking drone. The living room walls are playing footage of an urban firefight.

"I tried to warn you," I say.

"Warn me about what? What's happening? What's wrong?" Lisa taps the wall, but nothing changes. An explosion goes off in the kitchen floor, and a hi-def severed leg flies all the way through the kitchen, down the hall, across the living room ceiling, and behind the couch. I have to admire the power of the technology.

"Caspar D. Luckinbill!" shouts the stove, or maybe it's the bathroom mirror. "Caspar D. Luckinbill, look at what your negligence and apathy have unleashed! In a bloody escalation of urban warfare, renegade militias have overthrown the HAP party of the DRS.

Violent reprisals are underway. Dissidents have been purged and journalists persecuted. Soldiers as young as seven lie dead in the streets. Only two minutes ago, Paul Agalu, poet, ophthalmologist, and human-rights advocate, was attacked by a mob and torn to pieces in his home. Caspar D. Luckinbill, *you* are responsible for these horrors. Caspar D. Luckinbill, what are you going to do?"

Lisa is punching the wall. "It won't change. I can't even adjust the sound. Why do they keep saying your name?"

"Sit down." I draw her to the couch amid the bombs and rubble and screams and blood. "There's something I need to explain."

II

Recognition software doesn't violate privacy. Recognition software expands privacy. When every machine recognizes every user, the lived environment becomes personal and unique. Stores, cars, homes, and offices all learn to respond to individual needs. Private interest generates private experience. No awkward controls, no intrusive interface: what a user wants is what she gets.

That's what it says in the promotional materials my company sends to potential investors. I didn't write it. I don't believe it. At least, I don't think I do. I'm not quite sure anymore what I believe.

I'm riding in Armando's car. It's been a year since the terrorists found me. Or maybe ten months. Time seems to pass a lot slower nowadays.

The windshield of Armando's car is old-fashioned glass. I watch the trees go sliding by. I've come to appreciate trees lately. So non-judgmental. I like how they just couldn't care less. I like how they simply stand there, exhaling life and forgiveness.

The other windows of the car are not mere windows. Like most windows in my world, they are also screens. And like most screens in my life, they glow with bloody destruction. Young men stagger in smoke and agony. Something is hurting them; I can't see what. A sonic pain ray, perhaps. Maybe a laser. Something to do with deadly sound and light.

Gunfire rattles on the radio. Neither of us pays attention. I'm used to gunfire now. Violence is my music. When I sit near a radio, it sings of murder. When I stand near an advertisement, it cries.

All media recognize me. They conspire against me. Every magazine I open is a gallery of gore. Every book I read becomes a book of the dead. My news feeds tally the tortured, the vanished, the lost, the disappeared.

I can't sleep at home. The horror show plays day and night. I can't sleep at a hotel. I can't even sleep in a shelter. Are there any bedrooms left in this country that don't come with TVs?

The other day I bought some toothpaste and cheese. The store machine printed out a long receipt. It had coupons for bullets and first-aid kits. "Caspar D. Luckinbill," the receipt said at the bottom, "thanks to you, three hundred people were just massacred in the CPC's St. Ignatius Square. Do you suffer from loose joint skin? Try Ride-X. Have a great day!!!"

"Did I tell you?" Armando reaches for the radio, trying in vain to lower the volume. "I remembered about the FRF. It's an African country. A tiny place. Just one-tenth of a megacity. The name stands for Firstieme Republique Frasolee."

"That's not real French," I say. "That sounds like French, but it's not."

"Well, you know, it's a very backward country."

"Anyway," I say, "it's not the FRF anymore. Now it's the CPC. Before that it was the DRS."

"That's how it is with names," Armando says. "They're so ephemeral."

I disagree. It seems to me nowadays that names are all too permanent. In the early days of my affliction, I made a point of looking up names. I looked up names of people who had died, of landmarks that had been bombed, of leaders who had vanished. But the world has so very, very many names, and all of them, sooner or later, become the names of ghosts.

"At any rate," Armando says, "you really can't complain. At least you're keeping informed. At least you're learning about the outside world."

The screen beside me is playing footage of a burning river. The flames skid and ripple with a fluid surreality. I wonder, as I've wondered before, what if it's all just special FX? What if the gory images I see every day are doctored? What if the whole tragedy is made up?

In the early days of my affliction, I used to do a lot of research. I learned a lot, but the more I learned, the less I felt I understood. Now I don't do so much research anymore.

Armando gives up on the radio. "Have you . . . have you made any progress? Figured out a way to make it stop?"

I see that he is trying to be tactful. I sympathize. It's the people around me who suffer most. They haven't gotten used to the crash of bombs. They can't handle the screams and blood. They still think these things should be considered abnormal. People are very protective of that notion, normality.

"Have you tried canceling your accounts?" Armando says.

"I tried."

"Have you tried rebooting your identity?"

"I'm working on it."

"Have you tried law enforcement?"

"A dozen times." I tell the car to pull over at the next rest stop. "The problem is," I tell Armando, "fixing an issue like this takes patience and smarts and concentration. And those are qualities it's very difficult to summon in the middle of a war zone."

"I see," says Armando. "And have you tried tech support?"

I laugh. In the early days of my affliction, people made a lot of tech-support jokes. Everything was a joke back then. When I walked into work, the receptionist said, "Uh-oh, here comes the apocalypse." When I entered the staff room, my coworkers covered their ears. They called me Caspar the Unfriendly Ghost. They called me Caspar Track-n-Kill. They called me other, nastier things.

When I went home at night, Lisa would say, "How was your day, dear? Massacre any civilians? Eat any babies?"

Har-de-har.

As the weeks went by, there were fewer jokes. Soon even the stares stopped. No one wanted to make eye contact with the face that had launched a thousand gunships. It's a time-tested response under fire. Duck and cover.

One day at work, Sheila came to my cubicle. "I don't want this to be difficult, Caspar," she said. "I understand this isn't your fault. But I also need you to understand that we're all human beings, with thoughts and feelings and work to get done. And these days, with you in the office, Caspar—I don't want to put this the wrong way—but when I look at you, all I can see is a giant pile of murdered children."

"Maybe I should take a leave of absence," I said.

"Yes," said Sheila, "I think that would be wise."

The car pulls over in a picnic area. Armando and I walk far into the trees, the shade, the sweet green silence. It's a weekly ritual, this escape to the woods. Only here can I be at peace, amid the indifferent, ignorant trees. They don't recognize me, trees. They don't care. They don't know what things have been done in my name.

"This won't be easy to say," Armando says.

I sink to my knees in the soft pine needles. I know what's coming, but I don't blame Armando. I don't blame him any more than I blame the machines that scream and weep when I pass by. What else are they supposed to do, when innocent children are dying in the streets?

"I want you to know that I support you." Armando leans against a tree. "I even kind of admire you, Caspar. You seem so . . . connected to things, you know? It's just . . . it's getting a little hard to be around you."

"It's okay," I whisper. "I understand."

"I've got my own headaches, you know," Armando says. "I need to work on me for a while. And that's pretty tough to do when things keep exploding and dying all the time."

I don't answer. I notice a movement in the trees. A deer approaches, soft-stepping and shy.

"Be optimistic," Armando says. "That's my advice. Stay positive. I think that's the way to beat this thing."

The deer is an ad-deer, painted on both sides—something for the hunters to enjoy while taking aim. I read only half the message on its flank before it sees me and skips away.

Relax, the message says. *Don't worry. You too can have firm and beautiful knees.*

When I get home, the foyer is dark. But not for long. As soon as I enter, the door begins to weep. The ceiling fills with hurrying flame. Burning people run toward me from within the phantasmal walls. Even the floor is a field of carnage. As I walk to the kitchen, I tread on the faces of the maimed.

The kitchen cabinets tell me that churches are burning, that dogs are starving, that a human-rights worker has been killed by forced detegumentation. I open the fridge and take out a tub of four-milk, sumac-seasoned Georgian matzoon.

The living room is being strafed by an airplane. I sit on the couch as children run and scream.

People like to say that you can get used to anything. I know for a fact that this isn't true. You can get used to bombs. You can get used to gunfire. But you could live as long as God, you could see all he has seen, and you would never get used to the cries of suffering children.

When Lisa comes home, I'm staring into my tub of matzoon, surrounded by faces.

"There you are," she says, as though being here is a crime.

She goes into the bedroom, which has become a simulation of a torture chamber. Wires curl in curdled blood. A video cat bats a severed thumb. Lisa changes into sweatsocks and jeans. When she comes back into the living room, the faces are still here, hanging all around me, silent and staring.

"Who are these people?" Lisa says, waving. "Gangbangers? Apparatchiks? Assassins?"

I set aside my matzoon. Suddenly I'm angry. I don't know who the faces are either, but I know this: They are mine. They are faces I will see again, watching from the walls of trains, the tiles above urinals, the backs of cereal boxes. They are faces I will see in my sleep, the way a murderer sees his victims. They are my memories, my future, my dreams.

"What difference," I say, "does it make to you?"

Lisa stands over me. Her face is like the faces I see on the street, those strangers who turn to stare in disgust at the man who brings war and death in his wake.

"How dare you?" Lisa says. "How dare you take that tone? I'm dying, Caspar. I've put up with this for eight months."

Eight months—is that all it's been?

"You think I'm callous?" says Lisa. "You think I don't care? Look at yourself."

"What about me?" I say.

Lisa stares. The walls and her face become the color of fire. Something has been building, I see that now. Something has been developing, slowly, fatally, like a war.

"What am I supposed to say," Lisa says, "to a man who sits here eating yogurt while people are being tortured all around him? What am I supposed to say to a man who loafs around the apartment, day after day, watching rapes and massacres? What am I supposed to say to a man who barely turns his head when he hears a woman screaming?"

"I didn't ask for this," I say.

"You don't seem to mind it."

I stand. The matzoon container tips and rolls, dribbling white drool. I'm so upset I feel like I'm hovering, suspended in the center of an endless explosion.

"I've lost my friends," I say. "I've lost my job. I can't sleep. I can't think. You think this is hard for you? Maybe what I need right now is some support."

"So that's what it comes to?" Lisa says. "That your pain is bigger than my pain? Really?" She points at the wall. "What about them?"

I hold out my arms. I turn in a circle. The room is a killing field now, a farm of bones, and my hands move up and down slowly, as if to try and raise the dead.

"They're not me," I say. "They're not my problem."

"No," says Lisa, heading for the door. "They are."

When the door closes, I walk numbly through the apartment. Missiles arc overhead. Tanks roll.

"What are you going to do?" I say to the sobbing television.

Great works of culture are burning in the hall. "Caspar," I say to the bloody bedroom, "what are you going to do?"

Outside my window, ad-bugs mill in the night, patterned and phosphorescent, preprogrammed and minute, tiny pixies of light forming pictures of men and women with perfect chins and ears. I stare at these ideal people hovering in the dark, the angels of adspace, so familiar from a thousand daily visions, and realize that what makes them beautiful is not their shapely skulls, their tight skin, their healthy flesh, but their heroic unconcern—untroubled by conscience, unburdened by expectations, they smile for an instant before flickering away into the night.

I sink to my knees.

"Caspar D. Luckinbill," I say to the bedroom floor, "what are you going to do?"

In the floor I see a body, curled like a twist of wire. The face is obscure, but I would know this man anywhere. I would know him by his NVC alone—hunched with self-pity, shivering with guilt. And I know exactly what I'm going to do.

III

Mediaterrorism is not a concept. Mediaterrorism is an experience. Every day a new victim is targeted. Make no mistake: it could happen to you.

I wrote that for the voice-over of the teleplay of the documentary I helped to prepare for the British division of a Persian television network. I believe every word, but that's not what's important. What's important is that everyone else believes it.

It's a sunny summer day, and I'm walking to the downtown office of the nonprofit organization of which I am founder, spokesman, and president. I don't worry about jaywalking these days. The light on the corner recognizes me, arranges for me to cross. Money will do that for you. Money has its ways. And money, thank God, is now on my side.

The doors of the building greet me by name. No bombs, no blood, no assaultive sounds. The fake plant in the lobby waves a welcoming leaf. "Caspar D. Luckinbill," says the elevator, "welcome! What can I do for you today?"

Inside the elevator, an ad-droid is painting a picture on the doors. It's a picture of my face, from the cover of *Zeit-Life Magazine*. In this picture, my eyes have been artificially narrowed, my skin artificially loosened. Everything about me has been made to look harrowed and gaunt. *Special Report,* the caption reads. *The Human Face of Mediaterrorism.*

I ride the elevator to the fourteenth floor. In my office, Betty lies on her back, screening the new television special. Thanks to the office Ubervision, the image beams from the ceiling. The walls are a forest of virtual, tranquil trees.

"Is he here?" I say.

Betty sits up. "He's waiting for you."

Betty is my public awareness manager. She's also my girlfriend. She is young, smart, media-savvy, and takes care of herself. No loose joint skin on this young lady. She has the firmest, most beautiful knees I've ever seen.

"I think it's finally happened," Betty says. "I think we've finally reached critical mass."

I put my arms around her and rewind the TV special. The opener begins with doomful music. "Lurking in the shadows of cyberspace," a man's voice says, "lies a mysterious new hi-tech predator, on the hunt for human prey. It strikes from your TV, your phone, from the walls of your home, and no one knows who it will target next. Will you be the next victim of . . . *media-terrorism?*"

"Good stuff," I say. "The deadly part's a little heavy."

"We're covered," Betty says. "We've established links to suicide."

"In this special two-hour report," the announcer continues, "you'll learn about a person—a person just like you—a man named Caspar Luckinbill, who saw his life destroyed when the media he had trusted suddenly and unexpectedly turned against him. And you'll find out how to protect yourself and those you love from what may be the modern world's fastest-growing psychological scourge."

I pause the show. "How wide is the advertising?"

"Wide," says Betty. "Like, vast. Like, omnipresent. We're going after seniors first. Then moms. Then kids. By airtime we'll have total saturation."

"What about buzz?"

"Are you kidding? People can't get enough. They're intrigued. They're outraged. They're absolutely terrified."

The TV special is my baby. I was the one who reached out to the producers. I was the one who made the pitch. I'm chief consultant, assistant producer. And of course I'm the star.

It's a strange feeling. I'm not just in the charity game. I'm a one-man movement, the soul of a cause, the president of an ever-growing organization. I've become, as the magazines of the globe proclaim, the human face of mediaterrorism.

Betty and I run through other promotional channels—ads, radio, tie-ins, public appearances, even print. It's important to be comprehensive in this game. You've got to blanket the airwaves. You've got to speak up. People forget about the big issues, and reminding them is a full-time job. You've got to be ubi, omni, toto, round-the-clock. You can have too much of a lot of things in this world, but you can never have too much public awareness.

I give Betty a kiss on her perfect neck. "Keep pushing it. Don't let up. Let me know if you get overwhelmed."

"I never get overwhelmed," Betty says. "I do the whelming."

I give her another kiss. Then I go into my private office, where Armando sits waiting.

"Caspar D. Luckinbill," Armando says, rising, "you lucky s.o.b." He slaps my shoulder. "You're the talk of the town."

"I'd better be," I say. "We're paying through the nose for it."

"So that's your secret? Money talks?"

"Is it a secret?"

"Not many things are, these days," Armando says.

I shrug. I smile. I feel weirdly ashamed. The truth is, I never expected to be the talk of the town. I guess it's like a lot of things. I guess you have to hit bottom before you can climb to the top.

When I started my campaign to raise awareness of mediaterrorism, I didn't honestly hope to be heard. I'd lost my job, my wife, my home, my health. I needed to get busy. I needed to speak out. Speaking out was about the last thing I still had the wherewithal to do.

What I didn't know was that the reporters would run with it. What makes reporters decide to run with things? "It's a ripeness issue," one of the reporters told me. "This is a moment whose time has come."

What I didn't know was that there were fellow sufferers. So many, many fellow sufferers.

What I didn't know was that there were researchers of mediaterrorism—researchers who also wanted to be heard.

What I didn't know was that the donations I received would be numerous, large, almost reflexive. What I didn't know was that people would buy my book. I didn't even know people still read books.

What I didn't know was that corporations would get involved. Especially the media corporations. Ubervision alone gave $80 million.

What I didn't know was that the government would take interest, and that consulting with the government can be both lucrative and pleasant.

What I didn't know, in short, is that something on the order of a mini media and monetary empire can grow up around one man through a process of near-ecological inevitability. Why me? I often wonder.

"Why me?" I say to Armando as we sit in my office sipping South Islay single-malt twenty-three-year-old Scotch over cubes of naturally refrozen Swiss glacier melt. "That's what I still don't understand."

"It's obvious," Armando says. "You're a nobody, a nonentity. You're trivial, dull, not even very bright. Another TV-watching office drone who stayed in his mesh-chair and never made a fuss. You're all of us. You're an innocent victim." He crunches glacier. "For what it's worth, I've always supported you."

"That's why you're here," I say, and beckon him to my desk.

Armando listens while I explain what I need him to do.

"So what I'm hearing," Armando says, "is that you want this to be discreet."

"Use your judgment," I say.

"And you want it to be judicious."

"Use your discretion."

"Now it's my turn to ask," Armando says. "Why me?"

I look into his wide eyes. I feel sure I can trust him. Of course I never blamed Armando for turning his back on me. It takes a lot of energy, I've found, blaming people. It takes more commitment than I'm able to muster.

"You've always been someone very special to me, Armando," I say, and squeeze his shoulder. "You're my friend who knows about computers."

When Armando is gone, I go to the office window. Ad-clouds glide through the sky above the city, converted by projectors to flying billboards, sky-high beautiful faces smiling down. I have to go back out to Betty soon, to discuss the campaign for our new fundraising drive. It's a full-time job, attaining full-time exposure. It doesn't allow for a lot of freedom.

I hope Armando knows what he's doing. I don't want anyone to trace the donations. I don't want anything linked to my name.

Money circulates. Money gets around. Call it a rich man's sentimental dream. I'm the human face of a global cause, but I want my fortune to be infinitely sneaky, invisible as life-giving air or light. I want it to trickle through the world, working its influence unobserved. Above all, I want it to reach the FRF, or whatever that little country's called now. I see it percolating through the foreign soil, mingling with the graves and seeds and bones. I picture it gathering to itself a secret life, springing skyward as a stand of trees. I picture it inhaling and reaching for the air, and in my better moments I can almost see the details, the windy movement and the flickering leaves, now dark, now bright, like data, like grace.

DALE BAILEY

I Was a Teenage Werewolf

FROM *Nightmare Magazine*

Principal Ferguson's Testimony

BEFORE MISS FERGUSON found Maude Lewis's body in the school gym, none of us believed in the teenage werewolf. There had been rumors, of course. There always are. But many of us viewed Miss Ferguson's discovery as confirmation of our worst fears.

Not everyone shared our certainty. There had been only a fingernail paring of moon that late February night, and a small but vocal minority of us argued that this precluded the possibility that Maude's killer had been a lycanthrope. It was common knowledge, they contended, that werewolves only struck during full moons, often adding that one only became a werewolf by surviving the bite of another werewolf. No such attack had been reported.

The rest of us refrained from pointing out the errors in this fount of superstition. Instead we asked the skeptics to consider the facts of the case as Principal Ferguson reported them to the *Rockdale Gazette*. She had been working late, as she did most nights, partly, we believed, because she was lonely, having no family to go home to, and partly to accommodate Maude's practice schedule. Maude was a talented gymnast who harbored hopes of a college scholarship and often stayed well into the evening to practice her tumbling runs and stunts.

Around eight o'clock on the night in question, Principal Ferguson had heard a brief shriek of terror. What she found when she investigated sent her flying back to her office in a seizure of panic and horror. She would not soon forget what she'd discovered in the gym. Some creature with superhuman strength—surely it could not have been a man—had snapped Maude's back like a twig and draped her supine body over the balance beam. It dangled there like it had no bones at all. Her abdomen had been torn open, spilling out glistening loops of yellow entrails. The stench was terrible. You wouldn't think a pretty girl like Maude would have had such smells within her, Miss Ferguson said.

The Arrest of Tony Rivers

In a press conference the following afternoon, Police Chief Baker dismissed the rumors of a teenage werewolf and announced that Detective "Don" Donovan, the lead investigator on the case, had already made an arrest.

Tony Rivers, a junior, had also been in the school that night. Tony had been working after hours as the custodian for almost a year by then, ever since his father had succumbed to brain cancer, leaving Tony and his mother to make their way as best they could. Tony had told some of us about his father's transformation as the tumor ate into his brain. A gentle man, Ted Rivers had by the end become foulmouthed and prone to fits of rage. To those closest to him, Tony had confided that though he tried not to think about his father's death, it weighed constantly upon him: when he was doing his homework or watching TV, when he was pushing a broom down the halls of Rockdale High. It was the first thing he thought about when he woke up. It was the last thing he thought about when he went to sleep.

This was the grief-stricken young man the police had found standing over Maude Lewis's body. Tony's explanation for his presence was perfectly reasonable: he too had come running in response to Maude's scream, arriving scant seconds after Miss Ferguson had locked herself in her office to call for help. Detective Donovan had taken him in for questioning anyway. Under interrogation, Tony said that he always escorted Maude home after Miss Ferguson locked up the school. It seemed unwise to let her walk alone, given the rumors that a teenage werewolf stalked the streets of Rockdale. Tony also admitted to an unrequited crush on Maude. And yes, she had recently—the night before her murder, in fact—rebuffed an invitation to join him at the junior-senior prom. Had her snub angered him? Detective Donovan wanted to know. Did he approach her again the night of the murder? Did he lose his temper when she rejected him? Where was he when Maude died?

Tony barely had time to respond to one query—often incoherently—before the next arrived. His panic mounted, and when Detective Donovan confronted him with the final and most damning question of all—why had his hands been so bloody?—Tony's answer made no sense. *I couldn't stand to see her all torn up like that,* he said. *I was trying to put everything back inside her.*

Detective Donovan consulted the police chief. Tony Rivers was in a cell soon afterward.

The streets of Rockdale were safe, Chief Baker told us at his press conference. We had nothing to fear.

Other Cases of Teenage Lycanthropy

Our situation was not unprecedented. Other towns had been plagued by rumors of teenage werewolves: strange tracks in the snow, lupine howls in the lonesome morning hours.

Usually the rumors came to nothing. But in some few cases, what began as uneasy whispers escalated into outright horror. Missing pets, mutilated livestock, and worse. Much worse. The captain of the football team had been arrested for decapitating the head cheerleader in Bailey Downs, Indiana; the star mathlete detained for disemboweling his algebra instructor in Beacon Hills, New Hampshire; the homecoming queen taken into custody for slaughtering her entire court in Baker's Park, California. These had all been crimes of unparalleled savagery and mysterious circumstance. No convincing motives could be discovered, no weapons capable of inflicting such appalling wounds.

Anonymous sources reported that the cheerleader and the teacher had been partially devoured. The homecoming queen had hunted down her friends on the court with uncanny speed, butchering six girls and their escorts in the space of two hours. In all three cases, the perpetrators had been tracked down in wooded areas hours after dawn. They had been uniformly drenched in gore.

The Rumors in Rockdale

None of us could have foreseen Maude Lewis's death when Jim
Whitt, a fifty-something graduate of Rockdale High, first set local
tongues wagging. In the year since his wife had skipped town with
a Bible salesman, Jim had taken to drink, often closing down the
Four Roses Tavern. By the time he hauled himself off his barstool
on the night of January 11th, he was more than a little unsteady on
his feet. Halfway to his dilapidated farm — three miles out of town
on Rural Route 41 — he began to nod. He pulled over to rest his
eyes in a wooded turnout just outside the city limits.

The howling startled him awake an hour later.

Just a dog, he assured himself as he pulled back onto the
pavement. But he hadn't gone more than a quarter mile before
something big sprang onto the narrow road in front of him. For a
heart-pounding instant, the creature — he did not know what else
to call it — froze there, pinned in the splash of his old pickup's
one working headlight, its knees coiled, its arms flung up before it.
Jim stood on the brakes, wrenching the wheel hard left. When the
truck skidded to a stop, he reached for the rifle mounted behind
him, but the thing was already gone, leaving him little more than a
confused impression of slavering fangs, wiry fur, and hateful yellow
eyes. It looked unnervingly human, he told Frank Lilly over bottles
of Pabst Blue Ribbon the next day.

"Could have been a bear," Frank said.

But no bears had been seen around Rockdale for years. The
whole thing was far more likely to be a figment of Jim's whiskey-sat-
urated brain, we concluded — and that might have been the end
of it but for the incident at Mike Talbot's farm. One early February
night, the hunting dogs Mike kept kenneled near his barn woke
him. When he walked out to check on them, shotgun in hand,
he found them in a frenzy. They snapped and bayed at the surrounding woods. They gnawed at the chain-link mesh of their run.
Then an answering howl clove the night — close, much closer than
Mike would have liked. A wild, rank musk filled the air. Mike's
dogs whimpered and shrank away, their lips skinning back in terror. Something thrashed in the undergrowth at the tree line. Mike
didn't hesitate. He lifted his shotgun and discharged both barrels
into the darkness. He was still fumbling with the breech — his

hands were shaking, he would later report without shame—when the creature, whatever it was, crashed off into the woods. The animal stench faded. He'd driven the thing off, at least for now. He had no intention of waiting to see if it came back. He reloaded, retreated to the house, and put coffee on the burner. He didn't sleep till dawn.

This was a more difficult story to dismiss. Mike was an unimpeachable witness. A deacon at the First Baptist Church, he'd never been known to take a drink in his life, so his testimony added considerable force to Jim's account of the creature on Route 41. Miss Drummond's poodle, Yankee, disappeared from his fenced-in yard a few days later. When his half-eaten remains turned up on the high school steps the following morning, rumors of the teenage werewolf began to circulate in earnest, and though none of us really believed them, we liked to pretend that we did.

It was a pleasure to be afraid. We shivered with excitement when Andy Wilson swore that he'd seen an inhuman figure lurking in the gloom behind his father's toolshed. We swooned with delight when Debra Anderson reported hearing something snuffling at her bedroom window. We jumped at shadows and hid under covers. We roved the streets in packs for safety, immersed ourselves in werewolf lore, and debated the teenage lycanthrope's identity over chocolate malts at Mooney's drive-in. Fear united us, and granted some few of us social opportunities we'd never had before. Tony Rivers wasn't the only one who seized the chance to walk home with a girl who might not have given him a second glance beforehand.

Then Maude Lewis died.

Rockdale High Reacts

A feverish elation seized us at school the next day. The glamour of tragedy is contagious. Its aftermath permits no strangers. Maude's close friends sobbed, and even girls who'd barely known her—even girls who had never spoken to her at all—wept. The boys—not without self-interest—tendered solace when permitted, and swelled with false bravado. And had we wanted to forget, to declare ourselves free of any obligation to grieve Maude or honor or avenge her, we could not have done so. The teachers were long-faced and solicitous, engorged with empty platitudes. Yellow crime-scene tape adorned the locked gym doors, and uniformed policemen patrolled the halls. Speculation rang upon every lip. Who could have done such a thing? we wondered. Did a teenage werewolf truly walk among us?

The news of Tony Rivers's arrest, when it came that afternoon, settled the question for most of us. The crime did not conform to what many of us believed about lycanthropy. A human suspect had been taken into custody, the investigation successfully closed.

But those of us who knew Tony could not countenance his guilt. He was, like his father before him, an essentially gentle person, soft-spoken, shy. Surely he could not have committed such a crime—a conclusion confirmed in our minds by the publication of Miss Ferguson's account of the brutal attack in the next day's *Rockdale Gazette*. It had to have been the teenage werewolf, we concluded. Nothing else made sense.

Detective Donovan's Doubts

Though we did not know it at the time, we were not alone in our misgivings.

What seemed like efficiency to Police Chief Baker felt like political expedience to his lead investigator. What seemed like homicidal madness to his boss—the boy had been trying to stuff Maude's viscera back inside her abdominal cavity, after all—made a kind of bizarre sense to Donovan. In a similar situation—had someone gutted, say, his own beloved daughter, Sharon, a freshman at Rockdale High, and strewn her intestines around the room like garland—Donovan could very well imagine doing the same thing. He could even imagine that it might seem reasonable.

In short, Donovan was skeptical. If Chief Baker hadn't ordered him to make the arrest, Tony Rivers would still be free. The narrative didn't hold up to scrutiny.

No one denied that Tony had had the opportunity—but he was hardly alone. The school had been unlocked, open to any passerby.

Motive, Donovan believed, was equally problematic. Chief Baker ascribed the crime to Tony's humiliation and anger at Maude's rejection. This made sense at first blush, but Donovan couldn't reconcile it with what he'd learned from Tony's interview. Maude had been kind to the boy. She'd brought a casserole to Tony's house after his father died. She'd attended the funeral. And she'd been gentle in telling the boy she didn't want to go out with him. She valued him as a friend. They would continue to spend time together. She hoped he would still walk her home after she worked out at night.

More problematic still, Tony was a good kid himself—hard-working, kind. Donovan knew this from his daughter, and he'd sensed it in the interview. Tony seemed to have taken no offense at Maude's rejection. He seemed, sadly, to have accepted rejection as his lot in life. And he'd been genuinely distraught at her death—hysterical, even. Grief-stricken and destroyed. No doubt a good prosecutor could make the motive stick at trial, but Donovan believed that it collapsed in light of any honest analysis.

As for means? Impossible. Tony had been a scrawny, ungainly young man before his father's illness. After Ted Rivers died, Tony had grown haggard and pale, attenuated, weak. Even in the grip of unmitigated fury, of a hatred that burned hot and clean, Tony Rivers simply wasn't physically capable of such a crime. Few men were. He could not have broken Maude's spine. Could not have disemboweled her with his bare hands. And could not have—

Donovan shuddered.

Tony Rivers could not have chewed off her face.

Detective Donovan had heard the same rumors as everyone else, of course, but he'd never believed in the teenage werewolf. Now he wondered. How else could he explain the tuft of coarse brown hair they'd discovered in Maude Lewis's death-clenched fist?

The Death of Helen Bissell

A week passed without incident, then another. Gradually Rockdale returned to normal. We no longer roamed the streets in packs for safety. We dismissed as superstition the werewolf lore we had studied so intently mere weeks before. Talk at Mooney's turned from the teenage werewolf to the junior-senior prom. Our younger siblings once again skipped rope and played pick-up basketball as the March dusk enveloped our sidewalks and driveways. After Maude's funeral, the crime tape came down from the gym doors, the police no longer patrolled our hallways, and the teachers turned their attention back to English and equations. At night we slept with our windows open, and in the morning we walked to school without fear. Even those of us with doubts let down our guard as the days slipped by.

Then the teenage werewolf struck again.

Afterward, we would question our lack of vigilance. Many of us would blame Police Chief Baker for lulling us into complacency with his blind assurances that our streets were safe. Detective Donovan would blame himself. Others would blame the victims, Helen Bissell and Arlene Marshall, both seniors at Rockdale High. How could they have been so careless? we would ask ourselves.

But at the time, with Tony Rivers safely behind bars, the decisions Helen and Arlene made that evening must have seemed perfectly reasonable. They'd met at the public library to study for a geometry exam, and time had gotten away from them. One minute they were trying to figure out how to calculate the surface area of an irregular prism, the next Mrs. Landon, the head librarian, was ushering them into the night.

The *Rockdale Gazette* later reported that she'd closed the library five minutes early, a matter of some controversy, though most of us could not see how five minutes would have changed anything. There were no other patrons that night, and she'd hoped to make it home for *Alfred Hitchcock Presents*. How could she have known that a teenage werewolf lurked in the darkness outside?

How could any of us have known?

If we had, Helen and Arlene might never have been at the library in the first place. Failing that, they might have called a parent to pick them up. And in the unlikely event that they *had* decided to walk, they would certainly have taken a different route home. Their houses—they were neighbors, friends since childhood—lay on the other side of McComb Park. But going around the park added fifteen minutes to their walk. They decided to cut through instead.

By daylight our park is warm and inviting. Sunlight slants down through ancient oaks, and old men gather on the benches to gossip and feed the ducks that cruise the lake. Lovers picnic on the lawn by the bandshell. Children climb on the monkey bars and chase each other through the woods bordering the asphalt path that bisects the grounds. At night, however, the park is an entirely different place, isolated and abandoned. The oaks loom like giants against the black sky. The monkey bars have a skeletal aspect. Inky pools of shadow gather between widely spaced lampposts (too widely, we would later contend), and the woods seem to press closer to the path.

Helen and Arlene were more than halfway through the park when a lupine howl shattered the pristine silence. Just a dog, that's all, they reassured each other, as Jim Whitt had before them. But rumors of the teenage werewolf asserted themselves with fresh urgency. Another howl split the night as they passed into the bright pool beneath a lamppost. They exchanged glances, their faces white with dread, and hesitated, unwilling to brave the darkness, terrified not to. The next light gleamed like a beacon through the trees, just beyond a long curve in the path, and beyond that, one more was faintly visible, a hundred yards before the stone-columned exit to the park and the safety of the streets beyond. Another howl sundered the air. Reluctantly, they slipped into the gloom.

Maybe a third of the way to the curve, Arlene would later report, they realized that something was pacing them in the darkness under the trees. They began to walk faster. Their unseen shadow stayed with them. They got the first hints of a rank, animal stench, and when the next howl rent the air—the thing couldn't have been more than twenty or thirty feet deep in the trees—the girls panicked. Dropping their books, they broke into a run. The next instant, the monster came crashing out of the trees upon them.

As it hurtled past her and carried Helen screaming to the pavement, the creature raked Arlene's face with razor-edged claws. She caught what followed in glimpses, through the blood sheeting into her eyes: caught a flash of the thing, wiry and agile, as it crouched over Helen on legs of tensile muscle, a flash of its outstretched arms and curving talons, a flash of its face, its snout lifted to the sky as it howled in triumph. When the monster looked at her, its yellow eyes blazing in the gloom, its fangs glistening, Arlene whimpered. It leered at her. It grinned in mockery—if such a thing could grin—and then it turned away, sweeping one massive hand down and across Helen's throat, silencing her in an arterial spray.

And then, God help her, it started to feed.

Arlene found her voice and ran screaming through the park

into the streets beyond. She collapsed, still screaming, on the front porch of the first house she came to. It belonged to Larry Phillips and his wife, Esther, a childless couple with a penchant for jigsaw puzzles. When the door opened, Arlene lurched inside. Larry Phillips took one look at her, slammed the door behind her, and flipped the deadbolt. A moment later he was on the phone for help. His wife, meanwhile, was trying to stanch the bleeding from the gashes the monster had carved in the girl's face.

Arlene Marshall would never be beautiful again.

To his shame, that was Detective Donovan's first thought when he saw her in the hospital room where they had stitched her up. She was groggy with painkillers, and it took an hour or more—over the doctor's objections—to elicit even a fragmentary version of what had transpired. Despite the evidence before him, Donovan reeled with shock and disbelief. It could not be, he thought. None of it. It must have been the morphine that accounted for her story. Yet the final detail she'd confided before the drug carried her off to sleep would not leave his mind.

The monster had been wearing a Rockdale Rams letter jacket.

The Aftermath of Helen Bissell's Death

Most of what we knew of that night was the product of rumor and surmise, though we had some few facts at our disposal. The park was closed indefinitely, the *Rockdale Gazette* reported, and the contingent of policemen Detective Donovan had dispatched to search the grounds did not find Helen Bissell until well after dawn. Though the article was circumspect in its description, it was clear that Helen was no longer intact when they located her—that what was left of her had been discovered scattered throughout the woods, torn apart and half-eaten. We knew as well—or thought we did—that the teenage werewolf had been wearing a letter jacket, though Donovan had sworn the attending physician to silence.

Tony Rivers was released, but Vic Miller, star forward of the high school basketball team, a jealous ex-boyfriend of Helen Bissell and proud owner of a Rockdale Rams letter jacket, was taken into custody. Released for lack of evidence soon afterward—his father was an attorney, a Rotarian, and a fast friend of the sitting judge—he returned to school, as did Tony Rivers, nursing a grievance. Tony's shyness had been replaced with sullen resentment and hostility. Vic's natural belligerence had been exacerbated.

Few of us—even the most skeptical—still doubted the existence of the teenage werewolf. Once again we grieved, ostentatiously, and with a kind of manic joy. It was exciting to be afraid, more exciting still to be feared—for now that the rumors had been confirmed beyond all doubt, we *were* feared. Tension gripped the halls of Rockdale High. Our teachers looked askance at us in their classrooms. Our parents sent our younger siblings to visit relatives in other towns. But why? we asked, smiling sly, secret smiles, because of course we knew. A teenage werewolf walked among us. Who could say who it might be? Who could say when—or who—it would attack next?

Yet we were each of us confident in our invulnerability. Maude Lewis and Helen Bissell had met terrible fates, but no matter how well we had known them—and some of us had known them quite well—they were strangers to us in the end. To the young, the dead are always strangers, in transit of some inconceivable horizon, both proximate and impossibly remote. We understood that we could die, that we someday would, but we did not *know* it, and though we took precautions—once again we roved the streets in packs and locked our windows at night—we felt at heart that they were not necessary. The teenage werewolf would strike again, but it would not strike us. We took comfort in our immortality, pleasure in our fear.

And we secretly thrilled in the power that the teenage werewolf had bestowed upon us.

For if we were both sovereign and slave to our terror, our teachers and our parents were slaves alone. As long as no one knew who the teenage werewolf was, it could be any one of us.

The Town Meeting

Two days after Helen Bissell's death—after the children had been dispatched into the safekeeping of faraway grandparents, uncles, aunts, and cousins, and after we ourselves had grown giddy with power and despair—placards went up announcing a town meeting. Such affairs were usually ill-attended, the speakers' voices booming in the half-empty hall. *My neighbor's lawn is an eyesore, weedy and ungroomed. A red light should be installed at Third and Vine—traffic has picked up since the new A&P opened its doors. The proposed trailer park on State Route 321 must be opposed, lest visitors to Rockdale be given the wrong impression.*

Such mundane matters interested few of us.

The teenage werewolf, however, engaged us all. Anticipating the turnout, the town fathers moved the meeting to the high school gym. We gathered in Section A, at center court, and watched our parents and our teachers, our coaches, our scout masters, and our pastors file grimly in. They did not acknowledge us. They did not speak among themselves. And when Mayor Flanigan called the meeting to order, there was barely a rustle as they settled their attention upon the makeshift stage. We wondered if they thought, as we did, of the bloodstains that had been scrubbed from the hardwood underneath.

Mayor Flanigan told us that we faced a crisis unlike any other that Rockdale had ever endured. He voiced our grief for Maude Lewis and Helen Bissell. He adjured us to cooperate with Police Chief Baker and Detective Donovan in the ongoing investigation. He quoted scripture and bowed his head in prayer. And then he summoned the witnesses. Jim Whitt was too drunk to testify (Mayor Flanigan summarized his account), but the rest of them took the stage one by one—Mike Talbot and Miss Drummond and Miss Ferguson, each of them building the case that something terrible haunted the streets of Rockdale.

Then Arlene Marshall mounted the stage, stitched up like a teenage Frankenstein. A whisper of shock ran through the gym. In the silence that followed, Arlene took the microphone with trembling hands and surveyed the crowd, letting her gaze come to rest at last upon us, her peers. We could not read her expression. We could not see beyond her ravaged face. The sutures—there must have been a hundred or more, black and knotty, the puckered wounds slathered with some glistening antiseptic balm—pulled her skin taut, her mouth into a snarl. Her voice was unsteady when she began, barely audible and difficult to understand, but as she shared her experience in the park she gained confidence. She held the audience rapt as she described the howling in the night, the stalker in the woods. Gasps erupted when the monster came crashing through the trees, and when she spoke the fatal words at last, when she said that the thing had been a teenage werewolf, clad in the letter jacket of Rockdale High, a single cry of sorrow and horror—it was a woman's voice—scaled the walls and echoed in the raftered vault above.

Arlene left the stage, and—though the teenage werewolf sat somewhere in our section, hidden in a human skin—she took her place among us.

Detective Donovan was the next to take the stage. He begged of us our forgiveness. He had failed the town. He had assumed, even in the face of his own doubts, that Maude's murder had been the work of a merely human killer—despite the impossible violence of the attack and the tuft of coarse brown hair he'd found in one clenched fist. He'd ignored the evidence. His imagination had failed him. He would refine the focus of his investigation.

Mayor Flanigan and Police Chief Baker were not so humble. They did not acknowledge their own failures and did not examine past error. For them, the only question was the course forward. New policies were to be implemented. A strict curfew would be established and enforced. All high school extracurricular activities—including sports—would be put on indefinite hold. And it went without saying (they said), that the junior-senior prom—a mere week away—would be canceled. We stirred in discontent at the first of these pronouncements. A chorus of whispers sprang up in response to the second. An active outcry broke out at the third. Did Mayor Flanigan really think a curfew would contain a teenage werewolf? Had he forgotten that the basketball team was in contention for the state championship? And what about the prom? We'd purchased our dresses and sent our suits to the dry cleaners, made dinner reservations, ordered flowers. Did the mayor intend to reimburse us for these expenditures—for a year's worth of yards mown and snow shoveled, drive-in food delivered, babies sat?

He hesitated. He didn't answer.

Police Chief Baker cleared his throat. He gave us a stern look, but we'd seen that look before. Our teachers used it when they caught us smoking behind the fieldhouse, and our parents used it when we came home late on Saturday nights. Our coaches used it when we took a bad shot or forgot the play, our pastors when we missed services. It no longer frightened us, that look. We knew it for an empty threat. We'd seen what a teenage werewolf could do, and we knew that Chief Baker too was afraid. What would we have him do? he wanted to know. Would we surrender the once peaceful streets of Rockdale to a reign of blood?

We didn't answer him.

Then someone—none of us saw who it was—yelled that half-measures wouldn't do. By all means impose the curfew and cancel the prom. But something more had to be done! Our townsfolk roared their approval. *Put extra policemen on the street!* someone cried. And someone else: *Issue the officers silver bullets!* And then a clamor of competing shouts—*wolf's bane* and *monkshood* and *lock them all away!*—this last plunging the crowd into a deep silence as our parents contemplated the lengths that they would go to tame or contain us—

A silence into which Arlene Marshall once again stood and approached the stage.

She leaned into the microphone.

"I always dreamed of going to prom," she said, and after what she'd been through, who could deny her?

Thus it was decided.

Our Thoughts About the Teenage Werewolf

Who would take Arlene to prom? we wondered.

Following her mutilation, Jonathan Bowling—her boyfriend—had rescinded his invitation (inexcusably, we agreed) on the pretext that she had not sufficiently recovered to attend. When we told him that his place then was at her side—and not at the prom—he had no counterargument. His face burned with chagrin, his eyes with fury. He clenched his fists and set his teeth. Many of us feared him. He was big, a tackle on the football team, and short-tempered. Yet even he had no strength to oppose the force of our unified opinion.

He reinstated his invitation.

Arlene, to her credit, refused him. Even if she had no other options, she told him, she would not deign to accompany him. As it happened, however, she did have other options—a plethora of them. The attack and its aftermath, most notably her solidarity with us at the town meeting, had conferred a kind of celebrity upon her. But she turned her suitors down and asked Tony Rivers to be her date. They were kindred spirits, she said. They'd both been scarred by the teenage werewolf.

But hadn't we all?

Hadn't the teenage werewolf come to shape and define us? Wasn't its existence, its endless capacity for violence, the single most important fact about us? Hadn't our townsmen—our parents—made that clear? They wished to curtail our freedoms, cancel our sports, deny us, most of all, the zenith of our year—the axis about which our entire social calendar revolved. As far as they were concerned, until someone identified the teenage werewolf, we were *all* the teenage werewolf—and if at one level we resented this, at another it empowered us. In trying to save us, they had sought to imprison us. In seeking to imprison us, they had set us free.

The Friday before the prom, we cast our votes for queen. That night we gathered to decorate the gym. We erected a bandstand, unfolded card tables and disguised them with white linen cloths. We inflated balloons and draped ribbons. We hung a glitter ball from the rafters, like a shining silver moon, and felt wild currents flowing in our veins.

The Massacre at the Rockdale Prom

We woke to rain the next morning, but the weather cleared by ten. We heaved a collective sigh of relief. Cars needed washing, shoes polishing. We arrived early at the florist to collect our flowers—and sighed when we had to wait because everyone else had had the same idea.

Cliques clicked and gangs gathered.

We gossiped as we dressed. Our mothers clamped bobby pins between their teeth, plucking them out one by one as they constructed elaborate coiffures. Our fathers helped us knot ties purchased to coordinate with the dresses of our dates. Our stomachs churned with the magnitude of the occasion. We giggled in excitement. We put on stoic faces.

The prom officially commenced at 8:00, but most of us drifted in half an hour later. It wouldn't do to arrive too early, and besides,

we had other things to attend to. Dates had to be picked up, cor-
sages affixed. Pictures had to be taken. Our dinner plans ran long.
We ate with mannered precision, conducting stilted conversations
over our food. We pretended at adulthood and found it all a bore.

This was not what we had expected at all.

We longed for freedom, not a preview of the pinched years to
come.

Upon our arrival, we were alarmed to see that chaperones had
attended in unusual numbers. Miss Ferguson was there, of course,
as were our teachers. But Mayor Flanigan and Police Chief Baker
had also shown up. Our pastors and our parents too. Detective
Donovan kept to the shadows, watching with a weather eye.

Even the gym's transformation disappointed us. The card tables
were rickety. The folding chairs betrayed the illusion of elegance.
The balloons drooped. The hors d'oeuvres left much to be desired. The cheese tasted ashy. The cookies were dry, the punch
thin. And while we told ourselves that the band was fantastic, we
knew that it was second-rate. Their covers were pale shadows of the
rock-and-roll we'd grown to love, their harmonies off-key.

Yet we danced as if our lives depended on it. We danced like the
twelve princesses in the tale. When the band played a slow song,
we clutched each other close — too close, our chaperones would
have said. In the shadowy reaches of the room they stirred as if
to intercede, but then fell still. And when the band swung into a
fast song, we whirled around the floor, waved our arms, drew each
other close, and whirled away again. Our parents looked on in
disapproval, but they did not speak.

The dancing became wild, frenetic, Dionysian. The staid adult
masks we'd donned over dinner slipped and fell away entirely. And
then the music stopped. We all froze, panting on the dance floor
as a spotlight illuminated Miss Ferguson, thin and pale upon the
stage. It was almost eleven by then, the climax of the night, time
to announce the prom queen. One by one, to squeals of triumph
and delight, her court was appointed: four handmaidens and their
escorts, arrayed in a crescent moon around the stage. And then,
with a drumroll, Principal Ferguson opened the envelope containing the prom queen's identity. She unfolded the page within, she
scanned it silently. She leaned in to the microphone and read it
aloud.

"This year's prom queen is Arlene Marshall," she said.

The room burst into riotous applause.

As Tony Rivers squired her to the bandstand, we stomped our feet for Arlene. We cheered, we roared as one, and when she dipped her head to accept the crown, we howled. We howled and howled, like wild things, like monsters and like wolves. Her tiara on her head, Arlene turned to the microphone. Before she could speak—had she even intended to speak?—her visage bulged grotesquely, stitches popping, and cracked along the fault lines of her wounds. We gasped when she reached up with her fingers and tore back her human face to reveal the muzzle underneath, slavering and snapping at the air. Her yellow eyes glowed with untamed freedom and with joy. She lifted her head, baying into the dark vault of the gym with its glitter-ball moon. And even as a tide of lupine transformation swept the crowded dance floor, as we too clawed apart our faces to free at last the ravening beasts that lay underneath, teenage werewolves each and every one—even as we assumed our true and long-hidden forms, unknown even to ourselves, our werewolf queen claimed her first victim, decapitating Principal Ferguson with a single swipe of her hand.

Our muscles tightened and grew tenfold strong, agile, quick. Our fingers sprang razor-edged claws, our pores coarse hair. And our senses sharpened. The gloom of the gym was blasted clean with white, hot light, and we could hear the pulse of blood in every human vein. We could smell it too, metallic and hot. We could smell everything—the sweet tang of the punch and the terror of our chaperones in their sweat upon the air, even our own rank and randy musk—and we wanted to wallow in it all, to fight and fuck and eat, eat, eat. We were famished and insatiate, bottomless pits of raw appetite. Nothing had ever been so awful. Nothing had ever felt so good.

We reveled in it. Leaped on tables and smashed chairs. Snarled and howled and took our chaperones down. They stood in shock before our fury. Police Chief Baker died with his revolver still holstered. Detective Donovan got off a single shot before a teenage werewolf bit off his hand and took him to the floor. Someone kicked open a door and we eviscerated them as they fled into the night—pastors and parents, coaches, teachers, the mayor and the city council too. We ripped out their throats and tore off their arms. We ate of their flesh. We drank of their blood. We killed them all and we devoured them, and then we stood on the roofs of their cars and howled our triumph at the moon. We were teenage werewolves and we owned the night.

We would never let them tame us.

JOSEPH ALLEN HILL

The Venus Effect

FROM *Lightspeed Magazine*

Apollo Allen and the Girl from Venus

THIS IS 2015. A party on a west-side roof, just before midnight. Some Mia or Mina throwing it, the white girl with the jean jacket and the headband and the two-bumps-of-molly grin, flitting from friend circle to friend circle, laughing loudly and refilling any empty cup in her eyeline from a bottomless jug of sangria, Maenad Sicagi. There are three kegs, a table of wines and liquor, cake and nachos inside. It is a good party, and the surrounding night is beautiful, warm and soft and speckled with stars. A phone is hooked up to a portable sound system, and the speakers are kicking out rapture. It is 2009 again, the last year that music was any good, preserved in digital amber and reanimated via computer magic.

Apollo boogies on the margins, between the edge of the party and the edge of the roof, surrounded by revelers but basically alone. Naomi is on the other side of the crowd, grinding against her new boyfriend, Marcus, a musclebound meat-man stuffed into a spectacularly tacky T-shirt. Apollo finds this an entirely unappealing sight. That she and Apollo once shared an intimate relationship has nothing to do with this judgment. Not at all.

Speaking merely as an observer, a man with a love of Beauty and Dance in his heart, Apollo judges their performance unconvincing. It is the worst sort of kitsch. The meat-man against whom Naomi vibrates has no rhythm, no soul; he is as unfunky as the bad guys on Parliament-Funkadelic albums. He stutters from side to side with little regard for the twos and fours, and the occasional thrusts of his crotch are little more than burlesque, without the slightest suggestion of genuine eroticism. He is doing it just to do it. Pure kitsch. Appalling. Naomi is doing a better job, undulating her buttocks with a certain aplomb, a captivating bootyliciousness that might stir jiggly bedroom memories in the heart of the lay observer. But still. *We know that the tail must wag the dog, for the horse is drawn by the cart; But the Devil whoops, as he whooped of old: "It's pretty, but is it Art?*

Apollo cannot bear to watch this any longer. He desperately wants to point the terribleness of this scene out to someone, to say, "Hey, look at them. They look like dumbs. Are they not dumbs?" But Naomi was always the person to whom he pointed these sorts of things out. That's why they got along, at least in the beginning, a shared appreciation for the twin pleasures of pointing at a fool and laughing at a fool. Without her, he is vestigial, useless, alone.

He turns away from the ghastly scene just in time to notice a young woman dancing nearby. She is alone, like him, and she is, unlike him, utterly, utterly turnt. Look at her, spinning like a politician, bouncing like a bad check, bopping to the beat like the beat is all there is. She is not a talented dancer by any stretch of the imagination, and her gracelessness is unable to keep up with her abandon. She is embraced of the moment, full with the spirit, completely ungenerous with fucks, and possibly bordering on the near side of alcohol poisoning. Just look at her. Apollo, in a state of terrible cliché, is unable to take his eyes off her.

There is a problem, however.

Her heels, while fabulous, were not made for rocking so hard. They are beautiful shoes, certainly, vibrant and sleek, canary-yellow, bold as love. Perhaps they are a bit too matchy-matchy with regard to the rest of her outfit, the canary-yellow dress and the canary-yellow necklace and the canary-yellow bow atop her head, but the matchy-matchy look is good for people who are forces of nature, invoking four-color heroism and supernatural panache. Yet however lovely and amazing and charming and expensive these shoes might be, they cannot be everything.

The center cannot hold; things fall apart.

Her left heel snaps. Her balance is lost. Her momentum and her tipsiness send her stumbling, and no one is paying enough attention to catch her. The building is not so high up that a fall would definitely kill her, but death could be very easily found on the sidewalk below. Apollo rushes forward, reaches out to grab her, but he is too late. She goes over the edge. Apollo cannot look away. She falls for what feels like forever.

And then she stops. She doesn't hit the ground. She just stops and hangs in the air. Apollo stares frozen, on the one hand relieved not to witness a death, on the other hand filled with ontological dread as his understanding of the laws of gravitation unravel before his eyes, on a third hypothetical hand filled with wonder and awe at this flagrant violation of consensus reality. The young woman looks up at Apollo with her face stuck in a frightened grimace as she slowly, slowly descends, like a feather in the breeze. She takes off as soon as she hits the ground, stumble-running as fast as one can on nonfunctional shoes.

Apollo does not know what has just happened, but he knows that he wants to know. He does not say goodbye to the hostess or his friends or Naomi. He just ghosts, flying down the ladder and down the hall and down the stairs and out the door. He can just make out a blur in the direction she ran off, and he chases after it.

There is a man in a police uniform standing at the corner. Apollo does not see him in the darkness, does not know that he is running toward him. The man in the police uniform draws his weapon and yells for Apollo to stop. Inertia and confusion do not allow Apollo to stop quickly enough. Fearing for his life, the man in the police uniform pulls the trigger of his weapon several times, and the bullets strike Apollo in his chest, doing critical damage to his heart and lungs. He flops to the ground. He is dead now.

Uh, what? That was not supposed to happen. Apollo was supposed to chase the girl alien, then have some romantically charged adventures fighting evil aliens, then at the end she was going to go back to her home planet and it was going to be sad. Who was that guy? That's weird, right? That's not supposed to happen, right? Dudes aren't supposed to just pop off and end stories out of nowhere.

I guess to be fair, brother was running around in the middle of the night, acting a fool. That's just asking for trouble. He was a pretty unlikable protagonist anyway, a petty, horny, pretentious idiot with an almost palpable stink of author surrogacy on him. I think there was a Kipling quote in there. Who's that for? You don't want to read some lame indie romance bullshit, right? Sadboy meets manic pixie dream alien? I'm already bored. Let's start over.

This time we'll go classic. We'll have a real hero you can look up to, and cool action-adventure shit will go down. You ready? Here we go.

Apollo Rocket vs. the Space Barons from Beyond Pluto

There are fifteen seconds left on the clock, and the green jerseys have possession. The score is 99–98, green jerseys. The red jerseys have been plagued by injuries, infighting, and unfortunate calls on the part of the ref, who, despite his profession's reputed impartiality, is clearly a supporter of the green jerseys. The green jerseys themselves are playing as though this is the very last time they will ever play a basketball game. They are tall and white and aggressively midwestern, and this gives them something to prove. Sketch in your mind the Boston Celtics of another time. Picture the Washington Generals on one of the rare, rumored nights when they were actually able to defeat their perennial adversaries, mortal men who somehow found themselves snatching victory from the god-clowns of Harlem.

Fourteen.

One of the green jerseys is preparing to throw the ball toward the hoop. If the ball were to go into the hoop, the green jerseys would have two points added to their score, and it would become impossible for the red jerseys to throw enough balls into the other hoop before time runs out. The green jerseys are already preparing for their win, running over in their minds talking points for their postgame interviews, making sure the sports drink dispenser is full and ready to be poured upon the coach, and wondering how the word *champions* might feel on their lips.

Eleven.

But this will not happen. Apollo is in position. He reaches out with his mighty arm and strips the ball from the green jersey before he can throw it.

Ten.

Apollo runs as fast as he can with the ball, so fast that every atom of his body feels as if it is igniting. He looks for an open teammate, for he is no ball hog, our Apollo, but there are no teammates to be found between himself and the hoop. So he runs alone. He is lightning. There are green jersey players in his way, but he spins and jukes around them before they can react, as if they are sloths suspended in aspic. Do his feet even touch the floor? Is it the shoes?

He's on fire.

Three.

He leaps high into the air and dunks the ball so hard that the backboard shatters into a thousand glittering shards of victory. The buzzer goes off just as he hits the ground. The final score is 100–99, red jerseys. Apollo Triumphant is leaped upon by his teammates. Hugs and pats on the back are distributed freely and with great relish. The crowd erupts into wild celebration. *Apollo, Apollo,* they chant.

Patrick, the captain of the opposing team, approaches Apollo as confetti falls from above. There is a sour look on the man's face, an expression of constipated rage at its most pure. He balls his fingers into a fist and raises it level with Apollo's midsection. It rears back and trembles as an arrow notched in a bow, ready to be fired.

"Good job, bro," he says.

"You too," says Apollo.

They bump fists. It is so dope.

A small child limps onto the basketball court. He smiles so hard that it must be painful for his face. Apollo kneels and gives him a high-five, then a low-five, then a deep hug.

"You did it, Apollo," says the child.

"No. We did it," says Apollo. "They'll never be able to demolish the youth center now."

"My new mommy and daddy said they could never have adopted me without your help."

Apollo puts a finger to his own lips. "Shhhhh."

"I love you, Apollo," says the child, its face wet with tears. "You're the best man alive."

Apollo drives home with his trophy and game ball in the back seat of his sports car, a candy-apple convertible that gleams like justice. He blasts ~~Rick Ross~~ a positive, socially conscious rap song about working hard and pulling up one's pants on his stereo. The road is his tonight. There are no other cars to be seen, no other people for miles. For all his successes as balla par excellence, Apollo still appreciates the beauty and quiet of the country.

Suddenly a sonorous roar pours out from the edge of the sky, so powerful that it shakes the car. Before Apollo can react, a yellow-silver-blue ball of fire shoots across the sky and explodes on the horizon, for a moment blotting out the darkness with pure white light before retreating into smoke and darkness. Apollo ~~jams his foot on the pedal~~ proceeds in the direction of the mysterious explosion while obeying all traffic laws and keeping his vehicle within the legal speed limits.

"~~Holy shit~~ Golly," he says.

Apollo finds a field strewn with flaming debris, shattered crystals, and shards of brightly colored metals. He hops out of his car to take a closer look. Based on his astro-engineering courses, which he gets top marks in, he surmises that these materials could only have come from some kind of spaceship. He is fascinated, to say the least.

He hears movement from under a sheet of opaque glass. He pushes it away and sees that there is a woman lying prone underneath. At least, Apollo thinks she is a woman. She is shaped like a woman, but her skin is blue, and she has gills, and she has a second mouth on her forehead. Woman or not, she is beautiful, with delicate, alien features and C-cup breasts.

"Oh my God," says Apollo. He kneels down next to the alien woman and cradles her in his arms. "Are you okay?"

She sputters, ". . . Listen . . . ship . . . crashed . . . There isn't much . . . time . . . You must stop . . . Lord Tklox . . . He is coming to . . . answer the . . . Omega Question . . . He will stop at nothing . . . please . . . stop him . . . Save . . . civilization . . . Leave me . . ."

Apollo notices a growing purple stain on the woman's diaphanous yellow robes. Based on his theoretical xenobiology class, he hypothesizes that this is blood. He shakes his head at her, unwilling to accept the false choice she has presented him with. "I'll do whatever I can to stop him, but first I have to help you."

She reaches up to gently stroke his hand with her three-fingered hand. ". . . So kind . . . I . . . chose well . . ."

With his incredible basketballer's strength, it is nothing for Apollo to lift the woman. He may as well be carrying a large sack of feathers. He places her in the passenger seat of his car and gets back on the road lickety-split.

"You'll be okay. I just need some supplies."

He stops at the nearest gas station. He races around inside to get what he needs: bandages, ice, sports drink, needle, thread,

protein bar. With these items in hand, he rushes toward the register, which is next to the exit. He is stopped by a man in a police
uniform. The man in the police uniform asks him about his car.

"It's mine," Apollo says.

The man in the police uniform does not believe Apollo.

"You have to come help me! There's a woman in trouble!"

The man in the police uniform does not believe Apollo and is
concerned that he is shouting.

"~~This is ridiculous!~~ Sorry, sir. I am sure you are just doing your
job. Let me show you my ID and insurance information so we can
clear all of this up," says Apollo.

Apollo goes to fish his wallet from his pocket. His naked hostility, volatile tone, and the act of reaching for what very well could
be a weapon are clear signs of aggressive intent, and the man in
the police uniform has no choice but to withdraw his own weapon
and fire several shots. Apollo is struck first in the stomach, then
the shoulder. He does not immediately die. Instead he spends several moments on the floor of the convenience store, struggling
to breathe as his consciousness fades into nothing. Then, he dies.

What the fuck is happening? Seriously. Where is this dude coming from? I haven't written that many stories, but I really don't
think that's how these things are supposed to go. The way I was
taught, you establish character and setting, introduce conflict, develop themes, then end on an emotional climax. That's it. Nobody
said anything about killers popping up out of nowhere. Not in this
genre, anyway.

So hear me out. I think we may be dealing some kind of metafictional entity, a living concept, an ideolinguistic infection. I don't
know how he got in here, but he should be easy enough to deal
with. I think we just need to reason with him. He's probably a nice
guy. Just doing his job, trying to keep the story safe. He was probably genuinely afraid that Apollo was reaching for a gun. You never
know with people these days. Life is scary.

Besides, that story wasn't working either. That Apollo was a big
phony, totally unbelievable. Guys like that went out of style with
Flash Gordon and bell-bottoms. It's not just about liking the protagonist. You have to be able to relate to them, right? I think that's
how it works. That's what everybody says, anyway. To be honest,
I don't really get the whole "relatability" thing. Isn't the point of

reading to subsume one's own experience for the experience of another, to crawl out of one's body and into a stranger's thoughts? Why would you want to read about someone just like you? Stories are windows, not mirrors. Everybody's human. Shouldn't that make them relatable enough? I don't know. I don't have a lot of experience with this kind of thing. I thought smoking was a weird thing to do too, but then I tried smoking and was addicted forever. Maybe I've just never come across a good mirror.

So let's do a child. Everybody loves children, and everybody was one. Plus it's really easy to make them super-relatable. Just throw some social anxiety disorder and a pair of glasses on some little fucking weirdo and *boom:* you got a movie deal. It'll be a coming-of-age hero's-journey sort of thing, adolescence viewed through a gossamer haze of nostalgia.

Bully Brawl: An Apollo Kidd Adventure

This is 1995. A group of young people sit on the stoop of a decaying brownstone just off the L. The topic is television. Some show or another. Who can remember? Broadcast television in the year 1995 is terrible all around, hugs and catchphrases and phantasmal laughter suspended in analog fuzz. Is *Full House* on in 1995? Is Urkel? They don't know how bad they have it. Naomi leads the conversation. A skinny, toothy girl with a voice like a preacher. You can almost hear the organ chords rumbling in your chest whenever she opens her mouth. She jokes about what she would do if her own hypothetical future husband were to comically declare himself the man of the house, with the punchlines mainly revolving around the speed and vigor with which she would slap the black off him. She is sort of funny, but only because the television shows she is describing are not.

Apollo does not make any jokes. He is sort of funny himself (people laugh at him, at least), but he does not know how to make funny words happen. He is mostly quiet, only chiming in with the factual, offering airtimes and channels and dropping the names of actors when they get stuck on the tips of tongues. Six or seven of them are gathered, and Apollo believes himself to definitely be the or-seventh. He is wearing a T-shirt with a superhero on it. Not Superman. Superman gear can be forgiven as a harmless eccentricity if you're otherwise down. But Apollo's rocking some kind of deep-cut clown in a neon gimp suit on his chest. Remember, this is 1995, and this man is thirteen years old. Unforgivable. He's not just the or-seventh, he is the physical manifestation of all the or-seventhness that has ever existed in the world.

The new girl is sitting next to him. She might have been the or-seventh were she not new. Check that sweater. Yellow? Polyester? Sequin pineapples? In this heat? Worse than unforgivable. But who knows what lies under it? A butterfly? A swan? Any and all manner of transformative symbology could be hiding, waiting, growing. There's still hope for her. She may be four-eyed and flat-butted and double-handed and generally Oreoish, but there is hope. She can at least drop into the conversation sometimes, in the empty spaces after the punchlines. She has that power. For instance, after Naomi does a long routine on what she would do if she ever found a wallet lying on the sidewalk like on TV (in brief: cop that shit), the new girl says something about losing her own money and getting punished harshly by her mother. It is not a funny thing to say, but memories of belts and switches and tears are still fresh in their adolescent minds, and it is comforting to laugh it out. Apollo laughs the hardest, and he does not know why.

The sun is gone. Just a little light left. The new girl can't go home alone. Not in the almost-dark. This is 1995, not 1948. Apollo volunteers to walk with her.

"He like you," says Marcus, Naomi's not-quite-but-basically boyfriend, by way of explaining why Apollo is the best one for the job.

Apollo denies this so fervently that he has to go through with it, lest she think he truly hates her. The walk is quiet for the first few blocks. Apollo is not a big talker, and the new girl has been here for two weeks, and no one, except maybe the ultra-gregarious Naomi, has had a real conversation with her. Still, Apollo finds himself feeling strangely comfortable. Maybe it is the sweater. Perhaps the fact that it should be embarrassing her is preventing him from being embarrassed himself. Perhaps it is the sartorial equivalent of imagining one's audience naked. Perhaps she's just sort of great.

Apollo stops short just before they reach the corner. He holds out his arm so that the girl will stop too. There's danger up ahead. A gang of street toughs. Six of them. One of those multicultural, gender-integrated '90s gangs, a Benetton ad with knives. Red jackets, gold sneakers. One of them has a boom box. KRS-One, maybe? Early KRS-One. Stuff about listening to people's guns as they shoot you with them. Their victim is an old, gray-haired man. His hands are up. There is a briefcase at his feet. The gangsters taunt him stereotypically.

"Give us ya money, Pops!"

"Don't make me cut you!"

"Nice and easy!"

"Don't be a hero!"

"I need to regulate!"

Apollo takes a slow step back. He means for Shayla to step with him, but she does not. He pulls on her arm, but she is still. She has a look on her face like she wants to fight motherfuckers. This is the most frightening expression that can appear on a human face.

"We have to go," he says.

"No," she says. "We have to help him."

"C'mon."

He pulls on her arm again, hard this time, but she slips his grasp. She runs at the gang, leaps into the air, and tackles the nearest one. The gangsters are surprised at first, to see this little girl brazenly attacking one of their own, but they quickly pull her off him and throw her to the ground.

"What's your malfunction?!" one of them screeches.

The girl stands and pulls out, seemingly from nowhere, a fantastic-looking ~~gun~~ object that in no way resembles a gun or any other real-life weapon. "Stand down, jerks."

"Oh dag! She got a ~~gun~~ object that in no way resembles a gun or any other real-life weapon! Kick rocks, guys!"

The gangsters run off into the night. Apollo runs over to the girl.

"What's going on? What's that thing?"

"Don't worry about it. Forget you saw anything," says the girl.

"Exactly," says the old man. He begins to laugh, first a low, soft chuckle, then an increasingly maniacal cackle that echoes in the night. "You have fallen for my trap, Princess Amarillia! I knew you could not resist helping a stranger in need."

The girl gasps. "Lord Tklox!"

"What?" says Apollo.

Smiling, the old man reaches up and grabs his face, pulling it off to reveal pale skin, elegant features, and hair the color of starlight. His body begins to bulge and swell as he grows larger, eventually doubling in height. He laughs as a shining sword appears in his hands.

"Run!" shouts the girl.

"What is happening?!"

"No time to explain. Take this." She hands him her fantastic-looking ~~gun~~ object that in no way resembles a gun or any other real-life weapon. "I'll hold him off with my Venusian jiu-jitsu. Just go! Don't stop. Please. Don't stop. Just run. Don't let him get you like he got the others."

The girl takes a martial arts stance and nods. Apollo does not need further explanations. He runs in the opposite direction. He runs as fast as he can, until his lungs burn and he cannot feel his legs. Stopping to catch his breath, he holds the ~~gun~~ object that in no way resembles a gun or any other real-life weapon up to the light. He does not even know how to use it, how it could possibly help him in this strange battle.

So wrapped up in thought, Apollo does not even see the man in the police uniform. He does not hear him telling him to drop his weapon. He only hears the gun go bang. Later his body is found by his mother, who cries and cries and cries.

Did you ever read "Lost in the Funhouse"? I just reread it as research on solving metafictional problems. Not super-helpful. We get it; fiction is made up. Cool story, bro. But you know the flashback to the kids playing Niggers and Masters? Is that a real thing? Or is it just a sadomasochistic parody of Cowboys and Indians? I can't find any information on it online, but I'm sure somebody somewhere has played it. If something as cruel as Cowboys and Indians exists, why not Niggers and Masters? There is no way a game like that is only theoretical. It's too rich, too delicious. The role of Master is an obvious power fantasy, presenting one with the authority to command and punish as an adult might, without any of the responsibility. The role of Nigger is just a different kind of power fantasy, power expressed as counterfactual. In playing the Nigger, one can experience subjugation on one's own terms. There is no real danger, no real pain. You can leave at any time, go home and watch cartoons and forget about it. Or you can indulge fully, giving oneself up to the game, allowing oneself to experience a beautiful simulacrum of suffering. It is perfect pretend. There are probably worse ways of spending a suburban afternoon, and there is something slightly sublime about it, baby's first ego death. Sure, it's profoundly offensive, but who's going to stop you? But whatever. I'm probably reading too much into it. It's probably a made-up, postmodern joke. When I was a kid, we just played Cops and Robbers, and it was fine.

Anyway, that was a digression. I admit that it's difficult to defend the actions of certain uniformed narrative devices, but I'm sure there were good reasons for them. After all, there were gangsters with actual knives in that one, and Apollo was holding something that maybe sort of looked like a weapon in the dark. How are we supposed to tell the good ones from the bad ones? Can you tell the difference? I don't think so. Besides, this was to be expected. Children's literature is sad as fuck. It's all about dead moms and dead dogs and cancer and loneliness. You can't expect everyone to come out alive from that. But you know what isn't sad? Fucking superheroes.

Go Go Justice Gang! ft. Apollo Young

Oh no.

Downtown Clash City has been beset by a hypnagogic leviathan, a terrifying kludge of symbology and violence, an impossible horror from beyond the ontological wasteland. Citizens flee, police stand by impotently, soldiers fire from tanks and helicopters without success, their bullets finding no purchase, their fear finding no relief.

It is a bubblegum machine gone horribly, horribly awry, a clear plastic sphere with a red body and a bellhopian cap, except there is a tree growing inside it, and also it is several hundred feet tall. The tree is maybe a willow or a dying spruce or something like that. It is definitely a sad tree, the kind of tree that grows on the edges of graveyards in children's books or in the tattoos of young people with too many feelings, when not growing on the inside of giant animated bubblegum machines.

It trudges along Washington Avenue on its root system, which emerges from the slot where the bubblegum ought to come out and inflicts hazardous onomatopoesis upon people and property alike with its terrible branches.

Bang. Crack. Boom. Splat. Crunch.

Splat is the worst of them, if you think about the implications.

Various material reminders of American imperialist power under late capitalism, the bank and the television station and the army surplus store, are made naught but memory and masonry in its wake. The ground shakes like butts in music videos, and buildings fall like teenagers in love. Destruction. Carnage. Rage. Can nothing be done to stop this creature? Can the city be saved from certain destruction?

Yes!

Already Apollo Young, a.k.a. Black Justice, is on his way to the Justice Gang Headquarters. Even as his fellow citizens panic, he keeps a cool head as he drives his Justice Vehicle headlong into danger. When his wrist communicator begins to buzz and play the Justice Gang theme song, he pulls over to the curb, in full accordance with the law.

"Black Justice! Come in! This is Red Justice!" says the wrist communicator.

"I read you, Patrick! What's the haps?!"

"The city is in danger! We need your help! To defeat this evil, we, the Justice Gang, need to combine our powers to form White Justice!"

"Yes. Only White Justice can save the city this time!"

"Also, can you please pick up Pink Justice? She is grounded from driving because she went to the mall instead of babysitting her little brother."

"What an airhead!"

"I know. But she is also a valuable member of the Justice Gang. Only when Pink Justice, Blue Justice, Black Justice, and Mauve Justice combine with me, the leader, Red Justice, can our ultimate power, White Justice, be formed!"

"As I know."

"Yes. All thanks to Princess Amarillia, who gave us our prismatic justice powers in order to prevent the evil Lord Tklox from answering the Omega Question and destroying civilization!"

"Righteous!"

"Just as white light is composed of all colors of light, so White Justice will be formed from our multicultural, gender-inclusive commitment to Good and Right."

"Okay! Bye."

Apollo hangs up and gets back on the road. He picks up Pink Justice on the way. She is a stereotypical Valley girl, but that is okay, since the Justice Gang accepts all types of people, as long as they love justice, are between fifteen and seventeen, and present as heterosexual. They ride together in silence, as they are the two members of the Justice Gang least likely to be paired up for storylines, owing to the potentially provocative implications of a black man and a white woman interacting together, even platonically.

"Do you ever think that we're just going in circles?" asks Pink Justice, staring idly out the window.

"What do you mean?" asks Apollo.

"A monster appears, we kill it, another monster appears, we kill it again. We feel good about getting the bad guy in the moment, but it just keeps happening. Week after week, it's the same thing. Another monster. More dead people. We never actually fight *evil*. We just kill monsters. Evil is always still there."

"But what about justice?"

"What is justice? People are dying. I just don't know what we're fighting for sometimes, why we keep fighting. It's the same every time. It's just tiring, I guess."

"I think we have to fight. Even if nobody gets saved, we are better for having done it. Maybe the world isn't better, but it's different, and I think that difference is beautiful."

"Like, for sure!" says Pink Justice.

A police car flashes its lights at Apollo. He pulls over. The man in the police uniform walks to the passenger side and asks Pink Justice if she is okay.

"I'm fine. There's no problem," she says.

The man in the police uniform tells Pink Justice that he can help her if something is wrong.

"Everything is fine. Nothing is wrong."

The man in the police uniform tells Apollo to get out of the car.

"~~What is this about? What's your probable cause?~~ Yes sir, officer," says Apollo, getting out of the car.

The man in the police uniform slams Apollo into the side of the car and pats him down. Pink Justice gets out and begins to yell that they have done nothing wrong, that he has to let them go. This obviously agitates the man in the police uniform.

Apollo's wrist communicator goes off, and without thinking, he moves to answer it. The man in the police uniform tackles him to

the ground, sits on his chest, and begins to hit him with a flashlight. Apollo's windpipe is blocked. It continues to be blocked for
a long time. He dies.

Come on. Really? That one was really good. The white guy was
in charge and everything! This sucks. I'm trying to do something
here. The point of adventure fiction is to connect moral idealism
with the human experience. The good guys fight the bad guys, just
as we struggle against the infelicities of the material world. That's
the point of heroes. They journey into the wilderness, struggle
against the unknown, and make liminal spaces safe for the people.
That's how it works, from Hercules to Captain Kirk. It's really hard
to create ontological safety when people keep dying all the time.
Barth was right: literature is exhausting.

So I guess Apollo shouldn't have been in a car with a white lady?
That's scary, I guess. He didn't do anything, but he was probably no
angel. He was a teen. Teens get into all kinds of shit. When I was in
school, I knew so, so many kids who shoplifted and smoked drugs.
They were mostly white, but still. Teens are shitty. The man in the
police uniform probably had good intentions. Like, he wanted to
make sure the girl wasn't being kidnapped or anything. Why else
would they be together? I still think he only wants to keep people
safe, especially potentially vulnerable people.

I've fucking got it. This is 2016, right? Sisters are doing it for
themselves. Why not a lady protagonist? Women are empathetic
and nonthreatening and totally cool. Everyone is chill with ladies.
That's why phone robots all have feminine voices. True story. Why
would you just kill a woman for no reason? She's not going to hurt
you. This time no one is going to hurt anybody.

Apollonia Williams-Carter and the Venus Sanction

Naomi walks into Apollonia's private office just before 5:00. It is
a cramped and dingy room, lit by a single fluorescent bulb and
smelling strongly of mildew. Without greeting or warning, she
drops a thick yellow binder down on Apollonia's desk.

"Read this," she says.

The binder is marked A.M.A.R.I.L.L.I.A. PROJECT. It is filled
with photographs, exotic diagrams, and pages and pages of ex-

haustively researched reports. Apollonia proceeds slowly, taking in each and every fact printed on the pages, running them over in her mind and allowing them to settle. She feels a sinking sensation in her stomach as she journeys deeper and deeper into the text.

"Dear God," she whispers. "Can this be true?"

"Yes," says Naomi.

"This is absolutely disgusting. How could they do something like this? How could they sell us out to aliens?"

"They don't care about our world. Not anymore."

"What can we do?"

"I don't know. That's why I brought this to you."

Apollonia opens one of her drawers, retrieving two shot glasses and a bottle of whiskey. She pours a double and pushes it toward Naomi.

"Have some. It will calm your nerves."

Naomi throws the glass to the ground, shattering it.

"This is no time to drink! We've got to do something!"

Apollonia takes her shot. "We can't do anything if we can't keep our cool."

"You want me to be cool? The department would have my head if they even knew I am talking to you."

"My head's on the line too. I might be a vice president here, but they'd kill me as quickly as a break-room cockroach."

"So what do we do? I came to you because I have the utmost respect for your work with the company."

"We go to the press. It might cost us our lives, but at least the truth will be out there."

"Should we try to rescue the girl?"

"No. First we get the truth out. I'll handle this. Delete any digital copies of these files and meet me tonight at the Port Royale."

"Fine."

"Remember. Anyone you know could be one of them. Use caution."

Naomi nods and exits.

Apollonia takes another double shot of whiskey as she continues to read the binder. How could this happen? She had never trusted the powers that be, but how could they be doing this? How could they be killing people with impunity? The notes on the files indicate that it is in the name of safety and the greater good, but whose safety are they really talking about? Man or monster?

Apollonia leaves at 7:00, as she does every evening. She hides the pages of the binder in her purse. She puts on a cheerful face, smiling at coworkers and greeting the support staff as she passes. She takes the elevator down from her floor to the lobby, then the stairs to the parking garage. She makes sure no one is following her as she walks down the corridors of the unlit parking garage, turning her head every few moments to get a full view of her surroundings. She sees her car and breathes a sigh of relief. She is almost out.

"Hey there."

She turns to see a young man in a suit. He is at least six feet tall and aggressively muscled. He smiles brightly and broadly at Apollonia, as if trying to hide something.

"Hello, Patrick," she says.

"Where ya headed in such a hurry?"

"Just going home."

"Home, huh? I remember home."

He laughs. She joins him.

"Long hours, huh? I feel for you."

He sticks out his finger at her purse. She clutches it closer.

"Hey. Is that new? I think my girlfriend pointed that purse out at the store. I'm sure it was that one."

"I've had this thing forever."

"Do you mind if I see it? I just want to know if it's well made."

Apollonia swallows. "I'd really prefer it if you didn't."

The smile leaves his face, and his eyes begin to narrow. Apollonia takes a step back. She has been trained in self-defense, but this man has at least one hundred pounds on her and also might be an alien. She begins to slowly, subtly shift into a combat stance. If she times it right, she might be able to stun him long enough for her to escape. She just has to find the right moment. She waits. And waits. And waits.

Finally he chuckles. "You're right. That was a weird question. I haven't been getting enough sleep lately. Sorry. I'll see you later."

Apollonia gets into her car. On the way to the Port Royale, she is pulled over by the man in the police uniform. While patting her down for drugs, he slips his fingers into her underwear. She tries to pull his hands away, prompting him to use force to stop her from resisting arrest. Her head is slammed many times against the sidewalk. She dies.

*

She. Didn't. Do. Anything. And even if she did do something, killing is not the answer. That's it. I'm not playing anymore. I can quit at any time. No one can stop me. Look, I'll do it now. *Boom.* I just quit for two days. *Boom.* That was two weeks. *Boom.* Now I have to change all the dates to 2016. What's the point of writing this thing? What's the point of writing anything? I just wanted to tell a cool story. That's it. No murders. No deaths. Remember? It was just a love story.

I once read that people get more into love stories and poems in times of political strife and violence. What better way to assert meaning in the face of meaninglessness than by celebrating the connection between human beings? Our relationship with the state, the culture, the world, these are just petals in the winds compared to the love that flows between us. Fuck politics. I set out to do a love story, so I'm doing a love story. Plus I've got a plan. So far the Apollos have all died while messing around outside. The solution isn't relatability at all. It's so much simpler than that: transit. It doesn't matter if the guy can't sympathize with Apollo if he can't find him. There are tons of great stories set in one place. I'll just do one of those.

Apollo Right and the Architectural-Organic Wormhole

Apollo and Naomi sit alone on the couch by the window, the dusty brown one held together with tape and Band-Aids, quiet, listening to the rain and the night, watching the play of wind and glow on the raindrops outside, refracted lamplight and neon diffusing into glitter in the dark. His head rests on her lap, which is soft and warm and comfortingly "laplike," which is to say that it possesses the qualities of the Platonic lap in quantities nearing excess, qualities which are difficult to articulate, neotenous comforts and chthonic ecstasies of a sublime/clichéd nature, intimacy rendered in thigh meat and belly warmth. Her left hand is on his shoulder, just so, and her right is on his chest, and he takes note of the sensation of her fingers as his chest expands and contracts, and it is pleasant. He takes a breath, sweet and slow. There is a little sadness, because this moment will wilt and wither like all moments, and he does not want it to, more than anything.

"Remember this," he says.

"What?"

"I would like it if you would remember this. Tonight. Or at least this part."

"Why wouldn't I remember tonight?"

"You never remember any of the good parts."

"You say that."

"It's true. You only remember the bad parts. The before and after. Anxiety and regret. Never the moment."

"Who says this is a good part?"

"That's a cutting remark."

"I just think we have different definitions of the good and bad when it comes to certain things."

"So this is a bad part?"

"I didn't say that."

"Which is it, then?"

"It's good to see you."

"You know what my favorite memory of us is?"

"Leon."

"I'm sure you don't remember it."

"Don't."

"It's not weird or anything. One time I came over to your place, and you smiled that smile you have—not the usual one, the good one—and you gave me a hug. Just a long, deep hug, like you were just really happy to see me. Genuinely happy. Not angry or annoyed at all. Just cruisin', y'know. Just cruisin'. We made out afterward, and maybe had sex? I don't remember that super great."

"The fact that you don't see anything weird about that is why we had to break up."

"Whatever, lady."

The door flies open. The man in the police uniform shouts for everyone to get down. A flashbang grenade is thrown inside. Apollo pushes Naomi away but is unable to get away. He suffers critical burns to his head and chest. After being denied medical treatment on the scene, he dies weeks later in the hospital from opportunistic infections. Ironically, the man in the police uniform was actually meant to go to the next apartment over, where a minor marijuana dealer lives.

*

They didn't even get to the cool part. There was going to be a living wormhole in the closet, and all kinds of space shit was going to come out, and in the process of dealing with it they were going to rekindle their love. It was going to be awesome. We can't even have love stories anymore? What do we have if we can't have love stories?

Okay. Now I'm thinking that the issue is with the milieu. 2015 is a weird time. Shit is going down. It's politicizing this story. I'm not into it. What we need is a rip-roaring space adventure in the far future. That'll be cool. All this shit will be sorted out by then, and we can all focus on what really matters: space shit.

Apollo _____ vs. the Vita-Ray Miracle

The crystal spires of New Virtua throw tangles of intersecting rainbows onto the silver-lined streets below, such that a Citizen going about his daily duties cannot help but be enmeshed in a transpicuous net of light and color. A Good Citizen knows that this is Good, that beauty is a gift of Science, and he wears his smile the way men of lesser worlds might wear a coat and hat to ward off the cold damp of an unregulated atmosphere.

Lord Tklox is not a Good Citizen, and he rarely smiles at all. On those occasions when he does experience something akin to happiness (when his plans are coming to fruition, when he imagines the bloody corpses of his enemies, when he thinks of new ways to crush the Good Citizens of New Virtua under his foot), his smile is not so much worn as wielded, as one might wield the glowing spiral of a raymatic cannon.

"Soon my vita-ray projector will be complete, and all New Virtua will tremble as I unleash the Omega Question!" he exclaims to no one, alone in his subterranean laboratory two thousand miles below the surface.

Cackling to himself, Lord Tklox waits in his lair for those who would challenge his incredible genius.

He waits.

He keeps waiting.

Lord Tklox coughs, perhaps getting the attention of any heroes listening on nearby crime-detecting audioscopes. "First New Vir-

tua, then the universe! All will be destroyed by the radical subjectivity of the Omega Question!"

Waiting continues to happen.

More waiting.

Still more.

Uh, I guess nobody comes. Everybody dies, I guess.

So I checked, and it turns out there are no black people in the far
future. That's my bad. I really didn't do my research on that one.
I don't know where we end up going. Maybe we all just cram into
the Parliament-Funkadelic discography at some point between *Star
Trek* and *Foundation*? Whatever. That's an issue for tomorrow. Today we've got bigger problems.

It's time we faced this head-on. Borges teaches us that every
story is a labyrinth, and within every labyrinth is a minotaur. I've
been trying to avoid the minotaur, but instead I need to slay it. I
have my sword, and I know where the monster lurks. It is time to
blaxploit this problem.

Apollo Jones In: The Final Showdown

> *Who's the plainclothes police detective who leaves all the criminals dejected?*
> *[Apollo!]*
> *Who stops crime in the nick of time and dazzles the ladies with feminine*
> *   rhymes?*
> *[Apollo!]*
> *Can you dig it?*

Apollo's cruiser screeches to a halt at the entrance to the abandoned warehouse. He leaps out the door and pulls his gun, a custom golden Beretta with his name engraved on the handle.

"Hot gazpacho!" he says. "This is it."

Patrick pops out of the passenger seat. "We've got him now."

They have been chasing their suspect for weeks now, some sicko
responsible for a string of murders. In a surprising third-act twist,
they discovered that the one responsible is one of their own, a bad
apple who gets his kicks from harming the innocent.

"We've got him pinned down inside," says Apollo.

"He won't escape this time."

"Let's do this, brother."

They skip the middle part of the story, since that has been where we've been getting into trouble. They rush right to the end, where the man in the police uniform is waiting for them.

"Congratulations on solving my riddles, gentlemen. I'm impressed."

"You're going down, punk," says Apollo.

"Yeah!" says Patrick.

"I doubt that very much."

The man in the police uniform pulls his weapon and fires three shots, all hitting Apollo in the torso. He crumples to the ground. Patrick aims his own weapon, but the man in the police uniform is able to quickly shoot him in the shoulder, sending Patrick's pistol to the ground.

"You thought you could defeat me so easily? How foolish. We're not so different, you and I. You wanted a story about good aliens and bad aliens? Well, so did I."

"How's this for foolish?" says Apollo, pulling up his shirt to reveal he was wearing a bulletproof vest all along. Then he unloads a clip from his legendary golden Beretta at him. The man in the police uniform falls to the ground, bleeding.

Patrick clutches his shoulder. "We got him."

"We're not quite done yet," says Apollo.

He walks over to the body of the man in the police uniform. He tugs on the man's face, pulling it off completely. It is the face of Lord Tklox.

"This was his plan all along," says Apollo. "By murdering all those innocent people, he was turning us against each other, thereby making it easier for his invasion plans to succeed. All he had left to do was answer the Omega Question and *boom*, no more civilization. Good thing we stopped him in time."

"I knew it," says Patrick. "He was never one of us. He was just a bad guy the whole time. It is in no way necessary for me to consider the ideological mechanisms by which my community and society determine who benefits from and participates in civil society, thus freeing me from cognitive dissonance stemming from the ethical compromises that maintain my lifestyle."

"Hot gazpacho!" says Apollo.

They share a manly handshake like Schwarzenegger and Carl Weathers in *Predator*. It is so dope.

"I'll go call dispatch," says Patrick. "Tell them that we won't be needing backup. Or that we will be needing backup to get the body and investigate the scene? I don't really know how this works. The movie usually ends at this point."

Patrick leaves, and Apollo guards the body. Suddenly the warehouse door bursts open. Seeing him standing over the dead body, a man in a police uniform yells for Apollo to drop his weapon. Apollo shouts that he is a cop and moves to gingerly put his golden gun on the ground, but he is too slow. Bulletproof vests do not cover the head. He is very, very dead.

I wasn't trying to do apologetics for him. Before, I mean. I wasn't saying it's okay to kill people because they aren't perfect or do things that are vaguely threatening. I was just trying to find some meaning, the moral of the story. All I ever wanted to do was write a good story. But murder is inherently meaningless. The experience of living is a creative act, the personal construction of meaning for the individual, and death is the final return to meaninglessness. Thus, the act of killing is the ultimate abnegation of the human experience, a submission to the chaos and violence of the natural world. To kill, we must either admit the futility of our own life or deny the significance of the victim's.

This isn't right.

It's not supposed to happen like this.

Why does this keep happening?

It's the same story every time. Again and again and again.

I can't fight the man in the police uniform. He's real, and I'm an authorial construct, just words on a page, pure pretend. But you know who isn't pretend? You. We have to save Apollo. We're both responsible for him. We created him together. Death of the Author, you know? It's just you and me now. I've got one last trick. I didn't mention this in the interest of pace and narrative cohesion, but I lifted the Omega Question off Lord Tklox before he died. I don't have the answer, but I know the question. You've got to go in. I can keep the man in the police uniform at bay as long as I can, but you have to save Apollo. We're going full Morrison.

Engage second-person present.

God forgive us.

*

You wake up. It is still dark out. You reach out to take hold of your spouse. Your fingers intertwine, and it is difficult to tell where you stop and they begin. You love them so much. After a kiss and a cuddle, you get out of bed. You go to the bathroom and perform your morning toilette. When you are finished, you go to the kitchen and help your spouse with breakfast for the kids.

They give you a hug when they see you. You hug back, and you never want to let go. They are getting so big now, and you do everything you can to be a good parent to them. You know they love you, but you also want to make sure they have the best life possible.

You work hard every single day to make that happen. Your boss is hard on you, but he's a good guy, and you know you can rely on him when it counts. You trust all your coworkers with your life. You have to. There's no other option in your line of work.

After some paperwork, you and your partner go out on patrol. You've lived in this neighborhood your entire life. Everything about it is great—the food, the sights, the people. There are a few bad elements, but it's your job to stop them and keep everybody safe.

It's mostly nickel-and-dime stuff today, citations and warnings. The grocery store reports a shoplifter. An older woman reports some kids loitering near her house. Your partner notices a man urinating on the street while you're driving past. That kind of thing.

As you are on your way back to the station, you notice a man walking alone on the sidewalk. It's late, and it doesn't look like this is his part of town. His head is held down, like he's trying to hide his face from you. This is suspicious. Your partner says he recognizes him, that he fits the description of a mugger who has been plaguing the area for weeks. You pull up to him. Ask him what he is doing. He doesn't give you a straight answer. You ask him for some identification. He refuses to give it to you. You don't want to arrest this guy for nothing, but he's not giving you much choice.

Suddenly his hand moves toward a bulge in his pocket. It's a gun. You know it's a gun. You draw your weapon. You just want to scare him, show him that you're serious, stop him from drawing on you. But is he even scared? Is that fear on his face or rage? How can you even tell? He's bigger than you, and he is angry, and he probably has a gun. You do not know this person. You cannot imagine what is going through his mind. You have seen this scenario a million times before in movies and TV shows.

You might die.

You might die.

You might die.

The Omega Question is activated:

Who matters?

Contributors' Notes

Notable Science Fiction and
Fantasy Stories of 2016

Contributors' Notes

A winner of both the Shirley Jackson Award and the International Horror Guild Award, **Dale Bailey** is the author of *The End of the End of Everything: Stories* and *The Subterranean Season,* as well as *The Fallen, House of Bones, Sleeping Policemen* (with Jack Slay, Jr.), and *The Resurrection Man's Legacy and Other Stories.* His work has twice been a finalist for the Nebula Award and once for the Bram Stoker Award and has been adapted for Showtime television. He lives in North Carolina with his family.

▪ "Teenagers from Outer Space" and "I Was a Teenage Werewolf" are siblings, both born from my abiding love of the ultra-cheap sci-fi movies of the 1950s and both part of a larger project to use the risible titles of those films as inspiration for stories that engage the source material with some emotional nuance and thematic complexity. These particular titles (it seems to me) are endearing both for their absurdity and for their essentially innocent exploitation of a then-new niche in the ecology of the American consumer—the one inhabited by the teenager, a word that, the *Oxford English Dictionary* informs us, did not come into usage until the 1940s.

In retrospect, of course, the teen culture of the 1950s—from *Blackboard Jungle* to Buddy Holly—seems tame, but middle-class parents of the era must have felt as if their kids had undergone a transformation no less radical than Michael Landon's in *I Was a Teenage Werewolf.* Though the anxieties attendant upon that transformation are here veiled in nostalgia, they remain no less relevant today. Despite their titles, these are not—or were not intended to be—camp stories. In the note appended to the original publication of "I Was a Teenage Werewolf," I said that I was pretty sure that my own teenage daughter was a werewolf. I wasn't entirely joking.

Leigh Bardugo is the best-selling author of *Six of Crows* (a New York Times Notable Book and CILIP Carnegie Medal nominee), *Crooked Kingdom,* the Shadow and Bone trilogy, *Wonder Woman: Warbringer,* and most recently

The Language of Thorns, an illustrated collection of original fairy tales. Her short stories and essays have appeared in *The Best of Tor.com, Slasher Girls & Monster Boys, Last Night a Superhero Saved My Life,* and *Summer Days and Summer Nights.* She lives in Los Angeles.

• I had a college roommate from Penticton, a small town in British Columbia. When she would describe it—the cottage she shared with her dad, the fruit she picked off the trees for her breakfast—my city-kid imagination painted her hometown as some kind of idyllic haven between Avonlea (wrong coast, I know) and Bradbury's Green Town, Illinois. Years later I got to visit, and despite the miles of pristine pine forest we traveled through to get there, the town itself was a disappointment, full of fast-food drive-thrus and bargain water parks. But I was still obsessed with Penticton—the Ogopogo they claimed lived in the lake, the giant fiberglass peach where town kids worked part-time serving pie and smoothies, the rowdy tourists who found a way to roll that peach into the lake every summer until the owners finally weighted its base down with concrete. I like places like Penticton that are one thing to visitors and another to the people who live there year-round. I like the haunted feeling of towns where half the businesses shut their doors through the winter and the whole world seems to wait. When you're young, summer has power. It's this strange gap in the year that requires new routines and operates by its own rules, a time when you can be someone else, and maybe see yourself transformed. In Little Spindle, that magic is real. Many thanks to Stephanie Perkins, who edited this story and who has been known to cast spells down at the DQ.

Peter S. Beagle was born in 1939 and raised in the Bronx, where he grew up surrounded by the arts and education: Both his parents were teachers, three of his uncles were world-renowned gallery painters, and his immigrant grandfather was a respected writer, in Hebrew, of Jewish fiction and folktales. As a child Peter used to sit by himself in the stairwell of the apartment building he lived in, staring at the mailboxes across the way and making up stories to entertain himself. Today, thanks to classics like *The Last Unicorn, A Fine and Private Place,* and "Two Hearts," he is a living icon of fantasy fiction. In addition to his novels and over one hundred pieces of short fiction, Peter has written many teleplays and screenplays (including the animated versions of *The Lord of the Rings* and *The Last Unicorn*), six nonfiction books (among them the classic travel memoir *I See By My Outfit*), the libretto for one opera, and more than seventy published poems and songs. He currently makes his home in Oakland, California. His latest novel is *Summerlong.*

• There is one origin story for "The Story of Kao Yu" that I've never mentioned to anyone—even myself. I knew a lady long ago who was no pickpocket, no thief, no murderer, but for whom I would have come across the world—I did, more than once—to do her bidding, without the slightest issue of right or wrong ever raising its head. James Thurber ends one of his fairy tales with the moral, "Love is blind, but desire just doesn't give a good goddamn . . ." As with Kao Yu himself, she was my only true experience of not giving a good goddamn. I miss her still.

Helena Bell lives and writes in Chattanooga, Tennessee. Her fiction has previously appeared in *Lightspeed*, *Clarkesworld*, *The Indiana Review*, and *Strange Horizons*, among other places.

▪ "I've Come to Marry the Princess" began with the thought, *Wouldn't it be funny if a boy found a dragon egg, and instead of helping the boy save the kingdom, the dragon ate the boy in the end?* Eventually I settled on the idea of setting it at the summer camp my brother and I went to as kids because, again, the thought of it amused me. But the core of it came from some advice that Joe Hill gave me at Clarion West about a completely different story. He'd suggested that I make a character do something really terrible, unforgivable even. That advice stayed with me, and I liked the idea of framing a story around an apology that needs to be given.

Brian Evenson is the author of a dozen books of fiction, most recently the story collection *A Collapse of Horses* and the novella *The Warren*. His story collection *Windeye* and novel *Immobility* were both finalists for a Shirley Jackson Award. His novel *Last Days* won the ALA-RUSA award for best horror novel of 2009, and his novel *The Open Curtain* was a finalist for an Edgar Award and an International Horror Guild Award. He is the recipient of three O. Henry Prizes as well as an NEA Fellowship and a Guggenheim Fellowship. His work has been translated into French, Italian, Greek, Spanish, Japanese, Persian, and Slovenian. He lives in Los Angeles and teaches in the Critical Studies Program at CalArts.

▪ I'd had the idea for "Smear" some time ago, stemming partly from Kelly Link's terrific story "Two Houses," partly from Guy de Maupassant's "The Horla," and partly from reading M. John Harrison's and Samuel Delany's work that describes body modification of starship pilots. I like too the idea of there being something we're semiconscious of, something that's there hovering just beyond perception or that might operate more along our neural pathways than out in the open. For such a being, if *being* is the right word for it, the distinction between a human mind and the artificial mind of a ship might not be as distinct as it would be for us, and we might perceive it only as a shift or torque in reality, always doubting whether anything was there at all.

Joseph Allen Hill is a writer based in Chicago. His work has appeared in *Lightspeed*, *Liminal Stories*, the *Cosmic Powers* anthology, and this anthology, which you are reading right now.

▪ I've always liked metafiction, from Looney Tunes to Italo Calvino to comic books proclaiming in bold-print narration that the superheroes will die if I don't turn the page. It always gets me, no matter how corny or pretentious. Stories about stories are meaningful because our lives are made of stories. We tell ourselves stories about who we are and how the world works and what it is to exist and act in the world. I wrote "The Venus Effect" because I was exhausted by a real-life story. Let's call it the police brutality story. The names change, the setting jumps around the United States, a few plot details get switched up, but it's always the same structure and always the same ending. I imagine the police brutality story will play out at least a couple times between me writing this now and you reading this. I hope very much that I am wrong in this assertion, but history suggests that I will not be. It was this sense of inevitability that drove me to write the story, the slow, dull grind of knowing exactly what is going to happen and not being able to do anything. I wanted to capture that feeling of exhaustion and powerlessness. The story is about other things—who is and is not a part of society, respectability politics, the value of fiction in confronting real-world issues—but the core of it, I think, is that feeling, the agony of the inevitable.

N. K. Jemisin is the author of several novels, including *The Fifth Season,* which won the Locus and Hugo Awards (making her the first black author to win either award for best novel). Her short fiction and novels have also been nominated multiple times for the Nebula and World Fantasy Awards and shortlisted for the Crawford and the Tiptree. Her speculative works range in genre from fantasy to science fiction to the undefinable; her themes include resistance to oppression, the inseverability of the liminal, and the coolness of Stuff Blowing Up. She is a member of the Altered Fluid writing group, and she has been an instructor for the Clarion and Clarion West workshops. She lives in Brooklyn, where in her spare time she is a biker and a gamer; she is also single-handedly responsible for saving the world from King Ozzymandias, her obnoxious ginger cat. Her essays and fiction excerpts are available at nkjemisin.com. Her newest novel, *The Stone Sky,* came out in August 2017.

▪ Back in 2014 or 2015, there was a debate about the H. P. Lovecraft bust that embodied the World Fantasy Award, and substantial discussion of just how much Lovecraft's fear of "the other" informed his work. I'd read some Lovecraft a long while before, but somehow hadn't realized that his "sinister hordes" were immigrants, poor people, and people of color like me. Once I saw it, though, I couldn't unsee it. I started to notice Lovecraftian paranoia not just in his work but in the reactions of bigoted people in the everyday: the police officer who imagines that an unarmed black child is a terrifying monster; the doctor who believes his Latina patient can't feel pain the way ordinary (white) human beings can; the parent who sees a trans child as an unnatural freak. I'm also well aware that despite the paranoid fantasies of Lovecraftian bigots, historically it's marginalized people who have the most to fear from "the other" . . . yet we seem to manage without seeing every stranger on the street as a monster from beyond.

So then I got the idea to write a story about (basically) Cthulhu attacking New York City, as one does. And I decided that New York—the New York of my experience, which is filthy and "ethnic" and full of "perverts" and poor people and basically everything Lovecraft despised, by his own word—would tell the big C exactly where he could put his eldritch abomination. Maybe, just maybe, all the people Lovecraft hated, all us sinister hordes, are exactly what humanity needs in its direst hour. And maybe, just maybe, I could use Lovecraft's own material to battle the ugliness he helped to foment in the fantasy zeitgeist. Plus: giant monster fight! Those are always fun.

Alice Sola Kim's writing has appeared in publications such as *McSweeney's, Tin House, BuzzFeed READER, Asimov's Science Fiction, Lightspeed,* the *Village Voice,* and *Lenny.* She is a winner of the 2016 Whiting Award and has received grants and scholarships from the MacDowell Colony, Bread Loaf Writers' Conference, and Elizabeth George Foundation.

▪ I belong to a writing group that has existed since I was in college. The group has gone through many transformations—people have joined, left, and moved, necessitating both an East Coast and a West Coast branch—but it's essentially still the same group. When the *BuzzFeed* editors Karolina Waclawiak, Saeed Jones, and Isaac Fitzgerald solicited a story from me for *BuzzFeed READER* on the theme of being almost famous, I knew right away that I wanted to write something inspired by my gorgeous long-running miracle of a writing group—except completely scary and evil, which my writing group is only sometimes.

As in the story, a lot of us are East Asian and South Asian, and when we all started writing in college, there was this sense that there wouldn't be enough room for all of us—that our place in the white-dominated literary world would be as tokens and therefore maybe only one of us would make it. But literary publishing has slowly become, is still in the process of slowly becoming, more reflective of the actual diverse world, and I'm happy to say that, unlike in the story, all of us in the group are seeing each other succeed. It is unbelievable and wonderful and everyone has worked so hard for it—no one took the shortcut of feeding their friends to a giant snake woman, for which I am thankful.

A. Merc Rustad is a queer nonbinary writer who lives in Minnesota. Merc is a Nebula Award finalist for "This Is Not a Wardrobe Door"—definitely a highlight of the year! Their stories have appeared in *Lightspeed, Fireside,*

Apex, Uncanny, Shimmer, Gamut, and other fine venues. Merc likes to play video games, watch movies, read comics, and wear awesome hats. You can find Merc on Twitter @Merc_Rustad or on their website, amercrustad. com. Their debut short story collection, *So You Want to Be a Robot,* was published in May 2017.

  • I almost didn't write this. No, that's not quite right—I wrote it, and it scared me because it felt true and honest. This was all-out me on the page. I had read a lot of portal fantasies, and none of them seemed to follow through on the aftermath. The trauma of being locked out of your found-home, cut off from all your friends and the life(s) you built, unsure why you could never go back. I refused to let this be a downer, either; it needed a happy ending, and I had these nagging doubts that Serious Genre would want that. So I trunked the story for six months, and only at the last minute of *Fireside*'s sub window did I send it out. Well. You know the rest. I like happy endings. I'm so pleased by the warm, welcoming reception "This Is Not a Wardrobe Door" has gotten. It's the most rewarding aspect of being a writer: when you see people connect with a story, the characters, and find hope in the end. Let's all build lots of doors.

Nisi Shawl's alternate history/AfroRetroFuturist novel *Everfair* was a 2016 publication and a finalist for the Nebula Award. Her 2008 collection *Filter House* co-won the James Tiptree, Jr. Award, and she has been a guest of honor at WisCon, the Science Fiction Research Association, and ArmadilloCon. She is the coauthor of *Writing the Other: A Practical Approach,* and she coedited *Strange Matings: Science Fiction, Feminism, African American Voices,* and *Octavia E. Butler,* and *Stories for Chip: A Tribute to Samuel R. Delany.* Recently she guest-edited *Fantastic Stories of the Imagination*'s special People of Color Take Over issue. Since its inception she has been reviews editor for the feminist literary quarterly *Cascadia Subduction Zone.* Shawl is a founder of the Carl Brandon Society, a nonprofit supporting the presence of people of color in the fantastic genres, and she serves on Clarion West's board of directors. She lives in Seattle, taking daily walks with her mother, June, and her cat, Minnie, at a feline pace.

  • Located adjacent to *Everfair* rather than functioning as its sequel or prequel or holding any other position on that novel's timeline, "Vulcanization" is told from a viewpoint I deliberately excluded from all other *Everfair*-related fiction: that of Leopold II, king of the Belgians. The historical Leopold my character is based on was a nasty piece of work, and I had a hard time inhabiting his head even for these few pages. I didn't really want to use the racial slurs that came so easily to his lips, but that's what his entitled callousness demanded.

  Researching "Vulcanization" was a lot easier than writing it. I looked into rubber processing, the Royal Museum for Central Africa's layout and architecture, and the personal foibles of this particular Belgian monarch. But then I had to put on a Leopold-shaped suit and wade into his story.

Did I construct the suit well enough? Was it proof against the ick? I hope that as you read you didn't get any on you.

Jeremiah Tolbert is a writer, Web designer, and photographer. His work has appeared in *Lightspeed, Asimov's Science Fiction, Interzone,* and numerous anthologies. He lives in Lawrence, Kansas, with his wife and son.

▪ "Not by Wardrobe, Tornado, or Looking Glass" required more time to get right than any other story I've written. I began tinkering with the idea nine years before and even completed a draft, but I didn't know how to end the story. I was certain that my poor protagonist could never find what she desired most (a rabbit hole of her own), and in my relative youth, I could see this leading to nothing but despair. The original ending was too clichéd to even describe here. It didn't work, and I couldn't see how I could make it, so I set the story aside and moved on.

Years later, after having a child, my perceptions of life shifted in very profound ways. One day, while waiting for another story idea to percolate, I went through my folder of unfinished and unsatisfactory work. I found this early manuscript and remembered my past frustrations. Upon rereading, I realized with one of those rare lightning bolts of insight that what my protagonist required wasn't for her world to change; she needed to change her perspective of the world. It took going through a similar change of perspective in my own life to see what she truly needed most, and not just what she (and I) thought she needed. As a writer, this realization that my understanding of my own stories can change as I age has helped me feel less urgency in getting stories perfect right away. Sometimes they require a period of hibernation.

Debbie Urbanski's stories have appeared in *The Sun,* the *Kenyon Review, Interfictions, Highlights Magazine, Cicada, Fantasy & Science Fiction, Nature, Terraform,* and *The Southern Review.* She lives with her husband and two kids in Syracuse, New York, and is permanently at work on a linked story collection concerning aliens and cults.

▪ I wrote "When They Came to Us" at a time when I was convinced that ordinary people (such as myself, and perhaps you as well) were capable of great evil but we were all pretending otherwise. "Oh no, that would never be me," I felt we were telling ourselves falsely when watching, on the news, whatever horrors were being committed that day. Why did I think this? Perhaps it was the beginning of a bout of depression. But also I was reading some really heavy nonfiction. Erik Larson's *In the Garden of Beasts,* for starters, about 1933 Germany as seen through the American ambassador's eyes—a study in, using Larson's words, "what allows a culture to slip its moorings." At the same time I was researching Abu Ghraib and war crimes in general for a bleak novella. Some of the soldiers involved in Abu Ghraib—one in particular, a woman who took certain photographs—seemed so normal and recognizable in interviews, and I wondered with dread whether, in such an environment, I could have done what she did. I became interested in Robert Jay Lifton's idea of "atrocity-producing situations" in which ordinary people—"indeed, just about anyone," Lifton writes—"can enter into 'the psychology of slaughter.'" Eventually, after reading way too many books, I realized I was never going to figure it all out, so I should just write a story about it. That story became "When They Came to Us." I was interested in telling this story using the collective voice as a way to invite the reader to step closer toward the narrators—the reader becoming, perhaps, for a little while, part of the town. An act not done by *them* but by *us*. Thank you to the editors of *The Sun* for giving this alien story its first home.

Catherynne M. Valente is the *New York Times* best-selling author of over thirty works of fiction and poetry, including *Palimpsest*, the *Orphan's Tales* series, *Deathless*, *Radiance*, and the crowdfunded phenomenon *The Girl Who Circumnavigated Fairyland in a Ship of Her Own Making* (and the four books that followed it). She is the winner of the Andre Norton, Tiptree, Eugie Foster Memorial, Mythopoeic, Rhysling, Lambda, Locus, Romantic Times' Critics Choice, and Hugo Awards and the Prix Imaginales. She has been a finalist for the Nebula and World Fantasy Awards. She lives on an island off the coast of Maine with a small but growing menagerie of beasts, some of which are human.

▪ "The Future Is Blue" came from a fairly simple assignment: Jonathan Strahan asked me to write a story about global warming, about the rising sea levels and how we would live in the new world they will almost certainly create for us, for an anthology called *Drowned Worlds*. I turned the idea over in my mind for several months and kept returning to two things: a line I'd had in my notebook for about five years, and the idea that we would live as we always have, with the same dramas and shortsightedness and lonely children and longing for entertainment above almost all other things, only there would be much, much fewer of us and we would be seabound. The line was, "When I grow up, I want to be the Thames." And the idea became Garbagetown. I've always been fascinated with the Great Pacific Garbage Patch, in part because it sounds like something out of a children's book, but it is heartbreakingly real, a roving patch of garbage in the ocean the size of Texas. And how much bigger will it become when coastal cities are inundated? How much will it be a testament to everything we had and threw away? If I was going to write a story about the ruin of our world, I couldn't think of a better place to set it than on top of all our flotsam and jetsam, full of humans doing the same stupid and sublime things they've always done, the same tribal foolishness, the same hoarding, the same extremes of violence and revenge, the same fear of change and yearning for it.

I'd intended to explore Garbagetown in a third-person point of view, describing the world as much as the characters. But Tetley's voice took over, and her first line, "My name is Tetley Abednego and I am the most hated girl in Garbagetown," demanded to be left in charge of everything. I couldn't let go of that line, of the question it asked—when the world has already ended, what can a person do that is worse than everything that's already happened? And so it was her voice, her inexplicable cheerfulness, her crime, her punishment, and a child whispering that he wanted to become the Thames (appropriately, all clinging together like floating detritus of the mind) that I followed through a beautiful and horrible world of half-understood rubbish, which is, naturally, a perfect descriptor of the world at any time period. Beautiful and horrible and full of half-understood rubbish. That seems unlikely to ever really change. In "The Future Is Blue," it just becomes literal. How we will live if the seas take back the land will be only different in setting, because we are tragic animals in the end, and the seed of our downfall is buried deep in our nature, never to be entirely thrown away, along with teabags and spent candles and old earrings and advertising circulars and kerosene cans . . .

Genevieve Valentine is the author of *Mechanique, The Girls at the Kingfisher Club, Persona,* and *Icon.* Her short fiction has appeared in over a dozen best-of-the-year anthologies, and she has written *Catwoman* for DC Comics. Her nonfiction and reviews have appeared in the *New York Times, The Atlantic, The A.V. Club, NPR.org,* and elsewhere.

 • A lot of things found their way all at once into "Everyone from Themis Sends Letters Home"; some of them were concerns I knew I had, and some of them, as usual, are obvious only in retrospect. As someone who imagines herself to be a curmudgeon with a poor track record of correspondence, I didn't know how interested I was in the epistolary form, and how it affects the reading experience, until I started writing this story.

Greg van Eekhout has so far published six novels whose audiences range from adult to middle grade. His most recent work is the Daniel Blackland trilogy, beginning with *California Bones,* a modern-day fantasy about wizards who gain powers by eating the fossilized remains of extinct magical creatures. Upcoming work includes a middle-grade novel about dogs in space. Find him at writingandsnacks.com.

 • Among the biggest influences on my work are the crappy things I grew up on. Fast food. Hanna-Barbera cartoons. Corner convenience stores. Shopping malls. Hardly a Bradburian childhood to mine for material. Nevertheless, I keep coming back to the extruded product of my youth and examining what it turned me into and what about it is interesting, valuable, mythological, magical. When I was asked to write a science fiction story for an anthology inspired by the music of the awesome Canadian rock trio Rush (who never recorded extruded product, who are not crappy, who are in fact, as I said, awesome), I immediately thought of their song "Subdivisions," which evokes the stultifying existence of suburbia. The trick was writing something that would not only appeal to Rush fans but would also speak to people who hate Rush, or are indifferent to Rush, or have never even heard of Rush. These people exist. I can't even. The other challenge was to write something more than just a fan letter to my favorite band, but rather to make a statement of personal concern to me. So I wrote about extruded food product, social status, pets, commercial real estate development, quests, and friendship. For research I looked to *Tempest,* the video game featured in the early-'80s MTV video for "Subdivisions." I got the high score because hardly anybody else had played the game in a while.

Alexander Weinstein is the director of the Martha's Vineyard Institute of Creative Writing and the author of the short story collection *Children of the New World* (2016). He is the recipient of a Sustainable Arts Foundation Award, and his fiction has been awarded the Lamar York, Gail Crump, Hamlin Garland, and New Millennium Prizes. He is an associate professor of creative writing at Siena Heights University.

▪ "Openness" was a story that took three years to write. The idea for the psychic technology came quite quickly. I was on a crowded bus in Boston, and I suddenly thought of how useful/horrifying it would be if we could project our likes/dislikes/preferences onto a visual aura around our bodies. You could look across a room and know that a stranger enjoyed Tom Waits, or hated cats, or was originally from Maine, and in turn you could psychically message people who shared your interests. So the technology of the story was fully formed, but I couldn't yet place its human conflict. For my stories to feel successful they need the human element, so the technology becomes backgrounded (and part of the setting) and the humanity of the characters is foregrounded. Since I didn't yet have this element, the story was put on the back burner.

It was about two years later, as I was going through a breakup with a woman I loved dearly, that the human element of the story took shape. The breakup dealt with putting up emotional walls—and as we were navigating this, I suddenly understood how the psychic technology of layers could work in the story as a metaphor for the emotional barriers that arise in a romantic relationship. This became the central theme of "Openness," which explores the way in which we can retract our "layers" from those closest to us. Once I had this element, I was able to start drafting the story.

As for the idea of "total openness," I'm fascinated by the question of how much we share of ourselves with our romantic partners and our ability to be compassionate for our partners' flaws and their most deeply held secrets.

Nick Wolven's fiction has appeared in *Asimov's Science Fiction, Fantasy & Science Fiction, Clarkesworld,* and various other magazines and anthologies. He's particularly interested in near-future science fiction with a strong flavor of social commentary, not because he thinks anyone benefits from the commentary but because he's so often bemused by society. His favorite authors in the science fiction genre are Samuel Delany, Margaret Atwood, and Kim Stanley Robinson. Wolven has a shabby-looking, sporadically updated blog at nickthewolven.com. He's on Twitter, rarely, as @nickwolven. He lives in New York City with his family.

▪ A political spoof like "Caspar D. Luckinbill . . ." is too easily spoiled with explication. I'll say only that I think there's a natural affinity between science fiction and satire, since both depend in some sense on the art of exaggeration. Perhaps I can venture an exaggeration of my own, then, and say that science fiction sets out to make the strange seem ordinary—or anyway, plausible—while good satire often succeeds at making the ordinary seem strange. When the two are brought together, the effect can be dizzying. As Vonnegut reminds us, we all now and then come unstuck in time, unsure how we got to be where we are, dreading where we seem to be going. Nothing gives me this sense of being out of joint, out of place, and out of workable options like today's multimedia blizzard of ads, fads, and admonitions.

Caroline M. Yoachim lives in Seattle and loves cold, cloudy weather. She is the author of dozens of short stories, which have appeared in *Fantasy & Science Fiction, Clarkesworld, Asimov's Science Fiction,* and *Lightspeed,* among other places. Her debut short story collection, *Seven Wonders of a Once and Future World and Other Stories,* came out in August 2016. For more about Caroline, check out her website at carolineyoachim.com.

▪ I have terrible seasonal allergies, and for about a year I got allergy shots a couple times a week in hopes of reducing my symptoms. Allergy shots increase people's tolerance to an allergen by injecting them with gradually increasing doses of whatever it is they are allergic to. After getting an allergy shot, you have to sit in the waiting room of the clinic for thirty minutes, just in case you have a serious anaphylactic reaction. Local reactions (giant itchy welts) on the arm where they've injected the allergen are quite common. "Welcome to the Medical Clinic at the Interplanetary Relay Station | Hours Since the Last Patient Death: 0" was inspired by the many hours I spent waiting in a medical clinic with itchy arms.

E. Lily Yu received the John W. Campbell Award for Best New Writer in 2012. Her short fiction appears in a variety of venues, from *McSweeney's* and *Boston Review* to *Clarkesworld, Tor.com, Fantasy & Science Fiction,* and *Uncanny,* as well as multiple best-of-the-year anthologies. Her stories have been finalists for the Hugo, Nebula, Sturgeon, Locus, and World Fantasy Awards.

▪ "The Witch of Orion Waste and the Boy Knight" paced my mind for days before pouring itself onto paper one March afternoon in a coffee shop decked in *War of the Worlds* kitsch. Conscious inspirations for this story include Richard Siken's "Litany in Which Certain Things Are Crossed Out," Norman Rockwell's *Boy Reading Adventure Story,* Connie Converse's "Man in the Sky," an illustrated edition of "The Red Shoes" in Chinese that terrified me as a child, a dragon borrowed from a Patricia McKillip novel, and a long list of books on family systems, attachment theory, and insight meditation. This is not a complete inventory, since good stories, like thieves, rifle their writer's pockets and snap up all kinds of unconsidered trifles of life and mind.

In a sense, I wrote "The Witch of Orion Waste . . ." from a loving dissatisfaction with all of the aforementioned sources. For centuries we have insisted on punishing, on the one hand, Ladies of Shalott and Elaines of Astolat and girls who would dance in red shoes or ride as knights, or demanding, on the other, bottomless forgiveness and patience from wronged women, in the pattern of Griselda, Penelope, and more recently the second half of *Lemonade.* However pleasing each individual tale, the body of work as a whole, in constantly retreading these narrative paths, has worn them into a deep labyrinth, whose end remains suffering or death. I have written one way out.

Notable Science Fiction and Fantasy Stories of 2016

Selected by John Joseph Adams

THE BEST AMERICAN SERIES®

FIRST, BEST, AND BEST-SELLING

The Best American Comics

The Best American Essays

The Best American Mystery Stories

The Best American Nonrequired Reading

The Best American Science and Nature Writing

The Best American Science Fiction and Fantasy

The Best American Short Stories

The Best American Sports Writing

The Best American Travel Writing

Available in print and e-book wherever books are sold.
Visit our website: *www.hmhco.com/bestamerican*